also by Martin Clark

The Many Aspects of Mobile Home Living

_____ plain heathen mischief

Plain

Heathen

Mischief

—————————————————————————————a novel

Martin Clark

Alfred A. Knopf New York 2004

This is a Borzoi Book
Published by Alfred A. Knopf

Library of Congress Cataloging-in-Publication Data
Clark, Martin, 1959–
    Plain heathen mischief / Martin Clark.
        p.   cm.
    ISBN 1-4000-4096-5
        1. Ex-prisoners—Fiction.   2. Brothers and sisters—Fiction.
    3. Missoula (Mont.)—Fiction.   4. False testimony—Fiction.
    5. Ex-clergy—Fiction.   6. Baptists—Fiction.   I. Title.

    PS3553.L2865P55 2004
    813'.6—dc22   2003060475

Manufactured in the United States of America
First Edition

This book is in memory of my sweet mom,
Hazel Clark, who passed away on May 4, 2003,
and is dedicated to my father, Martin F. "Fill" Clark,
the last lion.

I lost my job a month ago, so I took a small vacation
I went out west to make the best of my lowdown situation
Moved in with my sister, you know she works every day
We don't see each other much, and I guess it's just that way.

—Robert Earl Keen
"Runnin' with the Night"

When they arrived at the place where God had told Abraham to go, he built an altar and placed the wood in order, ready for the fire, and then tied Isaac and laid him on the altar over the wood. And Abraham took the knife and lifted it up to plunge it into his son, to slay him.

—Genesis 22:9–10

_____ plain heathen mischief

After considering the possibilities for six days and six nights, it seemed pointless to mention sex or weakness or the girl, so Joel King decided his final sermon would be pale and simple, no more and no less than the ordinary things he'd said to his congregation in the past. There were, of course, several last-stand temptations he'd contemplated while staring at his laptop, and two he'd quixotically pecked to life even though he knew all along they'd never depart his study. The first composition was a blaze of fury, defiance and "how-dare-you" indignation. Jacked on coffee and Jonathan Edwards, he wasted an afternoon creating a fiery screed that would have him going out unbowed and bare-knuckled, every syllable a conflagration, every breath a test of will, the pulpit seething with brimstone and bitter jabs into the air. Then, on Friday morning, his wife called him a "pissant," and by that evening, during a long, drab rain, a flamboyant collapse seemed—for an hour or so at least—like a good choice. Midway through this one, he started to use a Pentecostal tongue, typed the word "Gawd" a lot and didn't worry about periods, just strung together sentences he could preach big-time, throwing back his head and squeezing his eyes shut, the snot and tears running on his cheeks as he finished his career with a sopping, over-the-top, tent-revival mea culpa full of biblical caterwauling and pitifully rococo pleas to the forgiving heavenly Father.

It was all foolishness, though, silly and self-pitying, because his temperament was neither angry nor dramatic, and in the end he wasn't going to turn nasty or cry like the caramelized hucksters on the round-the-clock religion channels. Despite his musings and indulgences, there was little doubt he'd settle on fifteen minutes of typical Baptist formula—a New

Testament passage, a homily anchored in humanity and levity, and a message whose three small themes combined to reveal a bigger picture.

Standing beside his high-back chair in front of fifty-eight crowded pews, Joel could hear the choir crank up behind him, close to sixty pious folks cloaked by awkward robes with zippered fronts. There were a couple of strong baritones in the mix and a single passable alto, the rest an earnest muddle, a high, flat trilling that sounded vaguely strained and far too formal. Out in his church, he saw men and women standing shoulder to shoulder and sharing hymnals, the women giving every note its due, most of the men mute or barely mumbling the song's refrain. He was searching for something to keep, something vivid and clear he could walk off with: a shaft of blue-tinted light from the stained glass, a boy's loopy grin above a shirt collar several sizes too big, the furrows of wisdom and contentment that marked a sage face. He looked for the Lord's kind alms, took in everything before him with the hope of seeing more than was there.

All he got at first was a thought, an odd realization that skittered across his mind. It occurred to him that almost every house of worship he'd laid eyes on—this one included—was carpeted in red. He actually opened his mouth and whispered the word into the music: "Red." The color of so many things touched by his trade. Obviously he discerned the Savior's shed blood in the crimson floor, the gift of death and resurrection stretching from entrance to altar in commercial-grade glory that didn't show wear and was hard to soil. The color of passion was there, too, passion in so many of its ways and varieties, from generous to brutal. The hue of fire, the devil's shade, the heart's stain—just about everything under the sun was covered in the red aisles of the Roanoke First Baptist Church. And perhaps that is what I will take away from this day, Joel concluded as he shut his hymnal. That, and nothing else.

He opened his sermon with scripture from the Book of Matthew as his flock sat expectantly, waiting for a hint, an explanation, an apology, a denial. When he hesitated at five minutes before noon to sip from a water glass resting on the edge of the pulpit, backs turned rigid, ears cocked and the church's weight rustled and creaked forward. Walter Butler began rolling the dial on his hearing aid. Peggy and Larry Rice—newlyweds Joel had baptized after Larry's drug rehab—mouthed "Please, Jesus," and held hands. Joel cleared his throat and finished his last point, said nothing they wanted to hear, and as he called for the closing prayer, very few heads were bowed or humble. He peered out at the bewilderment and mild anger of people who felt they were owed and not paid. The single satisfied expression belonged to Edmund Brooks, who was staring at him from the far end of the front row, nodding slightly in the way people did when they agreed with their preacher, when the message had found truth or mentioned something everyone thought needed to be said.

Joel looked away from Edmund, letting his eyes wander through his congregation until a bit of magic stirred up in the corner of his sight, a striking impossibility that spun his head and returned him to Edmund's pew seat. Joel saw a red blur he'd overlooked, a silky scarlet rope suddenly growing out of the rug, as if the red on the floor were pouring into Edmund, rising from the ground. What in the Lord's name? What the . . . Queer as it seemed, it was like the crazy world was finally coming apart, trying to wrap itself around Edmund's windpipe.

Joel had to blink and scrub his eyes before he realized what was happening. There was nothing aberrant or miraculous in his vision, no Revelation's horse or water turning into wine—Edmund was simply wearing a necktie the exact color of the carpet. He was hunched forward, his elbows were propped on his thighs, and his posture caused the tie to fall in an unbroken crimson path that began at his collar and widened into more of the same at his feet. Like he was bleeding rug from his throat, Joel thought, or the ground had latched on to his neck with a red tether and was pulling him down. Even though Joel was able to solve the illusion, he still kept watch on Edmund during the prayer, cheating through slits that appeared completely closed.

Edmund was a newcomer to Roanoke First Baptist, a businessman from Las Vegas who'd been in town for a year or so. Sitting in church, he was simultaneously still and kinetic, jittery and static in the same outline, like a kid's whirligig with a spinning center inside a stationary metal frame, the whole contraption set off by yanking a string. Every Sunday he dropped a hundred-dollar bill into the collection plate—yes, the preacher was aware of who generously tithed—and he engulfed Joel's hand with two palms and ten fingers the first time the men met each other after the service, Joel dressed in his preacher's robe, Edmund in a black dandy suit. Edmund was dark-haired, tall and handsome, with powerful shoulders and features that fit together well, but Joel noticed early on that his left hand was somewhat peculiar. Edmund's ring finger was much smaller than the rest, not ugly or deformed, but just grown in miniature, a tiny fourth digit with a nail the size of a match head. Perhaps to compensate, he wore a diamond band on his middle finger and fancy cuff links that complemented the ring.

At the conclusion of the prayer, Joel stood beneath the pulpit while the choir ploughed through "Nearer My God to Thee." This was when people would walk up the aisle to join the church or ask for baptism; they would lean close to embrace Joel, and he would speak to them in a low voice—not a whisper, just his normal tone dropped two clicks softer—as the choir repeated the first and second verses of whatever hymn was being sung. He began to fade out of "Nearer My God" for an instant, things went quiet in his head, and the red floor, colored windows and fine clothes gradually receded, ebbed away from him. He swallowed hard and tried to wet his mouth, felt dread, sorrow and shame cutting through his stomach. No one came to the front asking to be saved, so he made his way to the end of the aisle, a crackling buzz in his ears and a tremble in his legs, adrenaline and tension seeping into his limbs as if a sickness were about to begin, a voracious, leeching fever.

At the door, people passed by in a Cubist jumble of eyes and lips and noses and teeth. He was trying to stay steady, trying to escape from the shakes and weakness, struggling to slow the gush of fractured, spotty scenes and piece them into sense. A little boy and girl were running up and down the center aisle, rambunctious twins were clamoring around under the pews, Nancy Fitzpatrick was removing flowers from the communion table, and Austin Whitehead was shutting off the sound system. On any other Sunday, Joel would have waited for everyone to leave, then humbly knelt in his empty church and said a prayer of thanksgiving.

About ten people into the line, he found a few crumbs of equilibrium and began to get a better take on the smears and fragments streaming by him. He was aware of several more hugs than he was used to, and tears. Folks recalled old times, their greetings were more heartfelt and somber than normal, and a man who wouldn't quit probing his face offered him a small wooden cross, carved by hand, he insisted, not store-bought. It was a compassionate crowd; the doubters and finger-waggers and letter-writers who wanted him gone had either stayed away or were skulking out the side exit, packs of men and women wound up in muttered, grumbling conversations. Horace Ayers waited until he was far removed from the sanctuary and almost to his car before he told his wife of twenty-six years Joel King was a liar and a damn disgrace. Of all the mob with torches and rope, only Foster Pullins—the deacon who'd pushed the hardest for Joel's dismissal— met him at the door and wished him well, claiming he'd remember Joel in his prayers.

Edmund Brooks smiled and shook hands, his same ritual repeated without any change, as if he'd understood the meaning of what Joel had done and wanted to abide by his minister's last wishes. "Good message, Preacher. A good sermon." Edmund always said this.

"Thank you," Joel answered.

"See you soon. You take care, okay?" This instead of "See you next week," his usual remark.

"I will. Thanks for everything." Joel gave Edmund a limp embrace before he turned to leave, then said goodbye to the Clements, a sweet, elderly couple who smelled of mothballs and liniment and took a long time to shuffle past. He glanced outside, where he noticed Edmund chatting with Regina Patterson. Edmund touched her arm—right above her elbow— and when he started to walk off, both his eyes were still on her, lagging behind, pure white at one corner of the sockets, his dark pupils jammed as far left as they could go at the other corner. Regina gazed at him, and a tiny separation appeared between her lips, a little gap she didn't do away with until Edmund had corrected his eyes and moved on. A few moments later, Edmund greeted her husband with the same pleasant vigor he brought to every exchange, said something cordial and looked over his shoulder at the church's doorway. Joel saw the whole affair for what it was, and was relieved he would not be charged with sorting through the alpha and omega of three people's sinful distress.

About half the crowd had filed by when Julie Richardson arrived in front of him. Julie was married to an orthopedic surgeon who was as diffident as she was brash. She was a gradation above the high end of acceptable, five tennis bracelets too many on one wrist and a face job at age forty-six that pulled her skin so taut her cheeks and forehead appeared to be grocery meat tightly bound in shrink-wrap. Today, her smooth, stretched countenance was conspicuously set on grim, and her whole person—jewels, perfume, snug skirt, tanning-bed-brown arms—was stacked onto four-hundred-dollar high heels, waiting to crash against Joel like a country-club tsunami. Here it comes, he thought. Here it comes.

Julie grabbed both his hands and then stood there theatrically mute for the longest time. She and Joel looked as if they were frozen in the middle of some zoot-suit swing step or at the very beginning of "London Bridge Is Falling Down." A playful child's foot clipped a pew near the front of the church, made a deep, bass sound that bounced all over the sanctuary.

"Joel, I'm so, so sorry about this," Julie announced, still at arm's length.

"Thanks. I appreciate your saying that."

"So very sorry," she repeated.

"Most things happen for a reason. You and Howard have been fine friends." He felt Julie tighten her grip. "I'm disappointed to be going. I'll miss everyone."

"And I don't care who hears it, I'll say it right here in front of the Lord and everyone else, but I *know* you didn't lay a hand on that girl. You did not touch her, and I'll say to anyone and everyone that she's a damn tramp and her father's a rich fool and you're being railroaded. So there." She twisted around to face the people standing behind her. "Railroaded," she said loudly.

"Julie, listen, I appreciate the support, but this is not the place or—"

She lunged forward and seized him, circled her bony arms around his ribs and patted his back. "You keep your chin up, Joel King. You're always welcome in our house." She pulled away, transferred a kiss from her fingertips to Joel's cheek, then jingled and sparkled down the front stairs, headed to a fine car and three or four afternoon white wines.

Beyond the rest of the people waiting, anxious to say goodbye or thank him for a generous visit to a sickbed, he caught sight of Martha, his wife, leaning against the end of a pew. She wouldn't look at him, wouldn't give an inch, kept a lifeless, tight smile cut into her face and avoided as many people as she could. She wasn't going to run out or leave early or be brought low in her own sanctuary, but she darn sure wasn't about to stand at Joel's elbow or hold his hand when they left and walked to the van to drive away. She was as enigmatic as he about what had happened, albeit with a little more cool edge in the way she said her few farewells and accepted a needlepoint verse from her ladies' Bible study group. Joel watched her suffer in her inexpensive minister's wife's dress, saw her tuck an errant strand of hair behind her ear.

Cathy Reynolds was a dependable, practical woman, a schoolteacher with two mannerly children, and she was next in line, behind Julie. She stood erect and wiped her eyes with a balled-up tissue. "Good luck, Joel."

"Thank you. Thanks."

"I can be at the trial if you like. To speak for you."

He half-smiled. "There's no need. And it wouldn't be right to drag this church into court."

Cathy opened her purse and stuffed the damp knot of tissue inside. "We believe in you, Joel. We really do. And no matter what happened, that doesn't change the good and decent man you are. All the fine things you've done, the time you've given, the families you've helped—we won't forget."

Joel hung his head, blocked almost the entire church from his view. He saw his wingtip shoes on the carpet, his own legs, Cathy Reynolds's ankles and shins, and a stray bulletin someone had dropped near the door. He surrendered, finally starting to cry, kept his face angled down and his body upright so the first tears never touched skin but just fell straight onto the rug, three or four sprinkles that turned the red a fuller, darker hue. Joel stayed bent and thanked Cathy a second time in a voice sad and dismal.

He was moved because he understood her affirmation, her pledge to him, was really much more than that. If he was a fraud and a cad, then this was about her and her worship and where she prayed and the fundamental things holding her faith together. If her minister was a liar, then what of his gospel? If she couldn't believe in his innocence and divine goodness, then she was merely another gullible chump, no better than some penniless, misguided freak standing atop a western mountain on the seventh day of the seventh year since the seventieth whatever, expecting the clouds to crack open and heaven's steps to unfold like attic stairs out of a ceiling.

Cathy ducked and slanted her head, trying to see Joel's face. "Things happen for a reason, Joel. The Lord always has a plan."

Joel didn't answer, and Cathy walked away. He glanced at the rest of the line, saw a family standing in front of him—the Wilsons—one of the kids holding something she'd made in Sunday school, the parents clutching Bibles. Suddenly Joel couldn't think of any reason to finish what he was doing, standing inches inside his church to shake hands with people he'd bruised and disappointed. He risked another peek at his wife. "You have ruined us," she'd told him last night. "I cannot forgive you for this." He lifted his hand above his head and gave a quick, stiff-wristed wave, a subdued version of his customary ending for the service, the benediction blessing, where he held both hands high and boomed good words, an entreaty to the Lord to be with him and his church "now and forevermore." As he pivoted and turned his back on the remnants of his congregation, he realized he had neglected the benediction today, had simply taken a numbed walk down the aisle when the final song was finished.

Joel stepped through the door into a pretty November afternoon, brisk and windless, the tail end of chimney smoke from the house down the street playing out in the air, the Blue Ridge Mountains tumbling and rising behind the parking lot. "You have ruined us, Joel." Dopers and drinkers can climb back into the ministry, often with a roguish flair and charisma that come from hitting bottom and wallowing in filth, then pulling free with a hard-knocks faith and a clean start. Adolescents listen whenever the heroin addict rolls up his sleeves and shows the needle scars; people find frankness and redemption in a prodigal evangelist's story of a fortune handed over to liquor and limousines; and sin and tribulation—as long as they're several years past—are the standbys in any preacher's bag of tricks. But a sex scandal involving a teenage girl is simply a getting-off point to nowhere, a fall from grace so abhorrent that it would only draw rebukes and frigid stares if offered as evidence of a minister's devil-wrestling credentials.

Joel began walking faster, considered looking back but didn't. He thought someone might call out his name or chase after him, but no one did. He never ran, though, no sir. While he hadn't been bold with his theology or a barn burner in the pulpit, he had been a steadfast pillar for his church, a tall, strapping, honest man whose acts were full of diligence and reflection and whose thoughtful sermons went directly to the point. He had won his congregation's trust and affection because of his rapturous dedication to even the most distasteful aspects of his duties: He'd journeyed to Haiti with his tools and carpenter's belt to help transform a shanty into a sturdy schoolhouse; he'd comforted the AIDS-rotted hand of a forty-year-old First Baptist electrician named Joe Barbour while the emaciated man's boyfriend wept and declared there was no God, no Heaven and no fairness for mankind; and he'd honored his denomination's dogma without becoming hidebound, had installed a woman as youth minister, allowed the NA addicts to smoke in the fellowship hall during their meetings, and often yielded discreetly to his wife's superior judgment in matters of ecclesiastical significance.

He left swiftly, embarrassed and contrite and tarnished, but he was not afraid and didn't run.

Christina Agnes Norway Darden's mother carried her to term without the slightest hint of distress, showed only a whispery sway along her abdomen at six months and never got sick or swollen or achy in her joints. When Christy was born, she seemed too clearly perfect, almost monstrously so, as if she were a fairy's hoax or a changeling wrought by hands overqualified for the task. She slept and ate and burped on an exact schedule, rarely cried, and spoke and toddled sooner than normal and all at once, with scant warning or transition. Her eyes, though, her eyes were the giveaway and the riddle: for several years after her birth, she blinked slowly . . . cautiously . . . infrequently, and when people tried to study her closely or discover what was inside, they got nowhere, zero, found themselves stymied by a warren of baffles and trapdoors just behind her pure blue gaze.

Not long after her twelfth birthday, the first glitches came, the unmistakable warnings—stealing cigarettes, calling a social studies teacher a bitch, shoplifting a tube of drugstore lipstick—but her parents treated the misdeeds like a lug in a car engine or a hesitation in an electrical switch, buried their heads and pretended the delinquency was a fluke or hiccup, all the while realizing Christy would probably grow worse, that they were witnessing starts and not a conclusion. And they simply didn't know what to do, because they'd done everything already—loved her and coddled her and bought her the best, spoiled her in fact. "Who the hell can get a handle on kids?" Big Bill Darden had snapped at his wife after they'd received another call from the grocery store, informing them that their fourteen-year-old daughter had been apprehended at the dairy case again, sniffing the tops of whipped cream, glassy-eyed and buzzed from the pops of amyl nitrite.

At sixteen there was a brief lull. Christy became withdrawn and introverted and happy to be let alone, spent a lot of time talking on the phone to friends and reading about animals, especially tigers, elephants and giraffes, even said she might want to study veterinary science, travel to Africa. Her parents purchased a new BMW for her, and she squealed and leapt with delight, hugged them both, shocked by how beautiful the car was and how expensive it smelled, like leather boots straight from the box.

The free fall began near the middle of her senior year at Cave Spring High School. Christy read a *Cosmopolitan* piece about Oscar Wilde—"Men We Love to Like"—discovered an old copy of *Bright Lights, Big City* and finally found her view of the world, decided there was far more joy in archness and revelry than in girls' soccer and prom committee. She and her two best friends became the "know-betters." The cute name was a puerile takeoff on the gracious atom bomb often dropped by a set of Roanokers who still did things a certain way, still had teas and cotillions and black-tie doings to raise money for the local theater troupe. Christy couldn't count the times her mother had complained over a whiskey sour that so-and-so down the avenue or some philistine at the club "surely should know better." The phrase was also a hoary Virginia reprimand, usually coupled with a full recitation of the offender's given names and spoken with practiced astonishment: "Chistina Agnes Norway Darden—you *know better* than that."

Inasmuch as self-awareness appeared to be the bedrock of correct living, the know-betters' credo was simple: you could do whatever you wanted, no matter how decadent, bad or bitchy, so long as you recognized that the pissy deed or tacky earrings were beneath accepted standards. Knowledge was the power to act as you pleased, a philosophy that quickly became too sloppy to be ironic and far too hands-on to be mistaken for aloofness. Not surprisingly, Christy's final summer before college turned into an unbroken stretch of wild, self-indulgent tumults and carte blanche partying, and no one really called her on it, especially when word got around about what had been happening over at Roanoke First Baptist.

Christy heard about Preacher Joel's sorry departure two days after he'd fled the church. She was sitting in a Charlottesville restaurant, spacing on the ting-ting-ting sounds in the background of the Chinese music, eating the crunchy noodles served with the wonton soup and letting the rest of her meal go cold, when a friend from Roanoke stopped by her table and shared the news, then congratulated her for being so strong. Her parents had probably called, too, but she hadn't checked her messages since Friday, didn't feel like dealing with all that. "What's the sound I'm hearing in the music?" she asked the friend. "A flute or something? It kinda inhabits your skull, huh?" Christy and her date, a grubby Roman—as in numeral; he was a IV—had been drinking bourbon and vacuuming crank since ten that morning, and it was now dusk.

"Enchanting," the walleyed Roman declared, and he and Christy fell into a laughing jag, ignored the kind girl standing beside them and lost track of where she went and what she said as she left.

It was maybe a week later—Christy didn't really keep up with days and dates—when she decided to call Joel. She was sitting on the sofa at her condominium, dressed in a sweatshirt, panties and a pair of men's silk stockings that fit poorly, too loose in the calves, the heels climbing the rear of her legs. She couldn't recall where she'd come across the socks, but she did remember spending the last three days with a stockbroker named Josh, having sex and taking showers and eating Häagen-Dazs with her hands. She knew better, of course. Josh had dropped her next to Scott Stadium because she was winding down from some methamphetamine and gin and starting to freak a little, and for some reason she didn't want him to know her address even though he was severely gorgeous and drove a superb Porsche.

Her hands were shaking, the burning in her nose was poking toward her brain, and her elbow had been skinned, leaving a patch of torn red flesh that was just starting to scab. Things were slipping away . . . slipping away. Slipping away. She'd been to maybe ten classes all year, and here it was almost Christmas. She'd decided on the University of Virginia because it was close to home and seemed to have its fair share of weekday parties and Roman layabouts with guaranteed incomes, but she'd not figured on the place being so damn hard. The professors were old bastards full of bile and departmental grudges who heaped on work and had no interest in the short-skirt treats she obliquely offered. Her advisor was constantly hounding her, some counselor kept phoning and leaving shit on her door, and this self-important boy in a blazer from the student something-or-other came by to let her know he "was there" for her. Great.

What also was there for Christy was a problem so daunting—one of her favorite words—that all her father's considerable money and all her considerable allure might not be able to make it vanish. A vile crone who taught her horrible English class had charged her with an honor violation, which meant she could get kicked out of school. Christy had purchased her first research paper from the *Rolling Stone* classifieds, typed a cover sheet with a new title and her name, and turned in the fine work on Edgar Allan Poe a day before the deadline. It was early in the semester when some good parties were popping up, so she was anxious to get her nails done and shop for new shoes and find an afternoon bash. The first couple pages she'd skimmed seemed like okay stuff, so who could've guessed there'd be a stupid disclaimer at the end of the paper, warning everybody that the essay was written by a professor and should be used only as a research tool? So she submitted Professor Holt of Stanford's Poe discussion with the telltale message still attached, looked like a cheat *and* a dumbass.

She probably could ride this thing with Joel a tad longer though, and that might, just might, win her some sympathy in the honor hearing, if she could remember when she was supposed to show up for that kangaroo court. She'd written it down somewhere but hadn't even told her parents yet. She'd have to work herself into a good bawl for the confession, say over and over she had no idea how this had happened, and let *them* suggest it was because of the stress and trauma. After all, she'd had no problems with her grades in high school, just a few brushes with the law and some community service hours the judge made her do and a totally unfair DUI on graduation night.

Her hands wouldn't stay still and she really *was* going to call Joel, but first she needed to find Thomas and have him bring by some Valium to level her mood. This meant she'd have to screw him, and even worse, he'd want to hang around after they were done and play his ratty guitar. Perhaps he'd settle for something quicker. She felt bad about everything with Joel, but no way was she backing out of this now. Everyone would kill her, especially her father, and—duh—there'd be no payoff, no fat, liberating check from the church to compensate her for her suffering. It would be cool if she and Joel could somehow hook up, not forever, but just for a while. She really liked him, that's what she wanted to say. She should call and say hello and let him know how miserable and guilty she was about what was happening. And say something slutty right before she got off the line, like how hot his kisses made her, unroll the flypaper a little bit more.

Even after three calls, Thomas was taking a decade to get there, so she punched in Joel's number and listened to it ring and ring and ring. At the restaurant, her dopey friend had told her Joel didn't have to go to jail until after Christmas, so he ought to be around, and he probably wasn't doing anything important. But his wife answered the phone—a hazard she hadn't even considered in her addled state—and the whole idea got far too daunting. Christy didn't say a word. Her hand had this twitchy, mercurial palsy, and she could barely keep the receiver next to her ear. Her tongue was dead and useless, a giant, fossilized slug filling the space in her mouth.

"Christy, is that you? Christy?"

Fucking caller ID. Busted.

She hung up and looked out the window. No sign of Thomas. She remembered there was some champagne in the fridge, but it had been there for a long time, without a cork or stopper. She wondered whether the alcohol evaporates or only the fizz. She and Josh the stockbroker had done away with a fifth that evening, and she wanted some more booze to keep her buzz marching. When she checked, the bottle was still in the refrigerator, although she could tell from picking it up there wasn't much left to drink. She started gulping the flat dregs without a glass; the taste was stale and toothless, like cold water with a trace of something poisonous mixed in.

Thomas finally arrived at her condo, and he wanted to sing to her, but she was ready to get down to business, really wanted the Valium. So she put her hand in his pants, and she made him give her five pills. She took them all, washed into her gullet with the last of the spent champagne.

Before too long, he was on top of her, working like a busy bee, saying things that bounced off her ears and didn't sink in. The drugs did their job right away, put the kibosh on her tremors, and she started to feel loose and warm. The heat began at her toes, then filled in below her knees, felt like a gentle quilt being pulled across her. She looked past Thomas's jackhammering butt to see what was happening, discovered that both socks were missing and her legs were naked. The feeling crept into her stomach, and she reminded herself to breathe because her lungs were next, then her heart. She lost herself for a few minutes, and when she picked up again the cozy sensation had broken out in her wrists and hands.

She wondered when Thomas would realize she'd fallen unconscious. He'd probably keep humping and not even notice, then pull out the guitar and strum "Fire and Rain" like it was some huge treasure. Kiss her mouth before he left and not catch on that she was the same temperature as the room. The comfort slid into her neck and fingered her jaw, and she was gone except for the last little snatch of her face. She turned a cheek flush to the pillow and forgot about breathing. She wasn't sure she'd come to again, but a melancholy ending had been in the back of her mind for several weeks now. She'd seen the hobgoblins who were riding shotgun with the drugs and booze and handsome boys, knew what there was to know and simply didn't give a shit.

Seven months after his last sermon, Joel King is weaving laces into a pair of tennis shoes, watching his fingers lead the strings through the metal eyes, making small crosses from his toes to his ankles, and he's thinking that not many people know the difference between a jail and a penitentiary. The joint, the slammer, the pen, the hoosegow, the clink, the state's hotel, the can—it's no big deal to the bridge-club ladies or the go-getters at the Jaycee meeting, nothing but a slew of funny names for the same sordid spot. Even after he'd been convicted and herded out of the courtroom with an ornery bailiff's handcuffs biting his wrists, the distinction didn't seem very important to Joel, just more words in a will-o'-the-wisp, Lewis Carroll, tweaks-and-shades, hide-the-ball justice system that struggled to be incomprehensible, full of phonetic clouds and black velvet curtains.

Six months in *jail,* though, had taught him what was what. The pen is the big top, the zenith of time behind bars, the Olympus of isolation, a place crammed with fear and shivs, gangs and sodomy, endless days curling dumbbells, riots, constant tension and a stubborn, rich depravity that leaks from the prisoners, oozing into their gazes and coiling around their words. Penitentiaries are inhabited by men with only a cosmetic connection to humanity, men who have worn a victim's warm intestines as a necklace, men who have killed without giving it a second thought, men who have slashed and stolen and lied and peddled dope out of a Corvette window to fourteen-year-old crackhead girls and their worthless whore mothers.

Jail, on the other hand, is an altogether different place, a local cage filled with fools, losers, drunks, yahoos and riffraff, all chatter and threat, punk wannabes who will end up spending most of their lives at mom's apartment or grandma's rundown trailer. Jail is home to thirty-year-old ciphers and wastrels, small-timers whose eyes are always narrowed for one reason or another, the men and boys who talk big and then cry and fret in open court when they draw a few months for stealing a lawnmower or wheels from an old Mustang. These are the bush-league criminals, the failures at failing.

The deal Joel had accepted seemed good enough at the time: guilty pleas to two counts of contributing to the delinquency of a minor, twelve months to serve, twelve months suspended, and he could do the sentence in the Roanoke city jail, not Augusta or Powhatan or some other penitentiary packed with inked-up felons who would, as his lawyer put it, "bend you over and break you down like a shotgun." The charges were misdemeanors, there was no mention of rape or sex, he could turn himself in after Christmas and he'd only have to actually pull six months.

If he had it to do again, Joel is thinking, he might take his chances in the penitentiary, because the tedium of the city jail had almost smothered him. Each day was the same dull progression of idle chatter, crackpot philosophy, food complaints, hopeless escape schemes and jokes about the dandruff on the guards' brown shirts. Every inmate was planning to puncture the judge's tires or put sugar in the commonwealth's attorney's gas tank or "tell what he really knew," and on and on and on and on it went, played out against a backdrop of "Freebird," Metallica and afternoon game shows. Maybe living with a little menace and wickedness would be better than spending half a year in a crowded cell with men who didn't pay child support and dreamed about becoming NASCAR mechanics.

More than anything, Joel's jail sentence corroded his minister's optimism and caused him to look at people differently. Loving his neighbor—tolerating his neighbor, even—became a heavy labor when there appeared to be so little divine spark in some of the men he lived with behind bars. It wasn't as if these were worthy souls corrupted by Satan's bait or the devil had taken up residence in their bowels; it was worse than that. There were prisoners who seemed set apart, soulless like dogs or cats or cows, blameless for the most part inasmuch as the whole scheme of good and evil was not anywhere in them. They worked on impulse and instinct, locked out of salvation games they weren't skilled enough to play. All the explanations and all the noble instruction in the world couldn't move some of these convicts one whit, nor could the wiles of hell cause them to make the wrong choice. They were what they were. Hardly God's children, these were his unruly mock-ups, fistfighting for no apparent reason and occasionally masturbating after lunch with a foil packet of Thousand Island dressing and wiping the results on the wall, grinning like monkeys the entire time they worked themselves. Still, Joel struggled not to despise them. They were put on earth by the Lord, borne of mothers who came to visit on Sunday afternoons.

Joel finished lacing his sneakers and tied the strings tight against his ankles. It was the first time he'd worn comfortable shoes and his own pants and shirt since his day in court. The jail issued orange plastic sandals and orange jumpsuits, and he'd been allowed five pair of white briefs and T-shirts. When Joel had arrived to serve his punishment, he'd naively brought clothes and belts and books and razors and trail mix—"*fucking* trail mix," the jailer had hooted—as well as a ziplock bag full of Band-Aids, Handi Wipes and aspirin. "You want the moccasin kit or the water-color kit?" the officer processing him had asked.

"Pardon?" Joel was standing in a small room with a desk, naked except for his underwear.

"Which kit you want? The one to make shoes, or the one for painting?"

"I didn't realize I got a kit. I don't really know. What would you suggest?"

"What I would suggest," the officer said, smirking and shaking his head, "is you ain't at no summer camp, and you'll be leaving your swim trunks and all your other shit here with me."

"Oh. Well, then, what do I do about clothes and medical attention and—"

"We'll take care of that for you."

"What *can* I have?" Joel didn't know what to do with his hands. Ordinarily, they would have been in his pockets.

"Basically, what we decide you can," was the answer.

After he was through with his shoes, Joel washed his hands, sat down on his bunk, opened his Bible and read the beginning of First Corinthians. As he did every morning, he prayed, asked to be forgiven of his sins and begged the Lord to restore him to a virtuous life. A few minutes later, Will Cassady, his favorite jailer, appeared with a set of long, sturdy keys, unlocked a series of doors and nodded at him. "Today's the day, Preacher."

The four other men in Joel's cell stopped jawing and poring over a hot-rod magazine. At first they'd apologized when they cursed or mentioned sex, and for a month or so Kenny—a third-offense drunk driver—had talked to Joel about religion and his children and what he could gain from prayer. In February, though, Kenny wrangled a prescription for Xanax and that was the end of that. Once again, the cell was a cauldron of profanity, childish bickering and body stench, all hope reduced to cars, dope and girlfriends waiting in a motel room with a bottle of Wild Turkey, any notion of restraint or religious deference completely forgotten.

When Joel stood to leave, Kenny and the other three were quiet, the lot of them staring at him. Kenny flipped a magazine page. "Later on, man," he said. "Keep the faith."

"Hope you walk out of this shithole right into some good times," added Watkins Hudson. Watkins laughed, showing his teeth and pink gums. He'd been jailed since December for forging checks stolen from a sickly aunt.

Will took Joel by the arm and guided him into the main run. "I don't see how you stomached that for six months," he told Joel.

Will was one of the respectable jailers, a lanky boy who wanted to be a state trooper and was starting at the bottom of the system. He led Joel into the same cramped office he'd visited upon arriving, pointed at a chair for him, sat down and tore open a large yellow envelope. Will gave him back everything he'd brought to the jailhouse and had him sign a form. In the bewilderment of his first days behind bars, Joel had asked one of the church members to pick up his forbidden personal articles, but his snacks, food and trail mix were still in a locker, returned to him molded and rat-bitten, the wrappers riddled with messy holes.

Will sighed. "Why in the world did that get left here?"

"Who knows," Joel said, genuinely puzzled, and tossed all of it into a trash can beside the desk.

"Good luck to you, Joel."

"Thanks." Joel held out his hand, and Will shook it.

"So, are you goin' back to preachin'? Are you still a preacher?"

Joel considered the question. "I'm not sure what I am."

"You'll be okay." Will slipped the paper Joel had signed into a file.

"I hope so. It's kind of you to say."

"You mind if I ask you something? You don't have to answer if you don't want to. I mean, you've been tried and convicted and done your time and the case is over. I was wonderin', curious. A lot of folks don't think you were guilty. You sure don't seem like the type to me."

Joel lapsed into a battened silence, sat mute and stock-still as if he hadn't heard the question or—if he had—meant to repel it rather than answer. He was focusing on Will and choking the urge to tell this sympathetic boy that yes, you bet, there was more to the story than the obvious, run-of-the-mill tawdriness of an old-goat minister romping after a beautiful teenager, the same tired song and dance. It would've been nice to be granted a ticket back into common society for five minutes, briefly freed from the ranks of the shunned and reviled. But no matter how truthful his response, it would seem self-serving and convoluted, and it was well nigh impossible for him to explain his situation to a callow jailer. Also, critical portions of the tale were still mysterious to Joel himself, details he couldn't provide and gaps he couldn't close, so he'd sound just like any other convict, claiming he didn't know how the dope wound up in his sock or the pilfered TV materialized in his trunk, his defense a crude farce.

Will finally broke the quiet. "I didn't mean to upset you," he said apologetically, absorbing Joel's ferocious silence. "Or to pry."

Joel ended the debate with himself and opened his features. "Not your fault," he remarked, looking at his watch. The band felt taut and odd on his wrist since he hadn't worn any jewelry after entering the jail. "I pled guilty, Will. What else can I tell you? I've served my six months and would just as soon put all this behind me."

"Sure." Will tapped the folder's spine against the desk. "Okay."

Joel pitched him an unconvincing grin. "Hey, no one in this place is guilty, right?"

"So I've heard."

"No offense, but I hope this is the last time we see each other under these circumstances," Joel said. "Thanks for treating me so fairly."

"I got a couple more things to finish here, and we'll have you gone before you know it."

Joel left the jail with his Good Book tucked under his arm, stepped outside for the first time in a long while, into the heat and sounds of the city. He heard a car's motor turn over and take hold and the harsh, steady warnings of a garbage truck that was in reverse, backing down an alley. He pulled as much breath as he could through his mouth, tasted summer on his tongue and felt hot, syrupy air hang at the beginning of his throat. Mildly disoriented, he shaded his eyes and checked the horizon, trying to locate Mill Mountain, where a huge electrical star—a five-pointed landmark made from steel and neon tubes—capped a stout peak. The high site was visible from almost every quarter of the city, even during the day, before the sun dimmed and the juice was switched on. Buildings blocked Joel's view, though, and he wasn't able to find the star. Sprawled gum-popping in his bunk and dawdling through clichés and possibilities, he had wondered how this moment would feel, and now that he was out from behind bars— a free man—he saw and sensed hundreds of things routine and familiar and felt no different than he had the day before or the day before that.

There was no elation or relief, no sense of commencement or finality, only the nagging numbness of awaiting whatever might come next.

Roanoke had been a splendid fit for him, an agreeable city with a frank, homespun skyline, two liberal-arts colleges where the kids were always dancing, painting, acting and singing, a farmers' market and a civic center that booked New York production companies, weeklong circuses and famous rock-and-roll bands. The community, though, had never outgrown itself, and invariably Joel would cross paths with a neighbor in the soup-and-pasta aisle at the grocery or happen into a conversation with a stranger while eating a downtown hot dog and elbow-leaning against the counter at the wiener stand. He would very much miss this part of the world, all its people and its gracious, comely aspects.

He glanced at a crowded intersection and saw Edmund Brooks jogging toward him, doing his best to navigate an unruly sidewalk, veering around a woman and her small dog and snaking through people and a light pole and a rumpled panhandler who'd set up shop on the curb, just above the gutter. Edmund was wearing one of his fine suits, and his shirttail had started to work out of his pants during his dash down Campbell Avenue. He waved at Joel from a block away and slowed to a fast walk, bouncing and chugging for several steps as he changed gaits. When he finally pulled up in front of Joel, he raked his hand through his hair and wiped a sleeve across his forehead. "Oh my, I'm sorry to be late. I couldn't find a parking spot anywhere near the jail," he said. He was sweating clear streaks that started at his sideburns and trickled down to his jaws.

"It's no problem. I only got released a few minutes ago, and I figured you'd meet me here, not inside." Joel smiled and grabbed Edmund's hand. "I should be thanking you. You're kind to come and get me."

"Glad I could help. Least I could do, good as you've been to me." Edmund put his arm over Joel's shoulder. "I guess it's great to be done with everything, huh?"

"Yeah."

The two men departed the jail's front entrance with Edmund's arm still draped across Joel's shoulders. Several church members had written Joel while he was incarcerated, and a few had left him books or magazines at the administrative desk, but Edmund had been his most reliable friend, stopping by for Sunday visiting hours to talk about sports and restaurants and swap harmless jokes. One afternoon, Edmund seemed glum—unusual for him—and he'd asked Joel to pray with him. The two men bowed their heads and Joel offered a prayer; at the end they both said amen. A week later, when Joel mentioned that his sister in Montana had agreed to let him stay with her, Edmund clapped his hands together and promised him a ride west. "I drive to Vegas every couple months or so, gamble a little and check on some investments. Just let me know the date you're gonna need to travel that direction, and I'll work around your schedule. You'd be doin' me a favor—the company would more than make up for the detour. Anyway, what's a couple extra days on the road?"

They were leaving straightaway, as Joel hadn't seen any reason to loiter around town, and had walked three blocks when Joel heard someone shouting his name. He checked behind him, and Will Cassady was loping down the sidewalk, coming in a rush. Joel stopped where he was, watching Will get closer and closer.

"What in blue blazes is he doing?" Edmund wondered out loud.

Joel shrugged. "I'm not sure. You think they made a mistake or something? I counted the days myself. I've done my sentence, every second of it." He noticed a tingle in his stomach, felt his heart accelerate.

Will hurried to a halt in front of them. He was wearing his hat and didn't seem winded by the sprint. "Hey, Preacher." Will held up his hand.

"Hello, Will," Joel said. "What's the matter?"

"I'm glad I caught you. Some civil papers just come through, and I'm afraid I got to serve 'em on you."

"Civil papers?" Joel repeated. "I don't understand."

"Uh, they're divorce papers, sir. From your wife. She's filed for a divorce." Will looked at the ground as he was explaining his business.

"It seems safe to assume they're from his wife if it's a divorce suit," Edmund said. He was very poised.

"Right," the policeman answered, handing Joel a collection of papers. "I'm sorry to come racin' after you and all, but they just got to us and I knew you was leavin' for Montana and what a mess that would be, gettin' you properly served out there."

Joel didn't know what to say.

"Study 'em real good and hire yourself a lawyer. You've got three weeks from now to answer what she's filed."

"Why? Why would she . . . ? The timing, I mean." Joel looked at him. "Why would she do this the very day I'm released?"

"Well, sometimes it gets complicated to file for divorce when your husband or wife's in jail. A few of the judges make the other side pay for a guardian to look after the one incarcerated, so if you ain't got long to serve, it's cheaper and less hassle to wait. It's probably nothin' spiteful."

"She could've at least shown him the courtesy of telling him in advance," Edmund complained. "Pretty inconsiderate, if you ask me."

Joel turned through the sheets, saw numbered paragraphs and a big, gaudy lawyer's scrawl at the bottom of the last page. He folded the papers twice and stuck them in his hip pocket. "Not quite the fresh beginning I'd imagined, huh?"

"Hang in there, Joel. The worst's behind you." Will tipped his hat. "Sorry I was the one bringin' the bad news. Just doin' my job. Hope you understand."

"Certainly," Joel said. He gave Will a thin, weary smile. "Of course I understand."

"Okay then. You take care now." Will had started off when the radio on his wide, polished belt announced, "Dispatch to fifty-two," the voice a woman's, the words surrounded by cracks and static. He hesitated and then lifted the radio to his mouth. The radio's clip snapped when he pulled it from his side, metal sprung against metal. "Fifty-two. Go ahead."

Joel was rooted to the cement, deflated, the little surge of spirit his release had provided completely gone.

Edmund touched his arm, nudging him up the street. "Don't let it ruin your day, Joel. You're better off without a wife who won't stick with you through hard times."

"That's kind of distorting things," Joel said. "I suppose I knew this was coming, but—"

"Preacher, can you hold on a sec?" Will was fitting the radio back onto his belt.

"Wait here?" Joel peered at the policeman. "What for?" He made a beseeching sweep with his hands and raised his eyebrows.

"I need you to wait with me for another second or two."

"What the hell is it now?" Edmund demanded.

"Just some more papers. No big problem." Will's voice gathered an edge.

"I can't see any reason he has to stay here if he doesn't want to." Edmund folded his arms across his chest. "In fact, we're about to leave town."

The policeman stiffened, took up the slack in his neck and shoulders. "Sir, this is between me and Mr. King, so you may want to keep out of it."

"Keep out of *what*? I was simply asking a question."

"No sir. You didn't ask me any question. You directed profanity at me when I attempted to address the subject here about my radio dispatch."

Edmund shook his head and tightened his face, drew his eyes small and stern. "Pardon me? First, I merely asked a question. Second, I did not direct anything *at* you. Third, there's no need for *you* to start in with the *Dragnet* and *Starsky and Hutch* routine. 'Subject' and 'radio dispatch' probably scare the pants off the teenage smokers and skateboarders at the mall, but I ain't real impressed by it."

"Maybe you'd be impressed by an obstruction of justice charge."

"What? You *are* kidding, I assume."

"You heard me. You say one more word to impede me and I'll have to place you in custody, sir. This is your final warning."

Edmund tossed his head back and belly-laughed, a big roar full of swagger. He stretched his arms straight out in front of him, turned down his palms. " 'One more word to impede me.' " He recited the phrase snidely, mocking the officer. "There—I said it. So go on and call the paddy wagon. You'll love doin' security on the graveyard shift at the sewing plant, and I need a new Cadillac and a bigger diamond." Edmund's hands were still in front of him, and he wiggled his middle finger. The stone in his ring captured the light and fired off a quick, flashing arc.

Joel wasn't sure how things had been pushed this far. He'd missed a few sentences at the start, had been concerned about the divorce suit in his pocket and befuddled by the policeman chasing after him when he thought he was rid of that part of his life. He knew Edmund was taking his side, determined the police and their papers and their walkie-talkies would not get the better of either of them. Edmund was scowling at the jailer, still standing with his arms extended, diamond-Frankenstein waiting for the cuffs.

"Will, what is it you need?" Joel asked in a soft voice. "Let's not make this a hardship for anyone." He put his hand on one of Edmund's perpendicular arms and pushed it down. Edmund lowered the other limb by himself.

"Dispatch says there's another bunch of papers I have to serve on you," Will said. He remained locked onto Edmund, didn't look at Joel when he spoke.

"More papers? What kind of papers? About the divorce? I don't understand."

"I'm not sure, but they're on the way. That's all I wanted to tell you. Of course, your friend wants to get himself arrested over somethin' that basic."

Will and Edmund were still facing each other, both of them tense and raw. "I think, Officer, that you're the one who went to full-blown fury when—"

"We'll wait right here," Joel interrupted. "No problem. Hey, how much worse can this batch be than the ones I just got?"

"I never said we wouldn't stay. We never even got to that point. Certainly I want to do what's right." Edmund's words had a jot of disdain in them—probably not enough, Joel decided, to register on the jailer.

"Exactly," Joel agreed.

"Thanks, Joel," Will said. "I 'preciate it." He relaxed and finally ended his stare-down with Edmund.

Another policeman arrived with a second set of papers and gave them to Joel. The new cop stood beside Will while Joel read the latest pleadings from the court system.

"What is it now?" Edmund asked. "They leave somethin' out of the divorce?"

"No."

"So what's goin' on?"

"Well . . ." Joel paused to skim the pages again. "Well, it looks like Christy has decided to sue me for, uh, what happened."

Will stared at his feet for an instant, then raised up. "I got to be movin' on. Sorry, Preacher. And good luck. I mean it." He motioned to the other officer, a flabby man who'd just lit a cigarette. "Let's go, Pete." Will touched the brim of his police hat but didn't doff it. "See you later."

"Thanks, Will." Joel's arms were limp, the insides of his biceps resting against his ribs, the lawsuit barely hanging in his hand.

"Let me take a look, Joel," Edmund said. "I mean, if you don't mind."

Joel lifted the papers a few inches, left them swinging from his fingers. "See for yourself."

Edmund took the stapled sheets and held them in front of his face. He moved his head back and forth and read some of the lines aloud, slurred through several sections with legal terms, and impatiently said "Yeah, yeah, yeah" when he hit a bog on the second page. He flipped to the last paragraph, and his eyes popped. "Shit, Joel—sorry, sorry to say that—I mean, this thing is for five million dollars."

"That part I understood." He managed a faint grin. He saw a man toss the sidewalk bum some change.

" 'Sexual assault' . . . 'intentional infliction of emotional harm . . .' " Edmund was examining the suit papers again. " 'Two million dollars for compensatory damages, plus punitive damages in the amount of three million dollars . . .' " He shot Joel an amazed look. "This is unbelievable."

Joel sighed. "How many times can I get punished for the same mistake? I've been hauled into court, done my jail sentence, had my life ruined at age forty-two, asked to be forgiven and tried to clear the slate. Isn't there double jeopardy or something? Do they get to pound me till I die?"

"Right. Exactly. That has to be right. They can't keep draggin' this up forever." Edmund returned the papers to Joel. "Enough's enough."

"I don't have squat, Edmund. Nothing. We lived in the church's parsonage, and I signed over our sliver of savings to my wife months ago. I've got a thousand dollars in a short-term CD and some knickknacks and books in a friend's attic. I used my last hundred dollars to fund my canteen account at the jail and spent every dime of it."

"Look, you definitely need a lawyer. I don't think this is legal."

"I'm not going to fight it. And I'm sure not planning to contest the divorce."

Other than the panhandler, there was suddenly and inexplicably only a single pedestrian in sight, a man with a cane crossing the street at a corner. Joel watched him hobble along the pavement, saw the colors in the traffic lights, the white letters in the WALK sign, the plate-glass windows in a line of shops and storefronts. He and Edmund were alone, standing in a section of the city everyone else had abandoned for an instant, the sounds of cars and people's comings and goings two or three streets over, walled off by solid rows of brick buildings.

"You can't just ignore this," Edmund encouraged Joel. "You'd never get out from under five million dollars if they score that kinda money against you." Edmund waved his hands, became more animated. "Listen, if it's money for a lawyer that's the problem, I can help with finances. And I can hook you up with one of the best cape-and-hat guys in the business. He—"

"Cape-and-hat guys?" Joel cocked his head. "I'm not sure I follow you."

"It's what I call lawyers, 'cause lawyers are vampires and vampires wear those long capes and weird hats. At least the old ones did, the black-and-white ones like Bela whatshisname. Cape-and-hat guys. I know a bunch of 'em, given that I'm in a high-risk profession."

"Why should I fight any of it, Edmund? Why? My wife's entitled to ask for a divorce. I still love her and I wish she wouldn't, but I can see her side of things. It breaks my heart, but I don't know how to change her mind. As for the money Christy's demanding—good luck. I don't have anything and probably never will, and I certainly haven't done a whole lot that's affected her life one way or the other. But it's not worth the battle. I mean—and I'm not trying to be critical—the whole church is familiar with her background and problems, and our little episode doesn't amount to a fly on an elephant's butt."

Edmund chuckled. " 'A fly on an elephant's butt . . .' I like that. And it's the stone truth. Having sex with you was probably—well, sorry, you know what I'm sayin'. I wasn't suggesting you did somethin' wrong."

"I know."

Edmund gave Joel a square look. "Listen, I got a fine cape-and-hat I want you to talk to when we get to Vegas. I'm already scheduled to see him anyway. It won't cost you nothin', and I'll feel better about it. Just let him go over all this and see what he thinks. Can't hurt, right? Let's be sure we know everything there is to know. Half the time it seems to me they make up this law rigmarole as they go along."

Joel shrugged. "I appreciate the offer, but I'll have to think about it."

On their way out of town, Joel asked Edmund to stop at a strip-mall Kmart. It was still early, only a few minutes after ten, and the store was just stirring to life. A group of kids was set up near the business's entrance, selling green-and-white boxes of Krispy Kreme doughnuts from a card table. A slipshod, poster-board sign with glue-and-glitter letters was taped to the front of the table, the glitter so lean and off-center in spots that it was impossible to miss the black Magic Marker skeleton underneath. Two girls and two boys, probably juniors or seniors in high school, were pushing the doughnuts to raise money for the marching band. The girls were giggly and the boy sitting behind a poorly organized money box had his hat turned backward and was wearing sunglasses and an earring.

Edmund looked at the kids, then at Joel. "Go on in. I'm going to investigate a little nourishment."

"I like the chocolate-covereds if they have them," Joel said.

"I'll take care of it, Preacher." Edmund gave him a thumbs-up.

Joel walked into the store and searched the toiletries aisle for in-house brands and odd lots, and he found a table stacked with discounted clothes, priced for clearance because of some irregularity or obvious flaw. He selected a three-pack of underwear, two shirts, walking shorts and a pair of long pants with a blue stain on the crotch, a baseball hat, deodorant and a cheap razor. His wife had shipped all his belongings to his sister's in Missoula, this about two months into his incarceration. She hadn't visited him a single time and had written only twice, first to ask where he wanted his things sent, once more to inquire where he kept the keys for the backyard shed.

He didn't blame her for shunning him and continued to write every week. Sometimes his letters were personal and filled with reminiscences and retellings of things they'd done and seen, sometimes he wrote about how he passed the time in jail, and occasionally he broached the subject of his mistakes and explained how much he loved her and his hope that they might reconcile. For their anniversary he'd arranged for her to receive lilies and a chocolate assortment, had exhausted the last of his canteen account and gone without Nabs, chips and Dr Peppers for the final sixty days of his jail stint. She was aware he was willing to commit to anything that would result in his restoration, but she wouldn't lower the bridge to the citadel. Touching the wad of legal papers on his hip, he thought it remarkable that his failings could be distilled into such prim cant and carried around in his pocket.

There was no line at the register, and he walked out of the store with a few items in a flimsy plastic bag, starting over, about to ride across the country, disconnected in every possible fashion. He saw Edmund at the doughnut stand, planted in front of the table, pointing at the cash tray. The hat-and-earring boy and the two girls seemed agitated, all of them refusing to look at Edmund, and the other boy had moved several feet away from his friends.

"That twenty was already in the box, sir," the taller of the girls said. She stepped hard on the word "sir."

"I gave you a twenty," Edmund said calmly, "and there it is. The Krispy Kremes cost four dollars, so you owe me sixteen bucks. Now—you're simply going to have to give it to me. Otherwise, I'll complain to the security force here, have them shut you down and request they report you to the police."

"You can't do that," the hat-and-earring boy said, but there wasn't much conviction in his voice. It squeaked and fluttered on the last word.

Edmund laughed. "Why can't I? Don't you kids have an adult nearby, someone in charge?"

"Mr. Walters had to run back to the school."

"Well then, ladies and gentlemen, it's your decision. I'm not going to stand here all year and argue with you." Edmund leaned forward over the table. He was a good three or four inches beyond six feet, a year or so away from fifty.

"Just give him the money, Harold," the shorter girl said. "Even though I know he's wrong."

Edmund held out his hand, and Harold gave him a ten, a five, and a single. Edmund laid the dollar on the table and put the other bills in his wallet. "No hard feelings, guys. Hope you raise plenty of money. Keep the extra buck."

The boy smirked at Edmund. "Wow, thanks. That really makes our day. A whole dollar."

Edmund grunted and tilted his head, stared down at the kids and boxes and money. He picked up the dollar again, suspended it between himself and the students for an instant, then reached into his rear pocket for his billfold. "Smart mouth means no tip." He glanced at Joel. "Ah. My minister, children. The Reverend King. I guess it's time to go." Edmund tucked the dollar inside his wallet and strode off, Joel a few paces behind him.

"What was that about?" Joel asked once he caught up.

"Darn kids made a mistake with my change," Edmund replied.

They climbed into Edmund's white Cadillac, and he cranked the engine. Strangely, though, he kept them sitting there, didn't make any effort to leave the parking area. The air-conditioning came on in a burst, but there was almost no noise, only a flurry of air around Joel's face. Edmund flipped open the box and speared a doughnut with his index finger. "Help yourself," he offered.

"Thanks." Joel adjusted the vent and reached for the box.

"Nothin' in the world better than a fresh doughnut. I remember my mom would heat 'em up and feed 'em to us for breakfast, along with a big glass of sweet milk."

"Thanks for getting them." Joel took a bite. "I hope chocolate is okay with you."

"Chocolate's fine." Edmund used his free hand to reposition his seat and operate the outside mirror controls before continuing. "Joel, I need to talk to you about somethin', somethin' important. I want to lay my cards on the table now, quick as I can. And I don't want you to think I'm twistin' your arm or tryin' to take advantage of you." Edmund's voice was a mix of accents and rhythms, a peculiar amalgam of tongues: there were a number of flat, sparse pronunciations that seemed to come from the country's center as well as periodic lush southern vowels and an occasional pinched syllable that sliced a word short.

"What is it?" Joel swallowed his food.

"I have a proposal for you, an offer. I figure you're up against it right now, and this is a way to make a little money. I guess you need to get on your feet, right?" Edmund put the last piece of his Krispy Kreme in his mouth. He talked while he was chewing. "But I don't want you to feel trapped or beholden to me. Pressured. I'm not about to get halfway to Vegas and then spring somethin' on you, okay?"

"Sure. What's on your mind? My sister says she probably can locate a job for me, but it's going to be tough."

"It will be tough, Joel. No matter how hard you try, people are goin' to turn you down and look at you sideways. A man with a record has to be twice as good and three times as honest."

"It goes without saying I'd be grateful for anything you can do. You've already been a huge help—giving me a ride, stopping by the jail, keeping in touch." Joel looked at the box in the center of the seat, thought about eating another doughnut.

"Have another." Edmund grinned and motioned toward the box. "Well, let me do the preliminaries. See, I haven't ever traveled with a preacher before, haven't spent much time with somebody like you. I try to watch how I act, but I'm far from being a perfect man. To tell the truth—"

"No one's perfect, Edmund. We're all sinners, all less than God's ideal." The lines came instinctively, without thinking, the result of seventeen years in the ministry. "I mean, don't worry about it." Joel looked Edmund in the eye. "Heck, I'm the one with the criminal record."

"Well, like I was sayin', I drink a little, smoke a little, curse a little and like the ladies a little—okay, a lot—but I don't want us to have no disagreements or make you uneasy."

"I got out of jail two hours ago. I sat in so much smoke I thought a Kiss concert was about to commence any minute. I heard so much profanity I thought people were actually named Asshole. And by the way, there is no strong biblical injunction against profanity. There's a mention in Romans, but it's more of a social convention than a religious concern. I find it offensive, but there're worse things."

"Kiss, huh? You know about Kiss? Those guys with the frizzy hair and spooky makeup?"

"Believe it or not, my life didn't begin at age twenty-two on the steps of divinity school." Joel smiled. "I also know who Willie Nelson and Dwight Yoakam are, I enjoy Bruce Springsteen and Van Morrison and Jimi Hendrix, I think Lenny Bruce is funny even though I shouldn't, I like the taste and smell of Kentucky bourbon, I saw *Behind the Green Door* when I was in college—keep that under your hat—and I missed having sex with my wife while I was in jail. I'm an adult. A minister, not a cloistered monk from the Middle Ages."

"I didn't mean anything by it. I'm sure you've had all sorts of experiences. It's just that I don't want to do or say somethin' that upsets you."

"I appreciate your concern." The car had cooled down, and the fan automatically adjusted itself.

"Well, tell you what—let's talk business later. I'll get us on the road, then see if I can sell you on my idea. You're free to decline, tell me to go fly a kite. In fact, to be honest, it's a little close to the edge, a little risky, somethin' you might not want any part of."

"I'll tell you what I think, and there'll be no hard feelings. It's kind of you to take care of me like this."

Edmund shifted the Cadillac into drive and started to leave the parking lot. "I figure we can make it to Nashville tonight. Get a good meal and a good rest and hit it full blast in the morning."

"Sounds great."

When the car cruised by, Joel looked through the tinted glass at the kids and their fund-raiser. The hat-and-earring boy was talking to an adult, an older man wearing a golf shirt, and the boy was shaking his head and pointing at the money tray.

Kicked in the chest. It felt like Joel had been kicked in the chest and jolted and tossed from nowhere into a broken, skidding commotion. He'd been whipsawed from stark nothing into a startling racket and liquid images that were more color—grays, greens and tans—than form. The car was bouncing off something solid, and he heard the door metal give. He'd fallen asleep twenty minutes outside of Roanoke, two doughnuts contenting his belly, the Cadillac's leather and cool and steady ride the most comfort he'd known in months. When his eyes flew open, it was still daylight, the car was off the road and the sounds and suddenness of the collision were part there and part blurred in sleep. The shoulder harness had pulled strong against his chest and yanked him backward, jerking him up limp and surprised, and now the belt was too tight and Edmund was pointing at something behind them and shouting.

"You see him? There he goes, the crazy sonofabitch!"

The car had slammed to a halt against a tree. Joel dabbed his eyes and reached to release the seat belt. His breath was stifled, came in spurts. "Edmund?" he sputtered.

"Look at that idiot! He's flying." There was a web of blood across his teeth and a pink cut in the corner of his mouth. "Look at him. He's not even thinkin' about stopping."

Joel fumbled and groped his way to the square button that freed the restraints. The straps disappeared into the roof and floor, and he felt his chest expand with air. He turned and looked behind him, saw the rear of a white pickup driving out of sight, heading down a long stretch of two-lane road. When he'd fallen asleep, they were still on the interstate.

Edmund stopped staring at the highway and glanced at him. "You all right?"

"I think so." Joel coughed, then put his hand on his chest and felt along his breastbone. "The belt nearly squeezed me to death, but yeah, I'm okay. Wow. What happened?"

"I'll tell you what happened. That madman in the truck was completely on our side of the road, rollin' at us like a rocket. He almost killed us." Edmund made no effort to do anything about the blood around his mouth. "Didn't you see him?"

"See him? No, I was sleeping. The crash woke me up." Joel noticed the Krispy Kreme box was on the floor. The doughnuts were scattered on the carpet, and one frosted brown circle had landed on the dash. "Where are we?"

Edmund looked behind them again, in the direction the truck had gone. He was loud and out of sorts, his lips and teeth and chin red from the bleeding. "You saw him though, right? The guy who ran us off, the guy in the truck?"

"I saw a white truck driving away."

"That's him. He was doing seventy at least. Comin' dead at us." Edmund worked on his mouth, patting at the cut with his sleeve. Some of the blood wiped onto his suit coat, some stained the white cuff of his shirt. He opened the door and spit on the ground.

Joel's door was stuck, so they both left the car through the driver's side. The metal on the passenger's side was mangled from the headlight to the quarter panel, the wound full of crinkles and bends, and the paint had been altogether scrubbed off in one deep indentation. A tire was cartoonishly flat. The corner of the front bumper was pulled away from the body and wrenched into a silver frown. Hissing came from underneath the hood, fluid pooled in the dirt. Edmund looked at the wreck with his hands on his hips and made clicking noises, tsks and ticks that brought to mind a disappointed schoolmarm's scold.

"It's pretty bad, Edmund."

"I'll say." Edmund grimaced and rotated his head in a slow circle. He pushed his hand into the intersection of his neck and shoulder and massaged the muscles through his shirt. "I did something to my neck, Preacher." He wobbled two steps and sat down in a patch of weeds and tall grass. "How about usin' the car phone and callin' the police. Or the satellite gizmo on the dash—I think all you need to do is push the button and tell 'em what's happened. And I might need an ambulance." Edmund lay down. There was blood on his face and his neck, and it was difficult to see all of him because of the grass and scraggly growth.

"Are you going to be okay, Edmund?" Joel looked at the car and then at his friend.

"I'm dizzy and my neck hurts like the dickens, but I'm not dyin' or anything."

"Where are we?" Joel asked again. "I need to know our location for the police."

"I'm not positive. We're close to the Tennessee border, though."

A small tan Chevrolet eased off the road behind them, and a chubby man with a long beard got out. Joel started back to the Cadillac to call the cops. The bearded man walked toward Joel, and another car drifted onto the gravel shoulder, carelessly stopping with two wheels still on the pavement. "You need any help? Anybody hurt?" the first passerby asked. He was busy with his beard, kept tugging the ends of his whiskers while he was talking.

"Thanks," Joel said. "I believe we're okay. My friend's hurt some, but it looks like he'll be all right. I'm going to see if I can get a trooper and maybe the rescue squad."

The man from the tan car touched the battered side of the Cadillac. "Pretty bad damage there, friend. A real shame. What happened?"

"A truck ran us off the road."

The driver of the second car rolled down his window and asked if he could do anything. Joel thanked him and assured him there was no reason to stay. He wished Joel good luck and left, pulled away slowly and never gained much speed.

"By the way," Joel wondered, "exactly where are we?"

"Next to Abingdon. Abingdon, Virginia." The stranger continued to stroke his beard.

"Oh, okay."

"You want me to keep an eye on your partner there?" He was wearing camouflage pants and a T-shirt with a screen-printed design that was faded beyond recognition.

"Thanks. That'd be great."

The man squinted at Joel, kicking the ground aimlessly. He let go of the bush under his chin. "You guys got anything you need me to hold? Or help you, you know, keep low-profile from the police?"

Joel licked his lips, took a step closer to the man. Joel was near the front of the Cadillac, the stranger standing beside the caved-in fender. "Hold?" Joel wet his lips again. "I'm not sure I follow you."

"Hey, look, I ain't no friend of the police, okay? You got anything The Man don't need to be seein', give it to me or let's get rid of it now. Beer, liquor, drugs, guns, whatever. I'm just tryin' to be a good neighbor. I don't much agree with the state jumpin' into everybody's business."

Two cars drove by nose to tail and slowed down, but didn't stop.

"Oh, no thanks. We're fine in that department."

"Good deal." The man smiled and headed to the high grass and Edmund.

A middle-age state trooper came to investigate the accident, and a volunteer rescue squad arrived to take Edmund to the emergency room. Edmund described the wreck and the white truck to the patrolman, and the bearded man confirmed that he'd seen the same vehicle moments later, driving like a "wild man." While the policeman was walking around the Cadillac and taking photographs, the man in camo and the faded shirt nodded at Joel. Edmund was strapped to a gurney, and he touched his new buddy on the arm and said, "Thanks." The officer wrote down everything and decided Edmund certainly didn't deserve a ticket. He told them they were fortunate, that they probably would've been hurt worse if Edmund hadn't disabled the air bags immediately after buying the car.

Joel and Edmund spent three hours at the Abingdon hospital, and after being examined were given prescriptions for painkillers and muscle relaxers.

"What a day," Joel said as he and Edmund were sitting in cloth and metal chairs outside the emergency room, waiting for a taxi to take them to a hotel. "It's been so tumultuous that I almost wish I were back in jail." He gave Edmund a bedraggled look. "It's been like slamming into concrete walls ever since I left my cell."

"Don't let it bring you down." Edmund was wearing a cervical support, a white foam brace that came up as far as his jawline. His expensive shirt was open at the collar to accommodate the brace. He had his coat and tie neatly spread across his legs; blood had ruined the coat and also dried on his French cuffs. "Don't let it bring you down," he repeated.

"Well, on top of everything else, I don't have any health insurance. I wonder if the hospital folks have to wait for Christy to get her five million before they get their payment? I must be into them for two or three thousand for the stuff they did here."

Edmund arranged himself so he could see Joel, had to pick up his feet and swivel his whole frame. "I've got insurance on the car—full coverage. I'm sure you'll be taken care of. As will I." Edmund's eyes jumped and darted. "As will I."

"Really? That's good news. I'm glad I'll only be five million in the hole."

"We'll let the capes-and-hats worry about that. Remember, Joel, things have a way of workin' out. There're silver linings all around, everywhere. The Lord helps those who help themselves."

Joel picked up something strange in Edmund's expression, something

Edmund was showing him. There was an invitation, a challenge, a clue. His eyes were pain-free, and the corners of his mouth were working into a grin. "What're you getting at, Edmund? I mean, I appreciate the help with the insurance. That's a relief."

Edmund touched the neck support with his index finger. "You know what this is, Joel? Do you?" He tapped the brace several times. "A dollar-collar, my man. A dollar-collar." He closed down his face and shifted away from Joel. The chair moved when he changed positions, and there was a sharp, biting noise, the sound of metal twisted over floor tile. "A month from now, you'll be happy we took this little detour." Edmund was looking straight ahead, his hands laced together in his lap.

Just as he finished the sentence, a red-headed orderly in baggy blue clothes came through a door and told the men their cab had arrived. Edmund raised from his seat and fell back, grimacing. "Sorry," he said to the orderly. "Could you give me a hand? I'm really hurtin'."

three _____

Edmund Brooks, Joel discovered, liked to live large. Edmund directed the cabdriver to drop them at the Martha Washington Inn, an old, elegant building on Abingdon's main street. The hotel was the city's pride and joy, a strapping hostelry with a commanding porch, tidy grounds, muted lobby murals, uniformed porters and maids, and the well-mannered atmosphere of a place that had scarcely changed over the decades. Edmund insisted on separate rooms at two hundred dollars apiece, and immediately ordered an expensive bottle of port for his nightstand. "I like having my own bathroom," he pointed out when Joel mentioned his willingness to share an accommodation. "And I figure you could use a night of privacy yourself."

So Joel—who just that morning had awakened to the sound of Kenny's urine stream playing off the back of a metal toilet bowl and then scooped up the jail's watery scrambled eggs with a plastic spork—Joel found himself swaddled in ease and beset by eager lads wanting to carry his pathetic Kmart bag and get him settled upstairs. After a shower and change of clothes, he and Edmund devoted well over an hour to sumptuous dishes in the hotel's dining room, where they clinked water glasses to toast Joel's release. Joel finished his meal with a flourless chocolate torte from the pastry cart before climbing into bed under an avalanche of sheets, ruffles, shams, blankets and feather-filled pillows.

He woke up a few minutes after midnight, the rich food hectoring his stomach, and walked to the porch for some air. He took a seat in a rocking chair and watched a horse and carriage roll along the street, a tourist conveyance entertaining its last fare for the day. He sat by himself, listening to the trills and shrieks and rants of summer insects that seemed close at hand but impossible to pin down. He began closing his eyes every so often and lifting with his toes to even the rhythm of the rocker's bowed wooden legs, and he was nearly dozing when a wedding party stumbled from the inn, a group of young men and women who seemed to shimmer and float when their exuberance came through the door and into the outside world. All the boys had shed their jackets, and one of the girls was carrying her high heels, a single finger hooking the shoes' straps. They frolicked right past Joel and ignored him, didn't appear to see him pushing to and fro in his chair while the bug sounds passed through his drowsy head.

After lunch the next day, the two men set out for Nashville with Joel behind the wheel and Edmund braced and ailing in the passenger seat. The Cadillac had been made drivable, although there were still repairs that needed to be completed. The garage had installed a new front tire, but the bent bumper hadn't been replaced and the gash down the side was still present, a nasty metal mess that caught the air and whipped it into an annoying roar. Once they'd made their way back onto the interstate and driven about twenty miles, and after Edmund had put away his road map and selected a CD, he revisited the subject of Joel's job prospects.

"So what is it your sister's got lined up for you? As far as I know, there ain't a lot of opportunity in Missoula for a man tied to a record. Teachin' at the college—they won't let you do that, even with all your education and whatnot. Tourist industry—there's a possibility, maybe that's it. They don't have many factories or mills or plants, and I can't see you in the loggin' business—it's too damn dangerous and hard. Wonder what she has in mind?"

"I'm not sure. The good news is she has a place for me to stay and will help out however she can."

"That's family for you. Nothin' in the world like it." Edmund paused and tugged at his cervical collar. "So let me tell you about the chance I have for you." He turned the stereo volume down and leaned back cautiously. "Might as well go on and get around to it. You ready?"

"Ready," Joel said.

"I don't want you to think you're obligated, and like I told you, I don't want you to feel pressured. Plus I don't want you gettin' the wrong idea about me."

Joel was traveling in the right lane, the cruise control set dead-on the speed limit. There was a tiny vibration in the steering wheel, and the suspension felt skewed, the ride choppier than it had been before the crash. "Just tell me, Edmund. There's no need to make such a big deal out of it."

"Okay, Joel. I'll start by sayin' there are no bigger thieves in the world than insurance companies. Big insurance companies that earn a livin' by systematically denying claims and nickel-and-dimin' folks to death. And if they finally do pay you, it's always horribly late since they want to use *your* money for months and months before forking it over." Edmund focused on highway signs and billboards as he spoke, avoided Joel.

"You're not planning a run for public office, are you?" Joel grinned and peered across the seat at his friend, but Edmund continued to watch the humdrum scenery along the interstate, didn't meet his gaze. "You'll need to do better than that. Maybe work in something about 'the children.' " He laughed. " 'I took this junket to Aruba for the kids.' And education's important, too. What if the big insurance companies are stealing money from the schools? 'Edmund Brooks—he'll tackle the insurance giants to get what's right for our kids.' I could be your campaign manager."

"No politics for me, thank you," Edmund said curtly. "I figure Nelson Rockefeller was the last trustworthy man to hold high office. And Carter was a classy fellow. At any rate, a lot of my work involves keepin' insurance companies honest, makin' sure they don't get too rich from the sweat of the ordinary people they're trying to screw. See what I'm saying?"

Joel felt the vibration increase in his hands. A tractor-trailer rumbled by on his left, sped past the Cadillac at a good eighty miles an hour. "I guess. You're some kind of watchdog or regulator? An activist like Ralph Nader?"

Edmund chuckled. "Somethin' similar to that. Yeah. I definitely don't have any problem doggin' Allstate, if that's what you mean. So anyhow, here's my plan. My friend Abel Crane runs a cleanin' business in Vegas. Takes care of houses, commercial property, all sorts of spreads. Has access to a bunch of areas most people don't. Are you followin' me?"

Joel cleared his throat. The phrase "access to . . . areas" didn't sit well with him. "Yeah, sort of. Keep going."

"Here's how this project works. Abel has the capacity to get his hands on some very expensive antique jewelry from a house in Vegas. The folks who live there come and go all the time. Stay with me now, okay? This ain't goin' where you think. It's not about stealin' someone's diamonds and pearls. Stay with me. They leave for a month or two at a time—you know how wealthy people love to vacation. Of course Abel's got the key to their house and the code to their security system, right? He's 'licensed and bonded,' as they say in the trade. People eat that up."

"I'm listening." It seemed to Joel that the wind noise was gaining strength. He looked at the speedometer; nothing had changed.

"Abel will simply remove several items of jewelry, and there's where you come in. He'll give them to me, and I'll very quickly give 'em to you. We'll see to it that plenty of people know you have these valuables. In fact, you'll buy an insurance policy on them in Missoula. The agent will want to see 'em. The agent will take pictures and demand an appraisal, which you'll get from a reputable local jeweler who'll inform you that these fine keepsakes your mother left you are worth more than a quarter of a million dollars. If ever pressed on the issue, you'll say they were kept in storage or in a safe-deposit box. Do you have a safe-deposit box?"

"Uh, yeah. I did . . . we did, my wife and I, when I went to jail. It's empty except for some legal papers and a few odds and ends. An old ring. But—"

Edmund raised his hand. "Hear me out. If anyone ever leans on you, you'll simply advise them that these precious mementos were stored during your incarceration and you retrieved them when you got released. Naturally, you took 'em with you when you left Virginia." Edmund's tone was professional, very assured and measured. "Of course, you don't tell anybody that right off the bat. Just say they came from your mother, get an appraisal and act stunned as heck when the jeweler quotes you a value."

Joel checked his speed again, even though the cruise control was activated. "That would be a lie, Edmund. I couldn't do it. And this hardly sounds like a job."

"Don't bring the curtain down before you let me finish, okay? After it's real clear you own the stuff and the agent's seen it and we have photos and a jeweler's appraisal, you give the jewelry back to me and we return it. All of it. No theft, no crime, no nothin'. We just send it home to Vegas. See? Like I said, this isn't any type theft involving people or anything of that stripe." Edmund reached into his suit jacket and collected a pack of cigarettes, lowered his window to suck away the smoke. He fired the cigarette with a silver metal lighter and seemed to have finished his pitch. He sat quietly and blew smoke from his nostrils and thumped an ash into the crack.

"And?" Joel had to grin. "That's the end?"

"No, of course not. You want to know the whole prospectus, the whole deal?"

"Prospectus, Edmund?" Joel was smiling now. "Like this thing's registered with the Securities and Exchange Commission, and we're selling stock shares? You're offering me a salesman's job?" The Cadillac was boxed in between a van and a Buick poking along in the passing lane, so he tapped the brake to disengage the cruise control and waited for an opening.

"You could say that. The rest of the project unfolds a few months later. The bait's back where it belongs, and after, say, six months go by, burglars hit your home. Door's kicked in, TV's gone, house is turned upside down, things are stolen and—tragically—your mama's sacred stones wind up in the clutches of some junkie thief, never to be seen again. You should've taken them to the bank for safekeepin', but money was tight and you kept delaying, never got around to it. You, of course, will be at work or church or volunteerin' at the cancer hospice when the home invasion occurs." Edmund tossed his cigarette out the window and sealed the car.

"I see. Then I march to the insurance office, file my claim and accept a check for jewels I never owned?"

"Yep. Sweet, isn't it? Their agent's your best witness—hell, he's seen the goods and held them in his own hands and has the pictures to prove it. The jeweler—another total stranger—he's also seen 'em. Your churchgoin' pal Edmund will definitely say that he too got an eyeful of these fine gems. They'll have to cut the check. Six figures, no one hurt, only the bad guys stung."

"What if they discover the jewelry belongs to someone else? That kind of quality might be on record somewhere, or so distinctive they could trace the real owners."

"A diamond's a diamond, a sapphire's a sapphire. We're not goin' after Liz Taylor's stash. And two hundred fifty thou isn't all that much, not really. Plus we'll throw in a couple pieces of our own, just to scramble the pot."

Joel floored the car and shot into the passing lane. "I see. Well, I'm afraid my mom's still alive."

"She is?" Edmund's voice flagged for the first time since he'd started his spiel.

"Sure enough," Joel answered.

"Huh."

"She's very infirm, though. She has Alzheimer's and lives in a nursing home. I'm embarrassed to admit that we had to move her from Roanoke to Missoula and make her my sister's responsibility while I was in jail."

Edmund considered this for a moment. "Well, I don't know exactly how to put it, but as far as our project's concerned, that's not the end of the universe. Don't get me wrong, Joel. I hate it for you and your mother, I certainly do. I hear it's a wicked affliction, awful to deal with." He twisted his lips. "But dependin' on how bad it is, it might be a positive and not a minus. Can't you just see some cape-and-hat from the insurance company tryin' to put the torch to a fragile old sweetheart?" He allowed himself a cackle. "We could work with this situation, I do believe. Yessir."

Joel's features tightened, and the amusement and mirth drained out of him. He pressed the cruise button to reset his speed and zombie-stared at the road. "I've become a convict," he said, almost mumbling the words. "What in the world."

Edmund didn't know how to take the remark, didn't know how it stacked up against what he'd been proposing. "Don't worry about it, Joel," he finally said.

Joel turned and gave him a level look. Edmund kept his eyes to himself, kept his posture unnaturally erect. "What exactly is your business, Edmund?" Joel asked the question with a plain voice, didn't give anything away in his tone.

"My business?" Edmund repeated.

"Yes. How do you make money? Support yourself?"

"Oh, okay. Sure. I'll tell you. You see, Joel, I work the sag, patrol it from stem to stern, top to bottom. And you're gonna ask 'What's the sag?,' so I'll go ahead and explain. Sag's the sneaky tax and the holdback and the cushion and the reserve and the contingency and the ol' thumb on the scale. It's the markup that stores and companies and corporations factor in for the illusions we don't truly receive. It's all those dollars lost in green eyeshades or your congressman's payroll, all the premiums we pay State Farm and the Good Hands People for Swiss-cheese protection. It's the extra seventy-four cents on your phone bill each month that you're too damn weary to fight about, rounded-off decimal points and that tiny price increase at Sears because they *assume* they'll have a five-percent theft-loss this year. Well, I say let's make certain they do, because otherwise they're over-chargin'. To put it in plain English, the sag is somethin' nobody's got any claim to but somebody has."

Joel scratched his chin. "I understand the concept. But businesses have to prepare budgets that reflect real and reasoned possibilities. I mean, my goodness, we did it at the church, Edmund. We had a contingency fund for repairs and replacements or unforeseen events, and you're saying— what *are* you saying?"

Edmund locked onto Joel. "Listen, all I'm saying is that money ends up in the purses of people who have no right to it, and as far as I'm concerned there's an open season on it, a free-for-all. They won't miss it anyway—that's why I call it the sag. We're not talkin' shoestring budgets and powdered-milk shipments for the saucer-eyed babies; we're talkin' some fat cat's secretary ordering a friggin' ice swan for the company buffet."

"Ultimately, Edmund, you have to break the law to do most of this, correct? That's what I'm reading between the lines. Like the jewelry scam you're selling—it's just insurance fraud, pure and simple. Stealing."

Edmund wrinkled his brow, pursed his lips and filled his face with ruts and creases. He held the sour expression for several moments as if he were in pain, his features frozen in a long wince. "It's sure not stealin'," he finally said. "It's just doin' battle over what's available. You ask me, they're the ones puttin' it to folks. How's it stealin' when you get money some insurance company's sittin' on 'cause they arbitrarily refused to pay your doctor his total bill? Or claiming some treatment ain't covered by one of their hundred-page policies written in Sanskrit? Let's talk about who's really at fault."

"That's why we have laws and courts and proper methods to settle disputes."

"That's right, Joel. Take some big corporation to court." Edmund laughed sarcastically. "Just try. And see if a vampire will take your case if it ain't a biggie. They won't. They know the capes-and-hats on the other side will keep 'em tied in knots for years over your tiny rag of a case. And the miserable insurance companies are financin' the battle with the sag money they charged you in *your* payments."

"Not all companies are corrupt, Edmund. A lot of them provide real benefits. It's far too simplistic and convenient to think every corporation's a sinister bully."

"Let me finish. Even if you do find a lawyer and win in court, you still take a butt kickin'. Let's say you get dinged in an accident and you're due around five grand. They'll offer you maybe three. They know if you fight that, you gotta pay a doctor to testify and a third to your cape-and-hat. So you go to court, get your whole five and walk out with only two thousand in your pocket. Fair, huh?"

"I'm sure that can't be altogether accurate. You could ask for your lawyer's fee."

"Nope. No way. It doesn't happen like that."

"Well, whatever you call it, it's still illegal."

"Illegal?" Edmund snorted. "Illegal? The law ain't always right, and it seems to change all the time dependin' on who's writin' the checks. It was once the law that black people couldn't vote, you couldn't drink liquor and you couldn't get an abortion down at the mall in the clinic next to the

Chick-fil-A. You're a preacher, Joel. You of all people oughta know the law isn't always sound or even fair. And, hey, the law surely didn't do justice by you. Look at the way you got treated."

"I can understand your position, but I don't agree with it. I'm not a fan of anarchy and mob rule. And I have no problems with my punishment. I pled guilty and went to jail, and my troubles were of my own doing."

"I can't say you got a square deal. What chance did you have? And look what's happenin' now. You're right back in court, fightin' the same old trench war."

"That's hardly the system's fault. Christy filed the suit." Joel shrugged. "Anyway, I've already told you I'm planning to take what comes."

Edmund tossed his hands up and let his palms slap his thighs. "You're a tough hombre, Joel. You are indeed. Like I say, I can sure understand why you might not want to get involved. Just wanted to give you the opportunity. No hard feelings, I hope."

"Of course not. I'm a little surprised, though. I'd assumed your businesses were more, uh, conventional. I think I recall—didn't you once tell me you were in the meat-processing business? I believe I remember that."

Edmund showed him a satisfied expression, with a mote of smugness mixed in. He didn't say anything.

"Edmund?"

"Think about it."

"I am."

"Think harder," Edmund urged.

The gag finally registered with Joel. "Oh, right. *Meat* processing. I get it—it's the lard and suet you're whittling away at. The fat. The sag."

"Exactly. There you go. I told you the truth." He took out his silver lighter and began absentmindedly flipping the lid. "So now you know what I do."

"Yep," Joel said. "I guess I do." He paused, started to say something else but didn't.

"What is it?" Edmund asked.

"Nothing."

"You were goin' to say some more."

"Well, I . . . it's not important," Joel stammered.

"Tell me. Heck, you're not goin' to hurt my feelings."

"Well, Edmund, I was wondering whether you believe in the Lord. I hate to ask it like that—it sounds sort of pious—and it's really none of my business now. I suppose it's ingrained after so many years in the ministry.

Besides, I mean, you know, I'm in no position to ask anyone much of anything. There's not a whole lot sadder than a down-and-out preacher wearing the scarlet letter."

"You sure don't owe me any apologies."

"I imagine I do, in some sense. But be that as it may, I don't want to come off as a hypocrite."

"Why are you askin'?" Edmund wondered. "You know I was in church every Sunday." The accents were typical Edmund—a clipped "church" and a slurred, honeyed "I."

Joel waited a moment before he answered. "I guess I'm curious as to how your deceptions—your necessary untruths, or whatever you'd call them—fit into your world as a good servant of the Lord?"

"Man comes into your house and takes hold of your wallet, you have a right to do what's needed to get it back. It's sure not stealin', and as for the lying part of it, it's no different than the police callin' wanted criminals and tellin' them they've won the lottery or Super Bowl tickets and then arrestin' 'em when they show up at some swanky hotel to claim their prize."

Joel nodded. "So do you believe in God, Edmund?"

"I do. I sure do." He stopped opening and shutting the lighter. "I'm not as certain about the niceties and creeds and chants and original Greek and all the details that keep you guys in business, but I'm a believer. I don't know how He likes His suit cut or His hair parted or His martini made, but I believe in God. Yessiree."

"His martini?" Joel lifted his eyebrows.

"You know what I'm gettin' at."

"And *you* know what they say, Edmund, 'the devil is in the details.'" Joel tried to catch his eye but couldn't.

"The devil, Preacher, is in *too many* details."

"I see."

"And the best thing about being Baptist is that you can just throw up your hands and ask to be forgiven and it's done. Know it's a sin—doesn't matter. Do it over and over and over—doesn't matter. Beat a man to death with a claw hammer 'cause of a two-dollar bet in a poker game—same story. Simply ask to be forgiven and you're salvation bound. So there you go, bein' Baptist and believing like we believe works out just fine and dandy with what I do. Sorta like an all-you-can-eat buffet or a bottomless cup of coffee, that's how I think about it. I mean, assumin' I was into something sinful, which I'm not."

"I've often wondered about the expression 'bottomless cup.' Seems to me you'd never have anything in it."

Edmund laughed and rearranged himself in the seat. "That makes better sense, don't it?"

Joel forced Edmund to look at him. "You've got to mean it when you go to the Lord, Edmund. You need contrition and sincerity."

Edmund appeared perplexed. "Mean it? Mean it? You better believe I mean it. I da—darn sure don't want to wind up in hell. Of course I mean it."

"Good enough, then."

"I hope you don't think poorly of me, Joel. In my heart of hearts I don't feel I'm doing nothin' wrong."

"You're a friend and a good man, Edmund. We disagree on the sag, so let's just leave it there." Joel gave a subtle dip with his head to conclude the sentence.

"Great." Before the word had vanished, Edmund began a clumsy struggle to raise his leg from the floorboard. He joined his hands into a sling underneath his knee and hoisted and turned until the limb was on the seat. His foot ended up in Joel's lap, and his shoulders were pressed against the passenger-side window.

"Edmund? You okay?"

"Well, I'm in some pain, yeah. But I want to show you somethin' that might make things a little clearer." He grabbed his pant leg below the knee and hiked the fabric until his calf was bare.

Joel glanced at him, then returned to the highway. Edmund's leg was perfectly smooth and hairless, without any curves or veins or definition, a lifeless run of beige that disappeared into a blue sock. Joel took another peek, trying to scrutinize what was happening in the car and not miss events on the road. "What's wrong with your leg?"

"Not my entire leg. Not the entire shebang. Just below the knee, Joel." Edmund made a fist and rapped his shin, struck it three times with his knuckles. "Nice, huh?"

"Oh, my. It's not real. My goodness . . . you can't even tell. I never noticed."

"The best prosthesis money can buy." Edmund began maneuvering his leg out of the seat. "Of course, it's still plastic." He manufactured a smile. "What was the line in *The Graduate*? 'Plastics. Go into plastics, young man.' I wound up takin' it literally." He'd returned to his side of the car, was staring out the windshield.

"So this has something to do with an insurance company? Or a hospital? Is that it?"

"Puts things in a different light, don't it?"

"I'm so sorry, Edmund. What happened?"

"What happened is what happens all the time. Suppose you're a fifteen-year-old kid with a circulatory problem and your insurance company claims the surgery—which is damned expensive—that will save your leg is 'experimental' and isn't covered by your harried single mother's policy. What *is* covered is a nice, relatively cheap amputation and a clunky metal strap-on limb that rubs your new stump raw and causes you to limp and stumble and fall." Edmund spat out the words in dry tones, his eyes fixed on some distant point.

Joel was speechless. He bit his lip and felt his stomach turn heavy, his throat start to clog. Finally he managed to utter a slack-jawed "I'm so sorry" a second time.

"Hey, don't worry about it. I didn't mean to upset you. I get along okay, despite my handicap. In fact, I think I've done better than most."

"Yes, you have," Joel said. "You certainly have."

Joel and Edmund made it to Nashville in the middle of the afternoon, checked into the Hermitage, rented separate rooms—Edmund insisted—and had Edmund's luggage carried up while they talked to the receptionist about finding a good steak house. After dinner, they visited Tootsie's Orchid Lounge, a narrow bar with a purple facade and hundreds of photos on the wall, the ones closest to the ceiling turned a brittle yellow by decades of rising nicotine. Edmund put away three beers and tipped the band a five when they played a Marty Robbins song he'd requested. Joel ordered coffee and sang along on a couple choruses he knew. The front door stayed open as people came and went, drinking and talking, and Joel and Edmund laughed and clapped in time as the band ended a set with "The Devil Went Down to Georgia."

It took them four more days on Interstate 40—and stops in Little Rock, Amarillo, Albuquerque and Flagstaff—to reach Las Vegas. As they were walking out of their hotel into a blistering Arizona morning to start their last day on the road, two attractive, stylish women passed by them. The prettier of the women—a brunette with brash eyes—turned back and showed an interest in Edmund, looked at him with an explosion of bright lipstick and an unmistakable invitation. He slowed, but when the woman saw he was heading for the beaten Cadillac, she gave up on him and sauntered away. The incident seemed to vex Edmund; usually talkative and full of stories and quips, he was quiet, almost sullen, as he and Joel began the trip to Nevada. When Joel finally asked why he was so taciturn, he got only a hangdog stare and a big exhalation from his companion.

"For heaven's sake, Edmund, what's the matter with you? I hope I haven't done anything." Joel was settled behind the wheel, the safety belts aggravating the soreness along his chest.

"Nah. You've been fine company."

"So what is it? Something to do with those two women?"

"Well," Edmund said, "it's like this. I figure a man's got three things to worry about, three things to take pride in: his ride, his hide and his stride."

Joel made a quizzical sound, a quick "hmmm" that stayed mostly in his throat. "The ride part I get—"

"Your car, your clothes and the way you carry yourself. And here I am, limping into Vegas in a rent-a-wreck and lookin' like Joe Shit the Ragman. Sorry about the language, Joel, but I just hate for people to see me like this."

"You look great, and you can get the car fixed in no time at all. I can't imagine something so small and trivial would upset you."

"I know it shouldn't, but it does." Edmund grabbed his car-wreck collar with both hands and jerked it off. He tossed it into the rear seat and rubbed small circles on his neck with his palms. "There," he said, "that's better."

Joel drove into Las Vegas at night, when the city was loud and lit. Edmund woke up from a nap after the car came to a stop at a light, woke fresh and alert and recognized precisely where they were, pointed at an empty building and said it had once been an excellent restaurant. He directed Joel to the Golden Nugget, explaining that he enjoyed Vegas the way it used to be. Slick new resorts with French acrobats in the showrooms could never compare to bordello-red wallpaper, gangsters and molls, late meals and old gamblers hacking out unfiltered coughs while shaking dice over a table with a stain or two on the felt. Forget about art collections and roller coasters and pirate ships and fountains that danced to classical music. Despite the fact the city had tricked up the area with a hopeless light show, downtown was the place to be, the last little shard of the genuine thing and still the home of Binion's and the Four Queens, gaudy dens that were a little on the margins as soon as they were built and had never changed.

Edmund paid for a two-bedroom suite and set off to gamble, offering Joel a feeble courtesy invitation to come along and try the games. Instead,

Joel took a shower and found a cheap buffet at Sam Boyd's, went through the line twice and ate a mound of mushy, pencil-thin crab legs. He wandered the sidewalks and in and out of the casinos, and after an hour or so, it struck him that Las Vegas was not the devil's best work. There was a streak of Sodom in the streets and cards and slot machines, but the whole thing was so obvious, so gleefully corrupt, such a bolo punch, that you could spot the snares from miles away. The come-on for lethal sin was far more cunning: a secretary's hem an inch too high or a dab of cocaine after a round of golf, harmless distractions whose fangs at first are hidden. Las Vegas, Joel concluded, was to damnation what Cruella De Vil was to villainy: difficult to take seriously, outlandish and so predictable you could hear the cogs grinding before every move.

He bought a cold soda at a bar near the back of the Golden Nugget, dropped a quarter in a slot machine on the way to the elevators, hit two cherries and was paid ten coins, which he put in his pocket. In his room, he felt the cold marble floor brace his feet as he walked from the sink to his bed after brushing his teeth, and he fell asleep almost as soon as he lay down, pulled a pillow from beneath the comforter and didn't bother to get under the covers.

Edmund reappeared the next morning, wearing the same clothes he'd left in. He seemed sober and fairly composed, his eyes red but his pants still creased and his hair combed and neat. He told Joel to get the car keys, said they needed to visit his lawyer before heading north to Missoula.

"Edmund, I appreciate it, but I don't see why it's necessary. On top of that, I feel bad about you paying a lawyer for me. You've already spent a fortune on meals and rooms."

"Least I can do, and don't fret about it. Hey, I more than financed us last night. I got into a blackjack table that was flat-out boiling. Skinned the house for close to seven grand."

"You won seven thousand dollars playing cards?"

"Yep."

"Wow." Joel whistled. "How about that."

"So we're still ahead. Way ahead." He clapped Joel on the back. "Our friends at Binion's will be coverin' the cost of the trip *and* payin' for your cape-and-hat gouging."

"For what it's worth, I truly am grateful. But we really don't have to see a lawyer."

"No more fussin' with me. I'm goin' anyway, so you may as well tag along. Come on or I'll leave you here and let you walk to your sister's."

"Well, I did my part, too." Joel reached into his pocket and produced the quarters. "Here you go—I had a big evening also."

Edmund took the change and balled it in his fist. "Consider us even, Preacher. You're paid in full." He slapped Joel on the back again and unleashed a peal of laughter, a burst of noise that stayed in Joel's ears even after they'd left the room and started toward the elevator.

Joel and Edmund never took a seat in the lobby of Sa'ad X. Sa'ad's law firm. They walked straight through past ten or twelve other people and followed a dignified secretary down a hall to a huge office, where Sa'ad X. Sa'ad was waiting for them at the doorway. The room behind him was phenomenal, laid out in a large rectangle with Sa'ad's desk—an ornate mahogany monster—on a raised platform in the center of the space. Two steps led to the desk plateau, and four leather chairs were arranged at the foot of the steps. While the sheer size of the office was impressive, it was the horns and snouts and heads of dead animals protruding from the walls and jammed into every corner and cranny that mesmerized Joel. The main attraction was a stuffed bear, easily seven feet tall, standing on its rear legs, its shellacked nails pawing at the ceiling. The bear was kept company by a fox, deer heads, game birds, racks from a moose and an elk, a wild boar and a coyote with yellow marbles in its skull. An elaborate gun case was located within easy reach of the desk, and Joel noticed the stock of one rifle was finished in ivory swirls and the trigger gold.

Evidently Edmund had toured the menagerie before. He showed no interest in the surroundings and immediately wrapped his lawyer in a robust embrace that ended with them still connected from thigh to breastbone and their heads withdrawn and offset, the greeting brotherly, fervent and strangely Old World. Sa'ad finished with Edmund and offered his hand to Joel. "Sa'ad X. Sa'ad. Pleasure to meet you."

Edmund insisted that Sa'ad sit with them on the ground and not climb the elevation to his desk. Joel sat between the two men. Edmund had regained his cervical collar on the way to the lawyer's, but even with the bulky ring around his neck and despite a full night at the tables, he was a handsome, vigorous figure, not a scuff or blemish on his shoes, every stitch and button in his suit impeccable. Sa'ad was his equal, a tall, immaculate black man whose face seemed to be permanently rotating. A hodgepodge of expressions—threatening or inviting or demanding or good-humored—took turns in his flawless features without any warning which would come next. Sa'ad removed a pair of delicate, rimless glasses, folded them, placed them in a case and pocketed the case. "So what's on the table, Edmund?"

Edmund's air became grave. "The preacher here. Let's talk about his concerns first. He's bein' royally screwed by this system you guys run. He had a small problem back in Roanoke with a girl at our church. I think—"

Sa'ad interrupted. "So you're a minister, Joel?"

"I was."

"What kind, if I could ask?"

"A damn fine one," Edmund blustered. "Who got a raw deal."

"I was a Baptist minister for several years," Joel answered.

"Ordained or merely—how is it you put it—'called'?" Sa'ad spoke in a smooth, practiced baritone that was almost musical.

"I'm ordained. College at Indiana, graduate degree from Southeastern Seminary in Wake Forest."

Sa'ad chuckled. "Ah yes, the Demon Deacons."

"Well, the university and the seminary are actually different places."

"Arnold Palmer's alma mater," Sa'ad noted.

"There's a dorm named after him, but it's at the university," Joel said.

"This is all great, gents, but let's not forget the meter's runnin', Sa'ad. You guys can talk golf and campus tours another time. I'm here to do business, not chitchat. As I was sayin', well . . . jeez . . . let Joel tell you what happened."

"I simply like to learn a little about my clients, Edmund. Why so touchy this morning—bad cards last night?"

"The cards were lovely," Edmund said.

"I'm happy for you. I'd think you'd be more civil." Sa'ad winked at Joel, then relaxed in his chair and crossed his legs. "So, Mr. King," he said, prompting Joel with a nod and a meaningless smile, "I'm eager to see if I can solve your problem. You mind telling me what's happened?"

"Okay," Joel said, and as Sa'ad listened impassively, he recited his story from start to present, told of the criminal charge, his guilty plea, his time in jail and the arrival of two lawsuits, one seeking a divorce, the other demanding five million dollars.

Edmund had slid to the edge of his seat. "I advised him to fight the infernal thing, Sa'ad. It's double jeopardy, right? He's been tried and done his time—you can't bring it up again, correct? That's against the Constitution."

Sa'ad stretched his legs and sank deeper into the leather. "Oh, no. Not at all. He's been tried on the criminal case. This is *civil*."

"I sort of guessed that," Joel said, "from what little I know."

"Explain to me what you're sayin'," Edmund insisted.

"It's like this, Edmund," the lawyer said, "and you of all people should know something so basic. Double jeopardy means a person can't be tried twice by the state for the same offense. That's one concern—you and the state and the criminal charges. You and the victim—that's another, that's the civil end of the equation. For instance, say you get hit by a drunk driver. The state puts him in jail, but you sue him for money damages. Two suits—one criminal, one civil."

"So the suit's good?" Edmund asked.

"Well, it's not barred." Sa'ad sat up slightly. "Whether it's good or not is a separate issue. Depends on the facts."

"I don't plan on contesting it," Joel said. "I told Edmund that."

"What kind of a case do they have against you—factually, I mean?" Sa'ad inquired. "What evidence?"

"I pled guilty, went to court and admitted it. Then there's Christy's testimony. A groundskeeper saw her go into the church the afternoon this was supposed to have happened. And their big gun was this test, a PERK test, I think you call it—"

"Physical evidence recovery kit," Sa'ad interjected. "Semen swabs, pubic-hair combings, some other investigations. I'm familiar with the term."

"Yeah, right." Joel felt his neck start to color. "They found some hair from, uh, my private area when they . . . when they, I guess, inspected her at the hospital. The state lab matched it to me."

"I see. Certainly a better than average beginning for the plaintiff," Sa'ad said dryly.

"Exactly." Joel was looking at the floor.

"I don't believe none of her crap," Edmund declared. "Nope."

"It's not as bad as it seems," Joel added. "There's a lot that went into my decision to accept blame. And some other, unsolved issues."

Sa'ad arched an eyebrow. "I'm happy to listen, but it's hard to undo a guilty plea that's coupled with uncontroverted DNA evidence. I imagine that will be our starting point." His tone was patronizing, carried a defense attorney's jaded, heard-it-before skepticism.

"I understand," Joel said, realizing his legal options were limited. "I've dug myself into quite a hole."

"Do you have any assets, Mr. King?" Sa'ad was polite, made the very personal inquiry seem like casual conversation.

Joel shook his head. "No, I'm broke."

"I guess that's the good news—you don't stand to lose much."

"Is it fair to assume they're doing this just to be spiteful?" Joel asked Sa'ad.

"Perhaps. Of course, the judgment would allow them to intercept wages or any money you might earn in the future."

"Take a long time to get to five million that way," Joel said.

"True, but it's hard to live on two hundred dollars a month." Sa'ad cleared his throat. "Let me ask you this: How big is your church?"

"Relatively large, especially for our area."

"Interesting." Sa'ad pulled himself higher and straighter.

"We've got close to nine hundred members," Edmund said.

"Why do you want to know?" Joel asked.

"So this isn't your uncle's basement with a boom box, a few tambourines and a plastic cross in the driveway? This is a solvent, substantial institution?"

"It's an old, established church," Joel said, "with a good, middle-class congregation."

"You have the papers with you?" Sa'ad asked.

Joel took the pages from his pocket and handed them to Sa'ad.

Sa'ad only glanced at the suit for an instant, never got past the first page. "There's your answer, gentlemen. There it is. Your church belongs to the Southern Baptist Convention?"

"Well, uh, yes," Joel stuttered, "although, you know, we've been—we were, I should say—debating our membership, given some of their doctrinal positions."

"What's the catch, Sa'ad?" Edmund swerved toward Joel. "I told you he was sharp, didn't I?" He focused on the lawyer again. "What's goin' on?"

"I was just inflating your bill, Edmund," Sa'ad teased, "padding your charges, trying to pry another dollar from your miserly white hands." He sang through the words and finished with a big laugh.

"Kiss my ass, Sa'ad," Edmund said, but the rejoinder was playful also, without prickles or malice.

"I'm guessing there's a healthy insurance policy at the end of this rainbow. They sued you *and* the church. Your friend Christina's chasing the heavy-duty money. You work for the church, so the church is responsible for your conduct. Maybe even your governing body. Is your church insured?"

Joel struggled to recall, mashed the heel of his hand against his forehead. "I know we are for fire and so forth, but I'm really not involved in that part of things. Believe it or not, ministers don't do much of the business end. Everything was in place before I got there, and the finance committee keeps track of those concerns. I mean, they keep me generally informed, keep me abreast of our needs, but I've never discussed insurance. I know I have life insurance, but that wouldn't make any difference."

Edmund looked flabbergasted. "So *that's* it."

"Most churches and businesses and corporations have some kind of liability policy to protect them, especially if they have something to lose—as would your church." Sa'ad held up the suit papers. "Did you notice that you have been sued quote 'individually and in your capacity as an agent and employee' of your church? And the church is named as a defendant, too."

Joel sighed and flipped up his palms. "I didn't pay much attention to the details. I got the general theme and put everything away. To tell you the truth, I was more concerned about my wife leaving me."

"What does he need to do, Sa'ad?" Edmund asked.

"This is most likely a good thing. If he's insured, they pay, not Mr. King. And the insurer will probably provide him and the church with a lawyer."

"Great. Their attorney. I'm sure he'll really be hot to do all he can for Joel, take Christy and her vampires right to the mat. I want you to watch this for Joel. You keep an eye on this, Sa'ad. I don't care about the cost." Edmund's mouth was drawn, and he pointed at his lawyer when he finished talking.

"Actually, Edmund, I'm sure the insurance lawyer will fight like hell—it's their money. They usually try to keep it."

"Whatever," Edmund groused. "But you're Joel's lawyer as of right now."

"Only if *he* hires me, Edmund. Not you."

Edmund gave Joel a stern look. "Don't cross me on this. I mean it. I'll take care of Blacula here and you can pay me back or do somethin' for me when your affairs settle down. Believe me, Sa'ad needs to look into this."

"Edmund, I appreciate it, but it sounds like it might work itself out. I—"

Edmund leaned into him, crowding him with his face and shoulders. He didn't say anything, just set his head with a slight pitch to it.

Joel paused. He considered Edmund's offer and his consternation. "Hey. Okay. Why not? Thanks, Edmund. Okay. Sign me up."

Edmund retreated back into his own chair. "You're welcome."

"I'll see where matters stand," Sa'ad promised. "And leave your divorce papers here, too. I'm not completely familiar with Virginia domestic law, but I'll see if there's anything obvious." He hesitated, and the cadence in his voice briefly changed. "I'm technically not licensed in Virginia, so I'll be working exclusively through an associate or local counsel. I'll report to you and manage the case, but I'll not be formally involved. The bar is very strict in these matters. It won't cost you—well, Edmund—any more, and you can rest assured I'll personally review every development. Plus, I suspect you'll have insurance counsel very soon."

"Thanks."

"Don't mention it."

Joel puckered his lips for an instant, formed the rudiments of a smile. "So, Edmund, the insurance company may not be the bad guy in this piece, huh? They might be on the white horse, galloping to my rescue."

"Or else they'll try to wiggle off the hook and leave you to take the enema," Edmund said. "You watch what I'm tellin' you."

"Maybe, but I choose to be optimistic."

"I'll tell you who should be optimistic—the capes-and-hats workin' the sag on the other side of this. Talk about provin' my point." Edmund waved his hand, dismissing the whole subject. "I'm a piker compared to these scoundrels."

Sa'ad rolled his wrist and checked his watch. "Well, Edmund, it would appear another accident has come your way. I trust that you're not too badly injured." Bemusement spilled from every word.

"It's pretty severe. Almost constant pain, the car torn up."

Sa'ad's eyes were dancing a sly soft-shoe. "Let me guess. Let's see. Let me put on the turban and explore the Ouija board. I'm feeling . . . a hit-and-run driver? In Virginia? Barreling down on you from the wrong side of the road?"

Edmund kept a straight face. "Key-recht, Sa'ad."

"I'll have one of the paralegals start the paperwork. Do you have time to take the car by Richard's for an estimate?"

"Already phoned him," Edmund said.

"How about a chiropractor?"

"I thought I'd see our buddy Doc Holton while I'm out here, then I've got a guy at home who's on the team."

"Excellent." Sa'ad turned his attention to Joel. "How about you, Mr. King? Were you injured in the accident?"

"He was," Edmund interjected. "Took a ferocious lick."

Joel gave Sa'ad a good going-over, waited a minute before answering. "I have a little discomfort from the seat belt. That's about it."

"That can be quite a nuisance in some cases." Sa'ad had emptied his face. "Is this something you'd like to pursue?"

"I don't have any insurance," Joel said.

"Ah, but Edmund does."

"I don't want to sue Edmund or cause him any problems." Joel was distracted, simultaneously trying to talk to Sa'ad and also capture what was actually going on beneath the conversation.

"You wouldn't need to. You'd sue the car that ran you off the road, collect from him."

"It was a truck. Well, I guess it was a truck." Joel cut his eyes at Edmund. "Let's put it this way. When I woke up, there was a truck in sight. He never made contact with us, and I don't know the driver's name. So how would we sue him?"

"Joel, Virginia's one of the rare states that allows you to sue your own policy when an unknown driver runs you off the road, even in the absence of contact between the vehicles. The claim would be against a John Doe driver, and you'd collect from Edmund's insurance company."

"How about that," Joel said.

"You don't need to know the driver's name or anything, only a description of the vehicle."

"I see."

Edmund spoke up. "Check this out, Sa'ad. We have a witness, this guy who was passin' through. He told the cop he saw the truck drivin' fast and erratic immediately after it went by us."

"Really?" Sa'ad seemed puzzled.

"Sure enough."

"How'd that happen? I don't get it." Sa'ad's features clicked into a look Joel hadn't seen before.

"Hey, just a man tryin' to help his fellow man. Talk about the luck of the draw—guy who stops at the accident looked like he was on his way to the bunker with his canned food and batteries, and of course he don't like the police, and of course he doesn't want me to get a ticket. Even offered to hold our dope and guns."

"So he sees the truck—"

"Drivin' like a madman." Edmund finished Sa'ad's sentence.

"Bravo, my friend."

"It was a nice stroke of luck."

Sa'ad checked his watch again. "So you see, Joel, you are very much entitled to collect for your injuries. There's plenty of coverage and no downside for Edmund."

Joel pinched the bridge of his nose with his thumb and forefinger. He closed his eyes for an instant and dragged the tips of his fingers over his lids, rubbed back and forth. When he let the room in again, his vision was briefly contaminated with speckles of color and dark, heavy dots. "I think I'll pass, if it's all the same to you guys. I did see the truck after it went by us, if that's helpful in the long run."

Sa'ad and Edmund were quiet. "You're sure, Joel?" Edmund finally asked. "I mean, you understand the situation here?"

"I understand."

"Let me know if you change your mind," Sa'ad offered.

"Not going to happen," Joel said firmly.

Sa'ad abruptly stood up. "I can certainly respect that," he said. "I'll take care of your other matters and be in touch. Leave your contact information with the receptionist."

Joel and Edmund left their leather chairs and followed him to the door. "Oh. The check from that South Dakota project arrived today," Sa'ad said to Edmund as they were shaking hands. "You can pick it up with the other two. Jill's got everything ready."

"Wow. Huh. That's good news. You're a regular miracle worker, Otis."

"I thought it would take longer, too. Got a new adjuster; that helped move matters along."

Joel was on the verge of ill temper when he and Edmund arrived at the Cadillac. He got into the passenger's seat but didn't shut the door. The desert heat was everywhere, blasting out of the car's interior and rising in waves from the parched sand that encircled the city.

"You know, Edmund, I'm on probation. I go straight to jail if I get into trouble." Joel was gazing down the street when he spoke, his feet outside the car, his back to Edmund. "I'm grateful for your efforts to help me, and I value our friendship. You've done a lot for me. Yes you have. I can understand to some extent what you do and why you do it. But . . ." He brought his feet into the vehicle, planted them on the floorboard and faced Edmund. "I don't appreciate your involving me in something like this without my knowledge, and on top of that, if I'm reading this correctly—and I think I am—I'm not too thrilled about being driven into a tree. What if I'd been badly hurt? You had no right."

Edmund hung his head and sighed. He ran his hand through his hair, leaving a few strands tousled when he finished. "Joel, I truly am sorry. I wanted to give you a boost the best way I know how. I'm sorry. I've made a mess of things."

"I wondered why the heck we were off the interstate on some rural highway. And you're not really injured, are you?"

Edmund kept his head down. "I apologize."

He seemed so sincere, so disappointed, so chastised, that Joel found it hard to sustain any ire or disgust. "Don't brood about it, just don't get me into anything else. No more of your crazy schemes, okay?"

"You have my word." Edmund was still slouched in his seat, subdued and embarrassed. He hadn't cranked the car, and the heat was pulling out sweat on his brow and along the top of his lip.

"Good enough. I accept your apology."

Edmund remained slumped and shamed, didn't speak.

"It's okay, Edmund," Joel assured him. "Forget it." The scorched air was making Joel light-headed; according to the thermometer at the bank across the highway, it was 104 degrees.

Edmund gathered himself. "Thanks." His voice was quiet and pained. "You know, Joel, when you preached my daddy's funeral and opened our church for the service, when you did that after those sorry bastards up in Maine wouldn't give him a decent burial, I told you right then I owed you the moon and the stars. I'm just tryin' to repay you."

"I appreciate that. I do. So let's forget about it and get on the road."

"You're sure? You're not cross about it?"

"It's behind us, Edmund," Joel promised him. "I forgive you."

"Okay then." Edmund fit the key into the ignition. "You're a good man to be so understandin'."

"Why did you call Sa'ad 'Otis' when we were leaving?"

"You don't think Sa'ad is his real name, do you?" Edmund asked. He didn't seem caught unawares by the question.

"I hadn't given it much thought." Joel took a fast-food napkin from his pocket and patted the perspiration on his face and neck. "How about you, Edmund, is that your real name?"

"Names, names, names. What's the difference? I've got lots of names. You need 'em in my occupation."

"I guess so."

Joel finished wiping and dabbing with the napkin. Even though he recognized the sincerity of Edmund's efforts and had—for the most part— found their time together agreeable, he was glad they would be severed after a few hundred more miles, relieved he soon would be out from under his friend's shady beneficence. "How long to Missoula?" Joel asked. "Can we drive it straight through?"

"I'll sure bust my hump trying, if that's what you want. Drive every cotton-pickin' second I can," Edmund vowed. "And I'll put in the CD you like, that *Al Green's Greatest Hits*. You take it easy and enjoy the trip. I'm gonna do whatever it takes to correct my errors where you're concerned."

Dr. Neal Baldwin Johnson was a piece of shit. At least according to his former wife, Dr. Johnson was a piece of shit. He'd abandoned a damn fine radiology partnership in Atlanta and talked her into packing for Missoula, Montana, to get away, he'd said, from the stress and the bustle and the rat race that kept him preoccupied so much of the time. As it turned out, the only rat involved was Dr. Johnson himself—"the aptly named Dr. Johnson," she liked to note—who proved to be a beady-eyed fiend worthy of a crown and a toe dance through *The Nutcracker,* a true Rodent King. The piece of shit deserted her underneath an undeniably big and beautiful sky, took up with a sophomore from the university and moved to France. France. She always said it twice when she did the rehearsed version.

Dr. Johnson was more than double the scrawny bitch's age when he decided to commit adultery, and when he hit the road, he left his wife with Baker, their five-year-old son. He also left her with everything they owned, all the money, furniture, stocks, land, pensions, cars—everything. And that just made it worse, made it harder to accept. What a slap in the face: he was willing to walk off a pauper if he could simply be rid of her and have his miniskirted nymph. It was a wicked generosity akin to a marital bribe—no price was too steep so long as he got to dump his threadbare wife, the graying yesterday's news who'd brought him sandwiches when he was a poor, unshaven resident and stretched her stomach out of whack to carry his child. Enraged by the entire affair, his spouse of nearly two decades paid an extra twenty-seven dollars during the divorce to dispose of the one thing she hated most, and now she was Sophie Ellis King again, a mother whose school-age kid didn't share her last name.

Sophie was three years younger than her brother, Joel. She'd always been attractive in a fashion men found comfortable and women considered unobtrusive, and she was smart, perceptive and mischievous, although it seemed to Joel, seeing her for the first time in many months, that the last couple years had sifted some of the cleverness from her face and bearing. She'd been a popular girl during high school—but not a cheerleader or club president, for goodness' sakes—a history major at Ohio State who never seemed the slightest bit pressed by her studies, and a proud wife and complete mother who enjoyed both roles, content to preside over a home, love her husband and rear their baby boy. While watching a cupboard and tending to Baker, she also planted a vegetable garden every spring, kept a journal, published a long magazine piece on Millard Fillmore, painted a household's worth of trim and molding, cooked for a horde of in-laws at Thanksgiving, taught herself conversational Spanish before a three-week vacation to Barcelona and managed to absorb far more about politics, plumbing, tax forms, child development and the world's guts than did her golf-and-well-done-steaks husband. And this was the thanks she got, ditched a year and a half ago for no legitimate reason.

Sophie was in front of her house when Edmund and her brother arrived in the Cadillac. She was using a green garden hose to fill a child's plastic wading pool, holding the hose high and letting the water cascade from around her chest. Baker was sitting in the pool, dressed in his white under-shorts and nothing else, plopping his open hands into the water and whooping after every splash. Joel and Edmund had stopped only for gas, coffee, snacks and restrooms, had slept and driven in shifts and made the trip from Las Vegas without spending another night in a hotel. As prom-ised, Edmund had stayed behind the wheel until he was exhausted, putting in the first ten hell-bent hours before allowing Joel to spell him.

Joel was surprised when he saw his sister's home, nonplussed by where she was living. He recalled a Christmas photo and occasional snapshots that showed a sprawling log fortress on the banks of the Bitterroot River. He and Edmund had followed her directions exactly and were parked beside a small, low-slung house built mostly from painted cinderblocks with an aluminum-siding addition hitched onto the rear. The men got out of the car and headed toward Sophie, Joel waving at her with both hands.

She bent the hose shut, stuck the crimp under her foot and hugged her brother. Joel introduced Edmund, who said nice things in his charming way and immediately knelt to greet Baker. After only a few moments of encouragement, the child recited his entire name and slapped Edmund a wet high five. The three grownups chatted briefly in the hot sun, and

Edmund told a story about a midget he'd seen at a Vegas craps game, described how the wee man would belly-balance on the edge of the table and toss the dice. When she mentioned it, Edmund politely refused Sophie's offer of a meal and a sofa. He carried Joel's Kmart bag into the house, walked back to the Cadillac and took hold of the door handle.

"I apologize again for lettin' you down like I did," Edmund said as he and Joel were standing beside the car. "You know I think the world of you."

"I know."

"Well, all right then. I reckon this is it. I appreciate your keeping me company."

"Thank you, Edmund, for bringing me here. And thanks for your friendship—even the misguided parts."

Edmund smiled with half his mouth. "You're welcome." He still had a grip on the handle.

"Be careful. Be careful driving to Virginia, and be careful what you do. Don't step too far over the line."

"I try to stay right on it, Joel."

"You sure you don't want to spend the night here? You're welcome to. A little beneath your standards, but we'd love to have you."

"I'm goin' to leave the reunion for you guys. I see a big steak and a hot bath in my future. I'll find a hotel and take off in the morning."

"Thanks again." Joel stretched out his hand.

Edmund grasped it and squeezed and shook at the same time. He'd let go of the car so he could give their farewell its due. "If you ever need anything, I want you to call me. No matter what the request or how long it's been, dial my number. Collect if you have to."

"I will," Joel promised him, breaking their handshake. "We'll keep in touch."

"Anything, anytime—you understand? And that's the minimum I'd do for you."

"I'd say we're pretty even," Joel remarked.

"Not really."

"Before you get away, let me ask your advice on something that's sort of in your field of expertise." Joel swatted at a fly buzzing near his face. "Do you think it would be wise for me to speak to Christy about the suit? I believe if we sat down together, I could talk some reason into her. Or—"

"No. Don't. Bad idea." Edmund frowned. "That's a dead-solid loser. Let Sa'ad do the talkin'. She ain't goin' to throw in the towel on millions just 'cause you ask sweetly and remind her you're a good fellow. She's a mean, conniving little brat, and her daddy's probably pullin' the strings anyhow.

I'm not even sure all the way across the country is enough distance. That pretty clear?"

"Very. But I still think I could get this resolved if I had the chance."

"Don't do it, Joel. Take it from a pro—they'll twist and shape whatever happens till it bites you in the ass. Claim you were threatenin' her or sniffin' around for some more adventure. Remember me tellin' you about her little escapade at college last fall? The overdose that hit while she was havin' intercourse with some hippie kid? She's not a person you need to be breakin' bread with, not stable. No tellin' what she might say or do, and the capes-and-hats would have a field day."

"Thanks for the advice."

"You're welcome. I hope you're listenin'."

"I'll certainly consider it," Joel said.

"Take care, Preacher. And good luck." Edmund climbed into his white car and drove toward the main road. Joel watched him go, stood in his sister's gravel drive kicking at the small rocks, waiting for Edmund to tap his horn or blink the lights or lower the glass and shout a last goodbye. He never did, though, just turned onto the hardtop and accelerated until he vanished from sight.

Baker was still in his cheap pool, playing with an elaborate submarine and a red ball, and Sophie was leaning against the door frame, arms folded, one leg crossing the other at the ankle. "I don't like that man, Joel. Something about him. I'm glad he's moving on."

"He's a good guy, all in all. You'd have to know his story. He was active in our church and stuck by me through everything that happened. He's the same as most of us, Sophie. He has his faults, but he's been a friend where I'm concerned."

"I can sense it a mile away. There's something there I don't care for. He's entirely too glib." She didn't change her position in the doorway.

"I think you're being far too critical of someone you've met for all of ten minutes."

"Bad vibes, Joel. Trust me. I've felt them before."

"Well, he *is* a man. Maybe that's it." He winced, wished he could suck back the words as soon as he'd spoken them. "I didn't mean it like that . . . to say that. I was only . . . I'm sorry. I'm tired and bleary-eyed and wrung out. I'm sorry." He bit his lip. "I wasn't thinking. Too many days in jail and too many miles on the highway."

Sophie straightened up from the door frame and took a step outside, fixing Joel with an angry, baleful glare.

"I'm sorry. It was a stupid, rude thing to say."

Her scowl continued, full bore. "Yes, it was."

"I don't know where that came from. It just popped out."

Sophie didn't speak.

"I'm sorry. I'm on your side. If I could, you know I'd hunt down Neal and kick his tail for you."

Her stern expression began to soften around the edges. "I'd like to see that—Gandhi takes up arms. And you'd what? 'Kick his tail'?"

"Well, maybe I'd just drop a hunger strike on him or something. Or a general boycott. How about that?"

Sophie relaxed her features, and her brother caught a glimpse of a generous face that was immutable and pretty and entirely his sister's, unmistakable to a sibling's eye no matter how many wrinkles and pranks the years left behind. He flashed on a darling little girl in black shoes and an Easter dress, the two of them holding hands and picking up dyed eggs in their parents' midwestern yard.

"Come on, I'll show you to your luxurious digs."

Sophie led Joel into her house. He followed her through a living room full of toys, empty glasses, a solitary tennis shoe and crayons flung onto a coffee table, to a hallway door with a decrepit knob that squeaked when Joel turned it. They walked down a set of wooden steps, carefully foot-feeling a path to the bottom, the descent blind and musty, the smell reminiscent of earth and moist, decaying leaves. Sophie tugged a string hanging from the ceiling and lit a bare bulb above their heads. When the light came to life, she surveyed her brother's expression, saw the way everything had gone flat in him. They were standing on a cement floor, a water heater to their right. A beige washer and dryer were across the room; the top of the washer was angled open, and a pink plastic basket with an overflow of clothes had been dropped next to the dryer. There wasn't the first window in the room, just pipes, wires and four gray cinder-block walls.

"Welcome to my basement," Sophie said. She gave her brother a little bow, put her arm across her waist in a show of pretend formality.

"Indeed." This was the best Joel could muster.

"Surprised?"

"By what?" he asked.

"Oh, I don't know. By where we're living? By where *you'll* be living?"

"Is this my room? Down here? I don't see a bed or anything."

"Your bed's behind the partition." She pointed at a divider—three sections of dark brown paneling—extending into the room from a far wall. "There's a bed on the other side, and a dresser and a rug and a radio. The dresser and bed are especially expensive—Empire period, I think—and the radio's one of those Bose wave machines, cost close to five hundred bucks new."

Joel took her by the hand, and they sat on the last wooden step, twisting sideways so they both could fit. "What happened to the river house? I didn't realize you'd moved. This is . . . uh . . . new."

"This, Joel, is the world of a single parent who gets it from every direction."

He released her hand. "I don't understand—I thought Neal left you everything. You guys had a beautiful home and cars and who knows what else."

"And I got it all. I got a seven-thousand-square-foot castle that costs more to maintain than I make in a year as a secretary. After I finally sold it and paid the mortgage, I cleared, what, maybe sixty thousand? It costs an arm and a leg every time you raise the hood on a Jag, and talk about worthless in the snow, so now I have a more practical ride. I've got trinkets and gizmos and state-of-the-art espresso machines and a Peter Max and a set of Waterford crystal to go to war over, but I'd trade the whole heap for a reliable transmission and a pair of comfortable shoes." She made a grand sweep of the room with her hand. "Before you lies the kingdom of the wounded gentry. Bauble rich, cash poor. You're getting the picture, I hope."

"Don't you get some help from Neal? Child support? Alimony?"

"Ah. Alimony and child support. I receive a whopping thousand bucks a month. He sends it in francs. I swear I'm not making that up. He got off light because he gave me so much other stuff. Besides, he's in Europe and not practicing medicine, and what am I going to do about it?"

Joel was growing uncomfortable on the hard step. "What's he up to over there?"

"He's taking art classes. I imagine by now he has a goatee, and probably a beret and a sash. Maybe a plumed chapeau for special occasions. I hope he dies a brutal, ugly death, Joel. I know you forgive everyone for everything, but I will never forgive him for how he's treated us. He hasn't seen his son in over a year. Not a letter, not a call. And as far as sacked wives go, I'm damn lucky. I have a house and enough to make ends meet. It could be worse, believe me."

"I'm sorry. I can understand why you despise him, but it won't do any good to let your anger fester. You need—"

Sophie held up a hand, cutting him off. "Don't tell me what I need. What I need is to see Neal flayed on a hot rock with buzzards pecking at his liver." She kept her hand in the air and directed her index finger at her brother. "And do you want to know the last chapter? Neal will show up ten years from now, all mystery and promises and manhood, and he'll treat Baker like a prince, tell him some half-assed tale of woe and whisk my son right out of here after I've loved him and raised him and struggled to do right by him. I'll be the hag who grounded him and made him go to summer school, and Neal's the cool guy with vacations and football tickets. I can already hear it: 'You didn't get my letters? I wrote and called, Son. It broke my heart not to be able to keep in touch. Your mom must've thrown away the letters. And didn't she tell you when I phoned?'"

"I think things will be okay, Sophie. I know you're an excellent mother. Your son will appreciate that in the long haul."

"He's a good kid, a joy. That's the saddest part."

Joel put his arm around his sister. The side of his face pressed against her hair, and he could smell hot weather and what remained of yesterday's strawberry shampoo. "Thanks for putting up with one more problem in your life. I'm going to try to get on my feet right away."

"I hope so, Joel. I can't carry the three of us, and we've got Mom to worry about, too."

He still had her next to him. "How bad is she? I phoned her when I could but I might as well have been from Mars, and I faithfully wrote every week. I couldn't decide which was crueler—agitating her with three-minute phone conversations and puzzling letters or just leaving her be."

"She's like any seventy-nine-year-old with Alzheimer's. I think they used to call it 'hardening of the arteries,' didn't they? She's here and there and daffy most of the time. I can't imagine how terrible it must be, everything washing straight through your head and nothing ever sticking."

"I'll drive out to see her tomorrow," he said. "At least she isn't aware her only son's a jailbird. I suppose that's a blessing."

"It's like talking to a black hole. I don't know if it makes any difference, but I still go three or four days a week and every Sunday afternoon."

"Company has to help. I'm betting it somehow registers with her." Joel heard choppy footsteps on the floor above them and Baker shouting for his mom. "How about a quick prayer?" he asked.

"No offense, but that's your business, Joel. You can pray all you want. I have better things to do. It's fair to assume the Lord knows what I need without my pestering Him every five minutes, right? Sort of like psychics and the lottery—they should win every drawing." She separated herself from him. "And don't start with me about religion and church and whatever else. I don't want to hear it."

The next morning, Joel dropped his sister at work and drove her Taurus station wagon to the High Pines Assisted Living Center. The trip to the center took half an hour, most of it on Interstate 90. Joel traveled deliberately and tuned to NPR, grateful to be out from behind bars and the cacophony of Snoop Dogg and Metallica and 96.3 Classic Rock that kicked off every day in jail. He noticed the vehicle's interior could use a thorough cleaning, something he would take care of as soon as he finished visiting his mother. There was a pink stain on the passenger seat and smears all over the dash and windshield. He kept the windows down, let the morning air blow on him from all directions.

Helen King's room at High Pines was hot and smelled like pee and Vicks cherry throat lozenges. Joel's mother didn't seem to recognize him but was clearly happy to have a visitor. She'd painted on big rouge cheeks and crazy makeup and was dressed as if she were about to leave for a cattle roundup, looked like Carol Burnett in costume for an Annie Oakley skit. A pipe-cleaner-and-construction-paper turkey occupied the heart of her dresser, and an orange-and-black spook—a Halloween holdover, evidently— was next to the turkey. There were at least a hundred white plastic forks and spoons on top of a small refrigerator. Tissues covered in perfect lipstick mouths were arranged beneath her mirror, the red-orange prints the last part of her morning ritual, a delicate pucker and blot to do away with any excess color.

Joel took a seat on the corner of her single bed. "How are you, Mom?"

"I feel fine. I'm going home tomorrow." She was sitting in the room's only chair.

"Home?" Joel said.

"I'm not staying here, locked up like this."

"You're not locked up. You can come and go as you please. This is a nice place."

"Who are you? You look like a man on TV."

"I'm Joel, your son." He slid nearer her chair, as if proximity might improve her memory.

"I'm going home tomorrow. After I eat, that is. I'll have my meal, then I'm leaving."

"Great," he answered. In Roanoke, the locals had said the Alzheimer's sickness caused people "to go back." Slipping, spinning, failing, misfiring, regressing . . . going back. "Do you remember the last time we saw each other, when you were in Roanoke?" he asked her. "The day Sophie came to Virginia and picked you up?"

"Where?" One of her eyelids hung too low, kept a partial hood over her vision.

"Roanoke, Virginia. You stayed with Martha and me after you left Indianapolis, and then at The Glade, that nice place out by Vinton." He and Sophie had moved her to Missoula a week before he began his sentence, had refused to totally surrender her to a world of old-folks volunteers, hairnetted dieticians and aides in teddy-bear smocks, all of whom were big-hearted and conscientious but not the same as kin.

"I've never been to Virginia, have I?" Her voice was heartbreaking, searching and rueful and confused. Her eyes were cloudy, her movements guarded.

Joel got the impression she'd simply begun to separate from herself, that a corner of her soul had been cut loose and was flapping in the wind. "A while ago, yes."

"What day is it?"

"Thursday."

"Are you the doctor?" she wanted to know.

"No," he said patiently, "I'm your son."

"My son?"

"Yes."

"I'm leaving here and going home."

"Where's that?" he asked, curious to see what she'd come up with.

"Two hundred eight Wilton Road, of course. Indianapolis, Indiana." His childhood home, where she'd lived until her husband died, then for three years more.

They talked this way for several minutes, until a woman came on the PA to announce a bingo game in the activities area. Helen King stood and patted her gray bangs, passed by her son without another sound and hurried out of the room. Joel called after her, then caught up with her in the hall, but she was a juggernaut in a loud western shirt, determined to get a choice spot and her fair share of cards before the game started. He kissed her cheek while she was on the fly, told her he loved her. She made a noise that was not quite a word and didn't slow her determined pace. Joel stood still and watched her merge into a phalanx of walkers, canes, stooped shoulders and crooked spines. She turned left, into a set of double doors, and disappeared.

After ten days of living in his sister's basement with his convict's leprosy, Joel began to discover how difficult starting over was going to be. He had no particular skill, no experience he could count on, no marketable trade, no flashy degree or snazzy story to sell. He'd known this much was coming though, realized it soon after he'd landed in jail, and he'd resigned himself to a different kind of work, was ready to take on grim, monotonous hours and punch a clock at minimum wage. He would gladly grovel in a fast-food uniform or stock shelves with high-school bag boys. He would do whatever it took. He would be meek.

He found out in short order it wasn't going to be so simple. His life quickly became making do and cutting corners and skipping lunch and wasting Sophie's gas on one dead-end job interview after another. His second morning in town, at nine o'clock, he lined up at the unemployment office behind a man who'd already been drinking, the drunk swaying and humming and turning around every so often to ask Joel some cockeyed question and finally coloring the seat of his pants with urine. One Monday when he went into the kitchen to fix his breakfast coffee, Sophie had left him a five-dollar bill and a promotional coupon for a free slice of pizza, charity for her wretched brother.

Despite his best efforts, two weeks came and went without any work. He prayed every morning and every night, did his best to keep his faith intact. There was a country church about a mile from Sophie's, and he plodded the distance one afternoon, even though the preacher had posted a trite message on the signboard, spelled out in black letters: GIVE THE DEVIL AN INCH AND HE'LL BECOME YOUR RULER. The door to the church was bolted, so he sat in the grass and enjoyed the mountains and magnificent sky. He stared into the high wispy clouds and blue heavens that went on forever and asked the Lord what he needed to do.

His probation officer, a weasel of a man named Jack Howard, made his problems worse. He'd been twice to Howard's office without finding him there, and finally had waited in the lobby for an hour before he actually got to meet the man who'd be supervising him. Howard was fiftyish, an odd-looking sort with a slender neck, hardly any eyebrows and a pinched, feral face. His feet were on his desk when Joel walked through the door, grudgingly allowed in by a grumpy secretary named Mrs. Heller.

"Welcome, Mr. King," he said over the tops of his shoes, a pair of black lace-ups with rubber soles. "Take a seat and let's get to know each other."

"Thanks." Joel sat in a chair with a bright blue vinyl back.

"So what kind of 'vert are you, Joel? Boys or girls?"

"I'm sorry. I'm not sure I follow you."

"I get a misdemeanor, contributing-to-a-minor case from Virginia, I gotta figure you didn't give some kid a sip of champagne at his parents' New Year's Eve dinner. I figure it's a plea bargain on somethin' pretty important, and I'm guessing you were diddlin' a child. I want you to tell me if it was a boy or a girl. I'd like to know what kind of per-*vert* I got on my roster." He split the word to help Joel with the first reference.

Joel felt his face flush. "Oh, I see."

"So which is it?"

"I pled guilty to having sex with a girl."

"She past training wheels?" Howard asked. His tie was loose around his neck, and he wasn't wearing a jacket.

"She was almost eighteen."

"Hey, great. So she was seventeen, and you're what? Forty-five?"

"I'm forty-two. I'll be forty-three in August."

Howard leaned forward but didn't disturb his feet. "What day?"

"The eighth. August eighth."

"Well now, you just sit tight." He picked up his phone but didn't dial any numbers. "Sue, listen, Mr. King the pedophile has a birthday in August. Can you get something organized for him, say, a cake and presents? And a piñata—they really make things festive. And wings and beer and party hats. Hell, just shoot the moon. Only the best." He tossed the phone onto his desk, didn't hang it up, and Joel soon heard an off-the-hook beeping start in the receiver. "I don't give a rat's ass when your birthday is, Mr. King."

"Right."

"I'm your PO, not your social planner."

"I understand."

The phone continued to make a racket. Howard left it alone, let it lie bleating on top of a file. He put his hands behind his head so his elbows stuck out from either side. "Hang it up," he said forcefully.

"Pardon?"

"The phone." Howard drilled the words. "Get off your ass and hang it up."

"Are you serious?" Joel asked.

"What do you think?"

Joel felt anger and indignation roiling in his abdomen. He felt certain his neck was still red, and his fingers had curled into slack fists. He stayed in his seat, didn't budge, didn't speak.

Howard swung one of his feet onto the floor and unfolded his arms. "You have a hearing problem, Mr. King?"

"No."

"Then I suggest you snap to and put this buzzin' motherfucker back where it belongs." He lifted the other leg off his desk.

Joel took a deep breath, thought about what he should do. "What if I decide I won't, Mr. Howard, then what?"

"Then I violate your probation."

Joel snorted. "Because I wouldn't perform your phone chores?"

"No. Because you had a dirty drug screen or missed an appointment or anything else I choose to put in my report."

"I don't guess I have a choice then, do I?"

"You can choose between workin' with me or catchin' more time."

Joel was seething. He wasn't able to get enough air to his lungs, had to take in rapid slurps through his mouth. "So . . ."

"So." Howard gave him a satisfied look.

Joel stood from his seat, adjusted his pants, went to the edge of Howard's state-employee desk, picked up the receiver and placed it on the base. He glared at Howard, but the probation officer didn't flinch, matched him dagger for dagger, scowl for scowl.

"Nice work," he said after Joel had returned to his screaming blue chair.

Joel was silent, his fingers intertwined in his lap, his jaw clenched.

"Now, just a few more questions." Up went the feet again.

"Don't you have all this in a file or something? Didn't Virginia send you my history?"

"I suppose they did, but I'd have to pull the records and read thirty minutes of crap I'd rather just ask you about."

"Oh."

"Yeah. See the wisdom of my technique?"

Howard then launched into a tired monologue Joel had trouble following because his head and ears were clotted with temper. Occasionally Howard would ask a question, and Joel would give a terse answer or say "yes" or "no." He had Joel sign several forms and reminded him the first payment on his fines and court costs was due in forty-five days. "Two hundred and thirty bucks. Don't be late with it."

Joel glanced down the paperwork he'd been given. "Two thirty?" he asked.

Howard smirked at him. "Two hundred and thirty dollars."

"The court in Roanoke said it was two hundred." Joel held up a sheet of paper. "This schedule says two hundred. Where'd you get two thirty?"

"That's a special processing fee, payable to your local PO. Bring it in cash, every month."

"You're just adding an extra thirty. I owe two hundred—that's what I was ordered to pay, and that's what everything says. Show me in writing where this additional amount is mentioned, and I'll pay it."

"Unwritten rule."

Joel was coming unwound, goaded by frustration and uncut anger and a sense of helplessness. "I'm not going to pay it, and you can violate me or send me to jail or whatever. I don't care. At least I can get fed there and have a place to sleep. And I'll report you for extorting money."

"I'm sure your word will carry a lot of weight."

"Are we through?"

"We are."

Joel jumped up from his chair and spun away from Howard, took a hasty, clumsy stride toward the door.

"Whoa, Mr. King, one more thing. A story for you. Don't go anywhere yet."

Joel kept his back to Howard, stood as tall as possible and listened to his own erratic breathing.

"One day this old tomcat's crossing the railroad tracks. He's almost across, almost on the other side, when he hears the train coming. Choo-choo, clickety-clack. Suddenly, the train's right there, right on top of him, and the cat's worried he might not be totally off the rails, so he stops and looks behind him. Guess what happens?" Howard hesitated, waiting for Joel to say something.

Joel didn't move and didn't respond.

"When he turns and looks around, the train hits him and cuts his head clean off."

"Wonderful story, Mr. Howard."

"The moral of the fable, my criminal friend, is that you don't want to lose your head over a little piece of tail." Howard howled and clapped his hands, and he threw his legs off the table and stomped the ground, went into an all-out display of amusement even though he'd no doubt done the bit thousands of times.

Everything came to a boil on a Tuesday night, right before suppertime. Joel was now three weeks without a job, and he'd run out of places to apply. Employers from A to Z had a reason for putting him off—they had young girls working there or coming in as customers; they couldn't allow a convict to handle money; he had no cooking skills; he had no training; he wasn't a people person; he didn't have his own tools; he wouldn't look good wearing the company's uniform (this from a chubby Pizza Hut assistant manager whose shirttail wouldn't stay tucked inside his pants). He kept the house neat and the yard mowed, and that was the extent of what he was able to do. His first court installment was soon due, his mother's prescription bill needed to be paid, Baker had hopes of attending soccer camp and lightning had run in on the microwave oven, completely ruining it. Sophie had a friend take the Peter Max painting to a Jackson Hole gallery, but she got virtually nothing for it, and prior to Joel's arrival she'd already sold her engagement ring and two Persian rugs.

Tuesday morning, Joel was washing breakfast dishes when Sa'ad called with unhappy news: Martha wanted a divorce *and* alimony, and wasn't in a negotiating mood. On the heels of Sa'ad's report, a lawyer from Roanoke phoned to discuss Christy's case. The lawyer represented the church's insurance company and said he was anxious to defend both Joel and Roanoke First Baptist, although he warned Joel to expect some "discomfort" as the suit progressed. He and Joel made plans to speak again, and Joel printed his new counsel's name—Brian Roland—and direct-dial number on the cover of the Missoula directory. Then Alice from the temp agency finished the bloodletting, calling to inform Joel he wouldn't need to show up at Wal-Mart since they'd hired a college kid for the third-shift stocking job. Three calls and nothing but bad news, nothing on the horizon except Kool-Aid and tuna fish at lunch. By eleven o'clock he'd fed the chickens, pulled weeds, organized another closet and washed Baker's sheets. Sophie had taken to addressing him as "Mr. French" or "Alfred" or "Hop Sing," often with a trace of irritation in the joke.

Around six, he was resting on his antique bed in the basement when he heard Sophie's station wagon rattle down the driveway and stop at the front of the house. The drive dissolved straight into the worn, trampled beginnings of the yard without any break or proper transition, brought the vehicle so close to their home that the underpinnings and block walls vibrated until Sophie killed the engine. The Taurus kicked and wheezed before quitting, and a few moments later a pair of rusty, cantankerous hinges screeched in unison as the screen door opened. The sounds were always the same, a pattern of noise and movement immediately above Joel's head. He waited for the floor to give at the threshold, listened for the little sway his sister's feet caused in the two-by-eight joists, but the usual step never came. Instead, he heard a shriek and a thud and cursing and another shriek.

He rushed upstairs and found the living room and kitchen cloudy with smoke. Orange flame was rising in spiked, flickering tongues from a black skillet on the stove top and bouncing against the ceiling. Sophie was flailing at the blaze with a throw rug. Joel snatched a blanket off the couch and joined in with her, the two of them swinging and coughing, the smoke stinging their eyes as they got near the stove.

They beat the flame down quickly, but the damage was done. The ceiling was charred, a small pan was flipped on its side on the floor, and the kitchen and living room had an acrid, metallic smell from the smoke that would dig into everything and plague the house for days to come.

Sophie was holding the rug at her side. There was a grimy smudge on her forehead, and she was panting. "Where's Baker?" she asked.

"Baker?"

"Baker. My son. Is he in his room?"

"I thought he was with you," Joel said. "Is he outside?" He was bewildered.

"He's not in the house?"

"No." The frying pan sizzled and popped, then was quiet again.

"Didn't you pick him up from the Grahams'?" she asked.

"No. How would I do that? Or why? I don't have a car."

"Damn, Joel. I left you a note this morning. Kathy was coming by around noon, and you were supposed to take her to work and use her car to pick up Baker. I wondered why the car wasn't here. I mentioned all this a week ago."

"You said I *might* need to drive him somewhere, but there was never anything definite. That's the last I heard about it. And I didn't see a note."

"Are you blind?" she asked, pointing and shaking her finger. "It's right there on the damn refrigerator."

"Oh. Well, I just missed it. I mean, yeah, I guess I see it now that I'm looking for it, but it's stuck up there with a million other things. Plus, I've been staying out of the fridge lately. I feel guilty about the food situation, so I try to keep my visits to a minimum. Why didn't you come downstairs and tell me or leave the note on the table? You know I would've been glad to help."

"Well, Joel, like always, I was rushed and under the gun and you were in bed sleeping, so I'm sorry I only spoke to you once and left an eye-level note in an obvious place. But how did you not see Kathy? What, did you sleep the entire day away?"

"You know I stay busy around here. I was up and dressed by seven-thirty, thank you. I walked to the church after I fed the chickens and straightened the house; she probably came while I was gone."

"Great—you missed her because you were out for an afternoon stroll. And I was at a stupid seminar, no way for her to get anything but voice mail when she called the office. I promised the Grahams that Baker wouldn't stay past four, so now they're probably pissed at me, and I don't guess Baker's going to be ready for his friend's birthday party that begins in fifteen minutes. Damn." She stomped her foot. "Damn."

"I'm sorry, Sophie. Are you—"

"Sorry," she interrupted. "Sorry?" She swung the rug and struck him across the chest.

He jerked back, startled. "Why are you so angry at me? Hitting me with a rug?"

"Why?"

"Yes, why?" he asked.

"Because you've burned up my house, and you're deadweight who hasn't earned a penny in almost a month." She drew back the rug again but didn't follow through, just kept it cocked behind her.

"I'm doing the best I can. I'm sorry about the note and Baker—I'll take the blame for that. And I don't know how a fire started. I was boiling potatoes and had hot dogs in the skillet on low. Check the dials. It's not like I'm an idiot. I was trying to cook dinner for you and Baker."

"Look at this mess."

"Do you want me to go get Baker for you?" he offered. "It's fortunate in one sense—at least he wasn't here when the fire broke out. He could've been hurt."

She dropped the rug. "Shut up, Joel. Just shut up."

"What?"

"I'm sick of you. I'm sick of everything."

"Sick of me? Because of an accident? Because of a fire?"

"Why weren't you watching the stove?"

"I was. Well, I wasn't watching it every second, but what are the chances of boiling potatoes catching fire, or hot dogs on the lowest heat setting?"

"In this case," she snapped, "I'd say about a hundred percent."

"Perhaps it was the stove, the wiring or something."

"I'm sure it wasn't your fault. Not the mighty preacher's error. No way. It was the wiring. Or it happened for a reason, right? Something we can't understand. It happened because you let it happen, Joel." She wiped the back of her hand over her mouth. A tear was squeezing free from the corner of her eye, but there was no letting up in her tone.

"Things *do* happen for reasons we can't understand." Joel raised his voice.

"Bullshit. I'm smarter than that, Joel. Hey—I know where you could find a job. Have you checked the galleries and museums? Have you? You know why they'd hire you? Huh? Do you?"

"No. In fact, I applied at—"

"Because you guys live and breathe the same shitty ruse. Religion and high art pass off all grades of atrocities by convincing us we're cretins and fools. We just aren't smart enough to comprehend things. Well, I'm not buying into that."

"Suit yourself."

"You're so smug sometimes, Joel. So cocksure." The anger had turned to disdain. She wasn't as loud, the words weren't as caustic. "And look where it's gotten you."

"I made a bad choice."

"I'll say. Just like my philandering husband made a bad choice. There's no real difference is there? You crap all over your wife, and now you want to say you're sorry and have everybody forget about it. At least Neal was screwing a girl who was old enough to vote."

"I'd say my circumstances are a little different, Sophie. In fact, if you weren't being such a hard-nosed witch, I might tell you how I'm not that guilty." Joel's voice was sharp, a year's worth of disappointment and spleen breaking its seal. "But let's not dwell on it. I just wish I'd known how you felt before I got here."

"Let me tell you some more about how I feel. I think this Baptist minister thing is a big fat hypocritical scam. I'm surprised you even got a wrist slap for bedding the teenager, Joel. I really am. After all, the way I understand it, we're pretty much here for your convenience and little else. I mean, women can cook casseroles and fry chicken and bust their asses on bake sales, but you good Baptists won't let us stray too far. Only fine *men* like Joel King deserve the Lincoln and the parsonage, the expensive suits. Only fine *men* like yourself are privileged to stand in the pulpit and thunder about evil and injustice. We need to wear white gloves, spread our legs and keep our mouths shut. That pretty much sums it up, doesn't it?"

"No. And for your information, we drove a basic, economy-model van."

"You are worthless in so many ways." She said it calmly and thoughtfully, the fury gone.

He went to the stove and picked up the skillet. The handle was still hot, and it seared his skin when he grabbed it. He raised the skillet as high as he could, then slammed it against the counter, brought it down hard and fast, as if to obliterate the self-pity, the jail sentence, the loss of his wife, the unemployment, the disgrace and the months of indignity. The handle was punishing him, the heat and black cast iron burrowing toward his bones. He lifted the pan again and crashed it into the counter a second time, splintering the Formica and snapping the wood, then collapsed onto his knees and finally let go of the burning metal. There was a red gash running through the center of his palm, a painful streak he felt well into his arm, and he beat the kitchen floor with his fists, wailing and weeping.

Sophie was frightened at first; she gasped and covered her mouth. She'd never seen Joel anything but steady and balanced, always holding everything in check, always poised.

Joel stopped pounding the floor, and he and Sophie were quiet, a few feet apart in the aftermath of a kitchen fire. The counter was destroyed where he had struck it. There were potato pieces on the stove and the ground, and several shriveled, heat-split hot dogs were scattered near the sink. A refrigerator magnet had fallen off the door and landed facedown.

"Joel?"

He didn't answer.

"Are you going to say anything?"

"I'll pay you for the damage," he said, his voice dim and spent.

"Okay." She went to the sink and soaked a dishrag in cold water. "Here. Put this on your hand."

Joel stood up from the floor and looked at her, trying to gauge what she was thinking. He took the wet rag, had to reach out to his sister and pull it from between her thumb and forefinger. "I'll pay you for it, and I'll be gone from here soon." His voice quavered on every word.

She was about to say something when the phone rang, and she seemed grateful for the distraction. "That's probably the Grahams. I'll get it." She bobbled the receiver before it reached her ear, and once she recognized the caller, her face twitched, a small jerk that showed primarily in her lips. "It's your friend, the guy with the Cadillac." She tossed the phone into the seat of a recliner, scooped her purse from the floor and left the blackened kitchen to find her boy and bring him home.

Joel took the phone with his good hand. "Hello?"

"How you doin', Preacher?"

"Edmund?" He sat in the chair.

"The one and only," he said cheerfully.

"What . . . well, I . . . uh . . . I wasn't expecting to hear from you."

"You sound strange. Did I call at a bad time? If you're eatin' or sleepin' or runnin' late, I can call back."

Joel shook the dishrag off his burn and inspected the crevice the hot handle had made. "Oh Lord," he said when he saw the blisters and deep red gouge.

"Pardon?"

Joel couldn't stop looking at the center of his hand. "Edmund?"

"What? What's wrong, Joel? You don't seem to be hittin' on all cylinders."

"Cylinders?" He finally closed his fist around the injury. A long wooden splinter was dangling from the break in the counter, barely hanging on.

"You okay there, partner? Somethin' wrong?" Edmund hesitated. "Oh, wow, I hadn't even—you're not still cross with me about the wreck and so forth, are you?"

Joel was enthralled by the splinter, thinking it might fall at any moment. "Edmund?"

"Yes?"

"Do you recall our trip, driving across the country?"

"Of course I do. I truly enjoyed it."

"You were kind enough to offer me a job." Joel wasn't blinking; his eyes were starched, fixed and dry.

"I did. I remember."

"Is that still a possibility?" His voice had the same tame stupor as his inert eyes. "Something in the meat business?"

"I'm always lookin' for good help. But now, you know, Joel, you said my work wasn't exactly suited for you."

"What do I need to do, Edmund? Just tell me."

"Let's not discuss it on the phone. I don't want to give away any trade secrets. Never know who might be listenin'. I've got competitors, you understand. How about we meet and talk things over?"

"Tell me where, Edmund."

"Would Sa'ad's be okay? Has he been in touch with you and takin' care of your legal problems like I told him to?"

"I've talked to him," Joel answered.

"Then we'll meet at his office and go over the whole ball of wax."

"I can't get there. I don't have a car or any money for a ticket. Not even a bus ticket. So tell me what you want me to do."

"Hey, listen, here's what—"

"You tell me, and I'll do it." Joel talked right over him in the same weak monotone.

"Here's what we'll do. I'll overnight you some information. I might not be able to have it there tomorrow, but it'll be there the next day for sure. You left your address with Sa'ad, didn't you?"

"He has it."

"Good."

"Thank you, Edmund."

"Least I can do for a friend. That's why I called, to check in and see how you were. You sound terrible. Things a little tough so far?"

"You could say that."

"So what've you been up to?" Edmund inquired.

"Sorry, but I'm real busy right now. Can't talk. I'll see you soon, I guess."

"Sure. I didn't mean to catch you at a bad time. At least maybe I can hook you up with a job."

"Just let me know." Joel pushed the talk button and disconnected Edmund. He crouched and dropped onto his knees, then his hands. He crawled toward the stove, moving in a slow, addled drag like an old dog. The potato pieces were still on the floor, cold and raw and filthy. He and his sister had stepped on several chunks and mashed them into flat, mushy patches. Joel stretched his neck and started to eat the food on the ground. He had to lick and bite the crushed lumps to get them off the linoleum, but he never used anything other than his teeth and tongue, lapped up the white splotches and swallowed them with whatever else came along.

five _____

The next morning, Joel stayed in the basement until he was positive his sister and Baker were gone. He'd slept miserably, his hand ached and a summer cold seemed to be seeping into his throat and chest. Shortly after Sophie drove away, he heard a clunking, mechanical sound above him when the dishwasher changed cycles and began to drain, and in no time at all the discharge was flooding a noisy pipe beside his head. Even though he'd been residing in the cellar almost a month, he'd still not gotten used to the swooshes and vibrations, the sounds of sinks and toilets and the old avocado green dishwasher pouring out through his dank quarters.

He sat on the edge of his bed and watched ten minutes' worth of digital red numbers rise and fall, then went outside in his boxer shorts and T-shirt and flopped into a lawn chair. It wasn't quite warm yet, and the air retained enough of the night's chill to raise goose bumps. A huge black bug had landed in the wading pool and was buzzing frantically on the surface, struggling to pull free. Joel could hear its wings humming as it corkscrewed along the top of the water and bounced against the pool's sides, getting nowhere.

Tut, Baker's bantam rooster, was in the yard pecking and scratching and clucking. The bird paraded about on thin, scaly yellow legs and was topped off by a floppy red comb. The banty seemed suspicious of Joel, occasionally staring up and freezing a lone, skewed eye on him. A tan hen followed behind the rooster, attacking the ground with her beak and the sharp points of her feet. Joel looked away and gazed at the mountains, massive greenish brown climbs that remained burly and broad until the earth finally deferred to the sky. The heat soon drove Tut and his hen into the shade, and the bug quit its battle, just floated helplessly with its feet anchored in the water, waiting to become saturated and sink to the bottom. For hours, Joel sat there undressed, peering at the horizon, contemplating the doomed insect, trading glances with the chickens, wasting time.

He managed to skulk back to his underground room before Sophie returned home, and he lay in the dark listening to the evening unfold above him, heard Baker's backpack slap the floor, footsteps next to the supper table and snatches of sitcom voices when the TV turned on.

Around nine, Sophie opened the basement door and called down to him. "Are you still alive?"

"Yes."

"Do you think you could find time in your busy schedule to clean up the kitchen tomorrow?"

"Yes, I will. I realize I should've done it today."

"Thank you," she said, a trace of compassion leavening her tone.

"I'll tend to it first thing. I'm sorry."

"Good night."

He coughed, tried to loosen the weight in his lungs. Despite the sickness and his day at loose ends, he was beginning to recover, to quell the tremors and black shame that had afflicted him as he'd emptied his spleen in front of the stove. There was still a feeling of embarrassment, and he dreaded the painful discussion he'd need to have with his sister, but at least he'd driven out a bellyful of demons and could claim a fresh start.

Three days later, he was once again in Sa'ad's office, surrounded by stuffed beasts and big mounted birds with their wings outstretched, ready to clamp their talons around a field mouse or newborn rabbit. Edmund's FedEx package had contained a driver's license, a voter identification card and an e-ticket confirmation in the name of Henry Louis Williams, along with two hundred dollars in twenties and the street address for Sa'ad X. Sa'ad's law practice. Joel had left Missoula on a 6:00 a.m. flight, changed planes in Salt Lake City and been delivered to Sa'ad's office by a bossy, snaggle-toothed cabdriver.

When Joel walked into the reception area at Sa'ad's, he saw only one other client, a seedy man in a leg cast reading a back issue of *Popular Mechanics*. Well before he got near the lady at the front desk, the hallway door cracked and Edmund beckoned him inside. He strode past the receptionist, and she made it a point not to acknowledge him—she never turned away from her computer screen—although she had to realize he was in the room.

Edmund was dressed in casual pants and suede shoes, and he gave Joel's hand a vigorous pump before jerking him into a two-armed embrace. "Great to see you, Joel. The ID and travel arrangements go okay? Airports are awfully strict after those jihad bastards hit us. I ain't complainin', mind you—they can frisk and x-ray to their heart's content if it'll help."

"Yeah. No complications. Thank you." Joel noticed how healthy his friend looked—his skin was snug around his chin and eyes, his teeth were flawless and his hair was thick and shiny and perfectly barbered in half circles above his ears. Joel was dressed in his Kmart khakis, a pack of airplane nuts poking out of his shirt pocket.

"Excellent. Sorry for all the cloak-and-dagger shenanigans, but if we're goin' into business together, we need to be very, very cautious."

"I understand." Joel was almost back to normal, composed and grounded, the kitchen fire several paces behind him, the floor at his sister's cleaned and scrubbed, the counter patched together with a jackleg board and four mismatched nails. Before flying to Vegas, he'd left a letter for Sophie, a long, sincere apology that covered the front and rear of a piece of notebook paper. He'd take care of the rest when he returned, and soon, he hoped, he'd have a dollar or two in his wallet.

Joel entered Sa'ad's office ahead of Edmund, through a door that was already open. Sa'ad was standing in the raised center of the room, talking on the phone. He was imposing and striking, positioned so the snarling mouth of a bobcat appeared over his shoulder. A large man anyway, he was elevated three feet above everything around him by the buildup for his desk. He picked at some papers in a file, said a few words into the receiver and finished his call with a laugh and a promise to do the best he could, whatever that implied. "Reverend King," he said, spreading his arms wide in welcome. "Good to have you with us."

"Nice to see you again, Mr. Sa'ad. Thanks for agreeing to meet on such short notice."

"My pleasure." He dropped his arms and sat behind his desk. "I trust your trip was pleasant."

"It was fine," Joel said.

He and Edmund took the seats beneath the platform, had to scoot their chairs backward to get all of Sa'ad in the frame.

"So where should we begin?" Sa'ad asked.

"I don't care. You decide."

"Would you prefer to have Edmund leave the room? Your suit with Christy and your domestic matters are protected and confidential."

"I'd be happy to excuse myself, Joel," Edmund volunteered. "I understand if you want some privacy."

"There's no reason to," Joel answered. "You're welcome to listen. You know everything there is to know, so I don't see what difference it makes."

"All right, then," Sa'ad said. "Now, your divorce. As I mentioned on the phone, your wife is requesting alimony. If we continue to ignore the court proceedings in Virginia, she'll probably get it. Also, as you know, she's seeking a divorce based on a claim of adultery. I'm highlighting that only because you're a minister—a misconduct finding could obviously handicap you if you attempt to rebuild your career."

"I've really been burning up the job market so far," Joel said. "I can't imagine it having any impact. And I don't think I'll be returning to the ministry."

Sa'ad took off his glasses and held them by the earpiece. "So you're not working?"

"I can't get hired, and I've applied everywhere. As soon as they hear about my record, I'm booted to the curb."

"You've visited the unemployment office?" Sa'ad inquired. "Completed an application?"

"Sure, I go virtually every day. But these two little misdemeanors blow me right out of the water."

Edmund touched Joel on the knee. "Could I make a suggestion?"

"I'm open to almost anything."

Edmund took out his silver lighter. "Don't tell them."

"Don't tell them what?" Joel asked.

"Don't tell them about the convictions," Sa'ad chimed in. "Don't mention it."

"Exactly," Edmund said.

"But they always ask, everywhere I go. And the form at the unemployment office specifically has a section on criminal history."

"Leave it blank," Sa'ad said.

"You mean lie about my situation?"

"If that's how you want to look at it." Edmund had a cigarette in his hand, preparing to light it. "But what's the difference? Who gets hurt? You'll be an excellent employee, give your boss his money's worth and keep your nose clean, right? So who cares about the past?" He put the cigarette in his mouth.

"Don't you dare light that in here, Edmund," Sa'ad commanded from several feet above them.

"Why? It's not goin' to hurt a thing, Sa'ad. When'd you get so damn prissy about your office?"

"Put it up, Edmund. You can wait until you're outside."

Edmund slipped the lighter and cigarette into his pocket. "For heaven's sake," he grumbled.

"Thank you, Edmund."

"Don't mention it," he said sarcastically.

"Excuse me, guys," Joel interrupted. "You're both suggesting I mislead people about my background?"

"Only if you want a job," Edmund answered. "Otherwise, just keep doin' what you're doin' and starve to death."

"I hate not telling the truth. It's wrong. And what if someone hires me and then discovers my problems?"

Sa'ad still had the glasses in his hand. "First, no one's *going* to find out. Do you really think a restaurant owner can investigate every single waiter and busboy he hires? Second, if you're discovered, what's the worst that can happen? You get fired, and you start at square one again—who cares?"

"You'll need to tone down your resume, too," Edmund added. "Maybe say you've only got a year or so of college. It's a big red flag when a man with two degrees comes lookin' to mop floors for six bucks an hour."

"I think I'll stick to the truth," Joel said, "and see what happens."

"Your choice," Sa'ad replied. "I certainly admire your honesty."

"So what about this divorce nonsense?" Edmund blurted.

"Well, Reverend King will be subject to a monthly alimony payment if he doesn't contest this request by his wife."

"How can they make me pay when I don't have any income?" Joel asked.

"The court will impute income to you based on your last job," Sa'ad explained. "If you were dismissed and it's your fault, the court will use your most recent salary as earnings even if you're unemployed."

"And that's fair?" Joel groused.

"Actually it is, if you think about it. Keeps people from quitting work or getting terminated on purpose." Sa'ad paused, twirled his glasses in a slow loop. "So how do you want me to handle this?"

"You're the expert."

"I'll pick up the tab, Sa'ad," Edmund vowed. "You just look after Joel."

"Well, as I mentioned before, I'm not completely familiar with Virginia divorce law. I might have to associate someone there."

"I thought you already had," Joel said. "Because of your not being eligible to practice in other states."

"Correct. I've still been able to do most of the preliminaries, though. I might have to relinquish the case entirely—that's what I'm saying. I misspoke to some extent."

"So tell me again why I'm payin' you?" Edmund wanted to know. "Capes-and-hats. What a great gig you guys got goin'."

"You're welcome to manage the case yourself, Edmund." Sa'ad's voice was calm and firm.

"Maybe I will," Edmund said.

"Be that as it may," Sa'ad continued, "I'll try to negotiate a compromise with her attorney. If we can't agree, we end up in court, so I'll do my best to find something we can all live with."

"Okay. Thanks. I don't mind paying—it's simply that I'm broke. It's my fault the marriage ended and my fault Martha's having money problems, so I'd like to help. I still need to find work, though. You can tell her lawyer I'm willing to send a check as soon as I'm able."

"I'll probably hold off on that for the time being, Joel. I'm reluctant to start negotiations with my hat in hand." Sa'ad smiled. "I have good news on the Christy front, however. The church has four million in liability coverage, and we've talked to Brian Roland, the lawyer who'll be representing the insurance company. Parenthetically, Joel, when I say 'we,' I'm referring to my staff or my associates. I've never personally spoken with Mr. Roland, nor do I plan to. The name Sa'ad X. Sa'ad would mean nothing to him. He's on top of things, seems first-rate. I feel you're in good shape there. Now, since the suit's for five million, theoretically you and your church have a million dollars' worth of exposure not covered by insurance. I will continue to monitor things and do all I can to make sure the case settles within the policy limits."

"What does that mean, 'within the policy limits'?" Joel asked.

"I mean we want to make sure you're not *personally* responsible for anything. The suit's for five million, there's four in coverage. We don't care if they wind up with three or four million bucks, but everything over four comes from your pocket. Obviously, we want the case to settle at four or under." Sa'ad finally rested his glasses. "Of course, it could go to trial, but I don't see that as too likely."

"I understand," Joel said.

"The other news is that I've scheduled it so you can meet Mr. Roland in Roanoke. He wants to spend some time with you, then the other side will depose you. You know what that entails, don't you?"

"I think so." Joel glanced at Edmund, who'd rediscovered his lighter and was polishing it on his pant leg.

"It's simply questions put to you under oath prior to court. Don't get me wrong—it's an important part of the trial process. You don't want to fu . . . uh . . . foul it up, but it's done in a lawyer's office without a judge, a little more informal. You'll be asked all kinds of questions about the case, and you have to answer. As I said, you'll need to be careful, because your statements can be used at the trial itself and presented to the judge or jury."

"How careful do I need to be, Mr. Sa'ad," Joel scoffed, "given that I've already pled guilty?"

"That does take some of the pressure off, doesn't it?" Sa'ad grinned and tugged the knot in his tie. "Tactically speaking, I think it's wise to admit your wrongdoing without a lot of fuss. If you hedge and fib, it'll only make things worse." The last words were strangely hurried, almost melded together. "So I take it you're planning to concede the point?"

"Yeah. What's the alternative?"

"There really isn't one," Sa'ad answered. "You're being very smart about all this."

"So how's this good news?" Joel asked.

"Ah. Well, we've timed the trip to fit with Edmund's project. He tells me you've decided to come aboard, correct?"

"Yeah, I guess so." Joel had now made the decision with a clear, dispassionate mind, had actually committed when it counted. He'd turned the consideration away when it wormed into his thoughts in the days following his kitchen breakdown, had avoided revisiting the fugue-state plea he'd made to Edmund over the phone, figuring that each deliberation and acknowledgment was most likely a separate, distinct sin. And what choice did he have, even if the plan steered him down a crooked path? When he confirmed his intentions with Sa'ad, there was a fleeting burn in his middle, and he licked his lips, but the words didn't seem too bitter or serpentine as they crossed his tongue. He checked to see Edmund's reaction and discovered that his friend was still fiddling with the lighter, rubbing it against the fabric on his thigh.

"We need to get you to Virginia. The deposition will allow us to do so without any hint of irregularity. We need you in Roanoke to retrieve your belongings. Edmund mentioned that you have a bank box. Is that correct?"

"Yeah, I do."

"It would make sense, you see, for you to collect the last of your property. So we have a perfect cover, and the insurance company will be providing the travel cost."

"In other words," Edmund added, "they'll be payin' the lion's share of our project, and our project will ultimately take money from them or their evil kin in the same business." He flashed a toothy smile that was a combination of satisfaction and disdain. "I told you our buddy Sa'ad was slick, huh? Notice how there're no mirrors in here? No crosses or garlic?" The smile became puckish. "Capes-and-hats—what a racket."

Sa'ad altogether ignored him. "It would make sense, Joel, for you to start trying to sell some of your personal property, given your job dilemma. In the end, this bit of bad employment luck looks to be good for our endeavor. You go to Roanoke and leave a paper trail at the bank, show some jewelry around, maybe mention to Mr. Roland how money's tight and you're hoping to unload some of your mother's rings and necklaces. We might even have you pawn a piece or two. The bottom line is that it would be natural for you to withdraw jewelry from your safe-deposit box and take it with you to where you currently live."

"What about my wife?" Joel asked. "She knows I don't have any jewelry, and she knows what's in the box."

Sa'ad sat straighter in his chair. "If we're fortunate, she won't become involved, but we have to assume that she will. If she does, we simply hard-bluff her and insist the items were folded up in something or that she overlooked them. All she can say is that she never saw the stuff, not that it doesn't exist. Moreover, we let her know it's better for her if you have money, especially if she wants any kind of consideration from the divorce."

"She's very disappointed in me," Joel warned. "I wouldn't expect much help."

"Did your mother ever give either of you anything in the jewelry line, any family heirlooms?" Sa'ad inquired.

"Huh. Well, she gave Martha an old opal ring several years ago—it's stored at the bank. And there's also a bracelet in the box. It's old and ugly and the clasp is broken, but I understand the stones are not too bad. We were going to have it repaired."

"Excellent," Edmund said. "We can work that to our advantage."

Joel was becoming entangled in the planning. "And, you know, I have the only key, and Martha hasn't been in the box in over two years, so who knows what could've been deposited there, right?"

"There you go," Sa'ad said. "Who could say?"

"And a man with marital—well, you know, we'd *say* there was a marital problem—he ain't going to tell his wife all his money business, now is he?" This was Edmund's contribution. "We've got this nailed." He focused on Joel. "But you need to mention any potential traps that come to mind.

We've all got to operate together, like a team. Let us know your thoughts. You shouldn't be afraid to put the project to the test."

"Don't worry," Joel said. "I'll probably hound you till you're sick of me."

"No you won't," Edmund said jovially. "I understand how you must be feelin'."

"Will I actually have the genuine goods?" Joel asked.

"Most likely, yes. Make it a point to be careful with them. There's no room for error." Sa'ad's tone changed, acquired a streak of bass and turned purposefully somber. He brought his hands together and rested his elbows on the desk, then lowered his head until his face was obscured by a dark brown tangle of thumbs and fingers and bony knuckles. "If something goes awry, Reverend King, we're all on the griddle, and I can promise you there's not a lot of honor among thieves. We would do what we could, but . . ." Sa'ad broke open his hands and tossed them into a brief explosion, like a magician at the finale of a trick. "But I would imagine—sad as it may be—that you'd get the short end of the stick and catch most of the blame. No offense, of course." His nails, Joel noticed, were buffed and polished, clear offsets bordering against umber flesh.

"But nothin' like that's going to happen, Joel," Edmund assured him. "Never has, never will."

Joel didn't know what to say. "Right," he finally croaked. Some team.

"There are a number of critical guidelines, Joel, so listen to what I'm telling you." Sa'ad's voice turned pleasant again, and the stern angles rotated out of his face, replaced by an earnest helpfulness. "This is very important."

"Yeah, okay," Joel said, still unnerved by Sa'ad's dour warning.

"First—never talk about any aspect of this project over the phone. Never. Is that clear?"

"Yes. That seems obvious."

"I'm glad it does. If you need to speak with Edmund or me, call here, speak to the receptionist and use the code phrase 'this divorce is driving me crazy.' We will make arrangements to get you quickly in my office or meet you wherever you are. This office is a safe harbor. Attorney-client privilege affords us many protections from intercepts, wiretaps and so forth. Understood?"

"Understood," Joel repeated.

"Item next—if this project becomes compromised, if investigators, lawyers or police officers become involved, keep your fucking mouth shut. The only words you need to know are 'I'll have to speak with my lawyer.' No matter what they say or do or promise, keep your fucking mouth shut."

"I will," Joel said.

"Repeat the rule, please," Sa'ad said in his best professional voice. His expression was holding on solicitous.

"Keep my mouth shut, no matter what." The last of his cold flared in Joel's throat, and he ducked his head and coughed into a fist.

"That's not the rule. The rule is 'Keep your fucking mouth shut.' " Sa'ad uttered the sentence, profanity and all, without a trace of anger or menace.

"I got it," Joel assured him.

"What's the rule?" Sa'ad demanded.

"I don't use foul language, Mr. Sa'ad. But I fully grasp your message."

"Cut it out, Sa'ad," Edmund said. "Quit actin' the asshole. Here's your rule: Keep your fuckin' mouth shut. Keep your fuckin' mouth shut. There, I said it once for me and once for him. That ought to take care of things."

"Let's hope so," Sa'ad replied. "The police can be very deceptive, Mr. King. They might tell you Edmund has confessed, or that they have a strong case against you. They might offer to assist you, or they may threaten you. It doesn't matter how they come at it or what they suggest. 'I want to talk to my lawyer' is the mantra, and it's always the correct answer. Ninety percent of the people behind bars got there because of their own big mouths."

"I understand," Joel said. "I do."

"Joel's a bright man," Edmund offered. "He's gonna do great."

"How much . . . how much will the, uh, the project be worth?" Joel asked.

"Our partner Abel Crane has a skilled eye for jewelry—remember Abel Crane? I mentioned him to you when we were drivin' out here." Edmund returned his lighter to his pocket. "He estimates the profit to be between three and three fifty. More than I first told you."

"Three hundred thousand?" Joel asked.

"Yep."

Joel studied Edmund for a moment, then looked up at Sa'ad. "And my payment? What would that be?"

Sa'ad started to speak, but Edmund interrupted him. "We all take an equal share. Me, you, Blacula there, and Abel. Everybody gets a fourth. We take expenses off the top and divide the kitty equally."

"Sounds fair to me," Joel said. "More than fair. When do we get started?"

"By the way," Sa'ad leaned forward and summoned a nakedly challenging cast into his eyes, "you realize you don't go from the welfare line to the Jaguar dealership. You have to hide your money, camouflage things, create stories and explanations."

"I'd already thought of that. Give me a little credit, Sa'ad." This was the first time Joel had dropped the "Mr." when addressing his lawyer.

"We'll let you know," Edmund said. "We'll have to have the first phase completed before you leave for Roanoke. I'll take care of the details. You just head back to Montana and keep lookin' for work."

"Okay," Joel said.

Sa'ad stood and clasped his hands together in front of his chest. His necktie was mostly wine-colored and filled with minuscule white dots. "So we're all on the same page, yes? We have an understanding?"

"Sa'ad thinks he's Donald Trump or somethin'," Edmund said to Joel. "He likes to end his business dramatically."

"I'm ready," Joel said. "Thank you both for helping me." He and Edmund were also standing.

"You're welcome. Thank *you*. I'll get things cranked up right away." Edmund sounded enthusiastic.

"Then all we have left to do is celebrate the deal." Sa'ad gave Joel a big wink. "It's time to light the Bunsen burners and get the party brew boiling." He descended from his platform and put his arm around Edmund. "Dinner at Picasso's?"

Edmund frowned but didn't pull away from Sa'ad's grip. "First you get all fussy about your office, now we're goin' to a restaurant that doesn't respect dark booths and red meat? No, we go to Rosewood Grille like always, order the surf-and-turf and grab the big banquette in the corner."

Sa'ad laughed. "Fine with me, Edmund." He turned his attention to Joel. "Rosewood Grille suit you?"

"I've never been to any of the restaurants here." Joel hesitated, lowered his gaze. "You both know, I suppose, that I can't—"

"This one's billed to the business, Joel," Edmund said. "You don't need to worry about payin' for nothing."

"You don't mind? You're sure?"

"Hell yes, I'm sure." Edmund laid his arm across Joel's shoulder so the three men were connected to each other, linked like a chain of paper dolls. "Then we'll gamble on the Strip, visit the Crazy Horse at three in the mornin', eat the two-dollar breakfast at Barbary Coast and go to bed when the sun rises."

"I'll have to skip the gambling, and I'm assuming the Crazy Horse isn't a place I need to be either," Joel said. "But I'd be grateful for dinner."

"Nothin' wrong with a little blackjack, Joel," Edmund said. "No harm in that."

"Thanks just the same, but I'll let you two go on without me when dinner's over."

"I'll drive," Sa'ad said. "That way I'll be in charge of the music."

"The music?" Joel asked.

"Yeah. I can't imagine how you lasted more than a day on the road with Edmund."

"I'm not sure I follow you," Joel said.

"Did you notice anything strange about what you listened to? Discover any themes?"

"He had pretty fair taste as far as I can remember," Joel answered.

"Edmund only listens to music if the singer is alive," Sa'ad explained, his arm continuing to hang off Joel's shoulder.

"Come on." Joel laughed. "Are you guys kidding me?"

"He's tellin' the truth," Edmund said.

"Why?" Joel asked.

"I think it's eerie and creepy to listen to dead people's voices." Edmund let loose with a shudder that seemed visceral and genuine. "It's like from beyond the grave or somethin'. Weird, haunted, freaky—call it what you will, but it flat-out gets to me."

"So you don't listen to, say, Elvis Presley?" Joel asked.

"Absolutely not. Gives me the willies."

"Or Nat King Cole or Janis Joplin?"

"They're dead, aren't they?" Edmund replied.

Sa'ad was enjoying the exchange. "I'll bring my CDs, Joel. See the problem?"

"Mozart? Brahms?" Joel kept after Edmund. "I'm not a big music buff, but this seems a little strange."

"Mozart would be okay—most classical stuff, it's just music, no voices or singin'. It's hearin' from dead people that makes my skin crawl."

Joel was smiling. "Okay, how about groups or duos with a dead member?"

"Not on my playlist. It's a very basic rule."

Joel stuck his hands into his pockets. "My goodness—that takes a big bite out of your choices."

Sa'ad leaned around Edmund and spoke to Joel. "It's sort of like being afraid of the dark, isn't it? Or the tribes who think photographers can steal their souls." Sa'ad mussed Edmund's hair. "You should have seen him when George Jones had that wreck several years ago and was in the hospital. My man Edmund was cramming in all he could before George checked out, just gorging himself day and night, listening to hour after hour of that horrible hillbilly yammering. Then he heard one of the Eagles had cancer and loaded up on *Hotel California* for a month."

"Hey, everybody has their own peculiarities, Sa'ad." Edmund tried to sound indifferent, but Sa'ad had unsettled him and it told in his voice. He let Sa'ad out of his grasp. "You want to take your car, it's okay with me." He brushed his shirt, flicked his chest three times even though there was nothing visible on the fabric, no lint or dirt. "Everybody's got somethin' that worries 'em, depends on the person," he said, sounding embarrassed.

"How about you, Joel? What gives a minister the heebie-jeebies?" Sa'ad asked.

"Oh, I don't know. I can't abide dogs dressed in human clothes—poodles in vests and Great Danes wearing tam-o'-shanters. And I hate cigarette holders, except of course if you're Burgess Meredith or Marlene Dietrich." Joel grinned impishly. "Hope you won't think less of me."

When Sa'ad had finished taunting Edmund and the men were passing through the exposed teeth and fierce faces of the mounted animals, Joel noticed a new addition to the office. Sa'ad had placed a rack of bubble-gum machines—six of them, on a chrome frame—next to the door. The machines had red metal tops and glass fronts, appeared to be the kind that popped up at grocery store exits near the carts and real estate magazines. One offered Chiclets for a quarter, and the colorful gum squares were packed in a clear globe from top to bottom, creating a patchwork ball of yellow, crimson, white, green and black. The rest of the machines dispensed toys and novelty items: dice, key rings, puzzles, miniature playing cards, and rubber monsters that fit on the eraser ends of pencils.

"Those weren't here last time, were they?" Joel asked, pointing at the machines.

"No. A recent acquisition. A nice touch, don't you think?"

"I didn't realize you could hunt them," Joel said, keeping a poker face. "Must not be much sport—they seem top-heavy and couldn't possibly move too fast on those stubby metal legs."

Edmund laughed out loud and joined in, happy to be on the offensive. "What, Sa'ad, you hide a pistol under the loaf bread and slay 'em at the A&P?"

Sa'ad smiled, didn't seem ruffled. "They were a gift from a client, a gentleman who runs an amusement company. I actually asked for them. Fortunately, I didn't have to track them or shoot them."

"Seems out of context," Joel said. "I mean, with all the animals and guns and everything."

"It's just Sa'ad's way of tryin' to steal your last little bit of loose change before you escape from his lair," Edmund remarked. "Makes perfect sense to me."

Sa'ad chuckled. "Close, Edmund, close. The machines are my metaphor for the justice system. That's why I wanted them, as a vivid reminder to people as they leave my office. You see, gentlemen, exactly like the world of jurisprudence: if you have enough money to put in, sooner or later you'll receive what you're after." He gave them both a lively look. "You simply need the cash to turn the handle as many times as might be necessary."

"I see," Joel said. "How reassuring."

"I believe they make the point nicely," Sa'ad said.

Edmund had zeroed in on the six machines, was inspecting them with his head cocked and his lips nearly invisible from concentration.

"What do you think, Edmund?" Sa'ad asked.

"I think . . ." Edmund put a hand in his pocket, and Joel heard the sound of coins rubbing against one another. His hand churned and dug before reappearing. "I think, my old friend, that the legal system ain't always what it's cracked up to be." Edmund opened his hand. There was no money to be seen, only a flat pocket knife, probably two inches long. He walked to the machines and began working a blade in the lock slot on top of the closest one. The blade he'd chosen didn't do the trick, and he folded out a shorter, thinner tool. He jimmied and pushed and wiggled his wrists until he finally got into the raised silver lock just right and was able to turn the knife in a cautious clockwise circle. Edmund removed the lid and took out a handful of Chiclets, then tipped back his head and dropped several in his mouth. "Want some of Sa'ad's gum, Joel?"

Joel grinned. "No thanks. But I certainly admire your resourcefulness."

It occurred to Joel when he and Edmund arrived outside that he didn't have a place to stay. He had most of the two hundred dollars remaining but had no idea how much a decent hotel would cost. Before he could question Edmund about the subject, his new business partner volunteered that he'd reserved a room at the Golden Nugget under the Henry Louis Williams alias. He handed Joel a thousand dollars in hundreds and instructed him to pay in cash.

"It certainly won't be this expensive," Joel protested. "And I've got most of the two hundred left. I paid for a taxi in Missoula and one here, and that's it."

"Room will run you eighty-five and tax durin' the week. The rooms are great, too. Remember last time how classy the place was? Don't let the price fool you." He and Joel were standing in the parking lot under a crackling desert sun, waiting for Sa'ad to pick them up. "The rest is for you, some walkin' around money. WAM, we like to call it."

"I can't accept this, Edmund. I appreciate it, but—"

"It's an advance against your share, nothin' more, nothin' less. I don't want to see you livin' like a street person, Joel."

"You'll deduct it from my share at the end?"

"I will. You don't have to worry about that. As much as I respect our friendship, business is business." Edmund was holding a chunk of bills squeezed together in a gold clip. There looked to be several thousand dollars in paper money. "Sa'ad and me will drop you off downtown so you can spruce up and take care of check-in, then you catch a cab to the restaurant. I always treat Sa'ad to a drink at Caesar's Palace—our little tradition—and we'll meet you for dinner. Oh—tip the doorman two dollars and the cabbie three."

"Okay." Joel reached for his wallet, and when he was loading the cash inside, a Subway card fell out and fluttered onto the asphalt. The card had three stamps stuck to it, needed five more to earn a free sandwich. "Edmund, I'm only going to do this once. It's probably wrong on some level, and I assume I'm going to have to lie and who knows what else. I don't think you realize what it took to push me to this point, or how low I've fallen. One time, and no more. It seems to be my only choice, and I pray the Lord doesn't punish me too harshly for it." He recovered the card and crammed it between the hundreds and twenties, his wallet so bloated that it was difficult to fold in half.

Christy Darden's lawyer was standing behind her with his hands on her shoulders. She was sitting in a handsome leather chair, and she could hear his voice and smell his aftershave but couldn't see his face. He'd been speaking since she sat down, and Christy was only now tuning in.

"Leaving the University of Virginia, attending rehab, the accidental overdose—these events will bolster our lawsuit, make your position stronger."

Her mother and father were on her right, and another lawyer, an "associate" wearing a dull, baggy suit, was standing in the corner to her left, taking notes and pushing up his glasses each time he raised his head from his scribbling.

"There's no need to hide these matters, and no need to be ashamed. It's the same as a broken leg or a fractured ankle—these are part of the injuries caused by Reverend King and the church. You should, and will, be compensated for them."

When Big Bill Darden discovered Joel's misconduct, he'd hired his baby girl an attorney from Richmond—not Roanoke—and carried on about how Henry Clay Hanes was the "top dog" at Hunton and Williams, Virginia's biggest and grandest law firm. To Christy, Hanes seemed brilliant and mean as a striped snake, and he made her nervous, almost nauseated, every time she met with him to sign papers or talk about the case.

Hanes came around her chair and settled on the edge of his desk, not quite standing and not quite at rest. At least she could see him. "I want to make sure on some of the particulars, mostly having to do with the chronology, okay?"

"I guess." Christy sunk farther into her seat. "But haven't we been over this already? Like a zillion times?"

"This will make a zillion and one." He swatted her away, didn't seem at all put off by her petulance. "This is a multimillion-dollar lawsuit. We will be prepared, and we will leave not one breath to chance." Hanes wasn't looking at her when he spoke. He brought his gaze down and focused on her. "Would you like some privacy? I know this is difficult and emotional. It must be hard for you. I respect that. I have a psychologist who specializes in rape trauma on call if you feel the need. She can be here in ten minutes. I'm also bringing in a female associate to assist Oliver and myself with the case." He acknowledged the other lawyer in the room, and the awkward young man shuffled his feet and adjusted his glasses with his index finger. "Please let me know what I can do to make this tolerable. And again, let me point out that you have every right to talk to me without your parents present."

Christy was watching Oliver. She waited until he finally ceased writing and glanced up from his pad before she answered. "What you're saying, Mr. Hanes, in a kinda nice way, is don't fuck with me. Right?"

Christy heard her mother gasp, and her father's neck filled with blood. Henry Clay Hanes registered a hint of amusement and little else. He righted himself, took a step toward Christy and crouched in front of her. He was balanced on the tips of his feet, his face about even with hers, poised there with his knees akimbo like a mammoth toad, ready to leap. "That, Christy, is exactly what I'm saying. I appreciate your perceptive nature."

"But he's already confessed, right? How hard can this be?" Christy didn't want to slog through the story again, and doubted she could get all the details correct.

"I've spoken with Mr. Roland, his attorney. He's a most able lawyer. We have your deposition scheduled in a few weeks. I will depose Mr. King on the same day. My best assumption is that after you're questioned by Mr. Roland, and after he has reviewed the physical evidence, he'll make us an offer. He'll offer something unacceptable, I'll counter, and we'll wind up in the middle. I'm guessing this case will land between one and two million, depending on how you're perceived. If you come off as a sullen, spoiled party girl, we have a problem. If, on the other hand, you come off as a typical teenager who's suffering because of her minister's misdeeds, we have a lot more to gain. That's why the deposition is so important. I'm certain the church wants a quick settlement rather than months and months of bad publicity and a nasty trial, but their insurer holds the purse strings, and if the fine folks at Liberty Underwriters sense you might appear unappealing to a jury, we'll go to court. The insurance company won't give a damn about the church's problems if they can save several thousand bucks." Hanes rose from his squat. "You get what I'm saying?" His tone was completely neutral, constrained. "You'll need to put on your good dress and best manners for me at least once."

"The better I act, the more money you get."

"The more money we *both* get," Hanes replied. "So, would you like me to call the rape counselor?"

Christy didn't answer. She inspected the irregular edge she'd gnawed in her thumbnail, ignored her lawyer.

"Christy?" Hanes's voice remained steady and sterile.

"Christina, sit up straight and answer the man," her mother snapped. "And quit acting like a brat."

"Why would I need a rape counselor?" She drew her thumb closer to her face.

"I thought it might make you more comfortable," Hanes said, "but it's completely your decision. I'll have my associate Mrs. Patterson prepare you, if you'd like. She can handle the actual questioning. You tell me."

"It wasn't rape. I had sex. In fact, I liked it. I wanted to sleep with Joel."

"Great," her mother said. "Just great."

"So what'll it be?" Hanes asked.

"Can we do this some other time?"

"No. We may do it *again* on another day, but we're going to prep you now."

"I like you, Mr. Hanes. You don't take any shit, do you?" Christy dropped her thumb and changed her position in the chair, slid closer to the rounded seam at the cushion's lip. Her outright fear of Hanes had disappeared, although she still had the impression he wasn't someone to be trifled with.

"It would seem I just did, no?"

"How much could we get, like today? Without me having to give this deposition?"

"Why do you ask?" Hanes had returned to the front of his desk.

"Because I don't want to do it."

"I'm sure you don't, and I'm also confident they're not going to hand me a check without having a gander at you and hearing what you have to say."

"They won't give us anything? Right now, today? Nada? He admitted he did it, and you've got the tests from the hospital—what else is there? How good a lawyer do you have to be to win this one?"

Hanes sealed shut his eyes, pointed his face at the ceiling and emitted a laugh that was a few notches short of a howl. "Worried about your lawyer, are you?" he said when he finished baying at the roof. "I guess we'll soon find out how good I am." He put his hands flat against his belly and made the noise again. "See, we don't doubt the preacher's liable. What we don't know is how much it'll cost him. To know that, we have to know you. I could run over you with my car, but if you stand up without a scratch and in good spirits, then you have no damages and no case. Understand?"

"What if I just made this up? What if I told you that?" Christy looked at the paint on her toenails. Her mother had badgered her to wear proper shoes, but it was August and way too sweltering for anything other than sandals and a ponytail.

"I'd say you were understandably anxious about having to go through a difficult process and doing all you can to avoid reliving a horrible segment of your life."

"Maybe I'm just making all this up. Maybe I'll contradict everything."

"I'm guessing Reverend King didn't admit his crime and end his career because he's innocent." Hanes looked at Oliver. "When's the deposition set?"

"Two weeks from today, at one o'clock. In Roanoke at Mr. Roland's office." The young lawyer didn't hesitate, seemed to have the time and date committed to memory.

"Good. We'll have plenty of time to work with Christina. By the way, how are you spending your summer?"

"I'm serious, Mr. Hanes, what if Joel didn't do what I said he did? I'm having second thoughts about this."

"Oh?" For the first time, Hanes seemed unsure of himself. "Despite his guilty plea, and the fact the combings at the emergency room revealed his pubic hair in your private area and evidence of fresh vaginal tears?" He regained his composure, squinted at the girl across from him. "If there's truly something wrong or you've not told the truth, by all means let us know. I don't have any interest in tarring an innocent man, but hard as you might find this to accept, I genuinely believe in you and this case, and think it's horrible that a minister would break faith with you and your family. You need to decide if you want to pursue this and quit jerking everyone around. If you're in, great. If you're out, fine. Just don't sit here and waste my time."

"Christy, for once, just for once, please act like you have some sense," her father pleaded. "I know this has been terrible, and I know at times we've probably handled things wrong, but please let this man help you."

"I'm taking a class at Hollins and working part-time at the mall. They let me withdraw from UVA instead of expelling me, and I'm going to start at Sweet Briar in a few weeks."

"Ah. Good. It seems you're doing all *you* can to put this behind you." Hanes appeared satisfied with her response.

"And she goes to her AA meeting once a week," her mother added. "Every week."

"That so, Christina?" Hanes asked.

"I go every Wednesday night." In fact, she wouldn't dream of skipping it. At her second meeting after rehab, she'd met a woman named Celeste, a thirty-five-year-old divorcee with a house on Smith Mountain Lake. They'd burn a joint in the parking lot before each meeting and practically bust up every time a speaker mentioned the need for a "higher power" in day-to-day living. Afterwards, they'd drive to the lake and smoke more dope and sit on Celeste's dock and listen to music and scan the sky trying to identify constellations. Sometimes Celeste's boyfriend would come by with a boat full of friends and a keg of Bud Light.

"Stick with it," Hanes said.

"I plan to."

"Why don't you and your folks step into the conference room, relax for a moment, and then we'll get started."

"Do you want us to sit in with you, dear?" her mother asked.

"Whatever. If you want to."

"Moral support," her father said.

"You know . . ." Christy started, then stopped.

"What? What is it?" her father asked. "Tell us." The room became tense again.

"Well . . ."

"What?" her mother said, her impatience creeping into the single word despite her best efforts.

"If I'm going to have to do this deposition thing, I figure I'll need to look the part, right? So, I mean, I was hoping you guys would take me shopping while we're here, you know, for some cool outfits." She batted her eyes at her father at the end of the request.

"I agree," Bill Darden said, sounding relieved this was the limit of his daughter's extortion. "We'll go after we finish with Mr. Hanes."

"And if I have to get ready for this grilling from Mr. Roland, it would be nice if I didn't have to schlep to the mall every day for work and have all that pressure on me. I know I'll do better if I don't have to put in six hours of weekday retail and contend with snotty, rude customers. Mall employment can be extremely daunting. Plus school starts soon anyway."

Hanes interrupted Christy's negotiations. "Why don't you good people discuss this by yourselves while I locate Mrs. Patterson?" He touched a button on his phone and asked his secretary to show the Dardens to the conference room. A conservatively dressed woman entered the office and accompanied Christy and her parents down the hall. Hanes walked to the door, shut it and looked at Oliver. "I'll tell you one thing—as spoiled and headstrong as that worthless little bitch is, she's about the most beautiful kid I've ever seen. I can see why the rev was chasing after her—be tough not to. Talk about tying Odysseus to the mast. Jeez. There's something about our friend Christy, huh, Oliver? Like the red devil came at Joel King with his best pitch."

At the Rosewood Grille, Joel gave Sa'ad's name to a maitre d' with a mustache and dyed black hair, and the man acknowledged him with a pretentious sweep of his arm, whipped a menu from a stack near his post and swished Joel to the very end of the restaurant, turned the brief trip into a brisk, tuxedoed piece of theater that wound through tables, busboys and busy waiters. The restaurant was crowded and convivial, full of conversation and the sounds of forks clipping plates and ice sliding and rattling in heavy water glasses. The lights were low, and when the maitre d' stopped and gestured, Joel didn't recognize the group sitting at the table, three women and a man seated so Joel couldn't see his face. He leaned toward his host, smelled cologne and something distantly greasy. "I'm looking for Sa'ad X. Sa'ad's reservation."

"Yes, I know. And this is the table." A cheesy smile, a quick hand flourish in the direction of the three women and their companion.

Joel inspected the four people again. "I don't think—"

"Hello, Reverend King."

Joel heard the voice from behind him and felt a hand meet his shoulder. It was Sa'ad, dressed in the same splendid suit and speckled tie he'd worn at his office.

"Where's Edmund?"

"Right there." Sa'ad pointed at the man with the three women, and Joel finally registered the outline of Edmund's head. He'd been thrown off by the women and overlooked Edmund, hadn't seen what he'd expected when he arrived.

"Who's that, the three ladies?" Joel asked.

"Julie, Rachel, and Lilly. They're joining us for the evening."

Joel didn't move. He stuck his hands on his hips. "Joining *us*?"

"Yes." Sa'ad applied pressure and urged Joel forward.

Joel didn't budge. "Let me do the math. There are three of us and three women. Am I reading this correctly?"

Sa'ad chortled, but it was difficult to read his expression in the dim light. "You're free to interpret it any way you want, my friend."

"Is this a date you've arranged? A setup?"

The maitre d' had withdrawn to a wall and was watching them, the menu still pressed under his arm.

"We simply invited three friends along for the evening," Sa'ad answered. "No one, Mr. King, is holding a gun to your head. Stay or depart as you please."

Edmund had pivoted in his chair and was facing Sa'ad and Joel. "Joel. You're late. Come on and join us."

"Hello, Edmund," Joel said. He had Sa'ad blocked behind him.

"What are you waitin' for?" Edmund asked. "Sit down and enjoy."

"Okay." Joel took a seat, couldn't see where stomping his feet or raising a ruckus or storming off would accomplish much, and at its core this was simply another of Edmund's bad ideas, a bawdy, misguided effort at generosity. Edmund made the introductions, reciting each woman's first and last name as he toured the table. The six of them ordered lobsters and steaks, and the women drank two bottles of champagne that the waiter wrapped in cloth napkins and cradled like glass infants when he presented them to Lilly. She giggled and the three ladies jumped both times the cork was popped. It became apparent that Rachel had been assigned to Joel; he declined the champagne when she thrust the bottle in his direction and chatted with her about Wayne Newton and the Hoover Dam and the neat things her uncle did when she was a kid, such as throwing his voice and making his thumb disappear. After two hours, the table was strewn with highball glasses and champagne flutes and lobster husks and plugs of pink filet the women didn't eat. Joel finished every morsel of his meal from salad to entrée and ordered chocolate pie for dessert.

Edmund left eight hundred-dollar bills under a bread plate and announced it was time to cross the street and begin the evening's blackjack at the Mirage. Joel felt a keen emptiness as they were walking into the traffic and neon extravaganza that bracketed the city, Edmund and Sa'ad carefree and at ease, the three women skipping and dodging cars, acting silly, all of them as blithe as could be. Joel was absolutely alone, married but without a wife, jobless, essentially friendless, a teetotaler in a town that celebrated liquor and lust, waiting to return to a bleak underground hole at his sister's. He watched the women teeter past a cab in their high heels, saw Lilly blow a kiss to a limousine driver who braked to let them pass.

"I guess I'll call it a night," he said to Edmund.

"Come on, Joel, we're just hittin' our prime. At least go to the Mirage for a while."

Lilly, Rachel, and Julie had navigated Las Vegas Boulevard and were waving from across the street. Sa'ad looked at Joel but didn't say anything.

"Heck, Joel, you can stroll the lobby and look at the white tigers and sharks if nothin' else," Edmund urged. "You don't have to gamble or drink. Wouldn't you rather have some company than just sit in your room by yourself?"

"It's an impressive lobby," Sa'ad added.

The sidewalk was teeming with people, and the air was still warm, even after the sun had set. "I don't know . . . I'm not big on gambling," Joel said.

"It's a heckuva lot more than gambling, Joel. It's an upscale hotel with all kinds of attractions. Families and kids come here for their vacations." Edmund glanced across the street at the other half of their group. "If you were in Rome, you'd see Saint Peter's; if you went to London, you'd visit Buckingham Palace. You don't have to be a Catholic or believe in monarchs, right? It's just seein' the world."

"Well . . ."

"Look but don't touch. A trip through a museum," Sa'ad said.

"I don't . . ." Joel left the thought incomplete.

"It's a beautiful hotel lobby, not a saloon or speakeasy or somethin' dirty," Edmund explained. "It's the stuff you see on the Travel Channel."

Joel peered up at the gaudy gold letters spelling out the resort's name. "Why not? I might as well see what there is to see while I'm here, and I'm not crazy about sitting alone in a hotel room all night."

"That's the spirit. Now you're talkin'. " Edmund sounded truly pleased.

A cab pulled to the sidewalk, and a man got out, then an older woman in a bright pink pantsuit. Edmund approached the taxi and asked for a ride to the Mirage.

"It's right there," the driver said. He was wearing a baseball hat and had a yellowish film in one eye. When he spoke to Edmund, he wasn't brusque or condescending. He jabbed his thumb in the direction of the hotel.

"Exactly, sir, but we want a ride anyway. And we'll need to loop back and pick up those three beautiful ladies."

"Can't make no U-turn. Not here, not this time of night." The cabbie had his window almost completely down and was resting his arm on the slender strip of glass left in the door.

Edmund produced a C-note from his pocket and held it in front of the man behind the wheel.

"Get in," he said. "For that kinda fare, I'll make an exception."

"You're going to pay a hundred dollars to ride a cab for two minutes?" Joel was incredulous.

"It's only money, Joel," Edmund said.

"My goodness." Joel was shocked, astounded. "What about Sa'ad's car?"

"Sa'ad's been drinking, and we can't have him behind the wheel, now can we?"

"Just say no," Sa'ad joked.

"Let's go, people," Edmund said. "Our ride's waitin'."

"Is your leg bothering you, Edmund?" Joel asked. "Are you okay? I could get Sa'ad's car and drive. I'd be glad to, and I'm totally sober."

"I'm fine. Healthy as a horse. We're taking this cab, right now. Quit arguin' with me."

Sa'ad offered Edmund a curious look but didn't dwell on the issue. "Let's go then."

"You should always arrive at a casino by car," Edmund explained. "I hate going in all puffin' and sweaty. Takes something away when the people at the door watch you walkin' up the entrance road like a pack of teenagers."

"I'm not supposed to take six people in my car," the driver said.

"Damn, brother, we're paying you a hundred bucks for nothing," Sa'ad said. "It's not going to kill you to be a little more accommodating."

"I could lose my license," the driver said.

"You could lose a gig paying you three thousand dollars an hour if you don't get off your ass," Sa'ad reminded him.

Edmund bribed him with an additional twenty, and the driver found a way around the rule, horned and butted a route across eight traffic lanes until he was able to swing alongside the curb and collect Rachel, Julie, and Lilly. The three women piled into the rear of the car, and Rachel sat on Joel's lap. When the taxi accelerated, she bumped backward, and her neck touched the side of Joel's face. He smelled perfume and alcohol, felt the warmth of her skin transfer into his cheek and found the contact erotic, lowered the power window but got no relief from the hot, clingy air.

Joel was the last to leave the cab and the last to enter the Mirage. He had to admit that the casino was spectacular. White tigers were lounging in their habitat just off the lobby, sharks sulked in a mammoth aquarium behind the registration desks, and the entire enormous place was a jumble of squeals and voices and coins pouring down into the metal trays of slot machines while lights flashed and comely women tossed dice into felt pits adorned with numbers and chips. Joel's dose of melancholy continued as he wandered through the casino. He felt a weird disappointment because none of the games and attractions could bring him any particular excitement or lift him from his blue mood. Gambling, drinking, glitz and wholesale whoring were simply not the temptations that turned his head or struck his fancy, and it would've been oddly nice to have at least *wanted* to join in the revelry and feel a twinge of corruption, to *want* to sneak off and drink a glass of liquor and spin the big wheel-of-chance and petition the Lord for absolution the next morning.

He located Sa'ad, Edmund and the women at a blackjack table; everyone was playing, the men betting with black chips and sipping scotch. They seemed to be doing well, winning almost every time the cards went around.

"You better climb in, Joel," Edmund said. "We got a friendly dealer and a hot shoe, so you could earn some real interest on that money in your wallet."

"I'm not a gambler, Edmund. I don't enjoy it. What's a 'shoe'?"

"It's a box the cards are dealt out of, right there." He motioned toward a crimson-bottomed container on the dealer's side of the table. "And I ain't talkin' about liking it, Joel. I'm talking about makin' money."

"Oh. Well, I can't really afford to lose the rent check." Joel gave everyone a wan smile.

The dealer, an Asian woman with short hair, laid down a card and flicked her eyes over him.

"Just try it one time," Rachel wheedled. "It's a wonderful table."

"I don't know the rules."

"We'll be glad to help you, Joel," Sa'ad volunteered.

The dealer was drawing cards for herself and counting out loud. "Twenty-five," she said. "Dealer bust."

Lilly thrust her hands above her head, and everyone cheered and celebrated their good fortune. Sa'ad picked up his glass and swirled the brown whiskey but didn't take a drink.

"There's nothing to it," Lilly said. "Don't be a stick in the mud." She was wearing a shiny sequined top and a short skirt. She stumbled on the word "stick," slurring the *s*.

"You know, Joel, I don't enjoy getting up and preparing for work every day. But I do it. I do it to make money. That's what we have here—a legal chance to make some good money. Give it a try." Sa'ad still had his drink airborne.

"How much does it cost to play?"

"Twenty-five is the minimum bet."

"Wow." Joel made a face. "How much are you guys betting with the black chips?"

"Black is one hundred," the dealer explained.

Edmund suddenly clapped his hands, then elbowed Sa'ad. "Check it out, Otis. Twenty-one. That's sweet." Edmund had a black ace and a ten of diamonds in front of him.

"How much did you win?" Joel inquired.

"Bet two hundred. Blackjack'll pay me three hundred."

"Plus you get to keep your original bet, your two hundred?" Joel asked.

"Of course," Edmund said. A cocktail waitress came by the table and everyone ordered more alcohol. "That's three hundred profit," Edmund explained after he'd requested another scotch.

"I'll help you play," Rachel offered. "You need to hurry before the luck turns."

Joel stared at the table and cards and chips. "You just try to get to twenty-one, right?"

"Basically. We'll help you with the details." Edmund patted the empty chair next to him. "Hop in."

"I could sure use the money."

Sa'ad finally took a drink and looked at Joel over the top of his glass. "It's you and your seventh-grade friends playing twenty-one in the pup tent with your mama's bridge cards. Flashlights, graham crackers, sleeping bags, a transistor radio. Same harmless fun."

Joel rested his hand on the cushion in the vacant seat. "You forgot the BB guns."

"What are you talkin' about?" Lilly asked. "Transistor—"

She was interrupted by a yelp from Julie; another blackjack had appeared.

"It's an incredible table, Joel," Sa'ad said. He set down his scotch.

Joel reached into his wallet and took out one of the hundreds. "Where do I go to have it changed?"

"All right! Now we're cookin'. " Edmund was delighted. "Lay the money on the table, and she'll give you your chips."

Joel settled into his seat and held out the money for the dealer. "You have to put it on table," she instructed. Her name tag said Li and noted she was from Korea. "I can't take like that." She was kind, didn't scold him.

Joel received four green chips, which looked paltry compared to Edmund's massive stack next door. He pushed a chip into a square on the table and waited for his cards. When he swallowed, there was a brief catch in his throat, and a couple breaths came and went too quickly, one right after the other. Edmund raised his wrist to check the time, and things seemed to grind and lose purpose. Julie put her mouth next to Rachel's ear and whispered, and she took forever to finish three or four words. Joel's first card was an ace.

"Now we're talkin'," Edmund said. His speech was distorted and strangely slow. "That's a good start."

Rachel made a fist. "Now you need a ten." Her lips labored and her voice sounded drugged . . . stuck at thirty-three-and-a-third speed. "Paint . . . that . . . bad . . . boy."

Joel clasped his hands under his chin and squeezed until the feeling in the tips of his fingers disappeared. Sa'ad got a nine, Edmund a queen . . . The next card, his, was . . . an ace. Another ace, just like the first one. Both diamonds.

"How . . . what . . . is that right? I got the same card twice. Two aces of diamonds. Is this rigged or something? How—" His own voice wallowed out of his head.

"It a six-deck shoe," Li explained. There was a hitch . . . a jolt . . . voices and movements caught speed and herky-jerked into gear. Things returned to normal, ran in real time. "We play with six decks at once. No problem."

"There're six decks, all shuffled together," Edmund added. "Makes it harder to count cards or cheat."

"So I have, what, twelve? That's not so great." Joel rubbed his eyes and concentrated on his breathing. "Drat."

"Split 'em," Edmund said.

"Always split aces," Rachel agreed.

"Meaning?" Joel asked.

"You wager another chip, split the aces and you get one card on each ace," Edmund explained.

Joel sighed. "So I have to bet another twenty-five?"

"Yes."

Joel looked at Sa'ad, inviting his opinion.

"It's a no-brainer, Joel," he said.

"Okay. Okay, then." He placed another green bet. Li's hands darted to his cards and separated the aces. "Good luck," she uttered in a detached tone that made Joel think she frequently said it when people were in his circumstances.

The first card made a crisp, snapping sound when it exited the clear dispenser. A ten. "Twenty-one," Joel heard someone say. The next card appeared much more quietly, seemed to come from nowhere. A nine. "Twenty," Sa'ad said. "Good card."

Li finished dealing to the rest of the table and turned to her own cards, one exposed, the other facedown. She had a seven of spades everyone could see, and she pinched it at the corner and used it to flip over the card underneath. A red queen with a lazy smile rolled onto her rump, and the table cheered and broke into high-fives. "Dealer have seventeen," Li said. She slid two green chips to Joel, fifty dollars. More money than he'd earned in a month. Only Lilly had lost, and she didn't seemed too concerned about the setback.

"Nothing to it, huh, Joel?" Edmund said.

"Congratulations," Li said.

"Should I keep playing?" Joel asked. "Or are the odds against me winning again?"

"This table's a gold mine. Put your bet down." Edmund had been drinking for hours but didn't appear affected by it.

"You're sure?" Joel quizzed him.

"It's gambling, Joel, not banking," Sa'ad remarked. "The only sure bet is the ATM machine, and sometimes even that jams. But this is as good a run of cards as you'll find."

"How much should I put out?"

"Bet it all," Lilly said. She was smoking a cigarette, and a segment of gray and white ash collapsed and sprinkled the floor without her noticing it.

"Yeah," Rachel encouraged him. "Go for all of it."

"Don't pay them any attention," Edmund said sternly. "Bet the fifty you just won. That way you're playin' with the house's money."

"Makes sense," Joel agreed. He dropped two chips onto the table, and Li began giving everyone cards.

The same thing happened again as soon as the first card popped from the shoe . . . the Mirage bogged down, and the casino became sluggish and ponderous, congealed. Colors and shapes strung together in stuttering, piecemeal sequences and people moved like flipbook figures, leaving behind fleeting vapors with each step or reach or gesture. Joel saw a blackish vein across the top of Li's dealing hand, noticed the pattern and weave in the green fabric covering the table as a card closed in on his fifty-dollar wager. "A three," one of the women said, and she sounded as if she were submerged.

He noticed a man in a handsome suit, walking through the casino so slowly that he seemed mechanical. The man locked onto Joel and gradually released a smile, raised his hand in a leaden wave as if they knew each other. One tooth—in the top front—was outlined in gold, an image that lingered in Joel's mind even after the passerby had disappeared behind a cluster of people betting on a dice game.

"Sir, what you like to do?" It was Li, and the warped, weighted sound had gone from her voice. Her smile was formal and fixed. She was staring at him with one hand hovering above the shoe. He had missed a card, missed some time, gotten bound up in the freakish mire and the stranger's flashy smile.

"Uh, I . . . lost track there, sorry. It's strange the way things happen when, well, when the cards are coming. So, okay." He examined his cards. "Thirteen. That's low, isn't it? I guess I need to take one?" He turned to Edmund for help. "Right?"

"Lord no, Joel. Look at what the dealer's got showin'. She's riding a six. You stay where you are."

"I only have thirteen, Edmund. I'll never win with that."

Li hadn't moved, although her smile was gone. She shifted her weight, made eye contact with the dealer at the adjacent table.

"It works like this," Edmund began. "You don't care—"

Sa'ad interrupted. "We don't really care what you have. She has a six showing, and we assume she has a ten in the hole. That's sixteen, so she has to take a card. When she pulls a card, the odds are she'll bust. The object is to win. Thirteen wins if she goes over twenty-one."

"How do you know she has a ten underneath?" Joel demanded. "It could be anything."

"We're playin' the odds," Edmund explained.

Sa'ad hoisted his glass again. "It's not unlike your line of work, Reverend. A dash of faith and you're betting on something you can't see."

"So I don't take a card?"

"Exactly."

"I don't want any more," Joel said to Li.

"You have to make signal," she told him. "Like this." She showed him what he needed to do.

"Okay," Joel said, waving his hand palm down over his cards. "I'm not sure I understand, but I'm sticking with thirteen."

No one else took a card—they all shook their heads and made hand gestures and Julie said, "I don't think so." Li appeared to know what they were going to do and passed by them, quickly arriving at her own cards. She showed her hole card, an eight. An eight to go with her six.

Joel looked at the dealer, then at Sa'ad and Edmund. "I thought it was supposed to be a ten."

"Relax, Joel," Sa'ad said. "We're right on schedule."

"I should've taken another card," Joel griped.

"You do smart thing," Li said. She pulled the next card from the shoe, dragged it concealed across the table, peeked at its corner and then glanced at Joel. She shook her head, sighed and made a clicking sound. "Sorry," she said. "I hate it for you." She stood the card on its bottom edge and let it tumble forward. A jack, the jack of clubs. "Too many. Dealer bust." She started to laugh and everyone at the table laughed with her.

"So . . . oh, wow." It took Joel a moment to recover. "So I win, right? I win fifty bucks."

"Yeah," Sa'ad said, still chuckling.

"I figured I was cooked." Joel looked at Li. "That was pretty darn cruel. You scared me to death."

"Welcome to Las Vegas," she said. "We play rookie trick on you."

"By the way, Joel, would you like to go back and take a card?" Sa'ad asked.

"Pardon?"

"Add the numbers. Had you taken a card, you would have gotten that jack and pissed away your bet. You would've lost. Under the Sa'ad X. Sa'ad plan, she took the bust card, and we all win."

"You were right. Thanks." Joel rounded up his chips and clutched them inside a sweaty fist. "Where do I exchange these?"

"You're not stopping now, are you?" Rachel asked. "You're just getting the hang of it."

"Finish this shoe," Edmund urged. "Stay with us till she shuffles." His withered finger was especially apparent among the chips and cards.

"I don't have the nerve for it, and I'm a hundred bucks to the good. My position isn't likely to get any better." He was standing as he spoke.

"So why don't you mosey around and visit some more places—Caesar's is next door—then meet us for the next stop?" Edmund said.

"The next stop?"

"The Crazy Horse," Edmund said. "We'll catch a limo in an hour or so."

"And the Crazy Horse would be what? A Native American tribute with trick riders and medicine men?" Joel contorted his expression, pretended to be dumbfounded.

"Actually," Sa'ad said, "you're not too far off the mark."

"Well, I don't have any interest in more nightlife. I've had my taste of decadence." He opened his hand and inspected his winnings. "And the minister in me makes me want to warn you folks that a topless club isn't such a great idea."

"You're probably right." Edmund seemed contrite. "But it's a hard habit to break."

"Yeah. Maybe we'll all go ride the roller coaster at New York, New York," Sa'ad said. "Do something different and wholesome." His tone was so diluted that Joel couldn't tell if he was sincere or simply being acerbic.

"Okay. So . . . so I guess I won't see you before I leave, huh?"

"I guess that's the case," Edmund said. "And we'll handle everything else for now, so don't worry about the details. Everything will come to you."

"Sure."

"It was great seein' you," Edmund remarked. Li had finished dealing and was waiting for him to play his cards. "Have a safe trip home." He shook Joel's hand and returned to his gambling, then slurped his whiskey and good-naturedly commanded Li to throw him a ten. "Tell you what, Joel," he suddenly said. "In your honor I'm gonna put half my winnings in the plate next Sunday at Roanoke Baptist. How 'bout that?"

"I know it will be appreciated," Joel answered.

"We miss havin' you in the pulpit. It's not the same, you know—not by a long shot."

"Good night, Sa'ad." Joel touched his forehead with his index and middle fingers, presented the lawyer a faux salute. "Thanks for everything. Oh—thank you both for dinner. I enjoyed it. And ladies, good night to you as well. It was a pleasure meeting you. I wish you continued success at the table."

"I'll walk with you to swap your chips," Rachel volunteered. "Show you where to go so you don't get lost."

"Ah—there you have it, Preacher King. The chance to spurn another temptation. You must be close to getting out of the red by now." Sa'ad didn't look away from his cards as he spoke. He was fidgeting with one of his cuffs, extending a band of white shirt from beneath the sleeve of his jacket.

Joel stiffened. He was standing next to Edmund, waiting to squeeze through the small space between the seats. "I was out of the red, Sa'ad, the first time I asked to be forgiven. That's the way it works."

Sa'ad gave Li a hand signal—he scratched the felt with two fingers—and she dealt him a seven. "That's good to know, Joel, good to know. I thought maybe there was a sliding scale, whereby some fuckups would carry a bigger penalty than others." He stared at Joel and fingered a tower of black chips. "I didn't mean to ruffle your feathers. I'm hardly the theologian that you are, so I don't understand all the bylaws and fine print."

"Don't worry about it," Joel answered. "Ruffling my feathers, that is." He sensed that someone was behind him, then felt a tap on his shoulder.

"Is this seat taken?"

"No, I'm leaving." Joel took a step away from the table. "It's all yours."

"Thanks, pal," the newcomer said. He gave Joel a courteous smile and slid past him into the chair. His suit was even nicer than it had appeared from a distance, and the gold border around his tooth was bright enough to catch the false light raining from the ceiling.

Rachel showed Joel to the cage, and he exchanged his chips for cash. He'd never been concerned about money before, had for all his preacher years lived in this queer ether where finances were at best a means to an end and more often than not a sinful distraction. The charm of the pulpit was having very little but wanting for absolutely nothing. The church provided him with a home, health-care insurance and a satisfactory salary, and there were gifts and donations and summer vegetables and pound cakes and potluck suppers galore. The lady at the cage gave him two hundred-dollar bills, and he stared at them and reflected on how easy it had been for him to lecture his congregation about giving when it was damn impossible for some of them and painless for him.

Joel agreed to have a cup of coffee with Rachel at one of the casino bars after she mentioned she had something important to ask him and virtually begged him to spend a few more minutes in the Mirage. She ordered a bottled beer, and Joel asked for decaf with cream and sugar. Rachel's appearance had begun to turn slatternly—her hair was falling into her face, her skirt had a dark stain near the hem, and her makeup had worn thin in spots around her nose and cheeks. When she turned her profile to Joel, the makeup gaps caused her skin to appear patchy and mottled. Still, she was a pretty girl, probably thirty or so, with perfect teeth and a good shape.

"What did you want to ask me?" Joel said as the bartender was serving them their order.

"Huh?" Rachel was impaired, swaying a bit on her bar stool, but she wasn't drunk or sloppy. "A little tipsy" was the term used in Baptist circles.

"You wanted to speak with me about something important?" Joel assumed his minister's voice, concerned and compassionate yet studiously removed. In the past he'd usually known what was coming—garden-variety failings such as petty theft or a child who was "fooling with dope"—and he'd start the conversation with a confident blend of understanding and separation.

"Yes. Yeah, okay." The bartender had emptied part of her beer into a glass, and she added some more. She poured straight from the bottle into the glass, and a swollen rush of foam overflowed onto the bar. "Rats," she said, patting at the accident with a paper napkin.

"You wanted to talk?"

She looked up from what she was doing. "Are you really a preacher, Joel? Or is that just a gag between you guys?"

Joel considered his answer. "I'm an ordained Baptist minister. I pastored a church in Virginia for many years."

"Huh. So you really are." She fiddled with several loose strands of hair. "I figured you worked with Edmund in the meat business."

"So now you know." A cocktail waitress left the bar with a tray of drinks and longneck beers, brushing Joel's arm when she breezed by. "Was that your important question?"

"Well, sorta. That's part of it. I'm, well, I'm trying to get more spiritual, you see." She swallowed some of her beer. The napkin on the bar had soaked through and changed consistency, become a saturated lump. "I'm taking a yoga class at UNLV, and I was thinking about maybe signing up for tae kwon do—it's a whole lot more than just fighting and flexibility. It's deeper than that. A lot of it is about getting your mind and soul in harmony."

"I guess that's a start."

"There's just so much shit out there when it comes to religion, it's hard to know which one to pick. I mean, how could anyone ever . . . ever choose? How do you decide which is best for you?"

"It sometimes takes a lot of seeking. But I don't think yoga and kung fu—or whatever it is—are really serious options."

"What do you believe in, Joel?" Rachel asked. "You seem really centered and together, the way you have so much discipline."

Joel had his finger through the cup handle, ready to lift his coffee. Rachel's compliment caught him off guard, and he left the cup on its saucer. "I'm hardly the person you think. Far from it, in fact. But for what it's worth, I believe in the God of the Old Testament and the literal truth of the Four Gospels. That's the quick version."

"The Bible, right?"

"Yes. Absolutely." He sipped his coffee.

"I was raised a Presbyterian, went to Sunday school and church dinners and wore my granny's brown bath towel on my head for the Christmas play, did the whole thing pretty much, but it was so incredibly *boring* when I got older. I mean it was awful to sit in there for an hour every Sunday. And everybody was so uptight." Rachel stared into space for several seconds, as if conjuring up her time in church years ago.

" 'The frozen chosen,' we Baptists like to call them. I can promise you that Baptists are more demonstrative." A coffee rivulet had wandered down the side of Joel's cup.

"So what should I do?"

"Well, may I ask you something?"

"Sure."

"And I hope you won't be offended." He leaned toward Rachel and lowered his voice.

"Ask away."

"How should I put this? I wonder, I guess, how you ended up here tonight. What's your, uh, relationship with Edmund and Sa'ad?"

"You mean am I a hooker?" she said without dampening her tone.

"Yeah. Not to put too fine a point on it, but that's what I'm getting at."

"Why are you asking? What makes you think so?"

"Oh, I don't know. Maybe it's because you meet a broken-down wreck like me and turn giddy at the prospect of spending time together."

Rachel frowned. "Oh no. You're a handsome man. And you carry yourself like you are somebody. I could tell that right away about you. You're trim and tall and I love your eyes and your dark hair. Why would you say such a harsh thing about yourself?"

"So, are you?"

"Am I what?" she asked.

"A prostitute."

"No, I'm not."

Joel tried to assess her reaction. "Of course, if Edmund was setting this up, you wouldn't tell me anyway, would you?"

"True. Yeah." She wound a length of hair around her index finger. "You mind if I order another beer?"

"If you like."

"I'm not a hooker," she said. "I work at a clothing store. And part-time as a waitress at the Monte Carlo."

"I see."

"To tell you the truth, Lilly works for an escort service. Sometimes she invites me along." She was sailing now, talkative and a little juiced from the champagne and beer, the words tripping out one on top of the other.

"So Lilly's a prostitute?"

"Kind of, I suppose. She doesn't sleep with all of her dates. Sometimes they just want to hang out with her." She scanned the room, searching for the bartender. "If she thinks it'll be a good time, she gives me a call. But I don't sleep with people for money. Well, okay, once I did, one time, about two months ago. This icky little Japanese geek." She waved at the man behind the bar, and he started toward her. "Is that something you could, you know, bless me for?"

"Bless you?"

The bartender arrived, and Rachel asked for another beer. Joel wondered if she expected him to pay, wondered if that's why she'd checked with him before ordering.

"Can't you do that? You're a preacher, right? Isn't that what you do?"

"You mean forgive you?"

"That's it. Exactly. I'm sorry—I've been drinking. That's probably bad, too, askin' you to help when I'm close to hammered."

"You can ask for yourself. You don't need my intervention. Ask the Lord, and you'll be fine. I'll certainly say a prayer for you, though. I'd be honored to."

"I wish you would. That'd be so sweet." Rachel seemed touched. She blinked several times and bit her lip, then the sentiment appeared to pass and she was composed again. "I'm just bouncing around out here," she said. "I wanted to dance in the shows, but I'm not good enough. Half the time I'm just going through the motions." She shrugged, swallowed two gulps of beer.

"I suspect you have a great deal of talent and promise. Read your Bible again. Stop by a church. Try prayer—ask the Lord what He would have you do."

"Okay. Thanks." She reached out and rested her hand flat against Joel's knee. She left it there, and he wasn't sure what to think. He twisted away toward the bar, toward his coffee, and she folded her hands in her lap.

"It was a pleasure meeting you. I'm going to catch a cab to my hotel."

"Do you want me to come with you?"

"I'm flattered, but no. Thanks just the same."

"What's the best part of preaching, Joel?" she asked abruptly.

"The best part?"

"Yeah." She crossed her legs.

"Leading people to Christ."

"That's it?" she asked. "That's all?"

"That's more than enough."

"I mean for you, what do *you* get into—like golf or collectin' butterflies or sports or traveling or reading. Or the bad stuff—sex, drugs, and rock and roll. Understand what I'm askin'? You can't only be your job."

"Honestly, Rachel, nothing wicked really interests me. I'm blessed like that in a sense; I don't have any desire to chase women or use drugs or stay out all night carousing."

"That's hard to believe," she said.

"Although I have to confess that earlier tonight I wished for a little temptation, just to snap me out of the doldrums."

"Huh." The bartender arrived with a second beer and Rachel paid him for it, took several dollars out of a small purse. She didn't seem to expect Joel to satisfy the tab. "But there has to be something you like *doing,* an event or, I don't know, a moment you enjoy outside of bein' a preacher all the time."

Joel thought about her question. "Once a month, our church has a breakfast to raise money for our various ministries. The doors open at six, and folks are there at five to prepare the meal. I used to get to the fellowship hall about five-thirty, and my friend William Turner would fix a tenderloin plate for me—a nice piece of meat, gravy, fried apples, toast and an egg. I'd sit by myself in the kitchen with my food, and all around me my church—these fine men and women—were toiling and cooking and on the cusp of this remarkable feat. It was like being on the brink of pure goodness." He stopped talking. A man at a roulette table won his bet and hollered, "Hell, yeah!" Joel looked at Rachel. "I miss that so much," he said wistfully.

"Wow," Rachel said. "I can tell it really got to you." She made a quirky noise, part sough and part grunt. "So how come you don't go anymore? For the tenderloin breakfast with your church buddies?"

Joel suddenly felt like the worst kind of fraud. "Ah, well, you see, I'm not at the church now. I'm not the pastor there. In fact, I had to leave."

"Had to leave?"

"Yes."

"How come?"

"It's a convoluted story, and one I don't relish recounting." He forced a rueful smile. "Suffice it to say . . ." He paused, watched an old woman in a motorized wheelchair feeding coins into a slot machine. "Suffice it to say I had a problem with a temptation that doesn't even tempt me. How about that?"

"What?" Rachel scrunched her face, and the casino light hit a spot without makeup. "I'm not following you. What temptation are you talking about?" She struggled to stay perched on her bar stool.

"I guess you could say I suffered from Saint Augustine's curse."

Rachel scrambled off her seat so quickly that Joel thought she was going to chase after someone in the casino, thought she'd just spotted an old friend or seen Edmund and Sa'ad leaving her behind. She staggered for an instant when she first stood, then clapped her hands. "Damn. I know about him. I wrote a paper about him for my religion class at the community college. He got his maid pregnant." She looked at Joel, and her eyes cleared for a moment. "I always wondered how he could be a saint with an illegitimate baby on his record."

Joel was flustered. "Well, he was. And I don't think it was his maid, just a girlfriend. When he was a young man."

Rachel took a step closer to Joel, causing him to recoil without meaning to. "So you're not *really* a preacher? You got fired? Or quit?"

"Something like that." He got to his feet and laid a dollar and two quarters on the bar. "I'm not pastoring a church now."

"Well I think you're one fine specimen, Mr. Preacher." For an instant, Joel thought she'd said "spaceman," and he was silent while he tried to decipher what she meant.

"Oh, I . . . Well, thanks. Thank you. I think you're an attractive person, too."

"You sure I shouldn't go to your room with you? Or maybe somewhere else. We don't have to stay with these guys. How 'bout the topless clubs—I think it's a turn-on in a way, having another girl dance for us."

"No. Absolutely not. No thanks. I'm leaving." Joel tried not to sound prim. "By myself."

"You're positive? I really think you're cool. It's not a trick or anything. Let's just hang out."

"Maybe some other evening. You'd better get back to the party and find your friends."

Rachel gave him a look that was absolutely wanton and unstrung. "Okay," she said. "Can I at least hug you?"

Joel extended his hand before she had a chance to move in any farther. "How about we simply shake and wish each other well?"

"I guess I'm not going to be the temptation that gets you again." She was dangling her beer by her hip.

"I've learned my lesson there, I'm afraid."

"I hope you'll say my prayer. Don't forget."

"I promise," Joel answered. He took her hand from a distance, then walked away, headed for the exit to hail a cab. He stopped before he left the casino and looked back at Rachel. Like Lot, he thought, drawn to cast an eye over corruption at its bejeweled best. She was still drinking at the bar, watching him leave the gambling floor. Her balance wasn't what it should have been, and her lips, tongue and teeth were arranged in a wounded leer.

"Tenderloin," she called, wagging a besotted finger at him. "Just not mine."

seven_____

Joel knew.

He knew his prayers had been answered while he was away in Las Vegas plotting flimflam and eating high-dollar steak with Edmund Brooks. He knew as soon as he saw his mother's blue Volvo in Sophie's stone and dirt drive, parked between the rundown Taurus and the lawnmower shed. He knew he'd have a car, and most remarkably, he knew—even before the Missoula cabbie flipped the blinker and drifted off the main road—he'd have a job waiting on him, an offer for honest, Christian work. And he knew his sister had forgiven him, because she'd finally relented and retrieved the Volvo from outside their mother's window at High Pines so he could go places without having to walk or bum a ride. Helen King adored the Volvo, loved staring at it through the glass in the transfixed manner of the senile elderly, and it couldn't have been easy for Sophie to take the vehicle, her failing mother's last tie to normalcy.

He knew all this well before his sister talked to him and handed him the phone messages, considered his prospects as the driver crept down the driveway and gray gravel clattered in the wheel wells. More than anything, he realized the blessings to come were a test, a chance to separate himself from Edmund and Sa'ad and their slick plans. His requests—a car, a job, clean start—were about to be delivered in the most apparent, obvious fashion, the Lord stretching out His omnipotent hand, waiting for Joel to accept it. He shut his eyes, and the cab slowed until it stopped. The driver never got in a hurry, never touched the brakes, just let the speed play out of the taxi until there was nothing left.

Sophie had finished supper and was doctoring her ragged ferns and wilted potted plants; she bounded off the concrete stoop while Joel was still settling with the driver, didn't bother using the two uneven steps and cracked flagstones. She hurried to her brother and wrapped herself around him in an anxious hug, her head tucked and the limp fingers of her cloth gardening gloves jouncing from her rear pocket as she beelined across the yard. Baker appeared seconds later, tearing from the house in shorts and cowboy boots to grab Joel by the leg.

"What's all this?" he asked, the question equal parts relief and delight.

Sophie didn't say anything. Baker scuttled sideways and pointed two finger-pistols at him, shouted, "Pow pow pow," then ran behind the Volvo and hid.

"Sophie?"

She made some space between herself and her brother. "I'm glad you're here again, and I'm sorry I acted like I did. There's a lot on me, Joel, but that's no excuse. Besides Baker and a few friends, you're about everything I have in this world. You're welcome to stay as long as you need a roof above your head."

Joel folded her back into him. "Thanks," he said over her shoulder. "Thank you so much." Looking up at the sky, he saw a pair of colorful birds dip and bank and fly toward town. "A lot of what you said needed saying, you know?"

"Let's just put it behind us, forget it."

"I agree. You found the letter I left for you?" he asked.

"Yeah," she said. "Thanks."

"I meant what I wrote. I'm going to be a better person."

"You're already a good person, Joel. You just made some poor choices."

Joel leaned away so he could see her face. "It's a shame you don't get a mulligan on your first colossal mistake." He let her go, but she kept her hands fastened behind him. "I see you finally got Mom's car," he said. "I realize that had to be tough."

"Yeah, well, don't get too excited. *I'll* be driving the Volvo. You'll be riding the white bull."

"Fair enough." He glanced at the Volvo, saw Baker peeking out from behind the bumper, the boy squealing and disappearing when his uncle paid the tiniest bit of attention to him.

"I've got great news," Sophie mentioned as they were ambling to the house, her arm hooked inside his. "Calls from two businesses that seem really promising. I wrote down the info for you."

"That is great news," he said softly. He scanned the sky for the birds, but they were gone, and the daylight was beginning to weaken. He heard Tut crow, spotted him near the corner of the shed. The rooster flapped his wings, raised his hackles and drilled Joel with a single cock's eye.

Joel discovered he had two work opportunities, and he could easily juggle both jobs. He'd been offered a kitchen position at a restaurant and bar called the Station—from four to midnight, every weekday—and one of Sophie's leads had phoned with weekend hours at a fly-fishing service, rowing people down the Clark Fork and untangling their errant casts. He contacted the restaurant and made plans to report the following afternoon, then got in touch with Dixon Kreager at Royal Coachman Outfitters and arranged a Friday meeting. Before unpacking his duffel bag, he gave his sister five hundreds in Vegas money and said "Don't worry about it" when she asked about the cash.

"It's legal, isn't it?" she wanted to know.

"Of course it's legal. It's only five hundred dollars, Sophie. I have a few meager resources left. What—you think I robbed a miniature bank or something? I'm just trying to help, okay?"

"You're sure you don't need it?"

"Buy some groceries or put it toward Baker's camp."

"Thanks." Sophie wasn't interested in quizzing him on the issue. Five hundred bucks was five hundred bucks. "But I don't think I'll ask where you've been."

"Nowhere important, not really," he hedged. "Like the letter explained, just clearing my mind."

He poured himself a glass of cold Hawaiian Punch, plucked two Oreos from their shredded package, disappeared into the basement and lay on his bed without taking off his clothes or shoes. He smelled the scents of the laundry, detergent and bleach and the fragrance the softener sheets left around the dryer. There wasn't the first sound in the basement, and the floor above him was quiet, everything in the house calm and orderly.

The kitchen at the Station was hot and frenetic, four walls trapping clangs and shouts and the hisses of raw meat on the grill. Joel was happy to be in the activity, grateful for the work and content each time an hour passed, knowing he'd earned another six dollars. He washed dishes, scraped food off plates, swept up a broken bowl and jogged to the chef's car to fetch a box of spices. Though it was his first night, most of the waiters and waitresses made it a point to say hello or welcome him, and Frankie, who worked with him at the poor man's end of the food chain, was friendly and showed him where the scouring pads and cleaning products were located.

He was allowed a ten-minute break at eight o'clock, and he stepped out the rear door, found three other workers smoking and complaining about how expensive Missoula land had become, how river parcels were selling for millions. They were cordial and made an effort to include him in their conversation. When their break was over, they tossed their unfinished cigarettes onto the ground and went inside, left Joel standing alone in the warm evening. Despite a good stamping, one of the butts was still burning, sending up a white ribbon that disappeared before it rose as high as Joel's waist.

At the end of his shift, a woman walked into the kitchen. Joel was rolling white cloth napkins around silverware, listening to Frankie's story about the night Phil Jackson, the basketball coach, had come to eat at the Station. The woman was pretty, pretty in the face and pretty in the way she moved, but there was no vitality in her, no luster anywhere. The deep-fried air had marred her complexion, and the skin beneath her eyes drooped into yellowish sags. Joel guessed she'd caught a bad break somewhere along the line, had been the straight-A beauty who got pregnant on prom night, or the skittish girl who'd lived too long with a rheumatic mama and a daddy quick to use his belt. Lodged within her, Joel sensed, was something injured and permanent.

"Who's she?" he asked Frankie.

"Who?"

"The woman who just came in. I saw her two or three times earlier."

"Sarah, Sarah Aaron. Well, I guess to be accurate, I should say Sarah Daniels. She basically runs the place, although dumbass Ralph is technically the manager."

"Ralph hired me. Ralph Gardner. In fact, he gave me my assignments this afternoon. I thought he was the owner."

Frankie shrugged. He had a goatee, a nose ring and long, curly brown hair. "He lets on like he is. The Station belongs to his uncle, fellow by the name of David Wayne. Ralph has bombed out on every other job he's had, so we get the pleasure of his company here."

"Oh." Joel dropped a bundle of silverware into a plastic tub and glanced over to where the woman was propped against a stainless steel counter, speaking to the chef.

Frankie was wearing yellow rubber gloves and wiping a sink. "Sarah's good as gold, but she won't talk much till you've been here a month. That's her rule. Lot of turnover in this business, and she doesn't like to waste her time on the sort who aren't goin' to be dedicated."

"What's her story?" Joel asked.

"Local girl, always been gorgeous. Smart, too. Stayed in college about a year, then got married to a guy by the name of William Daniels. We refer to him as Jack. As in the liquor. His daddy did real well for himself, making the metal parts for typewriters. By the time ol' eighty-six-proof Jack inherits the business, computers have taken over and there's not much call for typewriters, so the boy's got a dab of money and scads of time. Business eventually goes bust, but he's too lazy to do anything else workwise, and there's your story. He comes and goes, stays drunk most of the time, cheats on Sarah whenever he has the chance and treats her like crap. Brought some woman in *here* 'bout a month ago, if you can believe that. He's a handsome fellow and a big talker but doesn't have a pot to piss in now. There was two guys from the finance company here recently, drove from Helena to repo his Explorer—Sarah stalled them and paid them cash out of her purse to get 'em gone."

Joel was watching Sarah the whole time Frankie spoke. She'd taken the weight off one foot, was listing farther into the counter and supporting herself with a hip and elbow. "You can tell she's had it rough." Joel paused. "They got kids? That must be why she sticks with him."

Frankie shook his head. "No kids, and there's no explaining it. I treated my girlfriend that way, she'd punch an ice pick in my temple."

"How long you been working here, Frankie?" Joel asked.

"Going on six years." He had an appealing disposition, appeared to be in his early thirties.

"You must like it."

"Weird as it sounds, I do. It's simple work, always the same, no surprises, no stress."

"Good for you."

"Yeah."

Sarah had finished with the chef and was checking her watch. She glanced up and noticed Joel staring at her. He looked away and returned to his knives and forks and spoons, but she refused to let him go, kept her gaze right where it had been when she'd discovered him. She didn't move until he sneaked another glimpse and forced a guilty, fretful smile.

"Were you staring at me?" she demanded from across the room.

Frankie and the chef and one of the waiters stopped what they were doing. Joel squared himself to Sarah, folded his arms over his chest and crammed his hands into his armpits. "Yes ma'am, I was." His cheeks and neck were embarrassed, but he spoke in a clear, firm voice. "I didn't mean to be impolite," he added.

Sarah studied him for a moment. He looked down and noticed the grout outlining the floor tiles, hoped he wouldn't be fired on the spot.

"Ah," she said. "So what have we here, people? An honest man? A man who doesn't lie for sport? Call the guys with the nets and tranquilizer darts—we've got the rarest of the species right here in the kitchen. Hell, we'll all be rich."

Dixon Kreager was a tall, rangy redhead close to fifty years old. He'd earned a chemistry degree from the University of North Carolina at Chapel Hill but had migrated west after a single year working in the research department for DuPont, where he tried to engineer better nylon products and did mad-scientist, beaker-exploding experiments with his lunatic supervisor. He'd guided the Clark Fork, Bitterroot and Blackfoot for almost three decades, could cast sixty-foot flies that hit the water like dandelion down and knew every riffle and eddy and swirl in the big rivers. He'd learned the ropes from Greer Watkins, the best there was, and he'd bought Greer's boat and hovel of a shop when the old man quit the business in 1984. For years, Dixon merely got by in the fishing trade, killed an elk for his freezer in October and substitute-taught a little school to make ends meet during the winter. His girlfriend helped cook at Blackbird's resort from early fall till the fishermen returned in May, and this was the way he lived, frugally and hand-to-mouth.

Then came *A River Runs Through It*, and thanks to Brad Pitt—who to Dixon looked more like a lion tamer with a nine-foot whip than a competent fly fisherman—everybody and his wealthy brother wanted to be on the Montana water, connected to the mystery in the streams and surrounded by inscrutable mountains while they sipped chardonnay from a portable table at lunch. Dixon's skill became much in demand and stayed that way, especially after *Esquire* magazine published a story on him and ESPN paired him with an oafish football player and filmed them catching over fifty fat trout in a single day. Soon his reservation book was full years in advance, and he was making shitloads of money and spending less and less time holding the heavy boat in the current so his clients could get a foolproof casting angle. He married his girlfriend, expanded the shop, published a newsletter, and hired a bunch of help to mollycoddle the would-be fishermen so he, his bride and his black lab could do what they damn well pleased.

The lady who managed his fly shop knew Sophie's boss, and word reached Dixon that there was a tainted preacher with a college degree looking for a job. Joel met Dixon at Royal Coachman Outfitters, found the lanky man sitting in a comfortable office drinking coffee and reading *Money* magazine.

Dixon stood and introduced himself, and he and Joel shook hands. "Coffee?" Dixon asked.

Joel considered the offer. "You know, that would be great. Thanks."

Dixon poured from a pot behind his desk, filling a cup with a picture of a Royal Coachman fly embossed on the front. "Here you go."

Joel inspected the cup, rubbed the fly image with his index finger. "I like the mug."

"Hell, it's a damn theme park 'round here. I make more on the trinkets and T-shirts than I do sellin' rods."

"Nothing wrong with that," Joel said as they both sat down.

"So you're looking for work as a guide?"

"I'll be glad to do anything," Joel said. "Whatever."

"Huh," Dixon grunted. "And I hear through the grapevine you've had a brush with the law, correct?"

"Yes, sir, that's correct." Joel gave Dixon a candid look and struggled to keep his poise. "But I've already been hired at the Station." He hesitated, unhappy with his response. "Please don't take that wrong—what I mean is I want this job, and I don't think you need to worry since someplace else already looked into it and put me to work."

"What is it you did?" Dixon swallowed some coffee. His mug was green and had a brook trout encircling it.

Joel pondered his answer, thought about not telling the truth. "Well, I got fouled up with a seventeen-year-old girl at my church. I was convicted of contributing to the delinquency of a minor."

"Sex, huh?" Dixon said.

"Yeah."

"Any other trouble?" he wanted to know.

"No, sir. None at all."

"What kind of preacher were you? What denomination?"

"Baptist," Joel answered.

"You know how to fly-fish, Joel?"

"I'm okay. A little rusty, so probably what you'd call an intermediate." Joel tasted his coffee; it was pungent and hot.

"You ever fish out here before?" Dixon asked.

"No, I haven't."

"Well, I'll give you a shot, see what you can do. Two of my guys are set-tin' up on their own, so I can use the help. You can row a boat, can't you? And tell entertainin' stories, talk the talk?"

"I'll try. I'm anxious to get the job."

"I suppose I need to make sure I only book you with men and marrieds, huh?" Dixon measured Joel over the rim of his brook trout mug. "Come by Monday morning at seven sharp. I'll carry you to the Clark Fork and see how you rate."

It was Joel's fifth night at the Station when the call came, around eight o'clock on a Wednesday. He was busy in the kitchen, mopping a corner where a waiter had spilled a tray of appetizers and drinks. The chef had cursed the waiter, and Sarah had appeared to learn what the clamor was about, had chided them both and told them they were being babies. She'd left and returned a few moments later, timing her strides so she never touched the swinging double doors, barreled in as a busboy went out.

"Call for you, Joel." She placed the portable receiver on a table. "Please bring me the phone when you're done," she said as she headed back into the dining room.

He took the phone from the table, plugging his open ear with his middle finger against the noise of the kitchen. "Hello?"

"Reverend. How are you?"

Joel blanched when he heard the voice, felt his stomach shrink and a bolt of anxiety disrupt his lungs. He'd put the insurance trickery out of his mind, ignoring it like a child with a hidden report card or a war bride with an unopened telegram, hoping dumb inertia would somehow grant him a reprieve. He was vacillating, betwixt and between, frightened of the bar-gain he'd struck but mindful he was penniless and sinking fast, floundering.

"You there, Joel?"

"Yeah."

"It's me, Sa'ad. Can you hear me?"

"Yeah, I can." Walking to the door, he stumbled into a rack and caused two skillets to bang together.

"I have wonderful news for you, my friend."

"Oh?" He was almost outside.

"Indeed. We've persuaded your wife to abandon her alimony claim. I just talked to our associate in Virginia."

Joel was out of the building. He shut the door behind him and rested against the wall. Someone had spray-painted a shaky heart and arrow with four runny initials on the restaurant's Dumpster. A bike was parked in the alley, fastened to a utility pole by a chain and combination lock.

"She what?"

"We've won the alimony game," Sa'ad said.

"How? How'd that happen?"

"You know when a divorce ends, Joel? When it's actually over?"

"I would assume when the judge signs the paperwork."

"No, not at all. Death or hot new romance—that's when it's truly finished. When they're either dead or in bed."

"So what're you saying?"

"Well, your wife's still living, and her lawyer wants to do a painless no-fault divorce. You connect the dots."

"You think she's got a beau?"

Sa'ad cackled. "My phone screwed up, Joel? Did you say 'beau'? Yeah—she and Ashley are probably picking out hoopskirts and buggy-riding and hand-holding and taking nature walks. That's what I think."

"So you're positive there's another man?"

Sa'ad caught the sadness in Joel's question. "Well, yeah, Joel. What can I say? She's moving on. After all, it's been several months now, and you can't expect her to let her hair go white and spend the rest of her life in peasant dresses and crummy old sweaters."

"I suppose." Joel slid his shoulders down the wall, felt the brick's scratchy bite through his shirt.

"I thought you'd be pleased. You're off the hook, Joel. This is resolved, favorably resolved." Sa'ad was sympathetic; all the taunting and cynicism had vanished. "And who knows, maybe she simply decided to cut you a break. That's possible. Or she and her lawyer decided it wasn't worth the effort, with you broke and in another state. Sometimes people just want to get it done. I'm only speculating about the boyfriend."

"It's just terribly heartbreaking when it finally hits home. What a horrible punishment. My wife's a good woman, and I'd always hoped we . . ." The words perished in his throat.

"You'll be over it soon. Trust me."

"Well, thanks for managing things for me. You certainly took care of your part." Joel was sitting now, completely collapsed onto the ground, his legs straight in front of him, flush against the pavement. He could feel heat from the asphalt grilling his butt and calves.

"By the way, your deposition in the other case is set for August twenty-second. That's right around the corner. As I told you, Mr. Roland is paying your travel expenses—I've got a plane ticket to Virginia he sent my associate, and you're to submit the hotel bill at his office when you leave."

"Right."

"August twenty-first," Sa'ad said, "you'll be flying to Roanoke."

Joel knew exactly what was not being mentioned. "How's Edmund doing?"

"Fine, I would imagine. I haven't seen him much." Sa'ad was terse.

"How'd you find me?"

"I called your sister, and she gave me the number. I'm pleased you located work. She said you were doing something for a guide service, too."

"Yeah. I've got two solid jobs."

"Congratulations. And good luck with the deposition. I hope everything goes well in Roanoke. I'm sure you realize there's a lot riding on how you do."

Joel sighed. "I figured that out."

The next morning, Joel stopped by the probation office for his scheduled meeting. Jack Howard was in his customary arrangement, sprawled in his chair with his feet on the desk. "Reverend King. You keepin' your nose clean, my criminal friend?"

"Yes." Joel took a seat.

"You got a job?" Howard asked.

"Two," Joel answered.

"Can you pass a piss test?"

"For drugs? Is that what you're referring to?"

"Right, Sherlock. For drugs."

"Of course," Joel replied.

"Then I guess our intensive, thirty-minute monthly contact is almost done. Did you make your monthly payment?"

"Yes. I have a receipt if you need to see it."

"Oh no. I trust you, Reverend. But I don't think you've gotten around to your local fee, have you?"

"No." Joel was focusing on a spot a few inches above Howard's head, determined not to be drawn into a skirmish.

"Well, we need to attend to that important business."

"If you say so."

Howard put down one of his feet and thrust his hand at Joel. Joel removed a ten and twenty from his wallet and placed the cash on the edge of the desk, next to a file and a posed picture of Howard and his two kids. "You realize you're taking five hours of my work," Joel said. "Five hours."

"Like I give a shit," Howard barked. "I expect you never had any problem sending the plate around a few extra times, huh Reverend? All the while you're humpin' some guy's minor daughter, and he's payin' you to do it? I don't give a damn if you go hungry and sleep under a bridge. You get my drift? You're nothing but a con artist with a Bible." He swiveled his head and spit on the floor. "That's what I think of you. Be glad it's only thirty."

"I assume I won't be getting a receipt for this portion," Joel said dryly.

"Get the hell out of here."

Joel left the office and walked outside, opened the door to the station wagon. A summer storm was in the offing, and the mountaintops were stacked with clouds, rampaging shades of black, gray and pewter that manhandled the sky. Joel let the burning air escape from the car and tested the cracked leather seat as he entered to make sure it wouldn't singe him. He turned the key, and nothing came of it. He tried again, and still nothing happened. He adjusted the shift knob, removed and reinserted the key, then turned the switch as far as it would go, pressing the ignition's metal notch with his thumb and rolled wrist. The Taurus would not crank. The thunderheads were striding across a high, jagged peak, and the breeze latched on to a discarded fast-food wrapper and danced it through the parking lot.

Joel crumpled against the headrest and forgot about shutting the door. He would never be able to shake Howard, and even with two jobs, his life was always going to be a series of pitched battles and daily labors simply not to go under. He could afford to live in his sister's basement and no more, dwelling in the dirt like a subterranean millstone, a middle-aged pity whose big contribution would be to bring home the occasional out-of-date steak from the Station and cart his decrepit mom to her doctor's appointments. Watching the angry sky advance, he vowed to do the right thing with the money—give a chunk to his wife, send a generous tithe to Roanoke Baptist, and repay his sister for her help and love. He'd only keep enough for a fresh beginning, and how terrible was it anyway, pulling a fast one on the insurance guys whose policies were as rigged as a carnival game or a three-card-monte bet? Cheating a cheater, conning a con. He was going to play the insurance game by their own rules and beat them at it. Edmund had a point.

He acknowledged, too, sitting in the steamy, balky wagon, waiting for the rains to hit, that there was a sad weakness in his decision—he missed his former life, yearned for stability and certainty and comfort, and was willing to swap a portion of integrity for a little breathing room. He was unnerved by the thin balance of his life since jail, hounded by possibilities and what-ifs, fearful of a slow cancer in his belly or an achy tooth or something as slight as the cost of a broken water glass deducted from his pay, completely alone and at the mercy of happenstance and hinky fortune, only a tic, stumble or stutter away from sheer ruin. He was tired of being patient, weary of stepping gingerly, defeated by the feeling he could be picked off at any moment. His heartfelt belief in the Lord's loving guidance had run smack into the price of a dozen eggs and the need for electricity, gasoline and the other commonplace, worldly staples he required to barely eke by.

He got out and opened the hood, even though he knew nothing about automobiles and their repair. He scanned the wires, pulleys, hoses and belts in hopes of discovering something obvious and easy to fix. Two fat splatters popped the windshield, and he heard the first rumbles of thunder. There was a blanket of fair blue sky to the right of the storm, the weather tame and sunny many miles to the east. Joel stared helplessly at the engine and wiped his eyes, felt the stinging upheaval in his nose and chest that precedes unwelcome tears.

"Problem with your ride there, buddy?"

Joel spun and discovered a stranger standing behind him, a giant of a man in jeans and motorcycle garb. "Well, it won't start."

"Won't start, huh? That's 'cause it's a damn Ford." The biker laughed. His frizzy Fu Manchu framed his teeth on three sides.

"I have no idea what's wrong with it." The serious rain was almost there. The pace of the fat drops was picking up, and the wind was whipping the flag in front of the municipal building, causing its big brass grommets to thrash against its pole.

"You work here?" the burly man asked.

"In Missoula?"

"Naw. I mean inside, for the town." He seemed unconcerned about the storm.

"No," Joel said. "I just finished some business."

"Oh. Huh. I'm looking for a map, tryin' to see if there's a scenic route to Sturgis."

"It's all pretty scenic around here."

"I'm just lookin' for a different trip. You know, see something new." He was wearing a leather cap that was too small for his head. Joel decided he was over six and a half feet tall, probably weighed two seventy-five.

"I don't know the territory so well. Sorry. I'm sure someone inside can help you. I couldn't tell you if they have a map." Right then, the rain poured down in a gusty, sweeping burst, and Joel was drenched in a matter of seconds, before he could react or take cover. His shirt became saturated and translucent, his pants were soaked and the deluge was so fierce he had trouble seeing the man standing next to him.

The huge biker took off his leather hat and tilted his head so the drops hit him in the face. "Damn, that feels good," he yelled. "Bring it on!" He opened his mouth, let the downpour bounce off his tongue and pelt his throat. "Oh, man, what a gully-washer!"

"You have any idea what I could do to get my vehicle going?" Joel asked.

"I'll take a look; you never know." He lifted his shirt and let the rain wash his torso for several moments, then crouched under the hood and squinted at the motor. Water dripped off his nose and chin, and the rain continued to beat him from behind. "Get in and try to fire it up."

Joel got into the car, twisted the ignition and heard only a faint clicking sound.

The biker poked his head around the hood. "Try it again."

Joel did and got the same result. Click-click-click-click.

The man dropped the hood and walked to Joel's door, covering the distance in two gigantic steps. "Starter's history."

"The starter? Is that something you can fix?"

The man smiled, bent closer to the window. His face was dotted with rain, his mustache wet and drawn flat by the weight of the water. "If I had the parts and tools and about an hour to spare, but there ain't no hope for it as things stand right now. Sorry 'bout that."

"You're sure that's the problem? It's not something we can correct?"

"Wish it was." The biker resumed his full height. "Nope, you need a mechanic."

"I just thought, the way you materialized out of nowhere, the coincidence and so forth, like you'd been sent to help me . . . I'd hoped . . . well, I thought things would turn out differently. Better news or something."

"Be glad to let you off somewhere, but that's about the best I can offer."

"Thanks. I'll wait here till the storm passes, then call my sister."

"Good luck, buddy."

"Thanks." Joel extended his hand into the rain and the biker took it. The large man went through a sequence of three grips Joel recalled from high school, started with thumbs entwined and ended with a regular handshake. "How much will the new part cost?"

"Probably find a good rebuilt starter for a hundred-and-fifty or so."

"That wouldn't include installing it, would it?" Joel asked.

"Nope—that'd be for the parts only."

"Well, thanks again. Have a safe trip." Joel rolled up his window and watched the man penetrate the clear torrent, saw him vanish as if he'd punctured a membrane and been sucked from sight. Joel sat in the car for twenty minutes while the rain pounded the sheet metal and the water pooled around the sidewalk drains, then trudged back inside to locate a phone.

Joel was certain his sister wouldn't do it—she'd lecture and rebuke him and consider the request a breach of faith—and that left only one person to ask: Frankie, whom he'd known for all of two weeks. They were loitering next to the dishwasher during a slow spell at the Station, trying to look busy in case Sarah visited the kitchen. It had been an excellent night so far. A boisterous, crew-cut North Carolina deejay named Jack Murphy had enjoyed his meal so much he'd stuck his head in the door, handed the chef a ten and slipped Joel a twenty for the kitchen to divide. A table of tourist fly fishermen, drunk and happy after a successful day on the Bitterroot, had given one of the waitresses a hundred-dollar tip. They'd asked her to paint the town with them, but she had to get home and tend to her child. Better still, the chef had told Frankie that Phil Jackson was coming from Whitefish and would be in Friday with a party of ten. It seemed like as good a time as any to ask, and Joel was not going to have many more opportunities. He waited until Frankie finished wiping the sink with a paper towel, then took a deep breath and tried to sound casual.

"Do you think you could help me with something, Frankie? A small favor?"

"I might. Depends what it is."

"Well, you see, I need a phone number. For a woman who lives in Roanoke, Virginia. I know her parents' number, but I can't call there. I need someone to phone them and get her number, find out where she is. She might be with her parents, but I doubt it. So that would be the favor, calling her house and helping me locate her."

A waitress busted through the door, and both Joel and Frankie turned to look at her.

"Why can't you call?"

Joel put his palms on the lip of the sink and rocked forward. "I'm not supposed to. I can't. Her parents despise me. And to tell you the truth, so you know what you're getting into, I'm court-ordered not to have any contact with her. You should be aware of that. You'd probably need to call from a pay phone and say . . . say . . . you're a friend of hers from the University of Virginia."

"Man." Frankie stroked his goatee. "Huh."

"It would mean a lot to me, but I'll understand if you don't want to become involved."

"Why's it so important to talk to her?"

"To straighten out some business. I give you my word it's nothing bad or threatening." Joel stood up from the sink. "She's filed a lawsuit against me, and I need to know what she's thinking. I'd hoped that if I could talk to her, just the two of us, maybe I could get the situation resolved."

"What's the suit for?"

"For, uh, supposedly having sex with her."

Frankie wrinkled his face. "Like rape or something?"

"Oh no, nothing like that. There was no force or anything."

"So how old is this girl, Joel?"

"She's eighteen or older now. For sure she's at least eighteen." Joel stammered on the last word. It came out "eight-t-teen."

"And you only want to talk to her? You're not stalkin' her or something?"

"I give you my word."

"Hmmm . . ." Frankie was shaping the point of his goatee again. "You seem like a good enough guy, but I don't know. I sure don't need a load of somebody else's police problems dumped on me. Let me think about it."

"Of course, absolutely. I don't mean to pressure you, but I've got to find her real soon. In the next couple days."

"Give me the parents' number, and I'll sleep on it. I want to be a pal and all, but I don't want to do the wrong thing. You understand what I'm sayin'?"

"I do. I can only promise you I'm not out to cause any harm. If I were after her or planning to hurt her, I wouldn't be in Missoula, completely across the country. The girl's name is Christy, Christy Darden."

"Okay." Frankie fumbled with a dish towel. "How old was she when, you know, this stuff between you happened?"

"She was seventeen."

"Damn." He folded the towel in half. "Seventeen."

Joel wasn't sure what to make of his remark, delivered as it was with a blank face and an ambiguous inflection.

Two large tables were seated at seven-thirty, and the kitchen became hectic. Joel took his break at eight, stepping out the rear door with a Pepsi and a small plate of chicken wings. He sat down against the building and placed the food on the ground beside him. It was still bright and hot, the very first hints of night starting to surface in a shadow or two. The city was busy, full of commotion and bustle, and a group of young kids trooped by in front of Joel. Most of them had skateboards, and they all said hello but didn't bother him or act like punks. A man was following behind them, probably fifty yards away, the declining sun over his shoulder.

Joel ate a chicken wing and threw the stripped gray bone onto his plate. The man was much closer now, the gang of teenagers gone from view. Joel cocked his head to swallow his soft drink, caught a snatch of azure sky and rooftops, and when he finished with the Pepsi and leveled his eyes, Edmund Brooks was standing directly in front of him. Edmund looked exceptionally large from Joel's slouched perspective, and he dropped the can, causing a puddle of brown drink to wet his lap. He sprung to his feet and took several frantic swipes at the mess he'd made, tried to clean off the soda before it stained his trousers. "Edmund! Gosh, you startled me."

"Sorry about that, Joel. I hope you're doin' okay." Edmund was wearing a baseball hat, sunglasses and a long-sleeved white shirt. He'd grown a mustache since Joel last saw him, and his sideburns were more pronounced.

Joel felt a flash of fear. He wasn't sure why—it was simply avuncular Edmund, arrived to deliver the goods—but there was something suddenly imposing in the way Edmund had hunted him down and taken him by surprise, his eyes hidden and his face different and shaggy. "I'm fine," Joel said. "Just taking a break from work."

"I can't stay long, my friend." Edmund surveyed the alley, then reached into his pocket and handed Joel a red velvet bag cinched by a yellow cord woven into its top. "Here you go, Joel. You know the plan. Show 'em at the bank in Roanoke, pawn the *small* diamond earrings while you're in Virginia, have everything else insured locally, and make sure the agent takes photos and gives you an appraisal. I'll be here about a week after you get back from Virginia to collect the stones. You gotta work fast."

Joel didn't speak.

"Okay? You're ready, right?"

"Yeah. I suppose. Just the way you appeared without any warning... I'm really anxious, scared some, now that it's actually happening." Joel stuffed the bag in his Pepsi-damp pocket.

"That's natural, Joel. All you need to do is take it easy and follow the plan." Edmund clapped him on the shoulder. "I gotta hit the road. You'll be fine."

"How come you can't give them to me when I get to Roanoke? Wouldn't that be safer?"

"The less time the stuff's in my hands, the better. To be honest, I don't like holdin' 'em, don't like the risk. If I was caught with this kinda stash . . . Well, suffice it to say I don't have any wiggle room in the insurance business. Also, as insignificant as it may seem now, I don't even want to be *near* Roanoke while you're there showin' off stones and hocking diamonds. If the plan—God forbid—should ever go south, I'm checked into the Golden Nugget miles and miles away, and we eliminate one possible link. On top of that, hell, if you get stopped or inspected, you can simply stick to the plan, say you're transportin' your mother's jewelry. I don't have the same luxury."

"Oh."

"Good luck, Joel." Edmund adjusted his cap and tramped off with his head bowed, his shoulders rounded forward and his arms tucked against his sides, a winter walk almost, like he was pushing into a cold, mean wind.

Joel kept the bag in his pocket while he worked, didn't take it out until he'd returned to the basement. He was nervous and jumpy carrying the jewelry around the kitchen, would pat his thigh from time to time to check the lump in his pants and talked more than he ordinarily did, told Frankie a rambling story about Baker finding Tut's hen and her seven off-white eggs. The house was asleep when he arrived home, and Joel was especially careful to keep quiet as he crept through the kitchen and down the stairs. He got on his knees beside the bed and shook the bag until it was empty. Rings, fantastic brooches, several necklaces, three pairs of diamond earrings, bracelets and an elaborate stick pin spilled onto the thin counterpane, the necklaces coiled and wound like red, green and white snakes, the rings sparkling and vibrant even in the dull cellar light. "Oh my," he whispered. Like a goofy teenager, he collected the baubles and hid them underneath his mattress, then tossed and turned for most of the night above someone else's extravagant wealth.

The next afternoon, Frankie was already at work when Joel arrived. He reached into his shirt pocket and offered Joel an opened, empty envelope that was folded in half. The envelope was from the power company, addressed to Frankie Jamison. Joel glanced at the envelope, then looked at Frankie.

"It's on the front," Frankie said. "Hell, I just stopped on the way here and called for you. That's all I had to write on."

Joel found the number on the other side of the envelope, tore it off, put the scrap of paper in his wallet and tossed the remainder into the trash can. "Thanks, Frankie. Thank you."

"No problem."

"What do I owe you for the call?" Joel asked.

"Not a thing."

"You're sure?"

"Yep," Frankie said.

"I hope I can do something to return the favor."

"Maybe," Frankie replied. "Don't worry about it though."

"How did everything go? Any problems?"

"Shit, what time is it, Joel? Like not even four here. So I called a few minutes ago and it's six-something in the East, and the mother is already snockered, all slurred and talkative."

Joel grinned. "Mrs. Darden likes her toddy."

"I'll say." Frankie unbuttoned his cuffs and started adjusting his sleeves, getting ready to stick his arms in the sink and scrub dirty dishes. "She was a trip."

"Did she want to know why you were calling?"

"Not really. I told her I was a friend from school, and the old bag was smashed and not too curious. But here's the problem, Joel. Your girl Christy's still living with mom and dad. She's leaving soon for college at Sweet Briar—I think I got the name right—but she's bunkin' with her folks for the short term. I was scared to death they were going to put her on the phone, but lucky for me, she was 'out for the evening.' " Frankie mimicked Mrs. Darden's haughty, intoxicated voice.

"Huh. I thought she'd be staying somewhere else. Sorry to put you on the spot—I'd have never guessed she'd be living at home. I believe I mentioned she *could* be there, but I'd have bet against it." Joel paused long enough to read Frankie's scribbling. "So what's this number you gave me?"

Frankie allowed a smile to come and go. "That, Joel, would be her private line. Like the Bat Phone or the hotline to the Kremlin, those digits will take you directly to her and bypass the drunken mom and pistol-packin' papa."

"I see. Good." Joel nodded his head several times. "I'm grateful."

"Glad to help. I hope things turn out okay for you."

"I'm optimistic," Joel said. He gave Frankie a quick shrug. "Who knows, huh?"

"I'm pulling for you. I'm not certain what you're after, but I hope you get it."

"What convinced you to help me?" Joel asked.

Both Frankie's sleeves were folded into neat, round bands at his elbows. His hair was pulled into a ponytail, held tight with a red rubber band looped three times. "No real reason, Joel. You've got a good vibe, and it kinda hit me when I was driving in that I believed what you told me, and I didn't see how I could get in trouble even if things go sour. Lots of times I just do shit on impulse, without wasting a lot of energy agonizing over it. I think that's the way of the world—people don't put a lot of thought into half the junk they do."

"Amen," Joel said, and then realized he didn't exactly hold with what Frankie was saying. He raised his index finger and pursed his lips. "Although there are people who plot and scheme and take everything apart and plan to the smallest detail. Some people are very calculating, some very rash."

Frankie had turned his back and was standing over the sink spraying the first plate of the night. "You can have all the plannin' in the world, but when it comes time to jump, to do the deed, it's mostly a matter of checking the wind and takin' a deep breath. Most of the time you don't actually know how things will end up."

Joel had mentioned when he was hired that he would need to miss a day or two of work in the near future and had alerted Ralph the moment he'd received the exact date for his deposition. He'd leave on Sunday, return late Monday and be at the Station for his regular Tuesday shift. Dixon Kreager—who'd hired him on a handshake after the audition at the Clark Fork—had agreed to let him have the weekend free, even though it meant Dixon himself would have to fill in on the river and baby-sit a novice from Sacramento. When Joel's night ended on Friday, he thanked Frankie again for his help, said goodbye to the waitresses, wished George the chef a pleasant weekend and walked to the front of the Station to remind Sarah he'd be gone when the new week commenced.

"Gone?" she said. She was seated at the bar, tapping numbers into an old electric adding machine, the paper tape inching out the top each time she hit a key. She didn't take her eyes off her duties while she spoke to Joel.

"Yes. To Virginia."

"Whatever happened to two weeks' notice?" The machine made several zipping, mechanical sounds, and the tape grew incrementally longer.

"Pardon?"

She stopped her tally and smacked Joel with a withering stare. "How am

I supposed to run a restaurant when you people quit me with no warning? You think I can get someone else here and trained by Monday?"

The bartender finished loading beer into the cooler, glanced at Sarah and disappeared.

"Oh, I'm not quitting. I'll only be gone a day. I told Ralph when I was hired I'd need the time. I mentioned it to him again not long ago, and he assured me there wouldn't be a problem. And then I reminded him on Wednesday."

"Ralph. You told Ralph?"

"Yeah."

Sarah flung her hands. "When did you inform *me*? Huh? Who do you think really manages this place and does the schedule? How many times have you seen our boy Ralph in here doing anything helpful?"

"I'm sorry. I thought he was my boss. I didn't mean to leave you in a bind. I'm assuming this is news to you, huh?" Joel couldn't look at her. He studied the floor and shuffled his feet. "I apologize."

"Of course Ralph didn't tell me. And why shouldn't you have a vacation, Joel? You must be exhausted after putting in two or three weeks."

Joel was in no mood to quarrel. "It's not a vacation," he said quietly. "Far from it. From now on, I'll make sure you are the first to know my plans. I'm sorry about the confusion. I've tried to be a good employee and handle this the right way."

"Great," she snorted.

"I'll see you Tuesday." Joel caught her eye. "Okay?"

She began working the machine again. "I won't hold my breath."

He lingered for a second or two longer than he needed to, watched her flip a ledger sheet and search for a number near the end of the tape. The thought had been in the corner of his mind when he went looking for her that he might be able to ask how she was doing or visit for a while or share some leftovers from the chef's special. This was not the night for any of that, but it was nice to have an interest, something to keep him going.

eight

The next day was Saturday, and Joel was awake early. Tut was atop the lawnmower shed's tin roof, his head jaunty and his yellow beak cracked open, crowing for all he was worth, the cries loud and rapid and piercing. Joel drove down the gravel entrance onto the main road, then five miles to a large convenience store to buy food for breakfast. On the way, he slowed to watch three horses, a big Appaloosa and two paints, loping and kicking in a pasture, their flanks embroidered with raised muscle as they glided across the grass. Twice the Appaloosa pinned his ears, and one of the other horses leaped and bucked in the App's direction, came off the ground with all four hooves. The horses were beside a ramshackle house, corralled by a makeshift fence that was part wire and part board, and two white pails were near the fence's rusted gate, the smaller one tipped on its side. The day was splendid, the road deserted, the sky flawless, the tops of the ponderosa pines and cottonwoods petted by an occasional breeze. September was waiting in the wings, and the morning was brisk, close to cold.

Joel bought a dozen eggs, bacon, biscuits in a soft cardboard can, a tomato, strawberry jelly, orange juice and a box of chocolate Pop-Tarts for Baker, and he'd been back home for an hour when Sophie wandered into the kitchen at eight thirty, wearing a football jersey that covered her knees and a pair of gray wool socks with red rings around the tops. He fixed her a full breakfast while she lounged at the table, and they talked about old times and Sophie's first dog, a crazy cur named Luther who could walk on his hind legs across the living room floor. She let Baker sleep, was grateful for the quiet and her brother's generosity. After Joel drained the grease from the frying pan and washed and stored the dishes, he poured himself another glass of juice and rejoined Sophie at the table.

"I need to talk with you," he said.

His somber tone immediately caused her to constrict her face and bunch her lips. "I should have known this was too good to be true. I'm guessing one of three things: you lost your job, you need money, or you're in trouble with the law again."

Joel placed his hand on top of his sister's. "Why do you think it's going to be bad?"

"Experience." She slid her hand out from beneath Joel's and jumped her chair farther away from the table. "So what is it?"

"I need to tell you something. It's not bad unless you assume the worst."

"Why do I feel like I've been bribed, like you were greasing the skids with all this breakfast hoopla?" She sighed. "And things were going pretty well here, too."

Joel maneuvered his chair closer to the table, until the wooden edge was touching his stomach. "I made you breakfast because I wanted to, and because I got paid last night and had a little cash. Calm down—it's nothing terrible. In fact, it's far more good than negative."

Sophie didn't speak. She lifted her legs, drew her thighs against her chest and bundled her shins inside her arms, balled herself into a flesh-and-bone fortress, her chin on her knees.

"Okay," he said, "here it is. When I get to Roanoke, I'm going to meet with Christy before my deposition. I called her last night and made the arrangements. No one knows except you."

"Are you just plain fucking stupid, Joel? Are you?" She didn't raise her voice, but the skin in her face was stretched so taut Joel thought her jawbone might tear through. "It's like you're on dope or something. Amazing."

"Listen to me before you fly off the handle. I just need to talk to her, and I'm meeting her at Tanglewood Mall, in the food court upstairs. A public place. I wanted to tell you in advance, so if something goes wrong it won't seem as if I was being sneaky."

"Talk about what, Joel? Sorority rush or when she gets her braces removed or what's hot in back-to-school fashion? Talk? She's a child."

"I'm going to discuss the case with her. I want to get to the bottom of this and try to keep her from taking the church's money. And . . . well, there's a lot nagging and biting at me. I need to fill in some blanks."

"Why? What good will it do? This is the girl you screwed when she was a minor. The girl who ruined your career and your marriage."

"I didn't have intercourse with her," Joel said. "And *I* ruined my career and marriage, not Christy."

"Say that again."

"You heard me."

"I thought I heard you say you didn't have sex with her. That's what I heard. That's why I want you to repeat it. Maybe say it fifty or sixty times, so I can be sure."

Joel plopped his elbows onto the table, craned his neck. "I didn't have intercourse with Christy Darden."

"Why do you want to sit there and lie to me, Joel? Don't disgrace yourself or make this worse than it already is. Hell, I can't stop you from seeing her."

"I'm not lying, Sophie. Would you hear me out? Let me finish?"

She blew a long exhalation, held her hands above her head, palms up. "Sure. Go ahead. Tell me." She lowered her arms.

"Okay." Joel wiggled in his chair and shoved away from the table. "I . . . I never actually had sex with Christy. Never had intercourse—"

"Thank goodness you didn't say 'with *that woman,*'" she interrupted.

Joel ploughed ahead, determined to finish his story. "I never had intercourse, okay? In fact, in one sense, I did very little. The popular term is 'heavy petting'."

"Are you serious, Joel? I don't understand what you're saying."

"What I did with Christy was wrong and terrible, but I'm not the ogre everyone thinks. Well, that some people think."

"As I recall, you admitted being an ogre, went to jail for it and threw your life away."

"Christy was assigned to the church to do community-service work. She was in dutch with the juvenile court system, was supposed to clean toilets and scrub floors and mow the grass. She was also directed to meet with me once a week for counseling. Most of the time she did absolutely nothing, leaned on a broom or smoked marijuana in the fellowship hall. I never caught her using drugs, but I could smell it and her eyes looked stoned almost every day. The place would have been filthy if we'd actually counted on her to keep things tidy. She didn't set foot in my office bathroom for over a month and looked stricken when I suggested she take a bag of trash to the landfill."

Sophie unwound herself, stood and started toward the coffee pot. "Keep going, I'm listening." Her tone was noncommittal.

"She spent more and more time hanging around, talking with me. She got credit with the court for the 'counseling,' and it beat doing any real work. She is—and I have to say this, even though you'll shudder—a beautiful, lovely girl."

Sophie had poured half a cup and left it black. She was back in her seat, facing her brother. "It's only sad and typical, Joel. Sad doesn't rate a shudder. Creepy gets a shudder—when you start describing her perfect alabaster feet, or how innocent she looked in her schoolgirl uniform, that's when I'll shudder."

"Her uniform was hip-huggers, high heels and a push-up bra, as best I can recall."

"Ah."

"At any rate, she's spending a lot of time in the office. She's pretty. She's very aggressive for her age, very flirtatious."

"Tell me again how old this seductress was?" Sophie said.

"Seventeen. And I was old enough to be her father—I'll save you the rhetorical effort."

"Thanks."

"I was a hundred percent wrong in letting matters get out of control. She flattered me, and I was vain. She tempted me, and I was weak. Probably five days a month, I'm sitting in my study with this attractive girl who's wearing halter tops and short-shorts, and she's talking about sex, my eyes, how she wants to kiss me just one time." Joel paused, licked his lips. "About ninety-five percent of life is not doing the things you have an urge to do. Keeping your head in the foxhole and avoiding trouble. Sin can be glorious fun in the short term—that's why it's such good bait."

"Jeez, Joel. That's a sanitized way of saying you wanted to screw a teenager."

"But here's my point: I never did. One afternoon, we sat on the sofa at my office and kissed until I finally asked her to leave. Two days later, she's there again and we . . . uh . . . we sort of do the same thing, this time a little more involved. And I can't lie, Sophie—I liked it. It was so . . . I can't give you the exact word, but to kiss someone and not know how it would feel, how it might turn out, what to expect . . . All the newness and excitement and—"

"Spare me the mad-love spiel," Sophie said. "Otherwise, I'll puke. I'll puke all over the kitchen. I like the basic version better: Most sorry men would delight in screwing a child, and most men are sorry."

"I'm not saying I was justified or anything. I'm merely trying to explain *why* it happened. Here's the good news, Sophie. That's the end of the story. Some kissing, and I stuck my hands inside her bra on the second occasion. There was never sex or nakedness or sneaking into hotels. The last time, I stopped and told her she'd have to go. She came back the next day, of course, and I explained to her I'd asked to be forgiven and that I couldn't see her anymore. I gave her another minister's name to help with the counseling. Oh—I apologized, too. Said I was sorry."

Sophie began rubbing small circles around her temples, squirmed in her chair. She was sitting normally now, both feet touching the ground. "This doesn't make sense. What are you conveniently forgetting?"

"That's the story. The whole truth."

"Then why, Joel, did you lose your job and your marriage? You've got to be omitting *something*. Got to be." She still had her fingers against her temples, but the circles had ceased.

"I've told you everything," he said.

"Okay, so tell me how you got from there to here. Why did you go to jail? Why did Martha divorce you? Why didn't you fight the charges? Why wait till now to tell me this version?"

"Let me give you a preface that'll make this easier to understand. When I was in divinity school, I had a professor by the name of Amos Stone. He was a take-no-prisoners Baptist, had wild, flamboyant eyebrows and a big round head with two white clumps of Bozo hair, bald on top. Had the ear thickets, too, bristles like you wouldn't believe." Joel paused, allowed himself a smile. "Dr. Stone—we called him Dr. *Brim*stone—taught Old Testament in the days before the church became concerned about membership drives and giving totals. Nowadays, we're so worried about getting people in the door, we deliver them a religion without any sting or grit. We never castigate anybody, never step on toes because we're afraid the banker or car dealer or canning-factory heir will take offense and spread their coin elsewhere, and there'll be no dollars for the splashy buses or the hotel-size addition. People make fun of the obsolete pulpit-thumpers who lit you up, pointed fingers, spewed damnation and spelled out the price you pay for stepping over the line. It's all so much nicer now, but the truth's the truth. Congregations these days want to do exactly as they please and have us validate it. We're the church of accommodation and sycophancy and scented candles."

"Is this going somewhere, Joel? I really don't give a hoot about church doctrine. And I hope you don't expect me to sit here while you preen through a twenty-minute sermon."

"I'm almost there."

"Preachers love to hear themselves talk, don't they?" she said, the glimmer of a grin underneath the jab. "Do you even remember what I asked you?"

"Sure, and I'm answering you. We used to have these highbrow ethics debates in Dr. Stone's class. You know—is stealing justifiable to feed your starving kids? If you knew your unborn child would grow up to be Hitler, is abortion acceptable? Topics like that."

"Important, real-world concerns. I understand. It's why you guys are so good at your jobs and have so much to offer." Sophie finished her coffee and set the empty white cup on the table. There was a lukewarm spot of brown remaining in the bottom.

"I don't want to get sidetracked, but I'm flat weary of people taking shots at us for addressing tough issues and actually believing in something other than smart-mouth skepticism."

"You holy men bring a lot of it on yourselves, Joel. What's the great Rita Mae Brown line—if God's so smart, then why does he hire such bad help?"

"We're not perfect, okay? At least we try." Joel locked Sophie in a stare, daring her to push him any farther.

"Okay," she said. "Forget I said it."

"There are missionaries rocking famished babies, and priests who've treated sin and distress for thirty years still living in a freezing room with a hard bed. There are soup kitchens and food pantries and shelters and day-care centers and vacation Bible schools—a whole empire of charity and compassion supported by people of faith. Do you really want to discount all that and poke fun at millions of honest, devout people because a few cads and charlatans dishonor the pulpit? Beat on your chest because you believe in nothing?"

"I said okay, Joel. I do believe in God. I just haven't made a career out of it."

Joel stayed stiff, remained silent long enough to let her know he was distressed. He finally leveled one last stern glare at her. "Anyway, we'd have these rip-roaring debates, and at the end old Dr. Brimstone would yank off his glasses and give us the same speech. You don't get to average good and evil, he'd say, don't earn the Lord's blessing if your deeds tip the scales a tad in your favor, don't get to choose the middle road or the gray solution. There's the straight, correct, narrow route, and the rest is just plain heathen mischief. There is no alloy in righteousness, no shades and degrees in morality." Joel recited the words with conviction, his eyes animated and earnest.

"That's bullshit, Joel. It's a fine story, and you preach it well, but things aren't quite so simple as you make them out to be. The world isn't black-and-white, though life would be easier if it were." Sophie toyed with her coffee cup, rotated the handle until it pointed toward Joel. She peered at him without speaking and did her best to read his expression. "But you truly believe your own nonsense, don't you?" she said after studying him.

"Yeah." The answer came out hoarse. "I do."

"And where does this take us, Joel? I'm still not sure what you're trying to get at."

"Well, what I did was wrong. And wrong is wrong—it's an either-or situation. There's no such creature as a minor sin. I believe that, and I deserved punishment. Bad conduct invites suffering, right? Not much room for dispute there."

"So you make a mistake and then simply surrender for the remainder of your life? Touching a breast is the same as axe murder?"

"My particular mischief left me without any options. Once Christy told her parents and the police became involved, what could I do? I mean, what's my defense? Ethically and practically, I'm dead in the water. I could lie and fight to keep my job or just leave. You can bet the ranch that if I admitted to necking with a teenager, I'd be tarred and feathered and chased out of Roanoke on a rail. So my only choice was to lie—to the police, to my church and to my wife. I couldn't do that. Also, if I tried to save my own skin by attacking Christy's honesty, I would split my church apart and polarize my congregation, become a distraction. So I was stuck with the consequences of my misdeeds, unless I wanted to up the ante and add more wrongs to my list."

Sophie crossed her legs and adjusted her socks. "From what I understand, your lying options were pretty limited, weren't they, Joel? Didn't they have DNA evidence against you? Correct? Pretty difficult to bob and weave past the guys in thick glasses and white coats, huh? Which brings us back to square one. You screwed a child and couldn't lie your way free."

"I'm still puzzled by the tests. I can't solve that part," Joel said, "and it's worrying me to death."

"No kidding."

"I've considered a number of possibilities. Her father is wealthy and well connected, so perhaps he used his influence. Or maybe the police set me up."

"Or maybe it was the CIA, or Mossad, or the black-helicopter operatives, or the same people who nailed Princess Di and Dodi. What about the Queen of England? Remember how she brought down Lyndon LaRouche? Give me a break, Joel. The police framed you?"

"It's also possible the lab made a mistake. They're not infallible." Joel was agitated again, rushed his words. "You read about legal errors all the time. Heck, people are set free from death row."

"Yeah, Joel, they're set free because the science proves their *innocence*. Not exactly your case, is it?"

"Well, whatever. I didn't have intercourse with her. I didn't. Period. The tests are wrong or fixed or bought and paid for." He paused, slowed his speech. "I know this is difficult to accept, given the facts against me."

"We're dangerously close to the Richard Pryor defense, Joel. Remember the routine? Man's wife catches him in bed with another woman, and the man says to his wife as she stands there looking at him and his girlfriend: 'So who you gonna believe, me or your lyin' eyes?' "

"I hadn't heard that one. But I take your point." He grinned, attempting to lighten the mood. "Here I am reciting theology, and you're quoting a lesbian author and a drug-ravaged comedian. Nice."

"Yeah, well, I guess Hell will have an unrivaled variety show." She smirked at him. "So why did you go to jail if you weren't guilty? Why plead guilty?"

"I am guilty of *something*. And what chance did I have in court? I get on the stand and say I simply kissed her, touched her breasts? Lot of good that would do me—who'll believe that story? And the prosecutor would make it sound really sick and stunted, use the word 'fondle' a million times. Even my own lawyer didn't think I was being truthful. Plus he tells me some of the men on the jury will think I'm a loser for *not* having sex with her, conclude I'm some kind of troll or pervert and lower the boom. Don't ask me to explain the logic there. Also, they threatened to charge me with rape, forcible rape, a felony, up to life in prison, and who knows what crazy Christy might say. Would you take that gamble, see what's behind door number two? Risk going to trial? I don't think so. And even if they believed my version, I could still be guilty of 'taking indecent liberties,' which is also a felony—or so my attorney told me. In the end I took the safe, certain deal. It's not unfair I was jailed because of what I did. It's just how I got there that's so vexing."

"And of course you spared your church the pain of a nasty battle. Fell on your sword for the benefit of Roanoke First Baptist."

"To some extent," Joel said. "It was a consideration."

"What about Martha? I'm supposed to believe she left you over a few kisses and a sofa grope?"

Joel was silent. He looked around the kitchen and out the window over the sink, then at the floor. There was a hint of collapse in his eyes and mouth, trembles and strains that threatened to spread and crumble his face. He made a gulping noise, shook his head and buried himself into his palms. He sat there concealed behind his hands for several minutes, said nothing, didn't stir. When he finally uncovered his face, a slight tear had formed and was ready to break loose on his cheek. "I, uh, wasn't honest when she first asked me. She blindsided me at breakfast one morning, said she'd heard rumors, and I denied everything. What an idiot, huh? When I tried to tell her the truth, I had no credibility. Then she gets wind of the test results. She believes to this day that I committed adultery. I begged and pleaded and apologized and did everything in my power to convince her otherwise, but I just didn't have much to work with. I should've been truthful from the git-go." He dabbed the corner of his eye.

"I don't know, Joel. I just don't know." Sophie sawed her teeth along her bottom lip. "Why'd you wait so long to explain this to me?"

"I shouldn't have," he said. "And I sort of mentioned it when you were berating me about the kitchen fire."

"Yeah."

"You don't believe me either, do you?" he asked.

She stared at her white cup.

"Sophie?"

"I see the wisdom of Dr. Stone's theory," she said cryptically. "What else can I tell you?"

"I don't follow you."

"Let me put it like this. You know how people say that things aren't always as they seem? Well—"

"Exactly. That's my point. It looks bad for me, looks—"

"Hush, Joel. Listen to me. Things aren't always as they seem. It's just the case about ninety-nine percent of the time. Like when I mentioned to one of my friends I suspected Neal was having an affair, and she told me I had to trust him, that things aren't always as they seem."

"Well, you'll see soon enough. I have a plan, a way to redeem myself."

Christy sashayed into the Tanglewood Mall food court fifteen minutes late. She was dressed in a short top and low-riding pants that missed her belly button by two inches of bare skin. She was wearing tiny blue sunglasses and had a red and purplish dragonfly tattooed on her forearm. A man eating a pizza slice spied on her over the top of his magazine, and two young boys with voluminous, knee-length shorts were trailing along behind her, laughing and elbow-poking each other. A husband and wife followed her as she passed their table, their heads shifting in unison, their stares absolute ice and disdain. They stopped chewing and eating, watched Christy until she flounced in beside Joel at an orange table with four black chairs. The couple transferred their stares to Joel, bore down on him for an instant, then returned to their food.

Christy immediately unnerved Joel when she sat beside him instead of taking a seat across the table. He noticed her hair was longer and seemed lighter, perhaps from the summer sun. He said hello, took a sweeping look around the mall. His stomach was queasy, his eyes were blinking too quickly and his breathing was erratic, a string of staccato fits that shorted his lungs. It was Sunday, the dog days of August in Virginia, and he had traveled directly from the airport to the mall, still had his unpacked bag and a sheaf of legal papers and someone else's expensive jewelry in his rented turquoise Neon.

"Kiss me," Christy said as soon as Joel had croaked his nervous hello. She scooted closer to him and swung her legs so their knees hit. "I'm, like, thrilled to see you. I couldn't believe it when you called."

"Okay. Slow down." Joel rearranged his legs and sat formally in his chair. "It's nice to see you, too."

"A cheek kiss, like friends do."

"I can't kiss you, Christy. I tried to make the purpose of our meeting clear when we spoke."

She didn't change her expression. "So where do you want to go? I wish you could've been here last night. There was a superb bash at the lake. A huge boat tie-up and major alcohol, but I couldn't totally focus on the party because I was so excited about you coming to see me. The adrenaline kept smotherin' my buzz."

"Do you want something to eat?" Joel asked.

"Do you?"

"I thought maybe I'd try the Chinese."

"Let's go somewhere else. This place is so lame. It's not even the good mall."

"It's good enough. May I get something for you?"

"Let's go to Fiji Island, how about that? They have the best shrimp and lobster sauce and a cool bar with these kick-ass drinks in hurricane glasses."

"We need to stay right here. Do you want something or not?"

"A diet Coke. If that's not available, bottled water, but only if the label is predominately blue."

"Okay." Joel went to the cashier and ordered a combination plate with an egg roll and two diet Cokes. While the lady behind the counter was piling food onto a stiff, white disposable plate, a girl stopped to visit with Christy. Before she left, she and Christy both looked in Joel's direction, and he turned and pretended to be studying the packets of sauce and plastic forks next to the cash register.

"Who was she?" Joel asked when he returned to the table. He sat down opposite Christy.

"Why don't you sit over here?" she asked.

"Not a good idea."

"Do you think I'm gross or something?"

"No, I don't. Who was your friend?"

"Jan. We were in high school together. We're really not friends. I just know her."

"Oh." Joel sipped his drink and spun lo mein noodles onto his fork.

"I guess you're, like, really pissed at me, huh?"

He rested his fork on the side of his plate, left the noodles wound around the prongs. "I'm a little confused. And upset—that would be fair to say."

"I don't really want to talk about where we've been, you know? Can't we just disappear for a while, maybe get a cold case and some quality pot and go to the coast, stay high and mellow. I mean, I know you're not into partying, and you don't have to stay fucked up and all. I just want to hang out. I really like you, Joel. And I know it's probably infatuation and you're too old and you'll be limp-dicked and liver-spotted when I'm in my thirties, but why not catch the moment?"

"There's no good in it, Christy. None at all. Simple as that."

"Shit." She opened her drink, and the metallic click and carbonated hissing seemed loud, magnified.

"So why this lawsuit and the exaggerations, the falsehoods? Why are you doing this?"

"I don't want to talk about it."

"I'll certainly admit my wrongs. And I apologize. Again. I'm truly sorry. I've been punished, and I deserve what I got. I've lost my job and my wife—my fault. But you're suing the church for five million bucks. Their insurance won't cover the whole claim, Christy. They're a million dollars short, and I'm on the hook for the same million. As I understand it, you could ruin our church, take its assets, property, building funds, everything. I'm not saying you don't deserve something, not saying that at all. Millions of dollars, though, for what we did?"

"I have a friend from AA who has this hooked-up house at the lake. She said we could hang there tonight if we wanted to. Let's just banish the mall and spend time together. We can do whatever you want."

"We're doing it," Joel replied.

"If I talk about the legal shit, will you go to the lake with me? To my friend's house?"

"We'll see."

"No. You've got to swear."

"I can't make any promises," he said.

"What do you want to know?" She sunk into her chair, deflated herself and pitched her head forward so her hair curtained off most of her face. "I can't believe you're, like, forcing me to do this. It's extremely daunting and thoughtless."

"No it's not. Quit being a brat, Christy."

"You realize I really have a thing for you, right? I think you're so superb." She poured most of the Coke into a waxy paper cup.

"I appreciate your telling me. I'm flattered." Joel had calmed down and recaptured his senses. "But what's the story, Christy? I'd love to know."

"Know what?"

"Why did you do this to me?"

"Why do you think?" Her features were almost completely obscured by her hair and the tilt of her head.

"I have no idea. I truly don't. I've assumed for a long while you did it because you were angry with me, because I stopped what we were doing and you felt hurt, or rejected."

Christy took hold of the Coke can but left it on the orange Formica. She scrubbed the can back and forth in no particular pattern, the aluminum bottom and tabletop scraping out obnoxious, random noise. She didn't seem inclined to answer, kept moving the Coke and stayed withdrawn into her chair.

"Or I thought it was possible you told a friend who told a friend and word got round to your parents, and they were behind the suit. No offense, but you don't seem like someone who would dig in and pursue a court case and demand that I go to jail. I would've thought you'd just shrug and laugh and trot off to the next party."

Christy stuck her hair behind her ears, cleared her face. She was still slouched in her chair, but she'd stopped scratching the can all over the table. "Well, I wish it hadn't gotten so complicated. I *was* mad when you were mean to me and led me on and then dumped me, but I didn't see any of this coming. I feel so bad. I want you to know none of this is what I expected."

"How could that possibly be true? What did you *think* was going to happen? At one point, my lawyer's telling me you said I raped you. Did you say that?"

"Only for an hour or two."

"Only for an hour or two?" The anger caused Joel's voice to boil. "Why?"

"I don't know. I shouldn't have."

"You know I never did anything close to that. Never. What were you thinking, Christy?"

"I'm sorry."

"Did you report me? Did someone find out? I mean, how did this even get started?" Joel had completely neglected his food. The fork was still balanced on the edge of his plate, cocooned in a swirl of noodles.

"Here's all I'm gonna say. And after this I'm not sayin' another word. Right now everybody's leaning on me, and I can't stand it. I feel like I'm going to explode and die at any second. When I first got the idea, I never knew how shitty this would be for you, how everything would crash on your head. It was explained to me I could collect some major dollars, and I figured I'd finally be out from under my heinous parents' reign of terror. I could have my own money without any strings and not have to beg cash from Mom and Dad. That's why I did it, Joel, okay? The dollars. Are you happy now?"

"Explained? By whom? The lawyers? What do you mean?"

Christy inserted an imaginary key into her lips, twisted it and chucked it over her shoulder.

"But you'll admit we never had intercourse, right? We never had sex. I just want to hear you say it, say you fabricated almost everything. I would appreciate that small courtesy." He was trying to sound natural, trying to keep his voice consistent and his eyes from derailing. He inched closer to the table, closer to Christy, and he moved his arms to the side so they wouldn't block the tape recorder. "You know we never actually had intercourse." He was pressing some, estimated he had about fifteen minutes remaining on the cassette. He was postured like a proud bird, his arms pulled back and his chest shoved forward, the recorder aimed straight at her.

"What difference does it make?"

"Would you simply admit it? Tell the truth? Give me a whiff of decency?"

"I'm through talkin' about it."

"Just tell me," he pleaded. "Why can't you give me some tiny satisfaction after everything you've done?" His voice was stressed, corroded at the end of every word.

"Let's go to the lake. You promised."

"Not until you admit to me how you've lied about our having sex."

The recognition first appeared as a small jolt in her mouth, then swamped her face and limbs. She pushed off the armrests with both hands and sprang out of her seat, flew completely across the table. She slapped Joel's food onto the floor, backhanded the plate before he knew what was happening. "You motherfucker. You *motherfucker*. You're trying to get over on me. You've got a wire, don't you? Don't you, asshole?"

Joel recoiled when she hurtled across the table, and his hands were raised stick-up style, as if someone were pointing a gun in his direction. "Let me explain." His Chinese food was strewn along the floor, a trail of noodles, rice, green peas, sauce, chicken and broccoli. A boy in a McDonald's uniform stopped what he was doing, froze with a scoop of fries in one hand and an empty bag in the other. Every diner, every passerby, every worker, every teenager and every shopkeeper rubbernecked to get a view of the girl climbing over a table, her pants revealing too much flesh when she erupted, her mouth spouting profanity.

Instead of retreating, Christy crowded Joel more. Her knees were in her chair, and she was balancing herself on one arm. "Where is it, you piece of shit?" She searched his shirt pocket, then grabbed it and ripped one side from the rest of the fabric.

Joel knew he had to leave. He flashed on his cell, imagined himself returning to jail for another six months because he'd violated his probation. He bounced his chair back and bolted, didn't say another word. She crawled over the table and followed after him. He kept a lookout for mall security and familiar faces, fell into a hasty walk that quickly became a jog, hurried down a flight of stairs to the ground level, then past a shoe store and a tuxedoed mannequin in the window of a haberdashery. He rounded a corner, Christy right behind him, shouting his name, calling him an asshole. Two old ladies in walking shoes and wind suits interrupted their loop around the mall and watched the commotion, the taller of the two yelling "What's going on?" when Joel sprinted by them.

He made it outside and changed speeds, slowed. From behind, Christy took a wild, running swing at him, missed, then seized his shirt collar and yanked.

"Stop it, Christy. Just stop it." His voice was raspy, his air blocked by the cloth pulled tight against his windpipe.

"Give it to me."

"Okay. Let me go."

"You are *such* a bastard." She had moved partially to his side but still had his collar. Her face was an angry, contorted knot.

"Let me go, please. Let's keep walking and not make this any worse than it already is." He took a step and heard the stitches in his shirt stretch and tear.

"Give it to me right now."

He tried to walk but couldn't shake loose from Christy's grip without catching her arm. He was afraid to touch her, didn't want to get into a full-blown fight. "Take your hands off me and I will. Please."

Three teenagers passed them, then a young husband and wife, and the man stopped and asked if everything was all right. His wife stood at his side, her arm around his waist, her expression anxious and wide-eyed.

"Go the fuck on," Christy snapped. "Keep your nose out of other people's business."

"So you're okay?" he asked.

"Super." She loosened her stranglehold and gave Joel slack.

"Okay, then." They glanced back several times as they scurried to their car, and the man took out a cell phone as soon as he got inside.

"I'm sorry," Joel said. "Would you let me explain?"

She released his collar. "Give me the fucking tape. I know you're trying to trap me. You don't give it to me right now, I'll rip your fuckin' clothes off and raise so much hell every cop in Roanoke will be here. I don't think you want to get sent to jail again for not stayin' away from me."

Joel unbuttoned his shirt. He'd bought a small recorder and a roll of duct tape at the Wal-Mart in Missoula. The recorder was fastened over his sternum, held in place by two silver bands of tape ringing his trunk. "There you go. Could we keep moving? The gentleman who just tried to help is calling the police." Joel pointed at the man and his wife. He could see the man through the car window, holding the phone in one hand and waving the other while he reported what he'd witnessed.

The machine was still running, two plastic wheels rolling the last moments of tape from one spindle to another, the play and record buttons engaged, pressed even with the side of the recorder. Christy grabbed it and ripped it from the silver strips. "I can't believe you'd do such an evil thing."

"I don't feel bad about it. I was trying to protect myself and the church from what *you*'ve done. And I don't know why you're having such a fit—there's nothing damaging to you on the tape."

"You were trying to trick me," she said.

"You're right, I was. But you've been tricking a few people yourself, Christy."

"No I haven't." Once the device was in her hand, her wrath seemed to turn to disappointment. Her shoulders sagged, and she hesitated when

Joel began a purposeful walk to his car. "Joel?" She took a step toward the parking lot but didn't go after him. "Joel? Shit. Are you just going to, like, abandon me here after treating me so rudely?"

He was standing at the edge of the curb, where the cement turned to asphalt, waiting for a line of cars to pass. He noticed a cigarette butt and a wad of pink gum in the gutter, and he started speaking before he turned around to face Christy. "I'm sorry to have upset you. I hope you'll give some thought to what you're about to do. Lying is wrong. Destroying a church is wrong. Hurting innocent people for a few dollars is downright shameful. Try to be fair tomorrow."

She took a few halting steps closer, seemed uncertain, stranded between ire and sorrow. "Are you really leaving? All you wanted was to talk about the stupid church and court junk? Why can't you spend time with me?"

The traffic had passed and the route was clear. Joel hitched his trousers and headed for the Neon. He considered saying goodbye but decided against it.

"Joel, come back. Joel . . ."

He could tell she was moving by the sound of her voice, getting nearer, but he didn't speak, had nothing else to say. His shirt was unbuttoned, the dead summer air hot against his belly. The two silver bands of tape were still stuck to him, torn in the middle where Christy had wrenched out the tape recorder. He felt oddly composed, his mind settled, his thoughts honed, floating through the kind of stale tranquillity that comes on the coattails of a pure debacle, fortified by the feeling that nothing worse could happen, like a farmer looking at a crop decimated by freakish hail, or a family standing in their yard, watching the last wisps of smoke as the firemen reel in their hoses and depart what was once a priceless home.

"Please don't leave."

He arrived at his car, unlocked the door and started the engine. Christy was three spaces away, stationary for the moment, her expression a jumble of emotions, the black recorder still in her hand. Joel rolled down the window. "I'll see you tomorrow. Try to think about the horrible damage you can do. There's a lot more to this than simply collecting a check and getting your own apartment."

She stayed where she was, and the two of them considered each other. A woman and her daughter strolled by, the girl carrying a shopping bag and discussing shoes and skirts with her mother. Joel was sweating, had grown damp around his hairline and sideburns and in the center of his back. He finally blinked several times and looked away, put his foot on the brake and shifted the car into reverse.

"Don't you ever call me again, Joel. You prick. Next time you want something from me, you can call my fuckin' lawyer."

He eased the Neon out of the parking space and cut the wheel.

"I've got nothing to say to you. Nothing. Talk to my fucking lawyer. From now on, that's the magic phrase where you're concerned—you can talk to my fucking lawyer. And I'm going to report you to the police, tell them you're stalking me and how you've violated the court stuff about keepin' away from me."

"Do whatever you have to do, Christy. I just hope you can live with yourself. I hope—" He slammed the brake pedal, stopped the car abruptly. He felt as if his bowels and kidneys and ribs had been pulverized, and nausea blitzed through his stomach and stopped at the top of his throat. He tasted an acidic, fetid gush on the back of his tongue and swallowed several times to keep the puke from spreading any farther. The sweating worsened, causing his hair to stick to his forehead and his underarms to leak. "What did you say?" The vomit was churning, barely in check. His throat burned, his guts ached, his head was spinning.

"I said I'm going to call the cops and have you sent to jail."

"Before that. What did you say before that?" Everything above his chest was now—suddenly—out the window, hanging over the door, but he rolled his eyes so he could see her. The phrase was whipping around his skull: *my fucking lawyer . . . my fucking lawyer . . . my fucking lawyer . . . my fucking lawyer.* Right behind it came the other wicked cue: ". . . it was explained to me I could collect some major dollars . . . explained to me . . . explained to me . . ." The fragments did Roller Derby circuits that followed the banked contours of his head, faster and faster, louder and louder, until he was positive the whole orbiting train of words was going to bust out of him.

"Before . . . what?" She moved closer. "You okay, Joel? You look ill or something."

"What did you say about a lawyer?" Jeez, he was dizzy.

"I said you could talk to my lawyer instead of me." She was cooling again, winding down, her moods quicksilver crazy. "I didn't mean to be so harsh."

"You said 'talk to my effing lawyer,' didn't you?" A wave hit his middle, a ferocious push, and the explosion ran into his esophagus, flushing everything ahead of it. The vomit broke its bonds, overwhelmed him, and liquid stench flooded his mouth and trickled from his nose. Some of the awful heave splattered the parking lot, and some dripped down the bright green side of the car.

"Oh my God, what happened? I didn't mean to make you barf." Christy started creeping closer but changed her mind, walked on the balls of her feet and pinched her nose shut before coming to a halt a few yards away from the Neon. "It's not, like, spreading or something? I can't catch some disease from you, can I?"

"That's what you said, isn't it?" He wiped his lips with the back of his hand and sucked in clean air through his mouth.

"So what? But I, you know, was just saying it because I was mad. Is that why you're throwing up, because you thought I'd never talk to you again?" Her tone was nearly cheerful. "That would be sorta cool."

"No."

"No? What do you mean?"

"How well do you know a man named Edmund Brooks, Christy? Or even better, how about a fellow by the name of Sa'ad X. Sa'ad?"

For a moment, it appeared that Christy was going to join Joel in his distress—her knees went soft, her face melted and her neck and cheeks filled with startled blood. "Oh shit," she said and stood there, transparent and undone. She slid her foot to the side, almost staggered, then clutched her stomach with both hands. "I don't know anyone like that. Why?"

"I'm sure you know Edmund. He goes to church at Roanoke First Baptist."

She seemed at a loss as to what she should do with her hands. From her belly, they went to her hips, and she rocked forward, appeared to lose her balance. "This shit is way too daunting." Her voice was weak, confused. "I'm splitting."

"Edmund put you up to this, didn't he?" The question hemorrhaged astonishment. "This is one of his scams." Joel tried to sound more certain. "You and Edmund and Sa'ad hatched the whole scheme to rip off the insurance company. I'm just a collateral concern on the way to the jackpot."

Christy had stopped staggering and swaying and had braced her legs underneath her. She looked at Joel, and it was apparent to him she was weighing what she should do, how much she should admit. A police cruiser entered the parking lot from the far end, and Joel could tell by its speed and path that the trip wasn't routine. The car bounced on its springs when it went over a small dip and zigzagged through empty spaces instead of following the marked routes and painted arrows. Christy noticed the police as well, and she gave Joel a curious, ambivalent smile, raised her hand to her lips and blew him a kiss. Her nails were painted a stark shade of red, and she had a thick silver ring on her thumb. The colors jarred him when her hand flicked in his direction, came through the air like five sharp darts and a bright circle, appeared to separate from her fingers.

She spun toward the mall, and Joel let off the brake, tried to steer out of the lot without calling attention to himself, a patch of vomit drying on the side of his small, tacky car, his shirt unbuttoned and ripped, and silver duct tape stuck to him as if he'd just been hastily repaired. He kept watch in his rearview mirror and took the closest exit from the lot, made it onto the main road and blended into traffic. What a fiasco, he thought. What a fiasco. He had been stymied by an eighteen-year-old party girl, his efforts at subterfuge so clumsy that the likes of Christy had seen right through him. And he'd been ruthlessly betrayed by Edmund, sacrificed for the sake of the sag and some easy insurance dollars.

He stopped at a red signal and checked the highway behind him: no sign of the police. He buttoned and tucked his shirt while he was waiting at the light, spat out the window. The residue from his vomit still plagued his mouth and clung to his nose, and there was a viscous spot the size of a quarter on his pant leg, a splatter that would probably leave a stain, no matter how thoroughly he scrubbed and soaked it.

As the car in front of him started to accelerate, it dawned on Joel that his misadventure with Christy had actually been a good thing, perhaps even Heaven sent. Despite the embarrassing, wretched argument and the dash through the mall, despite getting so sick that the upheaval had poured from his head, and despite being frightened and on edge and scared, this was a great and marvelous revelation. Now he knew where he stood. Had his plan worked, had he been able to tape Christy saying what he wanted her to say and then left without incident, there would've been no confronta- tion and he never would have heard her recite Sa'ad's profane mantra. Without the chaos, he'd still be a sucker and a dupe. "Thank you," he said aloud. "Glory be."

Joel drove five miles to Brambleton Avenue, turned right and then traveled until he located a convenience store. He pulled into the lot, parking the car away from the street and behind a van that made the Neon difficult to spot. The store was busy, and Joel waited in line to pay for a cappuccino and a pack of Wrigley's gum. The coffee came self-serve, and he placed his cup underneath a machine and held a button while two jets shot milk and coffee till he'd gotten his money's worth. He took the coffee along with two napkins and sat in the Neon, debating what he should do next. The cappuccino chased the bittersweet taste from his mouth and throat, and he blew his nose into one of the napkins, did his best to rid his nostrils of the vomit scent.

As he considered his plight, he drank the coffee and began biting a circle around the top of the styrofoam cup. He finished with the cup and chewed a piece of the gum until it lost its flavor, folded it in the wrapper and started on another stick. People and vehicles came and went. A family filled the neighboring van and left, dropping an empty bag from the window as they were backing up. An SUV stopped beside Joel soon afterward, and two skinny, rambunctious boys jumped out and squared off and flailed karate moves, their hands held high in cartoonish poses and their kicks and punches nowhere close to landing. They would shout "Haaa!" every time they changed stances or took a swing, and they kept at it until their father made them quit.

For half an hour, Joel pondered what he should do. He finally decided to call his sister, the only person on the planet who wouldn't betray him and who cared what happened to him. He found a pay phone outside the store, attached to the wall. The metal box enclosing the phone was scratched and defaced by initials, numbers, names and trite vulgarities. The plastic binder for the phone book hung empty at the end of a slight chain, the book probably ripped out by kids or late-night drunks. Joel called collect, said his name into the receiver when a computerized voice at the other end prompted him. Sophie accepted the call and came on the line. He could hear the TV in the background.

"Joel? Where are you?" she asked.

"I'm in Roanoke."

"I hope this isn't your one call from the station. You're not with Danno and McGarrett, are you?"

"I'm fine. Actually, I have some good news."

"Great." She told her son to cut down the TV volume. "You'd sometimes think Baker is deaf," she said when she returned to her conversation with Joel.

"Listen, here's what I need you to do. Go to a pay phone and call me back, okay? Don't tell me where you're going, don't say the location, just go and call me here."

"Why?"

"I'm afraid someone might be listening to our conversations."

"Who?"

"I don't know for sure, but I'm not going to take any chances. Would you please just do it and not debate the issue for the next two hours?"

"How, Joel, can I call you? I don't know your number."

"Area code is 540. Then our old street address, and the month and day of Dad's birthday. Add three to the last digit."

"Let me find a pen."

Joel heard a kitchen drawer open and Sophie hunting through the clutter. He repeated the sequence, and she wrote down the numbers and recited the code back to him. "Will I need a password or cloaking device for the car? Trench coat? How about one of those fountain pens that turns into a rocket ship?"

Joel laughed. "Call me as soon as you can. I'll be waiting for you." The plan seemed imperfect if someone was indeed tapping Sophie's phone, but it was the best he could do and better than nothing. He was suddenly very paranoid, a new arrival in the world of deceit and backstabbing.

Sophie phoned in less than ten minutes, and Joel could tell she was outside, could hear traffic passing and something mechanical in the background, an engine or a compressor. "Joel? Is this my brother Joel?"

"Thanks. That was quick."

"How do I know it's really you?" Her tone was playful, mocking.

"Because it is." Joel leaned against the store wall, supported his weight with his shoulder.

"I need to test you."

Despite everything, he smiled. "Go ahead."

"My first boyfriend."

"Freddie Morris. We called him Hollywood on account of his horrible sunglasses."

"Okay. You pass," she said. "So what's the big secret? I hope this warrants all the hype and suspense. I'm wearing a scarf and sunglasses, you know. Got Baker dressed in his Halloween costume."

"I have a lot to tell you, a lot I've learned."

"Give me the short version, please. We're using my calling card."

Joel told her what had happened, recounted his meeting with Christy and his discovery. "But I don't know what to do, Sophie. I'm absolutely hemmed in," he said. "I know I've been set up, but there doesn't seem to be any escaping."

"Well, I'm glad you've managed to find a better explanation than the ones you left here with. I told you that Edmund was slippery, didn't I? I told you the moment I laid eyes on him, and you chastised me. Remember?"

"I'm sorry. I knew he was a little shady, but never in a way to hurt anyone. Or so I thought. I'm heartsick at what he's done to me, absolutely disappointed."

"I don't have any trouble believing he'd skin you alive for a dollar or two. He's got the smell, Joel. You were a dolt not to see it."

"I suppose so," he said.

"And you're sure he's behind this? The girl told you?"

"Pretty much, yeah."

"She admitted it?" Sophie was still not completely sold.

"She almost collapsed when I confronted her, and she looked like she'd seen a ghost and said 'oh, shit'—pardon my language—and ran. I know what I know. This was a calculated plan to scam money, no doubt."

"So she didn't completely confess?"

"She might as well have." He watched four college boys leave the convenience store, each carrying a case of Natural Light beer. "I'm certain this whole deal is crooked, and Sa'ad's the mastermind."

"Well, it makes more sense than anything else you've come up with."

"They were planning to do this no matter what. If I'd never laid a hand on her, she was still going to say I did. She was in the church, with me, by herself—everyone knew that. Even if I'd kept my hands off her, even if I were completely innocent, it would've been a swearing contest, and with the infernal DNA tests they'd still be in the money. I just made it easier for them by kissing her a couple times. My own stupidity."

"Quite a fantastic story, Joel."

"Do you believe me now?"

"I don't know what to believe. I'm the skeptical one. I think Michael Jackson *did* have a little surgery done, and I wouldn't be surprised if there's price-fixing among big oil companies." She sighed, and Joel heard voices near her, several people talking at once. "But your solution is easy, isn't it? Tell the police and your lawyer. The girl sounds like she'll fall apart if things get tough. And maybe they'll be able to turn up something on Edmund."

"I can't do that. It won't work."

"Won't work?" Her voice spiked. "What do you mean?"

"I've already thought about it, and it won't work. It'd be my word against theirs, and I'd have nothing to prove what I'm saying. Even if Christy flip-flops—and who knows with her—it would still be difficult to convince anyone this is a scam, especially at this late date, after I've already pled guilty and sat on my hands for so long. It'll just look like I'm trying to avoid paying what I owe, or trying to protect the church. If I knew how they manipulated the tests, I could make some headway, but right now I don't think the police will be too impressed. Of course, the one thing we can count on if I visit the cops is they'll send me back to jail for contacting Christy and violating my court order."

"Well, certainly you should tell your lawyer, this Roland guy. What's the harm there? I'm sure he'd like to know your theory before he questions

Christy. With so much money at stake, I'd think the insurance company would want to investigate your angle. Common sense tells you that."

"It's not an angle—it's the truth."

"So tell him, Joel. Why wouldn't you? At least he can ask her some questions and observe her reaction. He doesn't have to admit you saw her, doesn't have to mention any of that. Right? And he could talk to Edmund, find him and put him under oath."

Four motorcycles arrived in the lot near the pay phone, and for a moment it was too noisy for Joel to continue talking. The bikers revved their engines before shutting them down, took off their gloves and helmets and sauntered past Joel, toward the store's entrance.

"What were you saying?" Joel asked. "I missed part of it."

"You should tell your lawyer so he and the insurance company can look into your theory."

"Well, besides the fact that they have all the cards right now, there's another reason I can't turn them in. This thing is a tar baby." He recalled Sa'ad looking at him from behind his tangled hands and discussing who would be "on the griddle" if the jewelry scam failed. He had several thousand dollars' worth of stolen jewelry in his car, and they would no doubt cut him loose if he betrayed them, leave him to explain *his* efforts to bilk *his* insurer or possibly get word to the authorities that he had the missing goods. He was as guilty as they were, in just as deep, and he was the one with two convictions in his past. It was sly and cunning the way they'd tied him up, making him both a victim and a collaborator, keeping him close at hand, barricading his exits should he somehow piece together what was happening. "I can't discuss it over the phone, but suffice it to say they've got some leverage where I'm concerned. We might all drown together if I cross them. As I see it, trying to convince the police or my lawyer I've been set up has nothing but downside—no one's going to believe me, it'll come out I saw Christy when I wasn't supposed to, and Edmund and Sa'ad are in a position to retaliate big-time."

"I disagree, but do what you want. How are they going to retaliate?"

"I can't discuss it now."

"I thought that's why we're talking on pay phones."

"I'm not taking any chances," Joel said.

"Quite a fine mess you've gotten yourself into, Ollie," she said, assuming a Laurel-and-Hardy voice.

"I'll say." Joel pushed away from the wall, looked at the traffic passing by on Brambleton Avenue. "The way I see it, I've pretty much got one option, and it's not an altogether attractive one."

"How about this option: Forget about it. Go there tomorrow and tell the truth—whatever that happens to be—and come home. What do you care about the rest? If these people rip off an insurance company, who gives a damn? Didn't you tell me there's four million in insurance? I can't imagine she'll receive anywhere near that kind of money, so you and the good Baptists are safe. Why get yourself in more trouble over a squabble with a bunch of con men and a stupid slut?"

"It's not that simple. They shouldn't get rich by lying and cheating and taking advantage of me. Edmund and Sa'ad deserve nothing, and Christy should receive, at most, a couple thousand bucks. If I can put a stop to this, I'm going to."

"I don't know, Joel. It sounds to me like you're a little too eager to keep your hand in the action. I think these people are rubbing off on you. You ought to walk away and let everything unfold on its own. You act as if you can't let go when you can be done with this nonsense in a heartbeat."

"I'm not going to sit by while these louts profit at the expense of my good name."

"Your, uh, good name?" she said.

"They're destroying my reputation to make a buck."

"What are you going to do? What's the plan?" The playfulness was completely gone from her attitude.

"I need you to help me. One more time, I need you to do something."

"Joel—"

"I'm sorry to have to ask, but I need you to call Christy and have her meet me again. As bad as it sounds, she's my best hope right now."

"What for?" Sophie asked. "What do I need to tell her?"

"You're a good sister. Thanks. I love you."

"I haven't said I'd call yet."

"But I'm almost certain you will—I'd do it for you. And in the end—in the end—you'll be rewarded and blessed for doing the right thing."

nine————————————————————————————————————

Christy had been boozing when Joel met her three hours later at the parking lot of Mac and Maggie's restaurant. He could smell the alcohol soon after she got inside his car, and she occasionally added a "th" or a combination of spit and unfinished letters to the conclusion of her words. Her mood was difficult to decipher as she emerged from her BMW and toe-crushed a cigarette, though she seemed more stable and in kilter than she'd been earlier. Her purse arrived before she did, carelessly tossed through the open door, and there was a spurt of sound when the handbag hit, a jangle of keys and neglected change and something plastic. She flopped into the passenger seat, and the outside lights brightened one side of her face and left the other side dark, the illumination splitting her in two any time she looked straight ahead. The dim half was closest to Joel, showed him virtually nothing no matter how hard he strained to see.

"I know you're just tryin' to screw me over some more. I almost didn't come." Her tone was morose. "All that shit your sister said about you wantin' to hook up with me to apologize is a big fat lie."

"So why are you here?" he asked.

"I don't know. There's not much else to do, I guess, not on Sunday night in Roanoke." She turned and gazed out the window, lifted a handful of hair away from her nape and held the strands in a makeshift ponytail. "So what's up?" she asked, not looking at him. She dropped her hair and combed through it with her fingers. The light missed the majority of her head and face now and showered the console and the edge of her seat. A small patch of brightness, the size and shape of an egg, overflowed onto the carpet beside Joel's foot. The glass was down on his side, and he'd changed clothes, but the interior still reeked, smelled like vomit woven through coffee, cologne, muggy air and spearmint gum.

"I care a lot for you, Christy, probably too much, okay? That's no secret. And I do regret my conduct at the mall. I'm sorry. I want the best for you, and I hope we can come out of this with a good long-term relationship. Maybe more than friends." While he'd waited for her, Joel had rehearsed what he was going to say, had imagined Christy sitting in his rented car and practiced his apology aloud.

"Would you take me to the Virginia-Duke game in Charlottesville? I know a ton of people who'll be tailgatin', and my friend Michelle told me for sure Dave Matthews is going to be at Miller's. How deluxe would that be? It's not like, you know, announced, but it's a very definite rumor."

"When is the game?"

She pivoted and the light divided her face again. "September twenty-ninth. It's a night game, too. We'd have a blast." She looked directly at Joel for the first time since climbing into the car.

"It sounds fun, but I'll be gone by then. I'll be in Montana."

"Could I come out there? I could fly to see you, like maybe for spring break."

"I suppose it's possible."

"Really?"

"We'll see," he said, not revealing much in his voice. "Who knows."

"I probably could come before then, blow off class and—"

"But we need to settle everything else before we start discussing new plans."

"Damn. So we're back to the same old crap." She crossed her legs and exhaled.

"Not exactly."

"Are you taping me again?" she asked.

"No." He elongated the reply.

"I want to see. Undo your shirt."

"Let's get out of the car, and I'll be glad to show you."

"I want to search you," she said, suddenly flirtatious instead of sullen.

"I think I'd be more comfortable if you simply look."

"Forget it then. What if you have a wire hidden underneath your pants?" She put her elbow on the console and hunched closer. "And I want to visit in my car, not yours. You could have this ugly-ass thing bugged. I've got some forties, too. In my cooler. You want to kill one with me?"

"Forties?"

"Big beers. And there's some vodka left."

"Oh, no. But thanks for the offer."

She laughed and crinkled her nose. "So are you going to, like, let me investigate you and then chill in my car, or should I leave?"

"Let's step outside and see what kind of compromise we can reach." He opened the door and a buzzer sounded. He removed the ignition key to stay the noise but left the door swung away from the frame, the interior light burning. Christy walked behind the car and kept coming toward him without breaking her momentum, didn't slow when she got nearer. He thought perhaps the drinking had affected her ability to judge distance and reinforced his shoulders and legs, anticipating a bump. She halted awkwardly, the last stride a childish hop, and planted herself right in front of him, so close that everything beneath her neck didn't make it into his vision.

He retreated a step, then another. "Okay," he said. "Stay there. Don't move." He unbuttoned his shirt, held it by the tail and spread it into two cloth wings, rotated in a circle. "See? No recorders." He began fastening the shirt, got a button out of sequence, backtracked and started again. "And I give you my word there's nothing concealed anywhere else."

"I want to frisk you." She made a show of shifting her weight so her knee bent and her hip jutted out. Her hands were stuck against her waist, her elbows angled and protruding, the pose reminiscent of B-movie vixens and railish magazine models. "That was the deal."

"That was *not* the deal. There is no deal."

"Then I'm gone."

"Why do you want to complicate this for me?" he asked.

"Do I have 'dope' written across my forehead? You tried to trap me six hours ago and now it's like trust me, I won't come in your mouth? I don't think so."

Joel flinched, embarrassed at what he'd heard. "I'm giving you my word."

"And we'll both enjoy the experience." She pronounced the final word with a lisp.

"No we won't." He glanced at the sky. A good portion of the moon was exposed, and stars were abundant. It was bright enough for him to distinguish the shape of a cloud immediately over them, a gauzy blemish that was easing across the heavens, scarcely moving.

"I'll be real quick and promise not to hurt you." She pressed closer, and Joel could smell alcohol inlaid with the sweetness of wintergreen mints.

"What if I do all the talking and you just listen? There'd be nothing for me to record."

"Nope."

A white Ford drove into the parking area and stopped next to the entrance of Mac and Maggie's. A man left the car idling and tried the restaurant's doors, discovered them locked for the night and departed the lot.

"Please don't turn this into something inappropriate, Christy."

She squatted slowly, all the while keeping her eyes fixed on Joel's face. She touched his ankles, then ran her palms inside his pants along his calves and shins. When she slid her hands out, one of the trouser legs bunched above his sock, didn't completely let down. She raised into a half crouch and felt the backs of his thighs, positioning her face directly in front of his crotch, so close that there was no space visible between her mouth and the fabric. Joel took hold of her arms, pushed her away. "Satisfied?" he said.

"I'm not through. We're just gettin' to the good part." She stood upright, tugged free of Joel's grip and launched a new adventure. Her hands started at his belly and probed erratically until they began to disappear beneath his belt line and fan across his abdomen. He clamped her wrists and removed her fingers from inside his britches, then gave her a stern, disapproving frown. "Enough," he said.

She relaxed her arms, and Joel let her go. "You want to search me? What if I'm the one wearin' something this time?"

"I'll take my chances."

Without any warning, she reached around him, wrapped her hands over his rear and shoved into him with her pelvis. She was slammed against him, her hands clasped and ringing his behind. They were coupled from knee to high stomach without any interruption. He acquiesced at first, and she tried to kiss him, canted her head and floated toward his mouth, her eyes not quite shut and her weight mostly on her toes. He allowed her to do it, let her touch his lips for a second before turning his cheek and wedging his arms between their chests and gently pushing her away.

"A little more," she coaxed. "That was cool."

Joel's effort to distance himself was puny and incomplete—they remained snug at the belly, his forearm was sunk into the curve of her breast and he'd done nothing about her hands. "We can't stand here carrying on in a public parking lot," he said, the remark more elliptical than he'd intended. "Quit." He stood perfectly still, realized he'd not been allowed the slightest taste of intimacy or affectionate flesh for months, felt her offer more of her breast into his arm. There was a sublime power in the way she mashed and leaned and made him aware of her breathing, a primal summons that caused his mind to riot, his physical senses to goad him.

"One good kiss, just one. We can do it in the car if you're shy about being out here."

"That's not what I meant. This is wrong." He sidestepped her and clutched the crook of her arm, managed to wrestle himself free and avoid his own base impulses. "Let's finish our discussion—certainly it's obvious I'm not taping you. And I'll be glad to talk in your car." He guided her forward, and she laid her head against his shoulder and mouthed something he couldn't understand, a word or two barely above a whisper.

Inside Christy's BMW, she took a beer from her cooler and stuffed it into a brown paper bag that failed to cover several inches of glass neck. She set the alcohol between her legs, and as she was screwing the top off the oversize bottle, she asked Joel if he wanted a drink. He declined, and she never mentioned it again, didn't nag him about it. "So what's Montana like?" she asked.

"Nice. Beautiful, and very different from this part of the world." She took a pull from the beer, and Joel changed the subject while the bottle was on her lips. "I know you don't want to revisit the topic, but we need to talk about what's happening tomorrow. I can promise you that the wise thing to do is walk away from this, just forget it. You're an adult and you can call the shots. Tell your lawyer you want to terminate the suit, ask the Lord for forgiveness and leave with a clear conscience. Integrity and getting square with God are worth more than any amount of money."

"Maybe. But I'd be a retard to go through all this shit and stress for nothing. This has been extremely daunting. It would be like workin' at my horrible job in retail and then not pickin' up my check on Friday." The bag made a rustling, crackling noise when she jammed the bottle between her thighs.

"It's poisonous money, Christy. Cursed. You won't enjoy it, won't profit from it. Sin never, ever works out in the long run. You can't find happiness by lying and cheating."

"How do you figure I'm doing some gigantic sin? It's not like I'm stealing from grandmas or murderin' people."

"Christy, listen—"

"Let's go to the lake, like you promised," she interrupted. "It's still warm enough to swim, even after dark. We can stay up all night and burn a joint. Sleep on Celeste's dock till we have to meet the lawyers."

"How about this? How about you agree to a fair settlement? What about that? My wrongs where you're concerned are worth how much? Five thousand dollars? Ten? Heck, ask for twenty and leave knowing you haven't sold your honor."

"Shit, Joel. Right. And I do all this and come away with, like, a Yugo and an ensemble from Fashion Bug?" She snorted. "Why would I take twenty thousand dollars when I can just as easily get millions?" She reached for the switch, took hold of the key and prepared to start the engine.

"Whoa. Wait a minute. What're you doing?"

"Traveling. We can't have a proper party here." The words were a little thick, a little too wet.

"Okay, listen. Don't go anywhere yet." He put his hand on her wrist, just laid it across her, didn't squeeze or grab or try to pry her from the key. "Here's another proposal, one I suspect you'll like much more."

"Talk talk talk talk—I'm sick of talking." She cranked the car. Joel still had his hand draped across her wrist, and when he didn't move it or attempt to stop her, she hesitated, kept the key between her thumb and first finger and her arm extended.

"Try this. Hear me out, and then you can leave. The best option is to completely cut this loose, just dismiss the court case and forget the whole stinking idea. You're not planning to do that, correct?" He continued to touch her, hadn't disturbed his hand.

"Hell no, Joel. I'm not going to forget about tons of dollars *and* have my parents whale on me because I dragged everybody through this nightmare and changed my mind at the last moment."

"Right. The next best thing is to simply take a fair payment for the suit, not a ginned-up one based on lies and deceit. That's not in the cards either, as I understand what you're telling me?"

She placed her free hand on her temple, dropped her jaw in an idiot's gape and feigned serious thought. "Uh, gee, let me think . . . uhhhhhh . . . No. No. Nope. But thanks for the excellent suggestion."

"So how about this." He rubbed the back of her wrist and beginning of her hand, felt tiny, inconsequential hairs and shoots of delicate bones underneath her skin. "Think about this." His fingers became quiet again, stopped their soft incursion. "There's no reason for parasites like Edmund and Sa'ad to benefit from your efforts, to ride your anguish and suffering. Why should they receive one thin dime?"

"What're you saying?" It was dark in Christy's BMW; none of the outside light made its way through the windows. She was a murky outline, her face rudimentary like a child's sketch, a collection of inky, vague features that lacked color and shape and depth.

"I'm saying eliminate them. If you insist on doing this, at least don't cut them in on it."

She took her hand off the key and away from Joel's mild grip. The engine was running and the dash and gauges were lit, mostly in tranquil white with occasional spots of red and green. "Edmund and Sa'ad? The lawyer Sa'ad?"

"They're behind the whole scheme, aren't they? This is their baby from day one."

She didn't say anything. She moved around without purpose—shifted her legs, tossed her hair, twisted her silver ring, bit the corner of her thumbnail.

"They set this up, didn't they?"

She traced the circumference of the steering wheel with her index finger, staring at the windshield.

"There's no need to deny it. I know, okay? I could tell by how you reacted at the mall."

"So what if they did?" she said almost before he'd spoken the last word.

"Listen. You tell me the truth about Edmund, and I'll fix it so you can be rid of him and double the money from your lawsuit."

"You mean get paid more?"

"Exactly," he said.

"Well, maybe I'm saying Edmund was sorta involved, okay? Why's that do anything for me?"

"How, Christy? How could you let such a glib, seedy man talk you into this? You're a child, and this is horrible, serious stuff. What on earth could he have told you?"

"Edmund's just real sincere and real, like, you know, convincing. He seems totally okay."

"Didn't you know this would devastate me and my family? Was it worth it to destroy my marriage and bring down a church of fine, honest Christians? You had to know how ugly everything would get."

"Edmund said a million times that things like this are always handled behind the scenes. I thought it would be kept secret, so as not to embarrass the church. I'd tell my parents, maybe hire a lawyer, and I'd get the money without anybody finding out. No matter what, we'd never go to court, the lawyers would handle the details and some big insurance corporation that ripped off sick kids would pay me beaucoup green. From what I'd heard—Edmund's told me stories about some of the shit he's done—this would be over in a few months and nothin' would happen to you or anybody else. That's one of his rules: No innocent people get screwed."

"How could you possibly believe such nonsense?"

" 'Cause it made sense," she said, exasperated. "I never thought my father would go ballistic and take such an interest. He's too busy worryin' about his golf score and his zoning board meetings and his stupid baseball cards to even remember my name. You know 'Big Bill Darden'—I was sure he'd be humiliated and sorta blame me and be all worried his daughter was damaged goods and try to keep the story hush-hush. And my mom—shit, she'd just buy an extra bottle of vermouth and turn up Simon and Garfunkel a few decibels louder. But before I realize it, I'm talkin' to some dumbass policeman and nothing's on schedule. Except, you know, I'm going to get the money. The plan was okay there."

"Even if I do get skewered, it's nothing to Edmund." Joel was thinking out loud, almost mumbled. "He doesn't care as long as you tell your lies and you guys collect the money. And you truly believed word would never get around?"

"Damn, Joel. How many times do I have to say it? The church bosses and their lawyers don't want the bad pub, and my parents don't want the bad pub and probably won't give a shit, and I'm getting money—"

"That really doesn't belong to the evil people who happen to have it. I'm acquainted with the theory."

"Right, so don't act like I'm stupid as a cow or somethin'. It makes good sense, every particle of it. And, screw it, the money's coming soon, so I guess I'm not so dumb after all." Her tone had become defiant, her words crisper.

"You could've quit any time, Christy. For instance, right before I went to jail would've been a good point to tell the truth."

"Well, you did make out with me, now didn't you? Uh-huh, yes you did. You're the one who pled guilty. And my friend Arthur—he's in law school—he told me I'd be charged for giving a false report to the police if I changed my story. Plus my parents would've absolutely slaughtered me—I was already in trouble for the DUI and some other crap. It came down to me or you, and I chose me. I could catch major wrath and get zero, or I could leave someone I like in a bind and receive huge dollars and my parents' sympathy forever. Sorry, but that's life."

"So is all this infatuation part of the scam?" Joel asked.

"No, Joel. No it's not." Her demeanor changed again, became solicitous and girlish. "I've thought you were way hot since the first time I heard you preach. And then, when I had to have the meetings with you, for my punishment by the court, I thought you were such a superb person." She seemed delighted to have the upper hand, was gratified by Joel's uncertainty and blatant curiosity. "We could fuck right now if you wanted. Right here in the car."

"Why do you talk like that? So foul and rude? Is it for the shock value?"

"It's just how I talk. Some boys like it. I guess you don't."

"It's pretty rough," he said.

"What would you prefer?" she asked. "How would you say it? Seems to me I'm bein' accurate."

"Whatever. So your interest in me isn't an act?"

"Of course not. Why do you think I'm even tryin' to explain myself? I want you to see how at the same time, like simultaneously, I can be totally into you and still have gotten you caught up in all grades of trouble. I don't want you to be completely pissed at me and, like, brand me a total bitch. I was supposed to get the money, and nothing uncool happens to you."

"So, did you like me and *then* decide to falsely accuse me or hatch the plan first and then grow to like me?" Joel paused, thought for a moment. "I'm not sure which is worse, but I'd like to know."

"What?"

"When did you and Edmund decide to do this?"

"When?"

"Yes, when. That's not a tough question." Joel was perturbed by her stalling.

"Oh, yeah, okay. Let me think. He was like standing behind me when we were leavin' church, when everyone lines up to shake your hand, and he heard me say something about our counseling, and he could tell I was into you."

"Did you even know him?"

"Nope. I'd seen him at church, when I had to be there. I went on Mother's Day, and you know, like Christmas I went, and when I needed a little slack around the house or a cash boost from my parents I would go with them. Sunday service was always worth a few bonus points."

"And he approached you straight out of the blue?" Joel asked.

"Pretty much. He talked to me after the service."

"A total stranger? A total stranger asks you to tell horrible lies about your preacher, and you just enroll in the program as quickly as possible?"

"Of course not, Joel. He talked to me and got to know me and gave me presents and seemed interested in what was going on with my life. At first I thought he wanted to get with me, but he never tried, never did anything like that. He had two tickets to Key West he couldn't use, and he let me and my know-better friend Cammy have them. He—"

"He what? He gave two seventeen-year-old girls tickets to Florida?"

"So what's wrong with that? And Cammy was eighteen."

"Did he go?"

She switched off the engine but left the electrical system on, didn't turn the key all the way to last position. "No, he didn't. He never did anything other than be nice to me. He told me his daughter had been killed in a bad car wreck, and he thought a lot of me. I reminded him of her. When he was gone he let us use his house, stuff like that, but he never so much as bought us a beer or patted our knees."

"Unbelievable. I'll bet he never even had a daughter."

"I'll bet he did, Joel. I saw her picture."

"So how did he rope you into this dreadful scheme?"

"I don't know. I was just like, you know, complainin' one day about how wretched it was to have no money unless I begged my parents and how four years at some stupid college was going to get me what—a cubicle and a boring job at a marrow-sucking corporation in Atlanta or Richmond? On Fridays I could dress down, and maybe I'd be paid enough to take a trip to Myrtle Beach with my old roommates once a year. Hit the free appetizers and dollar draft at every 'Wild Wednesday,' collect donations for the United Way, wear Sam and Libbies, shit like that? No thank you."

"So Edmund persuades you to tell a horrendous lie without regard to any of the consequences?" Joel scratched his chin with his thumb and forefinger. The radio volume was turned low, and he could hear bits and pieces of a rock-and-roll song coming from the speakers, thumps of bass and occasional guitar notes. "Amazing."

"To tell you the truth, I more or less asked him to help me, not the other way around. He, like, totally understood my dilemma, and he has several businesses based on, like, the Robin Hood principle, to take money that nobody will ever miss."

Joel had to laugh. "Right, and Robin Hood needs a new Cadillac and a custom-tailored sharkskin suit. And, I imagine, the new BMWs will be in the showroom any day now. I'm sure you and the rest of the oppressed, penniless band of merry men don't want to miss out on a sunroof or the leather interior or the sport package. Robin Hood indeed."

"Screw you, Joel. See, you have no clue what I'm saying. He let me try a few small projects to make some cash, and it was just like he promised. He knew what I wanted and didn't make fun of me. So who could know my plan . . . the thing with you . . . wouldn't be perfect like all of his, like all the rest? I knew it was a big deal, serious. I considered that. But I suppose you've never done anything wrong, never lied or cut corners."

Joel considered what she was asking. He thought of Edmund's plastic leg stretched across the Cadillac seat, recalled the battered pride in Edmund's voice when he talked about overcoming his handicap, how there'd been a hint of sadness but no rancor in his words. He remembered how the cold potato lumps had tasted when he licked them off his sister's floor, how fine grit and dirt had mixed with the mush in his mouth and scraped his teeth. And now, in his rented car, there was a bag of jewelry, looted from someone else's home, the grist for an illegal scheme that was nothing more than old-fashioned stealing. "Nobody's perfect, Christy," he answered after a few minutes of silence. "Especially not me. I can understand why you're doing what you're doing. Edmund can be very convincing when he's telling you the things you want to hear and dolling up sin in its Sunday best. It's impossible to walk away sometimes even when you know you should. I certainly blame him more than you, and I want you to understand I forgive you. This is behind us now, okay? I'm not angry where you're concerned."

Joel's genuine charity caught her off guard, the change in his attitude swift and unexpected. "Okay," she said cautiously. "If you say so."

He touched her arm again, this time near her shoulder. Her top was sleeveless, and he kept his hand on her longer than was necessary to gain her attention. "I hope you don't think I was browbeating you or, I don't know, being sanctimonious," he said as he removed his hand. "You can understand why I'm trying to discover what's happening to me?"

"Yeah." She seemed uneasy.

"Getting back to what I was saying earlier, if you don't want to drop the case or compromise for a fair amount, why not eliminate Edmund and Sa'ad? They're nothing but leeches. You're the one with all the risk, who's done all the work and had to live with the stress and anxiety. Why let them free-ride your sweat and efforts?"

"Are we going to the lake?" She took a swig of beer and washed up a burp, then covered her mouth. "Sorry."

"Maybe. We might. Or perhaps we can just drive around and listen to music. We'll see. So you truly enjoy spending time with me?"

"Yes. I told you. Why would I, like, be here now if I was faking? I mean, you know, I've already done everything I need to do to get my money."

"So why not ditch Edmund and his parasite lawyer?"

"What difference does any of this make?" She sounded cross. "How am I gettin' more cash by tellin' you about Edmund and his lawyer?"

"Did you meet Sa'ad? Go to Las Vegas?"

"Yeah, I did. Edmund found me a fake ID so I could play the slots. I loved it. I only was able to stay for two days 'cause I had to trick my parents into thinking I was at my friend Nancy's in Arlington. You wouldn't believe how superb the shops and hotels are, like this place Bellagio and another one called the Mirage that has live sharks swimming in the lobby."

"Imagine that," Joel deadpanned.

"It was completely deluxe. I met one of the dealers at the Mirage, and he took me to a cool club in this huge, amazing pyramid. I suppose that somehow makes Edmund a bigger jerk?"

Joel added his final incentive. "It doesn't appear you've truly thought this through. If you've spent time with Sa'ad, you have to realize these guys will double-cross you the instant they have the chance."

She acted offended. "I never admitted to half the shit you're comin' up with, Joel. You're the one who put Edmund in control of everything, not me. And I'm not a total dunce, okay? I made over thirteen hundred on my College Boards."

"Why did you need them to begin with? After Edmund gave you the blueprint, why bother to include him and Sa'ad? Assuming you were going to do this, once you got the idea, why didn't you complete it by yourself and cut Edmund out?" Joel's voice became high-pitched with disbelief.

"Who knows, Joel. You need to quit floggin' me with this Edmund crap. Enough already. Jeez." She had finished her beer, and she took the empty bottle from the sack and dumped it into her cooler. "I'm thoroughly sorry you got in trouble, but there was no turning back."

"Okay."

"And I swear I felt rotten when you had to go to jail, really depressed and bummed. When it was time to report you, I was really liking you and I almost didn't do it. But you *had* already blown me off. And I did squash the rape shit immediately, okay? That was the original story, my first plan. I told my mom and she told the cops, but when the cops came I knew better than to put that on you, so I convinced them my mom was hysterical and hadn't heard me like she should. I begged the stupid police and the stupid prosecutor not to do anything to you, but by now I've got my parents doing this circle-the-wagons production and the cops tellin' me all the shit that'll happen if I change my story."

"Plus, I'm guessing that, as much as you liked me, the money was pretty important. More important than everything else, huh?"

"Yeah, well, that's why I got involved—the cash. And, like, I had a boy-friend then, so I'm not exactly sure how long-term our romance could've been. I'd like to get with you and all, but I'm not, you know, going to be your wife and do preacher's wife's deeds, hang around the church basement for the covered dishes and take turkey dinners to the shut-ins. Which doesn't mean I'm not crazy about you—I am. And I *am* sorry."

"I'm sure you are."

"Have you been talkin' to Edmund? It really freaked me out today when you mentioned his name at the mall."

"No, not recently. You said something though, something I've heard Sa'ad say."

"What, the part about talkin' to a lawyer? What's so strange about that?"

"Well, when you brought up the lawyer . . . and some other things. I just kind of put the puzzle together. Different facts, here and there."

"So you think Edmund's involved because of me getting mad and sayin' crap about a lawyer? I'm still not sayin' he is—I've never totally confirmed it, okay?" She punched a preset button on the radio and added volume. A rap song was playing. "I probably shouldn't have even discussed stuff with you, but like Mr. Hanes says, it's my word against yours now and you've already pled guilty. I'm all caught up in the middle, likin' you and feelin' guilty and still wantin' my money, so I figured I could at least give you a scrap."

"I'm not trying to cause you any problems."

"Excellent. I kinda trusted you were cool like that."

Even in the poor light, Joel was able to see her smile. "Here's my, uh, suggestion, what I've been leading up to. I say we punt Sa'ad and Edmund, and you and I go partners from here on." He loitered on the "we," waited a beat between words. He caught himself wringing his hands and stopped, was thankful the dark concealed his darting eyes and anxiety and jittery, spring-loaded limbs.

"Say what?"

"You and I finish this and split the money." It was easier to propose than he'd anticipated.

She extracted another large beer from her cooler but didn't shroud this one in the brown bag after opening it. "So you're trying to persuade me to hose them?"

"If you were to go along with me, things will turn out better for you in every regard. First, you can have a clear conscience where I'm concerned, even the score for what you did to me. You'll be able to cure the wrong you've delivered into the world. Second, you'll be able to shortchange Sa'ad and Edmund, who deserve nothing. Third, you and I sort of wind up together, maybe spend a day or two trout fishing in Montana and picnicking on the Bitterroot." He glanced at her to see if this last overture had the desired effect. "Finally, I guarantee you'll make more money. Much more. Financially, you'll be significantly better off."

"How? You keep sayin' that, and I'm to my second beer and you still haven't told me squat."

"I have a plan, a good plan."

"I hope it's better than the last one you had, sittin' there with a tape recorder glued to you and your eyes all buggin' out."

"Yeah, well, it's an improvement, I think. I'm putting this together as I go."

"I can't believe you want to become involved in all this scheming and shit. It's not the kind of person you are."

"I *am* involved, okay? I've been for quite a while, including the delightful months I spent in jail. The question now is *how* do I want to be involved. I can do nothing and continue on as a mark, a fool and a doormat, or I can attempt to salvage a little something, take the bull by the horns. Those are my options. I've asked you to totally come clean and you've refused, so that's where I am."

"You're kinda going to play the game, right?" She hadn't paid much attention to her new beer, hadn't taken a drink yet.

"You could put it that way. Yes."

"Are you serious?" she asked, her voice gaining enthusiasm. "You think we could pull it off?"

"I believe we can."

"So what's the plan? I want to hear it."

"First, I want you to tell me something, something important."

"What?" she asked, her tone bottoming.

"How in the world did you fake my DNA?" He could see her eyes open and close several times, saw her moisten her lips.

"You tell me this deluxe plan, then I'll tell you about the DNA. Like a trade."

Joel nodded and slipped closer to her. There was a muted cloth-on-leather sound and a faint squeak at the corner of his seat, springs and foam recovering from his weight when he changed positions. "Fair enough. Here's how we can make this work to our—"

"Are you sure you should be leaping into this side of things, you being a preacher and so honest and upright? Isn't it like . . . like worse if you do it than an ordinary person? Like when the cops break the law?"

"What do you mean? You don't even know what I'm proposing."

"What about that 'money is the root of all evil' saying and 'the wages of sin is death' stuff? It's got to go double if you're a preacher." Her voice was curiously deep, the giddy, scattered timbre gone. The words didn't immediately vanish; instead they seemed to take residence in the dark, lurking and reverberating. Her eyes and mouth were impenetrable banks of shadow in the weak light, two pitchy ovals and a horizontal black gash.

Joel squinted at her, tried to determine how much of the metamorphosis was real and how much was in his mind. "It's not where I want to be, Christy. I know exponential sin is no better than simple sin. I know that, and I know two wrongs don't equal a right. How many times have I stood in the pulpit and warned people there is no buffer zone between good and bad, no DMZ? So, yeah, I'm worried about this. I am. Perhaps I should simply walk in tomorrow and tell the truth and hand the situation to the Lord and go about my business, leave it in His hands. My sister tells me that's the smart choice. But even though I know better, I'm hoping . . . hoping, well, I don't know how, in one sense, I can honestly justify wading into this. I guess if 'the wages of sin is death,' I'm only planning to work part-time and maybe my payment will be a boil or pustule or trick knee, not the whole amount. With any luck, I'll catch a few locusts or a two-week famine." Joel chuckled at his sophistry and peered out the glass. He'd raised his hands to his chest, and his fingers were interlocked, his thumbs in line with his chin. "The Lord can be merciful despite our not deserving it."

"Damn, I just hope you know what you're doing." Her voice was normal again.

"Well, that makes two of us."

"So, I'm prepared now. Tell me this great idea."

"Okay," he said. "Here's how it goes." He separated his hands and lowered them to his lap. Before he could say any more, a siren began, a mile or so distant from Mac and Maggie's, and it became fiercer and louder, the shrieks and whoops bearing down on them until the hubbub was right there, the vehicle ready to appear. Joel and Christy looked at the highway and saw red and white lights strobing and flashing across the pavement, heard a horn sound twice. A boxy ambulance raced by in the passing lane, a cross painted on its side above the words RESCUE SQUAD. They watched the screaming vehicle disappear but didn't say anything about the scare it had given them both, kept their thoughts to themselves.

ten

The shirt and tie were spectacular, but the Bible, the Bible was even better. The shirt was purple, made from slick polyester that aped silk, and the tie was cut from the same bold, shiny stock. Fourteen ninety-nine at Suit City, and the talkative Pakistani gent who ran the store threw in a matching three-point pocket handkerchief, a sporty accessory of the variety favored by low-rent bankers and small-town funeral directors. "You can look like TV Regis," the proprietor said more than once as Joel sifted through the different colors and sizes. "Very special shirts, like TV Regis." The Bible was huge, a white leviathan with gold lettering and a wide gold border. It was a pulpit Bible, designed to be stationed on a podium and referenced in dramatic fashion when a compelling piece of scripture was needed. Joel had purchased the Bible first, then the shirt and tie, and he'd tried to find clothes that matched the gold script on the Good Book, had explored an entire shelf and two bins without any success. The Bible was bought at a strip-mall store not far from Suit City, and both stops had been convenient to Mac and Maggie's, allowing Joel plenty of time to locate everything and shut the two bags in the Neon's trunk prior to meeting Christy.

It was Monday morning in Roanoke, and he was standing before the broad mirror of a Hampton Inn bathroom, assessing the knot in the new purple tie. He'd opted for a double Windsor, wanted the triangle at his throat as large as possible and the length a little stunted, had pulled the front and rear sections almost equal so the ends didn't reach his belt buckle. He was fussing with his hair, trying to comb it straight back, pasting the strands in place with a flimsy comb and perfumed CVS styling mousse. No matter how much mousse he applied, his hair wouldn't lie flat, so he wound up with a greasy, bouffant pile parted in the center and swept back on the sides. He was wearing one of his dark suits, a classic Hart Schaffner & Marx he'd unpacked from his wife's shipment to Missoula and brought along for the big day. He walked out of the bathroom and returned with the enormous white Bible, posed in front of the mirror and rehearsed a smarmy smile.

It was a few minutes after eight when he left the hotel, and he was supposed to meet with his lawyer at ten-thirty to go over his testimony and prepare for the deposition. He and Christy were scheduled to be questioned at one. He drove to a Waffle House and ate breakfast, kidded with the waitress, drank three cups of coffee and read the "Extra" section of a *Roanoke Times* someone had discarded in his booth. "You in sales?" the waitress inquired at one point as she was warming his coffee and plucking two cream containers from her apron. Joel looked up from his plate and said, "For today, at least, I am." She grinned and asked if he wanted anything else.

He wandered out of the restaurant and started driving. He traveled on Route 220 to the Rocky Mount exit for Smith Mountain Lake, through the speed trap in Boone's Mill and past the roadside attractions with beer and gas and whatnots and crude wooden sculptures carved by a man using a chainsaw. He took the road toward the lake, following a single lane into the countryside. A woman in cutoff jeans and a bathing-suit top was mowing her lawn, bouncing along on a faded Snapper Comet, contrails of dust blowing from the blades when the metal scalped the ground or she hit a bare spot. Joel caught up with a family towing a boat and slowed, was stuck behind them for several miles before he was able to get around. He turned right on a gravel road not far from Hales Ford Bridge and headed into the woods. When he checked his watch, it was ten o'clock.

The house at the end of the road belonged to Roanoke First Baptist, donated by a childless widower named Albert Glenn. The church used the place for retreats and seminars, and Joel assumed no one would be there on a Monday in late August. He walked to the dock and turned a chair so he could face the water. Before he sat down, three bream darted between the pilings near the front of the dock, and a nice-size bass swam into view soon after, in no hurry at all, close enough to the surface that Joel saw a flash of silver when the fish rolled for deeper water. The sky was clear, the summer sluggishness and haze chased out of the air by a freakishly cool midnight shower, and the lake was at rest, a blue-brown tarp that stretched for miles without a wrinkle or swell.

Joel had come here to take inventory, to reflect on his situation . . . and to squander the morning. He and Martha used to visit the house on Friday nights, then eat Saturday biscuits-and-gravy breakfast at the marina and laze around the property. They'd fish off the dock with kernels of corn, float on the lake in black inner tubes, cut pink roses from the unkempt bushes near the porch and cook chicken and vegetables outside on the grill. Joel would pull out his reading glasses in the evening and give his sermon a final tweak, and Martha would pour herself half a glass of white wine and sit beside him while he edited. If he took too long or read too many passages to her, she'd blow in his ear or pinch his knee or pop his arm with her fist and call him Billy Sunday. Sometimes they'd have sex, and sometimes they'd take a blanket to the dock and listen to the radio, and sometimes they'd sit on the screened-in porch and swap stories and fit together the cardboard pieces of a jigsaw puzzle. When the lake was busy, they could hear laughs and shouts and boats ripping by until the sun set, and more nights than not, someone would shoot fireworks and burn the horizon with shimmering spreads of red, white and green.

And now he was alone at the very same place, stained by his mistakes, dressed in his best preacher's suit and a cheap purple shirt, his hair moussed and combed into a slippery joke. He closed his eyes and hung his head, imagined himself as the protagonist in a series of still photographs, each picture snapped from a more distant perspective than the last. Initially the camera was close to him, and the shot showed him from the waist up, captured his face and trunk and cut off everything else. The next view was farther away, perhaps taken from the end of the dock, included every bit of him along with a slice of background—bushes and water and riprap and the overhang of a willow tree. Then he was just a slight outline, photographed from the opposite side of the lake, and there was even less of him in the following frame, and the camera withdrew more and more until he disappeared, became a speck in a panorama that had the lake the size of a bottle cap. He knew the Lord could read his heart and understand that his intentions were pure.

He left his chair, walked to the gravel road, scooped up a handful of stones and returned to the dock. He piled the stones on a wooden slat in the walkway and tossed them into the water one at a time, waiting between throws for the concentric rings to disappear and the wound in the lake to heal. He thought about *The Wizard of Oz*, how it used to be aired only a single time each year. The King family would gather in the living room for the ritual, his parents on the sofa, he and Sophie on the floor. Their dad would twist the dial on the rotary antenna, and the picture would wane and strengthen while the control stuttered toward due north. They'd have a pallet of pillows and quilts and a quart of chocolate milk in the fridge, and the mean old witch always scared the heck out of Sophie, gave her bad dreams for a week. Now the movie was available on video and broadcast haphazardly on atheist Ted Turner's stations, in color from beginning to end.

Her mother would tell the ladies at her bridge club the next day that Christina had looked and acted "darling" at the deposition. She arrived at the eighth-floor offices of Gentry, Locke, Rakes and Moore twenty minutes early, about the time Joel was finishing off the final gravel from the pile on the dock. Henry Clay Hanes had posted a paralegal in the lobby of the law firm, and she greeted Christy and her parents and escorted them into a conference room where Hanes and his associate Oliver were waiting. When Christy entered the room, Hanes clapped his hands—they made a short, muffled sound as they struck—and shuffled his feet in an impromptu jig. He kept his hands clasped while his feet skidded on the carpet, and his grin was so deep that it exposed the wire arc of a bridge in his back teeth. "You look like a million bucks, Christy," he said. "Perfect. Thank you."

She was wearing a navy blue suit from Banana Republic, the pants stylish but not fitted, the jacket long enough to cover most of her rear. She had on simple shoes that matched the outfit and no jewelry except a watch with a silver band. There was a suggestion of color on her lips and that was it—the byzantine shades she usually painted around her eyes were absent, her skin blank and unadorned. Her hair was tight against her head, tied in a ponytail, and she looked at the floor and the walls and her hands far more than she looked at the other people in the room. Everyone was delighted— a diffident, vulnerable, beautiful child had arrived to tell her story.

Joel appeared at ten minutes past one and was quickly hauled into his lawyer's office.

"Where in the Sam Hill have you been?" Roland demanded, glaring at Joel. "It's already past one. You were supposed to be here hours ago." He had another lawyer with him, and the new lawyer glared, too.

"I'm sorry to be tardy."

" 'Sorry'? 'Tardy'? I don't think that's quite good enough. I called the hotel, and they said you left at eight. It takes you five hours to make it six miles?"

Joel chucked the huge Bible onto Roland's desk. "I apologize. I needed to gather my thoughts, and time kind of slipped away from me."

"This is a damned disaster, Mr. King. I've got to take you in there cold, completely unprepared. Henry Clay Hanes will eat us alive."

"We've talked on the phone and you've investigated the case, right? Hey, the truth's the truth, so what is there to prepare?"

"Did Mr. Ashe discuss any of this with you, prep you at all?"

"Who? Who's Mr. Ashe?"

"Your lawyer! The guy *you* hired? Remember him? From D.C.? He's talked to me three or four times, helped arrange your travel here. Ring any bells?"

Joel was truly flummoxed for a moment. He finally realized Roland was referring to Sa'ad or the "local counsel" Sa'ad was going to hire—probably Sa'ad with a cell phone and fake accent and bogus stationery. Or maybe he really did have an associate in this part of the world. Who knew? "Oh, right, Mr. Ashe. Sure. I thought you said 'Lash.' But no, Mr. Ashe really didn't give me much instruction. He's more of a big-picture man." Another layer between Sa'ad and any nettlesome trouble, Joel noted. Mr. Ashe almost certainly would be a will-o'-the-wisp if anyone ever attempted to locate him.

"I said Ashe."

"Anyway, I've fired him, so please don't have anything else to do with him, okay? Or anyone else. No contact, no more information. I'm very serious about this. He's off the case completely. From now on, everything stays between us. I've put that in writing." Joel handed Roland a sheet of hotel stationery containing his handwritten directions and signature.

"I'm glad you've been spending your time wisely, Mr. King," Roland said. "This is oh-so-important right now."

A secretary poked her head inside the office and told Roland that Henry Clay Hanes was impatient and ready to begin.

"Right, right, right," Roland said. "Tell him he can leave for all I care. We'll be there in a minute."

"What are you wearing?" asked the other lawyer.

"Who are you?" Joel was polite.

"I'm Allan White—I'm assisting Mr. Roland with this case. You look like Lex Luthor or something. Or Liberace or the King of the Gypsies. What's with the getup? I know Brian told you to dress conservatively."

"I thought I did. I have on a nice suit and a tie. This kind of shirt is very stylish."

"You look like a third world pimp, Mr. King."

"You think so?" Joel asked.

The secretary reappeared at the door. "Mr. Hanes says it's twenty after, and he's going to call Judge Weckstein and ask for sanctions if we don't get started. He's really being pushy."

"We're coming. Tell him we're on the way." Brian Roland stood and looked down at Joel. "Listen. Say as little as possible. Answer 'yes' or 'no' when you can. Don't answer questions you aren't asked, and don't volunteer anything. Always let Hanes complete his question before you respond. Understand?"

"I do." Joel felt sorry for Roland. He seemed to be a capable lawyer and, under normal circumstances, a considerate man. A picture of a child in soccer clothes was near Joel's Bible, a ten- or eleven-year-old boy kneeling in front of a net.

"What are you going to say when you're asked about having sexual relations with Christina Darden?" Roland asked. He was picking up papers and folders from his desk.

"I'll have to tell the truth and admit it. Sorry about that."

"Well, keep it at a minimum and act contrite."

"No problem."

"Follow me," Roland said. "Try not to get lost between here and the conference room."

Christy was to be questioned first. She sat at the end of an oblong mahogany table with Hanes at her elbow and a court reporter to their left. Hanes and Brian Roland began by arguing over the seating arrangements, Hanes insisting that there be an empty chair between his client and Roland, and Roland proclaiming that he'd sit wherever he pleased. They went round and round on the subject for ten minutes, wagging fingers and threatening this and that and reciting sections from the Code of Virginia. The court reporter tapped everything into her machine, her fingers starting and stopping in rhythm with the lawyers' harangues. Finally it was decided that Hanes could remove a chair—the chair next to Christy—to create some personal space for his client, and Brian Roland would occupy the next seat in line while asking his questions. "Just make sure you keep your chair where it is and don't crowd Miss Darden," Hanes warned Roland when they'd concluded their bickering. "I don't want you trying to intimidate this girl. She's been through enough already."

"Tell you what I'll do, Mr. Hanes. Let's adjourn, and I'll get the UN secretary general on the phone and he can send some peacekeeping troops over to guard your precious three feet of inviolate space. Would that satisfy you?"

Christy was a virtuoso. Despite being spoiled and undisciplined, she was a terrifically bright girl. She seemed able to anticipate many of Roland's questions and never had a problem with her answers. It became obvious that Hanes had given her two main talking points: how Joel had betrayed her, and how she was reluctant to trust anyone because of what had happened. She cried when she described the sex, sniffed, and wiped her nose and red-rimmed eyes with a tissue while she told how Joel had penetrated her "with his thing."

"I'm sorry to press you on this," Roland said, "but I have to ask you to clarify that. What do you mean by 'thing'?"

"His . . . thing. His penis," she said meekly. "You know."

"I'm not trying to embarrass you. I just have to make sure," Roland said. He was quiet and tentative, struggling to strike the appropriate tone.

She testified that she and Joel had engaged in intercourse on two separate occasions, each time in his office at the church. The first time she was "sort of overwhelmed and in awe," and she "kinda wanted to and kinda like didn't, probably more no than yes." But Joel never raped her—her mother was simply upset and alarmed when she'd reported as much to the police—and she still considered Preacher Joel her friend. She refused to face him until the conclusion of her testimony, and after meeting his eyes she sobbed and said she was trying not to hold a grudge. Hanes consoled her and poured her a glass of water from a silver metal pitcher. She took two timid swallows, then exited the room with her lawyer's big paternal arm encircling her, his monogrammed cuff and striking gold watch apparent to everyone still sitting at the table, his hands remarkably large and ruddy for a desk worker's.

The court reporter had Joel raise his right hand and swear to tell the truth, and he began his turn by asking everyone to join him in prayer, unleashed his giant Bible and rifled through a flurry of gilded pages.

"Pray?" asked Henry Clay Hanes.

"Yes, I'd like to pray."

"That won't be necessary," Roland said. "Let's just get started."

"Fine with me if he prays," Hanes said. "Technically, he's my witness and it's my choice. Have at it, Preacher." He was holding a thick, expensive pen, and he laid it on the table, then took off his glasses and placed them next to the pen.

"Do you want this on the record?" the court reporter asked.

"Of course. Absolutely," Hanes answered.

"Reverend King, as your attorney and the church's attorney, I'm strongly encouraging you to dispense with the prayer. In fact, I'm instructing you to do so." Roland's voice was strained. He was sitting beside Joel, the two of them having swapped positions with Christy and Hanes at the head of the table.

"He can do it if he wants," Hanes replied, happy to get a preview of Joel and his demeanor before they concentrated on business. "He's my witness."

"He's my client, Mr. Hanes. I don't know how you do things in Richmond, but here you don't tell *my* client what to do." He stared at Joel. "Let me see you outside, please."

"There's no need," Joel said. "Let's bow our heads."

"Joel, I'm insisting you shut your mouth and take a break." Roland was angry, almost yelled. He gripped Joel's elbow.

Joel ignored him and launched into a long-winded, meandering prayer that wandered from scripture to scripture and notion to notion but, to Roland's relief, dwelled mostly on Joel's innocence and the unfairness of his legal woes. He concluded by asking the Lord to forgive Henry Clay Hanes, "for he knows not what he is doing."

"Thank you, Mr. King. I appreciate your generosity where I'm concerned." Hanes took hold of his elaborate pen.

"Reverend King. I prefer to be called Reverend King." Joel made certain he sounded pompous.

Hanes put on his glasses. "Then Reverend King it will be."

Hanes was skilled at his trade. Joel thought it remarkable that the same man who had been so bombastic and childish earlier in his sandbox squabble over chairs could be so intuitive and effective. Hanes stalked and nipped and worked at his own speed, reversed course occasionally and repeated the same question three or four times if Joel was the slightest bit evasive. There was no bluster in his method, nothing at all threatening, just a methodical, unflappable doggedness that never subsided and seemed almost physically smothering.

It took Hanes half an hour to get to the first sexual event. He was quiet for a moment, looked Joel square in the eye and didn't utter a word. He tapped his pen across his meaty palm, waited exactly three counts between strikes: Pop—one, two, three. Pop—one, two, three. Pop—one, two, three. Joel felt an adrenaline pang sting his stomach, noticed his hands were pinching the edge of the table.

"Now, Reverend King, did there come a day, while meeting with Miss Darden in your church office, that you and Miss Darden engaged in sexual contact?"

Joel considered making Hanes explain the term, but decided against it, didn't see any need to prolong the process and get bludgeoned with five more questions. "Yes."

"This sexual encounter occurred within the confines of Roanoke First Baptist Church?"

"That's correct," Joel answered.

"And you were meeting with Miss Darden in your capacity as her minister?"

"True."

"You were counseling her?"

"Right," Joel said. He glimpsed a contemptuous look the court reporter sent his way.

"And during this session you knew she was a minor?"

"She was seventeen, almost eighteen."

"That would make her a minor, yes?" Hanes was clutching the pen, but only the tip was visible, sticking out from the bottom of his fist.

"She was a minor."

"My math suggests you were forty-one when this happened."

"Is that a question? Do I need to answer that?" Joel allowed the first trace of irritation to appear in his voice.

"Please."

"Your math is correct. I was forty-one. Maybe you should try logarithms and quadratic equations—you'd probably be more challenged."

"I'll keep that in mind. And it was during this counseling session at the church, inside your office, that you first had sexual intercourse with Miss Darden, sometime on or about May the third?"

"I don't remember the exact date." Joel was short with Hanes. "I'll take your word for it."

"Thank you. And did you have sexual intercourse with Miss Darden on that date at your church as I've described?"

Joel smoothed his gaudy purple tie, ran his hand from the knot to the end of the faux-silk cloth. He gave Hanes a full view of his features and displayed the embryonic stage of the brazen smile he'd practiced in the hotel mirror. "Yes, I did."

"I see. And did she consent?"

"She was nervous, but other than that she was willing. She consented, yes."

"How long did the intercourse last, Reverend King?"

Joel shifted his eyes in Roland's direction. "Do I have to answer? What does this have to do with anything?"

"Answer the question," Roland commanded.

"How long did it last? I don't know. Ten minutes, maybe? Fifteen?"

"Did you ejaculate, Reverend King?"

"Why are you asking me these questions? Are you some kind of voyeur or something?" Joel grimaced and closed his Bible, dropped the cover so there was a thud when the pages hit.

"You need to answer. It's a permissible question," Allan White said. He and Brian Roland were both seething, their disdain for their client poorly concealed, their curt language an unmistakable sign of their disgust.

Joel ratcheted up the smile, left it a whisker short of a sneer. "You guys are enjoying this, aren't you? Living vicariously? Am I right?"

Roland addressed Joel as if he were a child or simpleton, spoke to him with slow, exaggerated patience. "You see, Reverend King, as part of Mr. Hanes's case—their claim for damages—they are entitled to know if you put the plaintiff at risk for a pregnancy or a venereal disease. Also, it would be important to know if you stopped the act—perhaps felt bad about it— or concluded only when you were sexually gratified. They need to know how long Miss Darden was subjected to the encounter. Was it a minute or an hour? These are all relevant issues."

"Why don't you draw him a map?" Henry Clay Hanes complained. "Maybe write him a script."

"He asked a question, and I answered him, Mr. Hanes." Roland bore down on Joel. "You understand now?"

"Sure," Joel snarled. "Whatever you say."

"So did you ejaculate?" Hanes continued.

"The first time, yeah. I believe I did."

Brian Roland cringed. His forehead wrinkled into three parallel ridges, and the skin at the corners of his eyes shot full of webs.

"Did you use a condom or any other type of protection?"

"What do you think?"

"I don't know. I wasn't there. Did you use a condom or any other protection?"

"No, but she didn't turn up pregnant, now did she? And she didn't contract any disease. So what does it matter?"

"Could we take a break for about ten minutes?" Roland asked, a pitiful effort to interrupt Hanes's progress and to buy a few moments to talk some sense into his client.

"No, I'm sorry. I can't possibly fathom why we should stop." Hanes kept his focus on Joel and didn't even look at Roland when he spoke.

"We've been at this for over an hour," Roland said, "and I need a break."

"Why? Other than to impede my questioning of your client, why do you need a break?" Hanes was collected as always.

"I need to use the restroom, Mr. Hanes. Too much java, okay?" Roland stood. "And we will stop while I'm gone."

"I'm guessing your client's bladder needs relief also. You want him to be excused too? So you can woodshed him? Coach him?"

"Are you questioning my integrity?"

"Goodness no." Hanes practically drawled.

"I don't need to take a break," Joel offered, and both White and Roland attacked him with incensed glares. "I don't," he said in response to their incendiary looks. "Let's keep going."

"Ah, well. I guess that settles it," Hanes crowed. "The Reverend wants to continue. If he wants to stay here with us, why don't you go ahead on down the hall and take care of your restroom needs, Mr. Roland? We'll wait right here for you. 'Course you won't be able to meet with your client, but you can visit the toilet."

Roland's neck had covered over with saw-toothed splotches and his coat was crooked, pulled too close to his collar on one side.

"So you didn't use any sexual protection?" Hanes asked, simply began again with Roland hovering there, stewing and apoplectic.

"No."

"How about the second time you had sex?"

"How about it?" Joel remarked.

Roland was still on his feet. Allan White tugged his sleeve and spoke so everyone could hear. "Go ahead and leave if you need to. I'll cover this until you get back. Don't worry about it." Given the chance to save face, Roland squeezed his partner's shoulder and left the room, lifted a glass of water and held it at arm's length before departing, gave the impression he was considering whether he should empty it on Henry Clay Hanes, soak his sorry ass to the bone.

"Did you use protection the second time you had intercourse?"

"No."

"Did you ejaculate?"

"No," Joel said.

"Why?"

"I just didn't. She began complaining, and I stopped."

Hanes thought about the answer. "So she was—strike that," he said. "Forget it."

"What?"

"Let's move on." Hanes said, but was quiet for so long that Joel thought he might be through. "Tell me, Reverend," he finally said, "what your thoughts were each time you engaged in sex with this girl. What you were thinking?"

"I don't follow you."

Brian Roland came back into the room and leaned against the wall, next to a print of horses and hounds and men in red jodhpurs. The picture was matted in green, and there was a similar piece across the room, both of them in ornate gold frames.

"Well, what were your intentions? You were married at the time, correct?"

"I was married."

"Did you see this as a romance, a relationship with a future?"

"Hardly." Joel finger-sculpted the plastered, goopy sides of his hair.

"Well, what was it then? Simply a slip, a bad choice?"

Joel didn't answer.

"Reverend King?" Hanes prodded.

"Okay, listen. I'm smart enough to know you guys will take umbrage at what I'm going to say. I doubt you'll understand, but I don't want you to think I'm some weak, scabby pent-up little man who couldn't resist the first pretty girl who came his way." Joel turned loose the full smile. "Not at all. I had sex with Christy because I wanted to. I don't think it's a bad thing, don't think she's been damaged or scarred in any way. Better me than some drunk, pimply boy after her prom. It's part of my due, part of the whole spiritual cycle I manage as the Lord's instrument on earth."

"Your due?" For the first time, Hanes seemed surprised.

"Sure. I'm her pastor. Where she's concerned, I'm man but not of man." Joel was making up gibberish, anxious and scared and exhilarated. He opened the gaudy Bible with a flourish, spread his hands over the pages like a game-show host caressing a prize. "I know you will disagree, but the truth is in the Word. She's a part of my flock, part of me, and mine to draw close to the Father."

"Like a job perk? You are entitled to have sex with the women of your congregation?" Hanes had dropped his pen.

"Scoff and twist my words all you want. Go ahead."

Allan White appeared to have stopped breathing; his lips were parted and his nostrils were flared and everything about him seemed as if he'd sucked in a breath and seized up. Roland had gone from angry to resigned, was slumped against the wall with his neck dappled and his hands dangling.

"Oh, no. I don't mean to twist your words," Hanes said. "No sir. And I'm not judging you one way or the other. I just want to make sure I understand your position—no more, no less."

"Well, what don't you understand?" Joel added another vainglorious stroke of his hair, pinned the wings against his head with the heels of his hands.

"I think I'm clear. You feel because of your position as Christy's minister, it's acceptable to have sexual relations with her?"

"Exactly. Not everyone would agree—I understand that." Joel heard the cushioned pecking of the reporter's keys continue for a second or two after he finished his answer.

"I'm not here to decide the right or wrong of things, Reverend." Hanes was accommodating and generous, eager to give Joel as much leeway as he could. "But you feel what you did was good, a positive for Christy Darden?"

"Sure." The word hung, was hard for Joel to disgorge. "Absolutely. She's been especially blessed by having lain with me. I'm her minister, the steward of her faith, the Lord's conduit here on earth. Her union with me is a union with the Heavenly Father." Joel flipped his eyes at the ceiling. "How could anyone view it as wrong? A closer relationship with God, achieved through intimacy—what a blessing she's received. And let's face it—you gentlemen can sit here all day with your contrived disdain and fake indignation, and there's not a one of you who wouldn't sleep with her if you thought you could get away with it."

"I see." Hanes could have asked other questions, kept gouging and prying, but he didn't seem inclined to dilute the potency of his work by highlighting the obvious or providing Joel an opportunity to qualify a response. His case couldn't improve much more unless horns began sprouting from Joel's head or a pointed tail stirred in his britches. "Well, Reverend, thank you. Thank you for your candor. Those are all my inquiries. Your lawyers may have something to ask."

"By the way, Mr. Hanes," Joel added, "you didn't address this, but it's an important component of church doctrine and relevant to my relationship with Christy Darden. You need to understand the role of women in our denomination. The wife is subservient to the husband, the woman subservient to the man." Joel bent his index finger and tapped the Bible. "There's no disputing that. Of course, it's a two-way street. We respect women, love them and recognize our duty as men and leaders of the church to nurture them."

"I didn't mean to keep you from fully amplifying your answers, Reverend King. Thank you for the additional insight."

Brian Roland looked at Allan White, then at Joel. He studied the print beside him for a moment, most likely wishing he could dive through the glass and mount the big sorrel horse and ride away into the forest with the dogs and hunters, grow woozy on warm ale and go missing for several days. "No questions," he said.

The bank box and pawnshop were downtown, both within walking distance of Brian Roland's office. Joel had hightailed it out of Gentry, Locke, Rakes and Moore, Brian Roland berating him all the way to the elevator, saying over and over that Joel couldn't have done worse if he'd tried. Christy's father had jumped to his feet when Joel went scurrying through the lobby and had threatened to kill him with his bare hands, had called Joel a child molester and a fraud. Joel was relieved to be finished with the deposition and away from the discord, felt as if he'd been belly-crawling through land mines and barbed wire and somehow made it through alive. Both wracked and gratified, he'd taken off his jacket and undone his shirt at the top button by the time he reached the bank. He signed his name twice, then he and a redheaded girl in a summer dress simultaneously inserted their keys to open the box. "I'm here to pick up some jewelry," he told her. "I won't be long."

"There's no rush," she said as she was leaving.

"Thanks." He took the bag of borrowed goods from his pocket, lingered by his safe-deposit box and waved at the redhead and flashed the bright sack as he exited the vault. The sun and heat ambushed him when he left the frigid marble lobby, caused him to breathe through his mouth and completely remove his tie, the late-summer air trapped on three sides by brick, concrete, glass and pavement, so stale and stagnant it seemed a molecule away from solidifying.

He'd never noticed the pawnshop before, even though he'd passed by hundreds of times over the years. He hesitated as he walked to the entrance, surveying the huge display windows on each side of him to see what people had left behind, what they could do without if they were desperate, hopeful or in a predicament. There were several guitars and a solitary saxophone, a silver tea set, boom boxes and stereos, a man's brown leather jacket and a row of wedding bands and engagement rings. One diamond was in the three-carat range, and for a moment Joel wondered about its journey, how something so beautiful had arrived at such an unimpressive fate. An electronic tone sounded when he opened the door, two bleats in different octaves, a shrill, inhospitable greeting that warned the store someone was entering.

The man behind the counter was in his fifties, neatly dressed, wearing several rings and a chunky gold bracelet. He was short and compact, had on a knit shirt and smelled like cologne and strong soap when Joel got close to him.

"Can I help you?" he said pleasantly.

"I hope so. How are you today?"

"Fine, thanks. Just fine."

"Seems like a lot of musical folks wind up pawning things," Joel said.

"It's a tough way to make a living, even if you're good at it. Lot of drinking and drugs, too." The man glanced at the window. "You interested in an instrument? I got plenty more."

"No. My name's Joel King. Nice to meet you." They shook hands, and Joel felt the underside of the man's gold ring. "I'm actually looking to raise a little cash myself."

"Okay. I'm Rodger Adams, but people call me Doc."

"I have some jewelry I need to, uh, get a loan on. To pledge."

"I'll be glad to consider it, but I ain't moving much jewelry these days. I'll tell you what I can pay, and if we can do business, great. If not, I don't mean to offend you by what I offer. You might do better to try advertising in the newspaper."

"Sure. I understand." Joel was reaching into his pocket as he spoke. The store was cool; he could hear an air conditioner running, and the chilled air dried the moisture on his face and hands, left his skin feeling dirty and salted. He removed the bag of jewelry and handed it to the man without opening it. "Take a look and tell me what you think."

Doc set the bag on the counter, produced a black velvet pad and a jeweler's loupe, switched on a small lamp, emptied the contents into a pile and began inspecting the pieces one by one, occasionally picking up a bracelet or ring and holding it in front of his face. He squinted with his uncovered eye and spent a long time studying two of the pieces, moved them closer and turned them over and then held them between himself and the storefront windows to get a different light. "Where'd you come by all this?" He kept working on the jewelry, made a point of not looking at Joel when he spoke.

"My mother. It belonged to her, and she gave it to me."

"Your mother, huh?" His voice was a studied blend of interest and suspicion. "You from around here?"

"Used to be. We lived here for years."

"Where'd you live at?" He was touching some of the stones with the thin wire tip of a device he'd taken from a drawer and connected to an electrical outlet. Every time the tip made contact with a jewel, a green light came on and a buzzing vibration went up the gizmo's black handle.

"I was the pastor at Roanoke First Baptist. I'm living in Montana now. What're you doing to the jewelry? That won't scratch something, will it?"

"It's a diamond tester. Perfectly safe." Doc folded his loupe inside itself, quit his tests and inspections. "You the fellow they run off about a year ago?"

"Yep. I'm the guy." Joel flickered a grin and fingered his collar, even though he'd already unbuttoned it.

"My sister goes to church there. You know Shelly Ayers?"

"Why sure. Certainly. She was in charge of our missionary offerings and coordinated our Wednesday night church suppers. A fine lady. I thought the world of her. Phillip is her husband, right? He occasionally came to our services and seemed like a solid fellow as well."

"He's a bastard and a scumbag, but that's another story."

"Oh."

"My sister says you got a bum deal," Doc remarked.

"She was very kind to me, very supportive."

"Read in the paper where you'd been found guilty, though. Sexing some teenager, as I recall."

"I pled guilty to contributing to the delinquency of a minor. It seemed the wisest choice at the time, and saved the church a lot of grief and anguish."

"Yeah, well, that's one way to look at it. If it ain't dope or liquor, it's a man or a woman chasing after relations behind nearly every pawn I got in the shop."

"Huh."

"Yep," Doc said.

Two kids with sideburns and skateboards came through the door, the two-tone signal sounding for each boy.

"How much for the black Les Paul?" one of them asked.

"Gotta get six hundred," Doc said.

"You didn't pay no six hundred," the boy answered.

"That would be how I make money."

"You couldn't take four?"

"I *could* give it to you, but I ain't going to. Five seventy-five's the best I can do."

"Shit. You sure?" His skateboard was tucked under his arm.

"I'm sure."

"I'll think about it. I got a friend can find me a better price."

"Let me know," Doc replied.

"Later." The boys turned and left the shop, the door sounding again when they tripped the sensors, and Joel heard the boards' hard wheels hit the sidewalk and clatter away.

"Those skateboards are the worst," Doc said. "Oughta be outlawed."

"I've never given them much mind," Joel said.

"So you got this from your mom, right?"

"Correct."

"Well, this is some okay merchandise. Some nice stones, better than average. I reckon you knew that already, huh?"

"Not really. I just took them from my bank box."

"Platinum settings, some of the diamonds would go E or F, most all around IF clarity."

"I'm not familiar with gems or how you evaluate them."

"Have you taken them anywhere else, to any jewelry stores?"

Joel felt the first bit of con start to worm its way into Doc's delivery. "No. I didn't realize you could do that."

"The tennis bracelet's not so hot, and I'd have to steam everything, do some cleaning. What kind of money you looking for?"

"What can you give me?"

"Tough to say. I'd have trouble moving this. My clients are into sparkle more than quality. Antiques don't do well for me. Like I said, the stuff's nice, but it ain't what you'd call flawless. Know what I'm saying?"

"Sure. So what's your highest offer?"

Doc drummed his fingers on the counter, tried to keep from leaping out of his skin. "I could give you maybe five grand for everything."

"Wow. That's more than I expected."

"Yeah. Well, I ain't here to screw nobody. I want to make a fair profit and give people what I can. That's the reputation I've got. Ask anyone about Doc Adams."

"I really hate to let it all go, it being my mother's. What's the stuff worth? I mean, I understand you have to make money, but what would you say is the actual value of the whole bag?"

"I couldn't tell you that. Depends. Depends on who wants it and where you go to sell it and a million other things." Doc had acquired a slight tic; twice his right eye and the end of his mouth yawed toward each other while he was talking.

"Huh." Joel was enjoying the give-and-take, deriving a corrupt pleasure in having the catbird's seat and watching Doc feint and squirm and tell half-truths. Joel was finally in control, the hustle and grift altogether on his terms, and it was a satisfying feeling—even though it shouldn't have been—bracing and addictive, as if he could see around every bend and had hours to consider his answers, and Doc was small and impotent, about knee-high.

"I can't help you there, not really."

"So, what would be the least valuable piece?" Joel asked.

"The diamond earrings—" Doc interrupted himself. "No, come to think of it, the least expensive is this dinner ring here." He picked up a diamond and emerald ring. "It looks like a lot, but it's old, the setting's bad, and these are all commercial-grade stones. You can find something like this over at the mall for two or three hundred bucks."

"I see. I'm not sure about letting it go. Lot of sentimental value, been in the family a long, long while."

"So what are you needin' to get?" Doc asked. His eye and mouth did their small spasm.

"What were you going to say about the earrings, the small ones there? They're diamonds, aren't they?"

"Average stuff—mall quality. Dime a dozen." Doc accelerated his effort, pushed harder. "Tell you what. My sister's got nice things to say about you, and I'm figuring you caught a bad break. I know how damn holier-than-thou some church folks can be, and maybe this'll earn me some credit with the man upstairs, right? I shouldn't do it, but I'll go fifty-five hundred for the whole bag."

"Wow. That's awfully kind. Huh." Joel pretended to consider the offer. "I'm beginning to feel bad about this all of a sudden. What would you offer for just the earrings?"

"Not much. Maybe forty bucks."

"How long will I have to redeem them?"

"Thirty days. What would you take for the rest of the stuff? You tell me."

"You've been more than generous. It's not that. I appreciate your kindness and candor, but I'm getting a serious case of cold feet."

"How about I give you a thousand for the ring and the earrings?"

"I'm going to stick with the earrings. I may have to come back, but for now I'll take the forty." Joel reached for the rest of the jewelry, cupped his hand around the rings and brooches and necklaces, and dragged them across the countertop, his curved fingers and stiff wrist like a miniature vaudeville hook appearing to end the show.

"Okay, hang on a minute. How about ten thousand for everything. Whadda you say?"

"I appreciate it, but I've made up my mind."

"Name your price then. You tell me."

"Maybe some other time. I'm going to pledge the earrings today and try to get by with that. I'm grateful to you, though. Thanks."

"Give me your number in Montana before you leave, and I'll keep in touch. Here's my info." Doc took a business card from a plastic holder next to the register, handed it to Joel. "Let me see that again," Doc said, and Joel returned the card to him. "I'm goin' to give you my cell and my home number. You decide to do anything, how 'bout you contact me first?"

"You have my word."

Joel had several empty hours before he departed Roanoke, and after leaving Doc he roamed around downtown, spent part of his pawn money on a handcrafted candle for Sophie and a paperback copy of Paul Tillich's *Systematic Theology*. After purchasing the text, he chatted with a thoughtful bookseller named Robert about Tillich and Dietrich Bonhoeffer and Reinhold Niebuhr and Karl Barth. Joel ate free cookies and drank specialty coffee and had an amiable disagreement over precisely what Barth brought to the fray, finally conceding to the shop owner that Barth was occasionally disjointed and a tad too technical in his writings. They discussed theology and philosophy, proofs and syllogisms and the myriad contrivances writers and thinkers use to hog-tie gods, tiptoed to the banks of the Jordan but never got wet, sipped mocha hazelnut, nibbled bakery sweets and kept everything at arm's length, politely debated religion like mathematicians analyzing pi or historians wrangling over the Teapot Dome Scandal. They shook hands when they ended their conversation, and Robert accompanied Joel to the door, wished him well and invited him to visit again.

Joel delayed the most difficult decision as long as he could, waiting until he had only an hour left before he needed to arrive at the airport. He decided to drive to Roanoke First Baptist without making up his mind about much else, didn't know if he would stop or leave the car or go inside. The drive was short and didn't allow enough time for the air to blow cold from the Neon's vents, even though the fan was set on high and the control lever was pushed completely into the blue. Joel made a right turn and looked in his mirror, saw no one behind him. He slowed and watched the church inch by through his window, noticed two new buses and a fleet of matching vans in the parking lot. After another lap around the block, he pulled onto a side street, attended to the meter with two dimes and walked toward Roanoke First Baptist.

At first he felt a profound sadness, a swell of nostalgia and self-pity that weighed him down and caused him to gaze at the yard and building with his hands on his hips, sick to death over paradise lost. After a few minutes, though, he began to feel better, took some comfort from what he was seeing. The church was a feat of architecture, and the steeple was high and impeccably painted, not a flake or peel to be found, and the yard was perfectly cut, the walks swept. Inside, on the red carpet, so many things miraculous had happened—baptisms, marriages, confessions, transformations and forgiveness—and no matter how much these holy wonders had been dimmed or eroded or defiled by inattention and temptation after the fact, no one could deny that the mighty presence of the Lord God had dwelled under this roof and swallowed up people whole, made them pristine for an instant. The divine gift may have been gnawed to gristle by gossip, backbiting, avarice, coveting and false idols, but for a blessed while the church—his church—had been a repository of goodness, a bulwark against convenient choices and humanism's hollow enticements.

Joel turned without drawing any closer, wiped tears away and rubbed his purple polyester sleeve across his nose. He reached the Neon without taking another look at Roanoke First Baptist, drove north with the tears distorting his vision, relieved to know there was a rock in the world but heartbroken he'd been cleaved from it.

While he was waiting to board the plane to Montana, he began reading Tillich, recalled some of the passages from seminary, one particularly:

> . . . the theological truth of yesterday is defended as an unchangeable message against the theological truth of today and tomorrow. Fundamentalism fails to make contact with the present situation, not because it speaks from beyond every situation, but because it speaks from a situation of the past. It elevates something finite and transitory to infinite and eternal validity.

Joel read several pages and tossed the book in the trash, regretted paying ten bucks for it so as to have his unfortunate choices justified in print by a Harvard professor who thumbed his nose at orthodoxy and seemed to suggest that right and wrong changed with the day of the week. Staring vacantly at the trash can, waiting for his plane to board, he wondered if he'd ever again be certain of anything.

eleven

Even though his trip to Virginia had lasted only two days, the time zones and the air travel left Joel torpid and out of sorts when he woke up at his sister's on Tuesday, caused him to sleep through Tut's sunrise antics and a series of snooze-bar postponements. It took coffee with extra sugar and a burst of cold water as he was finishing his shower to return him to normal. He dusted the living room, washed clothes, browsed parts of the Sunday paper and made himself an early lunch, spread peanut butter on a dry heel slice of white bread and shooed the fruit flies from around a mushy yellow apple before slicing it into quarters. He put the half sandwich and apple pieces on a plate, then sniffed the contents of a milk jug, ignored the expiration date and filled Baker's plastic Ringling Brothers souvenir cup to the brim.

He watched the last segment of an ESPN fishing show, left his sister a cheerful note and drove the Taurus to Jack Howard's office, where he sat twenty-five minutes in the tedious reception area, reading pamphlets on sexually transmitted diseases, child abuse and drug-treatment programs. No one else was there except Mrs. Heller, the secretary, and Howard was busy with a crossword puzzle when Joel finally was allowed through the door.

"How's things going, my criminal friend?" Howard asked. The puzzle was a newspaper feature, and Howard had folded the paper to a fraction of its size. He erased a wrong entry and blew the rubber waste onto the floor.

"Just fine. I'm reporting for my monthly contact. I've got all my fees and so forth."

"Good. Hand 'em over."

Joel gave him a money order for his court obligations and thirty dollars in cash.

"I'm glad we're getting along so well. You still workin'?"

"Same two jobs," Joel said.

"Screwin' any teenagers?" He didn't bother to look up from the puzzle.

"No."

"See that you don't."

Joel did his best not to despise Howard. Condemn the sin, not the sinner, he reminded himself as he hunkered down in the uncomfortable chair. "I was thinking," he began, drastically lowering his voice, "about what I might have to do to be discharged from probation. I've heard that if I'm employed and the state's paid in full, I might be able to have my supervision terminated."

"Hell, you ain't been here but a few months. You got, what, three years with me?"

"True. But it was my understanding if I do well and pay all my fines and costs . . . and *fees* . . . I might get an early release."

"Hey. Whadda you know. Here's one you can help me with. Five across. 'Slang for inmate.' Three letters. You want to have a go at it?"

"Con," Joel said.

"Very good, Mr. King." Howard wrote in the letters.

"So is there any truth to that? I've heard through the grapevine that it's sort of policy. One of the jailers in Roanoke mentioned it, but he said it was probably the case everywhere."

"I have the discretion to release probationers if I think the court supervision has served its purpose. But you're with me for three years. Thirty-six lovely months."

"I understand. I figure by working two jobs, staying out of trouble and saving my money, I might be able to pay everything off in the next six or seven months. Everything," Joel added for emphasis, though it was apparent Howard was already calculating his dishonest profit.

"What'd you have in mind?" He leaned back in his seat, kept his yellow wooden pencil in his hand. The chair's metal swivel squeaked when he reclined.

"Whatever's necessary. I'm sure you have some type of guidelines."

"You're going to owe all your Virginia payments, then fees for thirty-six months, and on top of that an additional premium for the paperwork and filings I'd have to prepare for early release." Howard rocked back farther and put his feet on the desk.

"I've paid some already, so we're talking about, say, another thousand for you plus administrative costs added to that. Am I pretty close?"

"I'd guess about two thousand would cover it," Howard said.

"Of course, if I left Missoula for a better job in Roanoke, you wouldn't receive any local fees after I'm gone, correct? I mean, if I go home come January, your thirty-six months becomes very much abbreviated."

"I have to approve the transfer." Howard was smug, didn't seem concerned by Joel's bluff.

"True. But why wouldn't you? When I have a written offer from a captain of industry, when I've paid my court costs faithfully, when I've produced letters from the community welcoming me to Roanoke, why wouldn't you? As I understand it, if you won't, I'll bet your chief will, especially when my new boss and my attorney start raising Cain."

"You think you can threaten me?"

"Oh no. Certainly not. I was just thinking that if I were in your shoes, a thousand bucks and no fuss would probably be a fair arrangement."

Howard jerked down his feet, rolled his chair close to his desk and stretched as far as he could toward Joel. "You think you can chisel me? Come in my office and yank my chain? You're a two-bit, piece-of-shit criminal. You'll pay what I tell you and be damn happy to do it."

Joel leaned forward as well, met Howard midway across his desk. He spoke in a hushed, restrained voice. "The worst you can do is return me to Virginia, and I pull six months. You get zero, no thirty dollars, no thousand dollars, no two thousand dollars. And whether anyone believes me or not, I promise I'll report you to everyone I meet from Missoula to Roanoke. It's your choice, Mr. Howard. A thousand and we leave as friends, or nothing and we go to battle."

Howard raised from his seat, balancing himself with his arms. His nose almost grazed Joel's, and his warped, misshapen face blocked everything else in the room. "You think you're the first piece-of-shit jailbird ever to try to shake me down? I *will* send your ass back to the slammer. You go ahead and challenge me. You're nothing but a lowlife."

"So, Mr. Howard, are you. You just happen to have a tie and a state office," Joel said. They remained face-to-face.

Howard removed his right hand from the desk and slowly brought it to Joel's throat. "I'll cut off your head and drink your blood, you understand?" he said, clinching Joel's neck with his thumb and first two fingers. "You don't know half the shit I got in store for you. You think you can push me around? Say shit to me as you please? I don't see you leavin' my supervision for less than *three* thousand." He squeezed the soft pockets of flesh where Joel's neck met the curve of his jawbone.

Joel retreated and separated himself from Howard's grip. The sides of his neck stung, and it was difficult to swallow, felt as if something was massing in his windpipe. "Have it your way, Mr. Howard. I'll be gone soon, and you'll not see another red cent from me after that." He rotated his head, made two slow loops to work out the soreness. "You do what you have to do."

"You just bought yourself a boatload of trouble, my criminal friend." Howard was still humped over his desk, reminded Joel of a big chimp propped on its knuckles.

"I doubt it," Joel said with genuine confidence and then left the room. Howard stormed to the door of his office and screamed and cursed as Joel was walking through the lobby, but Joel didn't pay any attention to him, didn't break stride or parry the tongue-lashing.

By the time Joel arrived at High Pines, the marks on his throat had turned color, starting to darken into two bruises. He'd taken satisfaction in confronting Howard and felt certain the probation officer would calm down and relent in due time. He would wait a week or so and then call the greedy swine, say he was sorry, grease that approach for a while so the half man–half mole could regain his pride and brag to his friends how he'd taken another thug to school. In the end, though, Joel was optimistic he'd be done with probation when the new year started, and the cost would be a thousand crooked dollars, not the two thousand Howard had first demanded.

As usual, his mother was dressed for the hootenanny, her attire somewhere between Joan Baez and Dale Evans. When Joel opened the door to her room, she was sitting on her bed studying a piece of mail. Her lips mouthed every word, and her head followed the sentences across the page in the pattern of an old-fashioned typewriter carriage.

"Hi, Mom," he said.

"Shhh. Please be quiet while I'm reading. There are children dying, going hungry, no clothes. Naked children from other places. They've written me, and I've got to help."

Joel picked up an envelope from beside his mother, checked the return address, then peered at the letter she was clutching. From the Worldwide Children's Relief Fund, it showed a beautiful, poor child with doleful eyes and dirty feet, asked for a dollar a day—or more—if Helen King could find it in her heart to contribute.

"I've got to do something," she said.

"I don't know how these organizations get your name," Joel said, as much to himself as to her. "It's probably a scam. I know almost every charity there is, and I've never heard of these people. Probably ten percent goes to the recipients, ninety percent for overhead and administration and fund-raisers in Hilton Head."

"This little girl is hungry," she said, totally obsessed by the letter.

"Did you understand what I just said?" he asked her, and it occurred to him how completely cynicism had set up shop in him, how less than a year removed from the pulpit, he took nothing at face value, dissected every situation and second-guessed every motive, constantly kept an eye peeled for the sag in generous deeds and the hidden agenda in beneficence.

On the verge of tears, she held the letter closer to Joel. "Do you know this child? I can't remember who she is, but she's written me for help. I think she used to come to the library when I worked there. I was a librarian for twenty-one years. I believe she was one of my reading-circle children."

"I'm not sure who she is. We'll take care of her, okay?" He sat on the bed and put his arm around his mother, trying to comfort her. "We'll send her some money for food."

"Yes. Yes, we should do that. Send her money soon."

"We will."

"Where's my purse? I need to write a check."

"I'll send the money. You don't have to worry yourself." He took the letter. "I'll take care of everything, and the little girl will be eating a hot meal by tomorrow night."

"Thank you. You must be an angel."

He smiled. "I'm your son, Joel."

"I'd tend to her myself if I could. I would. But I can't. My children took my car from me, stole it." Her eyelids raised high enough for Joel to see the white above her pupils. "My Volvo. Joel and Sophie stole it from me."

"I'm Joel, and Sophie and I didn't steal your car."

"It had another ten years left. I had the oil changed like you're supposed to."

Joel took hold of his mother's hand and buried it in his. Her knuckles were deformed and several of her fingers were arthritic and skeletal, and the skin on her arm was as thin as tissue paper, mottled by black-and-blue ruptures. Eighty-one years had eroded her, taken the smooth color and suppleness from her small limbs, whittled her down to her last layer. He shook her gently, attempting to tune her in. "Mom, look at me. It's Joel, your son. The preacher."

"I want to go home," she said, her eyes back to normal, droopy and translucent with film.

"Okay. I think you should."

"I have a wonderful home in Indiana, filled with many expensive things. My grandparents adored me. They used to buy me licorice."

"Licorice, huh?"

"They lived like royalty and treated me like a princess. My daddy was a dashing man."

"He was. I've seen pictures." Joel hadn't turned loose of her hand.

"I need to go home," she said again.

"How about this? Would you like me to take you for a nice ride? Enjoy some fresh air?"

"I can't miss supper."

"It's two hours until you eat. I'll have you back in plenty of time."

"We line up at five sharp."

"I'll have you here before then. I promise."

"What a lovely picture," she said.

Joel searched the room for clues but had no idea what she was talking about. "While we're gone," he said, "we'll drop off the money for the child at the post office."

"All my children are grown. I give them money for their birthday."

Joel released her hand. "Do you still want to send money to the little girl in the letter?"

"I was a librarian for twenty-one years. What a lovely picture."

He showed his mother the letter, pointed at the pretty overseas girl who needed blankets, rice and clean drinking water. "What about her? Do you remember what we were discussing?"

Helen King was the dotty czarina of her own mismatched world, dwelling partly in the immediate moment, partly somewhere else, the starving child from the reading circle a cipher who'd sojourned in her head without leaving tracks or impressions or any permanent record. "I'm going home after my meal," she said. "My family's taking me out of this prison."

Sophie had told him the worst ones, at the end, gaze in the mirror and don't recognize who they're seeing, lose all sense of self and live in constant apprehension, terrorized by marauding strangers in their rooms and foreign faces tracking them from behind. He hugged and kissed his mom, pocketed the Children's Fund information and walked to the door.

"I love you," he said. "I'll see you soon."

"Come again," she answered. "I love you, too."

Sweet Briar College was just the place for Christy to resume her education. It was a single-sex school, no men admitted, and the curriculum included a number of courses in horseback riding, film studies and French. The curriculum also included mixers and dances and parties and cotillions and formals and boathouse bashes and trips to Hampden-Sydney, Randolph-Macon, Washington and Lee, VMI and her old stomping ground, the University of Virginia. The Sweet Briar rules were simple—show up for class, don't cause trouble, don't be a bitch, and convince the folks writing the tuition checks that, *oui oui*, thirty thousand a year is well spent to teach your daughter how to sit an English saddle and do dressage and speak a second tongue. Most important from Christy's perspective, the absence of men and the sheltered weekdays spent riding horses or playing field hockey or tackling the first chapter of *The Great Gatsby* or lighting candles for important vigils, all this restraint and denial granted the students an extreme license when weekends, holidays and special occasions came calling; it made good sense for the girls to break loose on Saturdays or Thanksgiving break, since they'd sacrificed and done without, paid their ascetic dues. Just don't get busted, turn up pregnant or puke on someone's riding boots.

A week into her new school year, at the beginning of September, Christy bought some mushrooms from a girl named Lisa who lived on her hall, skipped her last class and headed to Richmond in her BMW. It was two weeks after her deposition, and she'd been on the phone with Henry Clay Hanes almost daily. As agreed, she and Joel had not contacted each other. She purchased a beer with her fake ID when she left Sweet Briar, but she didn't sample the mushrooms, didn't want to meet with Mr. Hanes and have him melting and turning *Fantasia* colors while she was discussing her money.

Henry Clay Hanes was beaming when he ushered Christy into his office. He made Oliver fetch her a glass of ice and a bottle of water despite her saying she didn't want anything to drink, and he slyly produced an ashtray from his desk, let her smoke a cigarette on the condition she promise not to tell anyone. "Hell, I burn one myself every now and then," he said, giving her a conspiratorial wink. "Smoke-free building my ass."

"Thanks. And thank you for the water, Oliver." The lawyer adjusted his glasses when she acknowledged him. "So, uh, first off, I wondered if I could get you to do me a favor," she asked Hanes.

"By all means. Certainly."

"Good." Christy fitted her Doral ultralight into an indentation on the lip of the ashtray. "Here's the deal. I've sorta been talking to this other lawyer about the case, okay? Nothing against you or anything. A friend kinda recommended him. It's all very informal. Anyway, could you write him a letter and give me a copy?"

"I'm not sure I understand." Hanes was seated behind his desk. He picked up two pieces of paper stapled at the corner, then laid them next to a stack of books and files. "I haven't been contacted by any other counsel, or heard from anyone else about your case. Have you formally engaged another attorney?"

"No. Not at all. I've only, like, spoken to him. He's not after any money. A friend said to talk to him, and this was way before I got hooked up with you."

"I see. It's odd I haven't heard from him. Has he been monitoring the case? Does he have a lien I need to honor?"

She raised her cigarette, took a drag and blew the smoke toward the ceiling. "I don't have any contract or anything. And there's no lien, whatever that is. He's just a friend of a friend who wants to make sure I get what's fair. Anyway, I'd like for you to write him and, like, tell him I didn't do so hot in Roanoke."

"What do you mean?" Hanes asked.

"In my deposition. Let him know I was nervous and could've done better."

"What a strange request. I think you did an exceptional job. I'm not following you."

"I didn't do very good. I should know. It's me we're talkin' about."

"I disagree."

"If we'd practiced more, I could've given better answers." She was growing frustrated, impatient. "Shit. Why can't you just do what I ask? Isn't that the way this works? I'm like paying you a million freaking dollars and you won't even write a letter?"

"I'll battle to the ends of the earth for you—write letters and briefs, squeeze every dime from this claim, slay dragons, anything moral and legal, but I won't lie or say something I know is false. And I won't put my name on something unless I know what I'm signing. My integrity is priceless, Christy." Hanes's manner was genteel.

"Great. Good for you and your integrity."

"Sorry," he said.

"Well, what's the best you could do, like in a letter? I can't believe how you're being so damn unhelpful."

"You want me to write this lawyer a summary of the case, correct?"

"Yes."

"And you'll authorize me to release confidential information to him?"

"Yes," Christy moaned. "It's just a letter."

"And you want me to say your deposition went poorly?"

"Yep."

"Well, I'll be glad to write a letter detailing the case so far, but I won't say something I know to be false. I can certainly report that *you* feel you performed badly during your questioning, but I'm not going to suggest *I* feel the same way."

Christy perked up. "Excellent. Do that. There we go. And you'll put it on your, like, official stationery?"

"I'll use our letterhead." He turned to Oliver. "In fact, why don't you go ahead and draft something along those lines for me to sign while Christy's here?"

"Sure." Oliver sat on a sofa and began scribbling.

"Cool. Thanks."

"To whom should I send this?" Hanes asked.

Christy stubbed out her cigarette and bit her nails, started with her thumb and chewed in sequence until she reached her ring finger. "A guy named Sa'ad. 'Dear Mr. Sa'ad.'" She spelled the name.

"Do you have an address? A firm name?"

"Yeah, it's Las Vegas, Nevada. But *do not* send it. Give it to me, and I'll see it gets delivered. And certainly you have some flunky who can find his whole address."

Hanes pushed his tongue into his cheek, caused a lump to form on the side of his face. "You're not in any kind of trouble, are you? Let's not make a bad situation worse."

"I'd just like to do things my way, okay? Is that somehow not allowed?"

"You're telling me you'll deliver this letter to Mr. Sa'ad, and I'm not to mail it?"

"Yes. That's what I said like five seconds ago."

"And there's nothing amiss or wrong?"

"Everything's cool."

"You know, much of this information is public record. If Mr. Sa'ad wanted, he could most likely obtain transcripts of the depositions and see for himself what transpired. Especially if you've retained him."

"I'm not worried about him wanting to do that," she said. "I don't think he'll be lookin' at much of anything. He has no reason to." She smirked for an instant. "And if he wants to, more power to him."

"If he contacts me, should I discuss the case with him?" Hanes probed further, suppressing a sphinx's smile.

"I don't care. But he's not going to contact you. And don't you dare call him."

"Fine with me." He glanced at his associate. "Oliver, make a file note. We'll give you the copy before you leave," he told Christy. "Don't get into trouble with it."

"Good," she said. "Don't forget—the original stays here."

"It's hardly my place to meddle, especially where another attorney is concerned, but I would suggest that if you're dissatisfied with Las Vegas counsel, you simply terminate the relationship and pay him for the hours he's spent on your case."

"I'm not interested in firing him, Mr. Hanes. Okay? Why are you like harping on this forever and ever?"

Hanes shrugged. "I simply wanted you to know your options."

"Thanks. I'm completely informed," she said, making certain she sounded exasperated.

"Okay. Now, let's discuss a more pleasant topic." He toyed with a folder but didn't look inside or remove anything. "Mr. Roland and I have tentatively agreed to settle the case for three million, nine hundred thousand dollars. As per your request, none of that comes from the church or the good reverend—it's all insurance money, within their policy limit."

"What happened to four million?" Christy asked. "Aren't we, like, missing a hundred thousand here? I thought we talked about me getting the max and lettin' Joel and the church off for nothing."

"Exactly. You and I discussed that. Unfortunately, you and I don't write the check for the insurance company."

"So why won't they pay what they owe?" She practically whined.

"Who knows what they owe, Christy," Hanes lectured her. "That's the point. A jury might award you ten million, or fifty thousand. Realistically, as poorly as Reverend King did when we took his testimony, it seems fair to assume a jury will set him on fire. He was arrogant and despicable and self-righteous and dangerous. The case went extremely well in Roanoke. You were an excellent witness, and I was proud of you." He smiled at her, then continued: "Mr. Roland and Mr. White know we're in high cotton, know we have a blockbuster claim, even better than I thought when I first evaluated it. But if we insist on four million, they have nothing to lose.

That's the worst that can happen, so they simply appear in court and hope for the best and wind up no worse off if you get *twenty* million. They pay four and that's it."

"So . . ." Christy was nodding her head, absorbing Hanes's logic.

"So we give them a hundred thousand and get almost four million. Now they have something to lose, something to think about. Besides, if we go to trial, you'll have to pay experts and court reporters and miscellaneous expenses."

"When can I get my money?" Christy thought about smoking another cig, took the pack from her purse and slapped it against her hand until a filter appeared. She extracted a Doral but made no effort to light it.

"I'm not sure. Mr. Roland and I have a pretty firm agreement on the three-nine figure, but he has to sell it to his clients. They'll want to read the transcripts and take a look at the file before they start writin' million-dollar checks. Bottom line is that Roland will recommend they take the offer, and when they see the show the preacher put on in depositions, I imagine they'll be happy to go along. Of course they might buck him and instruct him to return to us with a lower settlement. Nothing's guaranteed yet."

"How long do you think it will take?"

"I'm guessing I'll hear from Roland within the next ten days."

"How long after that?" Christy asked.

"Well, they have to cut the check and prepare releases. I'd say another two weeks, if everything goes smoothly."

"Hurry them up as much as you can, okay?"

"I will," Hanes promised her.

She lit the cigarette with a cheap lighter, had to click the flint twice before the flame caught. "One other thing. Could you get them to make me two checks?"

"I'm not sure I understand."

"The insurance people. Will they, like, make two different checks that add up to the total amount?"

"Oh." Hanes paused and considered a request he hadn't seen coming. "There's usually a single insurance company check, for the full amount, written to you and me. We both endorse it, and I deposit it in my escrow account. I then write myself—well, my firm—a check for my fees, pay any costs and cut you a check for the remainder."

"So the check comes from you, not the insurance company?"

"Well, yes, the final check would normally be written from my escrow to you."

"Cool. So you could give me two checks, one big and one little?" Christy worked on an ash, tapped it loose from the tip of her cigarette. "You control that," she said, her tone brightening.

"In theory. Of course I'd have to know why I was splitting the proceeds and make sure there's no kind of tax dodge or illegality involved."

"Sure. I'm going to give part of the money to Roanoke First Baptist to, like, show there's no bad feelings."

"Really?" Hanes's mouth fell open, making a wet pop when his lips separated. "Well, good for you. How about that, Oliver?"

"Very admirable," Oliver said.

"How much are you planning to donate?" Hanes asked.

"Probably fifty thousand."

"So you'd want one big check to you, and a fifty-thousand payout for the church?"

"No, I'd want both checks to me. It's easier to give away if it's not all together, if it's not included in the big amount. My check would just be my check, and I won't have to deduct it. It's sort of a psychological thing."

"So why wouldn't I cut the other check to the church?" Hanes asked. "One for them, one for you?"

" 'Cause I might change my mind."

"Ah," Hanes said, growing skeptical of her intentions.

"Is this going to be another major production? I can't even get my money the way I want it? All I'm sayin' is give me two tens instead of a twenty—they can do that at friggin' Wal-Mart."

"We'll see to it that you receive two checks, if that's what you request."

"Deluxe. Thank you."

Joel was happy to be back in the Station kitchen, relieved to be offstage for a few hours, nondescript and insignificant again, another unremarkable employee behind two steel doors, scrubbing plates and folding napkins. Soon after he took his spot by the sink, Frankie arrived and gave him a high five and a delighted grin, then turned somber and discreetly shielded his lips. "Everything copacetic in Virginia?" he asked from the corner of his mouth.

Joel flipped him a thumbs-up. "Thanks to you, Frankie."

Joel was putting on rubber gloves when Sarah rushed into the kitchen, a menu under her arm and three dirty water glasses wedged between her fingers. She glanced at him while she was pointing at the menu and talking to the chef, but she didn't speak to him or do anything cordial, didn't wave or smile or nod. Business was slow—Tuesdays usually were—and Joel and Frankie took a couple extra breaks, stepped outside into the alley and split a Coke, talked about the coming winter and how cold Missoula would be.

Food orders had nearly ceased by nine—a handful of bar customers wanted wings and chicken fingers, and that was about it—and Joel and Frankie were completely caught up with their work. Sarah came into the kitchen and turned left, headed for Joel. She was wearing a white blouse and small pearl earrings, and her hair was completely swept from her face, fastened by two plain clips at the rear.

"Joel, right?" she said.

"Surprised to see me?" he asked.

"Truthfully, yes. How was your vacation to Virginia?"

"It wasn't a vacation," Joel said. "It was business."

"Good. I hope it went well."

"It did. And I apologize again for any misunderstanding." He was humble, ducked his head when he addressed her.

"Well, I'm glad you're here now, and we'll let bygones be bygones."

"I appreciate it." Joel stuck his hands in his pockets. He was wearing a white apron that tied behind him and covered his chest and thighs. "You didn't really have to guess at my name, did you?"

"I was fairly sure."

"I've been here a pretty good while."

"I've been here seven years," Sarah replied. "Help comes and goes."

"Yeah."

She took a scrap of paper from her pocket and handed it to him. "This guy called earlier and left these numbers for you. Said you could call collect or use the toll-free. Make sure you do—the phone bill here's plenty steep already."

"Thanks."

"You're welcome."

"So how've you been?" Joel asked, the transition clumsy and forced.

She scowled. "I've been here, Joel. Working."

"Oh."

"Yep," she said, the word quick and austere.

"I was, uh, wondering . . ." He looked around the kitchen, anxious for a measure of privacy. "If, uh, you're going to be here when we close."

"Of course I'll be here. I lock the doors."

"So, I wondered if I could maybe . . . visit with you, say hello while you're doing your final things."

She tilted her head, assailed Joel with her stare so there was no mistaking her mood. "Look, you're a handsome guy—I'm sure you're aware of that—very gentlemanly, very convincing with your shy, skittish, sincere approach. But you know what? You've either been there and screwed up, or you're never, ever gonna make it there. It's always one or the other. You wouldn't be washing dishes at your age unless you're carrying a lot of baggage or far too many impossible dreams and schemes. I don't have time to stitch you together again, to drive you to the methadone clinic or deal with your ex-wife or loan you money to fix your car. And if you're a poet or artist or singer, I'm not interested in waiting for Hollywood to buy the screenplay or the record company to come knocking. I've got my own problems."

"Sure," Joel stammered. "I understand."

"I'm flattered you'd ask, but I'm married and stressed." She gave Joel a little quarter, filtered some of the poison from her voice.

"I think you're a good person and, uh, wanted to get to know you. I didn't mean to offend you."

"You didn't." She nailed Joel with one last severe stare and started to walk away.

Frankie had been standing over the sink with the water turned off, wiping the chrome fixtures with a damp rag, pretending not to listen. "Ouch," he said good-naturedly. "Joel is singed."

"Shut your mouth, Frankie," Sarah said without turning around, and it was clear she meant it, wasn't amused in the least or pleased by the attention.

Frankie waited until she disappeared, reached beside a stainless steel range hood, took the fire extinguisher from the wall and aimed it in Joel's direction. "Hang on, Joel. I'll save you." The chef and one of the waitresses chuckled, and so did Joel.

"Oh shit," said the waitress. Her name was Jill. She was a happy-go-lucky girl who'd stayed in town after finishing college a year ago. "Check this." She was standing next to the radio, always kept low enough so as not to seep into the dining area. She spun the volume knob, twisted it to ten, and everyone stopped what they were doing, concentrated on the song coming from the plastic speakers. Frankie caught on first, then the chef, then Joel, and they all roared, laughed and hooted and wiped their eyes. Frankie slapped his thighs and Joel sat on the floor, collapsed and tipped over onto his shoulder for a moment before righting himself. It was Elvis—and that was funny for some reason—and he was singing "Burning Love," was tearing up the refrain when Jill adjusted the volume: ". . . a hunka, hunka burning love . . ." Everyone joined the King, singing along and laughing like loons, and Frankie convulsed and shimmied and bucked and danced across the floor, wielding the fire extinguisher as if it were a guitar.

After they settled down, Joel asked Jill to bring him the cordless phone from the hostess's stand. While she was gone, he and Frankie had another giggling fit, and two different waitresses hustled through the kitchen and couldn't figure out why everyone was maniacal, gave Joel and Frankie puzzled looks and said "What?" several times. "It's one of those nights, ladies," the chef told them. Jill returned with the phone and handed it to Joel. "Don't melt it," she kidded.

He stepped outside and punched in an 800 number. The keypad lit when he touched the buttons, and a woman answered and asked how to return his call, informed him that Mr. Sa'ad was eager to speak with him. He stood in the dark waiting on Sa'ad, and the illumination in the receiver shut off and he heard another bout of merriment break loose in the kitchen. He tapped his foot and stared down the narrow alley, watching people and traffic through a notch at the end of two high buildings.

The phone rang and lit white and Sa'ad was there, and it sounded as if he was calling from a party or a bar. "Joel, how are you?" he asked, as friendly and professional as ever.

"Good. I'm at work, standing outside."

"I'm glad your employment situation is going so well."

"It's better than nothing."

"I wanted to touch base, see how everything went in Roanoke." His voice was transparent and casual.

Even though he knew Sa'ad's deceitful plan and was on guard, Joel detected nothing unusual, not the faintest hitch or glimmer of conscience in Sa'ad's words. It was appalling, almost eerie. "Good news. Great news, in fact. Christy was terrible, really showed her true colors. I actually believe she was high or taking something." He didn't want to get too specific or spend too much time giving Sa'ad details.

"You mean she was impaired? Stoned or drunk?"

"Sure seemed so to me. And she 'fessed up to what I've been saying all along—admitted she was the aggressor, admitted all kinds of problems well before our contact, and, get this, she wasn't even able to say we had intercourse. She conceded she was so doped up at the time that everything was a blur."

"I'll be damned," Sa'ad said.

"Mr. Roland, my lawyer, was extremely pleased. I don't mean to boast, but he told me I did well. He thinks they'll get way, way less than five million. He was pretty sure they'd take forty or fifty thousand." Joel's mouth was dry, and his stomach was fluttering.

"What did you say?" Sa'ad asked. "How were you able to deny having sex?"

"In a nutshell, I told them we'd kissed and done some petting and that I was remorseful and accepted blame, but I denied actually having sex. I told them I'd resigned and pled guilty to spare the church. Mr. Roland thought it was very convincing."

"I see. So—"

"Look, my boss is yelling at me to get inside. I've got to go. But thanks for all your help with this. I'm confident the church and I are off the hook; looks like there'll be ample insurance money to pay Christy."

"I'm delighted," Sa'ad replied.

"By the way, I had another bit of good fortune while I was gone. I took some jewelry my mother had given me to a pawnshop, and the owner offered me ten thousand dollars on the spot. It's nice to have a little cushion. I had no idea it was so valuable." Joel wanted to confirm he'd done his part in Roanoke, signal Sa'ad that the plan was still on schedule.

"My, my, what a windfall," Sa'ad said, his tone silly and giddy and rife with feigned surprise. "You'll probably need to get it insured," he added, his voice virtually winking.

"Maybe I will. Thanks again for the help. I've got to run." Joel pushed an oval-shaped button at the top of the phone and disconnected Sa'ad. The space at the end of the alley was empty, no people or cars, the view straight across the street to the front of a bank.

Sarah let Joel and Frankie leave work early, appeared in the kitchen at ten-thirty and told them they could punch out and acted like she always did, as if nothing had happened between her and Joel. When Joel arrived home, his sister was still awake, dressed in jeans and a sweatshirt, lollygagging on the sofa, eating popcorn and watching *The Lion King*. The Whoopi Goldberg hyena was repeating Mufasa's name over and over and quivering with each syllable, the bit humorous or carnal depending on the viewer's age. Joel had watched the movie three times with Baker and thought it was enjoyable, loved the soaring redemption at the end.

"God, I need to get laid," Sophie said as he came into view. "A massage, a facial, a meal with wine, a good man and about an hour in bed."

"Can't have sex unless you're married," Joel said. He dropped the Taurus keys into a bowl and sat on the arm of the sofa. "Why are you watching *Lion King* for the thousandth time?"

"Baker had it in when I sent him to bed, and I would have to raise my weary ass from the sofa to switch things since the remote is broken. Besides, there's probably nothing on cable any better."

"True."

"Anyway, welcome home. I have to admit I missed you."

"I'm glad to be back," Joel said. He slid onto the sofa and put his sister's feet in his lap. "Thanks for all your help. You were a champ."

"So tell me the details. I'm ready for my debriefing." She wiggled her feet. "Put a little mojo on my aching arches while you're talking."

"You really want to know? Usually you're dismissive or upset." Joel started rubbing her soles and the undersides of her toes.

"I do. You promised me a handsome reward, remember? Why wouldn't I want to find out the rest of the story?"

"If things pan out, you'll get that and more."

"Did the girl show up after I called her?" Sophie asked.

"Yes."

"I felt like such a sleaze when I phoned—I'm old enough to be her mom, and here I am pimping and grovelling for my convict brother. It was not a pleasant experience." She knit her brows to underscore the point.

"I'm sure. I'm so grateful to you. I know—with the Neal experience and all the struggles and setbacks—what an effort this is. But you'll get ample blessings for being a faithful sister."

"Tell me what went on."

"Well, like I told you over the phone, I tried to record Christy without her knowing it, tried to trick her into admitting the truth. She discovered what I was doing and, uh, that plan basically exploded in my face."

"This is old news, Joel," Sophie reminded him. "I want to know what happened afterward. The new plan."

"Right. Okay, so I met Christy, and we came up with a scheme to essentially eliminate any profit for Edmund and Sa'ad, while at the same time funneling money to folks who deserve it." He was still massaging his sister's feet.

"I can hardly wait to hear this."

"I went to the deposition dressed like a lunatic evangelical and took a great big dive, said I'd had sex with Christy and acted bizarre and unrepentant. I did as poorly as I could. She showed up looking like Tinkerbell and said all the correct things. Based on my performance, her settlement is bound to increase. We, however, have told Sa'ad just the opposite, told him

Christy was stoned and stumbled through the questioning, and I came off like a hero. Sa'ad and Edmund will think the case has gone to pot—so to speak. Christy and I will split the bulk of a bigger settlement, brought about by my admitting to things I didn't do, and Sa'ad and Edmund will receive next to nothing."

"Joel," she said, her voice spiking with astonishment, "you didn't." She withdrew her feet. "Seriously?"

"It's a splendid plan. Look—Edmund and Sa'ad get a pittance compared to what they're expecting, and I get tons of money to give to you and the church. I'm only going to keep enough to pay my court costs. The rest is for you and Baker and Roanoke First Baptist. Christy gets far more than she deserves, but I did do wrong where she's concerned, so that's not altogether inappropriate."

"Are you fucking kidding me?"

"No. Why are you so upset?"

"Putting aside the question of what you really did or didn't do—and who knows what to believe about that—it seems to me you've managed to leap into the cesspool and become as corrupt and dishonest as your friends. This is terrible, crazy."

"Why? You tell me why."

"Okay, let's see. For starters, you lied. Lied under oath as I understand it. And you are stealing from the company that has to pay this bogus claim, ripping off people for a lot of money. You think everything is washed clean because you plan to donate the money to a church and your pitiful, ragtag sister?"

"It's the best outcome possible, given where I found myself," Joel protested. "The money's going to be paid regardless, right? So who should get it? You and the church and Baker, or two professional con men? Don't you see? And are you really rushing to the defense of an insurance company? Suggesting that those privileged fat cats are victims? You and I both know they're simply Sa'ad and Edmund with TV commercials and tax breaks."

Sophie grew stiffer, pressed her shoulders against the sofa. Mufasa had perished by now, done in by his brother's perfidy, and Scar ruled a parched, barren kingdom, surrounded by drooling yes-men. "I'm not going to argue with you, Joel. You're supposed to be the preacher, not me." She pointed a finger at him. "But understand this. I don't want one penny of your money. I don't want to see my son raised by foster parents while I do jail time. Keep me out of this, you understand?"

"Why did you help me? I mean, I told you I had another plan. Why'd you call Christy?"

"Because you're my brother, and I love you. And because I thought you were trying to get away from all the shit and scams and do the right thing, instead of using the meeting to hone your own thievery skills."

"Hey, I'll admit it's not a perfect situation, but I left things better than I found them."

Sophie kicked Joel's thigh, popping him hard with her heel. "Stupid," she said. "What has happened to you?"

"Nothing has happened to me. I'm still a good person. I still love the Lord. I've simply had to scrape the margins to improve my situation. You're the one always yapping about the real world and how I'm so naïve and impractical. Who can win with you?"

"You can't go from one extreme to the other, Joel. There's plenty of space you seem to have skipped right over." She appeared distracted when she was speaking, wasn't looking at Joel or anything in particular. "Damn," she said, raising her voice and suddenly drawing down on him. "You and this girl rigged this from the beginning, didn't you?" She kicked him again, this time not as energetically. "How else could she get your DNA for those tests? And so now you have to explain everything, make it look like something reasonable, go back and cover your tracks."

"How in the world could you think so poorly of me?" The accusation upset Joel, caused him to clamp his lips and return his sister's stare. "Huh?"

"Well?"

"I'll tell you exactly how they manufactured the tests. Christy let me in on that as part of our agreement. Remember her job at the church, cleaning toilets and mopping floors? Remember how I told you she'd go weeks without touching the bathroom in my study? She did that for a reason. She simply collected my hair—pubic hair—from the shower and from around the commode. They only needed two or three, and she kept watch and stored the hair till the big day. So, no, Sophie, I didn't decimate my church, ruin my marriage and end a career I loved for a few thousand dollars. I was set up."

"Sure, Joel. Whatever."

"I'm telling you the absolute truth."

"Just like you did in Roanoke, when you said 'So help me God' and raised your hand?"

"It's the truth." Joel didn't know what else he could say. He'd planned on divulging the jewelry scam to her, then delighting her with his scheme to once again take advantage of Sa'ad and Edmund and donate the money to her and the church, but he knew this was not the time, not with her so miffed and cranky.

twelve

Wednesday was the day to locate insurance for the borrowed jewelry. Edmund would soon be in Missoula to retrieve the rings, brooches, bracelets and necklaces so they could be returned to their owner, and Joel needed to purchase a policy as quickly as possible. Sophie was still sore at him, angry and annoyed from the night before, and she made it a point to start the gurgling, prehistoric dishwasher during her breakfast and stomp around on the floors every chance she got and blow the horn at Tut—like she was really going to hit him—after she'd cranked the Volvo, did all she could to treat Joel rudely in minor, offhand ways. He felt certain, though, that she would come to appreciate how well he was managing the betrayals and skeins of intricate zigzags, and when everything was said and done and the sag money was hers to keep, he knew she'd forgive him, understand he'd ridden roughshod over a gang of conniving, unscrupulous people.

Joel woke at six-thirty, but he didn't leave his bed until Sophie was gone. He rested under the covers, daydreaming about random delights and miracles, scenes that distilled transcendence and laid bare God's craft. He recalled saying grace over the platters of tenderloin and biscuits and fried apples in the First Baptist fellowship hall; saw the orange-speckled sides of a brown trout as it arched across the Clark Fork and smothered a tiny fly; and recaptured a middle-aged woman's beatific face rising through the water of the baptismal pool, her eyes closed, hair trailing behind, the lights and wetness turning her skin baby pale for the first second or two after he steadied her and she became upright and newly saved, her renaissance spilling into everyone who witnessed it.

He studied his Bible for longer than usual, recited several verses aloud and, out of habit, put together the beginnings of a sermon in his head. When he finished reading, he got down on his knees beside his bed and prayed. He was wearing boxer shorts and a Royal Coachman Outfitters T-shirt, and the cement was cold and unsympathetic, causing his naked knees to lose sensation.

The jewelry was once again between his mattress and box springs, hidden near the foot of his bed. He opened his eyes after saying amen, took the weight off his knees and then reached under the mattress to find the bag, turned his cheek and fed his arm deeper and deeper into the split, kept searching and sweeping with his hand until his entire limb disappeared and his neck touched the fitted sheet. For some reason, the jewelry was difficult to locate, didn't seem to be where he'd left it. He groped until he finally bumped the pouch with his fingertips, felt the red velvet just outside his grasp. The bed was completely jammed against the cinder-block wall opposite him—there wasn't even space to properly tuck the comforter—so he had to lift and balance the mattress to get at the valuables. The mattress flopped and wobbled when he propped it on its thin edge, and he used his shoulder as a support to keep it elevated.

A diamond and ruby bracelet was sticking out of the bag, and the top was not cinched, the pinched folds the drawstring made altogether missing, the fabric loose and relaxed over the sack's entire length. Joel grabbed the bag and snatched it from between the two bed parts. He took a nimble backward step, and the mattress collapsed when he withdrew his shoulder, falling shut like a giant toothless jaw. The impact spat fine, dancing dust into the basement air, tiny motes and particles that flitted through a passageway of light from a table lamp and irritated Joel's eyes, made him sneeze.

Setting the jewelry aside, he methodically ironed his trousers and shirt, starched and steamed a sharp crease in the pants and worked diligently around the shirt's collar. He wanted to have a good appearance and look well groomed when he showcased the jewelry and recited his story. He used a new blade to shave, trimmed and filed his nails, squeezed the bag into his pocket and embarked for town, followed a flatbed truck pulling a utility trailer until he arrived at the interstate. A mattock and a pair of shovels were lying on the bed of the truck, and Joel noticed one of the trailer tires was going flat, was deflated almost to the rim.

Given the reversal of fortune in Roanoke, he had considered abandoning the jewelry project, had debated his options as he sat crammed in coach flying home to Montana. He could simply relinquish the bag and tell his accomplices that he lacked the nerve and gumption to see the fraud through to the end. He'd recognized, though, that the potential windfall from the conspiracy with Christy was hardly guaranteed—her fidelity to him was the kicker in the deal, and what a kicker it was, a pitfall that could make him odd man out and leave his prosperity in her Prada purse or Sa'ad's eelskin wallet or Edmund's obscure Cayman account. Plus, he rationalized, since *he* would receive the insurance payment, continuing with the original plan might somehow provide him another opportunity to clip Sa'ad and Edmund while assisting his sister and his former congregation. And then there was the concern that a change of heart might stir suspicion in his partners, cause them to put the screws to him or double-check Christy's loyalty. A multitude of reasons, he'd told himself, to stay the course.

After consulting the yellow pages, Joel had decided to take his insurance business to a State Farm agent on Spruce Street. The man who ran the agency was nearing fifty, starting to decline through the stomach, and was dressed in a colorful sweater, khakis and shiny brown shoes. He was a handsome man in a plain, unimposing way, which was to say there was nothing patently wrong anywhere in his face or build—everything was within limits. There were numerous trophies on a shelf behind his desk, championships won by the Little League teams he'd sponsored over the years. James Scott was his name, but he informed Joel that everyone called him Scottie.

Scottie and Joel made small talk for several minutes, chatted about Virginia and the weather and how crowded the Blackfoot was on the weekends. There were two secretaries outside Scottie's office, and they both stayed busy, fielding phone calls and completing paperwork. After Scottie finished a story about vacationing at Colonial Williamsburg and the linens he'd gotten for cheap from an outlet mall there, Joel brought up the subject of his jewelry, told Scottie he'd brought his mother's gift west and wanted to make certain he was protected if, Heaven forbid, something should happen.

"Do you have an appraisal?" Scottie asked.

"You mean something stating their value?" Joel hoped to appear befuddled.

"Exactly. I need that, or else some kind of receipt, before I can write the policy. We have to know what we're insuring. It's as much for your protection as ours. We don't want you to have a loss and discover your coverage is short."

"Right. Well, I brought the whole kit and caboodle with me. I thought perhaps you could help me decide on an amount."

Scottie chuckled. "I wish I could. I sure do. I'd love to help you. But it's very easy to have them looked at by a professional."

"I figured maybe we could just agree on a value. I was guessing maybe ten or fifteen thousand dollars." Joel took the red sack from his pocket and placed it in front of Scottie. "See what you think."

"I'll be glad to look, but I'm hardly an expert." He untied the drawstring, tugged open the mouth of the bag and peeked inside. "Holy cow," he said. "There's a lot in here. Is this real?"

"I assume so," Joel answered. "Like I said, my mom gave it to me, and it's been in our family forever. Unfortunately, I don't know much about women's jewelry."

"If it's genuine, I imagine you'll need more coverage than fifteen thousand." He reached in the bag with his thumb and first finger and withdrew a sapphire ring. "This is awfully pretty. And old, a real antique." He looked at Joel, kept the ring displayed between his fingers.

"Thanks," Joel said. "My mom can't even wear the rings these days, her hands are so swollen. She has Alzheimer's and lives out at High Pines. Makes you realize, in a certain sense, how worthless and unimportant so many things are."

"I agree," Scottie said. "But now the jewelry's yours, right?"

"Oh yeah. She gave it to me years ago, when she was living in Roanoke. It's been in my safe-deposit box. I don't have a bank here yet, and I live with my sister. I thought she might enjoy it—my sister, I mean. Seems senseless not to get some use out of it."

"Sure. So I'll need to list you as the insured, not your mother?"

"Yeah, I guess. I'm the owner, if that's what you're asking. She gave it to me, and I've had it for years." The lies were effortless.

Scottie returned the ring to the bag, tugged the yellow drawstrings in opposite directions. "Great."

"So I need to have everything evaluated?" Joel asked.

"Definitely. I wouldn't feel comfortable writing your coverage until we see what you've got."

"That makes sense," Joel said. "Where should I go? I'd like to get this done today, if possible, without making another trip."

"Sure. You can use any reputable jeweler. Far as I know, almost anyone here in town will do. They may not be able to get it finished today, though. Never can tell how busy they'll be."

"Who would you recommend?" Joel asked.

"Well, the Diamond Store over on Main Street is good—lady named Wilma does their appraisals. You can tell her I sent you. The store's a few blocks down from the parking garage. Also, Riddle's Jewelry is okay. They're in Southgate Mall."

"I'll try the Diamond Store first. Thanks, Scottie."

"Thank *you*," Scottie said. He passed the bag to Joel and they shook hands, then walked together to the door.

Two teenagers—probably seventeen, maybe eighteen—were selecting a pre-engagement ring at the Diamond Store when Joel arrived. The boy had a silver loop through his nose and a tongue piercing and a dragon tattoo, and he was wearing a muscle shirt even though he was scrawny and trollish and the weather required something more substantial. His girlfriend had greasy black-and-orange hair and asked, "So how much is this one?" after she examined each tiny diamond-chip band. Joel loafed around the displays while waiting for the clerk to finish with the two kids, inspected a spinning rack of cigarette lighters and was careful not to smudge the glass counters. A stocky woman with frizzy hair appeared from the rear of the store, greeted him and asked if he needed help. Joel explained that he was interested in an appraisal, that he'd been sent by Scottie the insurance agent and was looking for Wilma.

"Then you're in luck. I'm Wilma Rand. Nice to meet you." She was far enough away that she didn't offer her hand. "What do you have?"

"Some rings and necklaces my mom gave me. I need to have them insured, and Scottie says I need an appraisal."

"I believe we can take care of that," she said genially.

"Would you be able to get to them now? I don't mean to be pushy, but I work two jobs, and I'd like to wrap this up today, if possible."

"I don't see why not. I'm doing repairs, but I could take a break if you're in a hurry."

"Thank you. I appreciate it."

She took the bag, sat down on a high stool behind a display case and progressed through the same ritual of squints, stares and tests that Doc had done a few days before. "Exquisite," she cooed once she'd scrutinized the entire velvet sack. "You're a lucky man."

"Why's that?"

"Your mother has some lovely jewelry."

"Thanks. I'm not positive, but I believe she's had the bulk of it for a pretty good while."

"I can tell. One of the rings is quite old. That's apparent from the settings and the wear patterns, and you don't see workmanship like this anymore." Wilma switched off a desk light and stood, pushed the stool back as she rose.

"I'm grateful to you for helping me on such short notice. Will you just get in touch with Scottie?"

"I'll actually do a written appraisal and give you a copy." She was holding the red bag.

"So what are they worth?" Joel asked. He looked at the floor, then up at Wilma, was careful to restrain his lips, lungs, and eyes, all the regions that might flag the swindle. His skin was sizzling, his nerves copper wire and voltage.

"Do you have any idea?" she asked.

"No, not really."

"None?" She was enjoying herself, had injected a lighthearted taunting into her voice, milking and building the anticipation.

"I asked Scottie about buying, say, fifteen thousand dollars' worth of coverage."

"That would certainly be adequate"—she jingled the bag—"for *one* of the pieces."

"What do you mean?"

She turned serious. "You've got some very nice jewelry. One piece, the diamond and ruby ring, is quite unique, very exotic. There's a bracelet that's run-of-the-mill, but this is a spectacular collection, very nice. All together, I'd say you're looking at close to two hundred seventy-five thousand."

"You're kidding." Joel tried not to appear *too* astonished, avoided pinwheel eyes and quaking knees. After rehearsing various reactions in the mirror, he'd decided to let his voice carry most of the weight.

"No, I'm not."

"Wow. I had no idea."

"Consider yourself fortunate," she said. "Most people come here believing they've got the Hope Diamond and leave thinking I'm a crook."

"Not me. This is something, a total shock . . . my goodness."

"I'm glad your surprise is on the happy side, not the other way around."

"Two hundred seventy-five thousand. Hard to imagine." Joel allowed some exuberance to bounce through his words. "My, my."

"My, my," she laughed.

"I don't know what to say—I'm grateful to you."

"Thank your mother, not me," she said.

He waited for Wilma to type his appraisal, paid her seventy-five dollars in cash, took a receipt and returned to State Farm.

Scottie was stunned when he saw the number at the bottom of Wilma's calculations, but he wasn't unhappy or reluctant to cover the jewelry, was eager to earn the commission for so large a policy. As Edmund had predicted, he took Polaroids of each item and snapped a final shot of Joel sitting behind the loot, smiling as if he'd just won the lottery. He laid the pictures in a row across his desk, and he and Joel watched the thirty-second alchemy, amiably joshing about Grizzly football while the blank white squares turned to glittery shots of gold and platinum and precious stones.

Scottie phoned the Diamond Store and confirmed the numbers with Wilma, filled out a personal articles binder for Joel and took a small payment, told Joel he'd be billed for the remainder in a week to ten days, after the underwriters processed the application. "I appreciate the business," Scottie said when the arrangements were complete and Joel was leaving.

Joel folded his receipts and papers in half and walked to his car, didn't dare look back and tried not to rush his departure, fought the urge to break into a trot and click his heels together. "No sweat," he said to himself after he shut the door to the Taurus. He closed his eyes and acknowledged the Lord, offered a brief prayer of thanks.

Joel loved his job with Dixon Kreager, looked forward to the weekends and his work on the big rivers. Initially, his shoulders and neck pained him on Monday mornings, but after several trips down the Clark Fork, he got used to rowing the drift boat, learned how to use the currents and position the oars and not wear himself out fighting the water. He and Dixon became friends of sorts, and Joel would arrive early at the Royal Coachman on Saturdays, drink strong coffee with Dixon and talk about fishing and politics and cooking and whatever else happened to pique their interest.

Joel had learned to fly-fish when he was a boy, had persuaded his mother to cash in her S&H Green Stamps for a nine-foot fiberglass rod that was heavy and cumbersome and difficult to cast. He'd liked the sport, though, and working as a minister gave him the opportunity to spend time perusing the streams around Roanoke. He could be on the Smith River in less than an hour, and the James—full of smallmouths and sunfish—was just up the interstate, a fifteen-minute drive. He was a competent angler when Dixon hired him, but Dixon took him behind the shop and showed him several tricks that made him that much better, changed his grip and slowed his casting rhythm.

During their first trip down the Clark Fork, when Joel was auditioning for the job, Dixon had explained to him that a big part of the business was providing "reasonable expectations," keeping novice fishermen interested and eager during an eight-mile float. "I've caught fish in just about every run, riffle and seam this river's got," Dixon had told him. "And I let folks know it, especially when things are slow and the fish have turned off. Keep 'em optimistic. I tell them I caught a big brown right here or a hellacious cutthroat from the hole right around the bend. Never let 'em think the fish aren't biting. This job's more than just rowing a boat and tying knots."

True to his word, Dixon had given Joel exclusively married couples and men, almost all of them tourists and beginners. He'd not let Joel attempt the Bitterroot with its hidden currents and wicked logjams that could take a boat quick to the bottom, had kept him on the Clark Fork and the tame sections of the Blackfoot. Dixon charged three hundred dollars per day for a guide and boat. He kept half the payment, and Joel received the other half minus the fifty he paid Dixon to use his boat and thirty bucks he spent on lunch and snacks for the customers. Joel also got tips, usually fifty dollars, sometimes more if the folks landed a big trout or drank a lot of wine at lunch. Normally, he'd bring home two hundred forty dollars for the weekend's work, along with leftover cookies and pretzels and sodas and sandwiches.

Edmund was due to arrive in Missoula any day now—Joel had no idea where and when—and Joel did all he could to keep his mind elsewhere when he went to work Saturday morning. Dixon was in his office, humped over a vise and a pile of fur, thread, chenille and loose feathers. He motioned for Joel to enter but didn't immediately interrupt what he was doing, finished winding a hackle around the front of a small hook and secured it with black thread.

"Good morning, Joel," he said as he was unclamping the tiny fly he'd just built.

"Morning. Looks like a fine day for it."

"Does indeed. You got a dentist and his wife today. They've never done much fishing, so it'll probably be mostly sightseeing and a long lunch." Dixon smiled. "They're here from South Carolina. Seein' the country, you know?"

"Maybe we'll get into a few nice fish for them."

"I hope so. Pull up a seat, partner. Sit down a minute." There was something odd about Dixon's tone, an anxiousness Joel hadn't heard before. Instead of pouring Joel coffee and stirring in two sugars and cream, he stayed behind his desk and began skating his eyes over the walls and floor. "You know September will be gone before you realize it?" he said.

"Right." Joel had no idea where this was headed.

"Then October, and that's it."

"It?" Joel stammered. "It for what?"

"The season, Joel," he said gently. "We shut down at the end of October. No fishing again till spring. I thought you'd know—most people around here do—but I got to thinkin' about it and figured you being new and all, you might not be aware of how things operate."

"I'd really not considered it. I mean, well, I just haven't thought ahead. So there's nothing, not a single trip?"

"Sorry."

"I'm getting laid off soon is what you're telling me?"

"I'll give you the first trip I schedule next spring," Dixon promised. "You're a good guy, Joel. I like you and you've been an excellent employee, honest and reliable. It's simply the way of the world in Missoula. Seasonal. Can you ski or hunt?"

"No."

"Not at all?"

"Nope."

"Well, I'm damn glad I mentioned it. At least you'll have a little lead time."

"Huh." Joel was speechless. He felt stupid, embarrassed.

"You still got your job at the Station, right?" Dixon asked.

"Yeah," he said forlornly. "I hope it's not seasonal too."

"Things will be okay."

"You don't have any work around the shop? I'd be more than happy to sweep floors, clean, whatever."

"I knew you were going to ask me that." Dixon slowed his eyes, allowing them to light on Joel. "I got Bo to pay all winter—he's been with me from the start—and I keep Cheryl on the clock to do my books and run the register. We get some mail order at Christmas, and sales here and there in March and April, but the sad truth is I'm already carryin' more people than I need."

"I understand. It's hard to imagine how I was so shortsighted and didn't see this coming. I've talked to folks about the winters here, the snow and cold. I don't know what I was thinking. In Roanoke, you can fish year-round. I mean, you know, we have ice and snow and so forth, but I've caught trout in December. I just thought things might slow down some, fewer tourists maybe, and I'd have to buy a heavy jacket and . . ." He sighed. "And . . . when do you start booking trips again?"

"Late April."

"Okay," Joel said. "Okay. I appreciate the heads-up."

"No problem."

"So how about my coffee?" Joel asked, full of false cheer.

"Sure, comin' right up. I'm sorry to have to tell you this. You know it has nothing to do with you—I don't keep any of my guides after October."

"I understand. You've been good to take me in and give me a job, and you've been a fine friend."

Dixon went to the coffeepot and filled a cup. He came around his desk and offered the cup to Joel, but didn't let it go when Joel took the handle. "Hell, if things get rugged, give me a call and I'll find something for you to do." The cup was still between them, both of them holding it. "I can pay you minimum wage to come by on Saturdays or maybe give you a little advance against next year's trips."

Joel noticed that the back of Dixon's hand was covered with faint red hair and freckles the color of brown beans. Dixon released the mug, and Joel stayed focused on the coffee. He saw the spotted hand, kind and awkward, long after it was gone, etched it within his mind and marveled at the span of a generous soul. "Thanks," he said before he tasted the first sip.

Joel could sense from the very beginning that the dentist and his wife were not on happy terms. The dentist walked in front of her to the store's entrance, never slowed or checked over his shoulder, and he went through the door without holding it open or waiting for her. She inspected hats and T-shirts two aisles away while Dixon started his canned speech about big fish and ancient mountains and introduced Joel to the husband.

The man's name was Karl, and he was chubby and had woolly black eyebrows. "That's my wife, Lisa," he said without so much as glancing at her. He walked out of the store several paces ahead of her and hogged the front seat of the Royal Coachman's jumbo pickup, making her take the jump seat in the rear. They didn't speak to each other, and Joel finally gave up trying to talk to either of them, left the cab quiet, the radio switched off, and drove thirty minutes in silence.

They were scheduled to do an easy float down the Blackfoot. Joel loaded the boat and put in by himself without any help from Karl and Lisa. As he was lugging the cooler down the skinned bank and uneven trail to the water, he noticed Karl glare at his wife and form several words Joel couldn't hear because of the noise coming from the stream. She didn't appear to answer him and turned her back on his nasty stare.

The day was splendid, maybe a little too bright and warm for active hatches and great fishing, but altogether agreeable for two tourists navigating the river for the first time. They'd catch some twelve-inch cutthroats and a few rainbows and maybe even luck into a respectable bull trout. Joel rowed across the river, latched on to a lazy current and handed them each a rod. Lisa was looking all around, her face receptive and amazed like so many Joel had seen on these trips, the uncontradicted majesty of the tamaracks, hill pines, mountains and endless sky awing her in a matter of minutes. The river was wide and changed colors all along its surface—white bangs spilled over rocks, pools turned from sandy brown to green to grayish as the water became deeper, and thousands of brilliant ripples and dents would appear and vanish depending on the boat's location and the sun's humor.

"It's beautiful, isn't it?" Joel said, holding the oars against the river's pull to slow them.

"Yes," she answered. "I had no idea."

"Let's find you guys a fat trout, and it'll look even better. Last weekend this stretch was truly hot. We landed about thirty, including a nice bull trout that went close to six pounds."

"I guess we're a day late and a dollar short," Karl said. He was sitting in the front of the boat and didn't turn around when he spoke.

After twenty minutes it was apparent that Karl had a vile temper and no aptitude for casting a fly. Joel switched him to nymphs—easier fishing— and gave him simple advice and put him directly on several pods of feeding fish. Karl cursed and thrashed the water and snarled his leader and said, "No shit, chief," when Joel mentioned he needed to be more delicate with the line. Lisa wasn't fishing, hadn't taken her fly from the keep, and was content to drift along on a pretty day, separated from her bully husband and enveloped by the remarkable sights.

"Lisa, you sure you don't want to wet a line?" Joel asked her.

"Oh, I'm great. I'm enjoying the ride. Down in South Carolina, you don't see anything like this."

"Why don't you let me tie on a big streamer?" Joel encouraged her. "You can dangle it off the back of the boat, sort of troll it. We're out of the really good bull trout water, but who knows what you might pick up. We've caught some big fish in the section coming up."

"If you say so," she said. "I couldn't be much better than I am right now, though."

"Yeah—a fuckin' three-hundred-dollar amusement park ride," Karl griped. "And I'm guessing Robinson Crusoe here is looking for a tip at the end of the day."

"Tips are completely optional," Joel said, unruffled. "If we don't land any fish, I wouldn't accept a tip and you shouldn't offer one."

"Don't worry," Karl said.

Joel persuaded Lisa to drop a line behind them, telling her to watch for logs and snags and hold on tight if a big one hit. Karl finally caught a fish, and he fought it like an excited child, horsing it out of the water and heaving it through the air into the boat. He made Joel beach them and take pictures of him and his ten-inch trout, then complained bitterly when Joel instructed him to return the fish and explained to him for the third time the importance of catch-and-release. Lisa stayed in her seat during the photo shoot, her fly hanging off three feet of line, blowing in the breeze.

Karl landed two more fish in the next hour, bragging to his wife after each and demanding more pictures. But he was nicer to Joel, seemed to be coming around. "This isn't so bad," he said after they'd turned back his last catch. He gave Joel several vigorous pats on the shoulder and thanked him for removing the hook.

They were in a quiet, glassy section of the river when Lisa screamed. Joel wheeled around, and he saw her rod pulled parallel to the water and knew she'd hooked a large fish. He stroked backward to give her some room, then started upstream toward the fish. At first he thought she had a big bull, but a huge rainbow erupted from the water, showing its deep red streak from gills to tail. The trout was strong, a slab of a fish, rolling line off the reel and charging for a sunken sanctuary. Lisa screamed again and asked, "What do I do?" over and over.

Still pushing against the flow, Joel pivoted quickly so he could face her. She was watching her line disappear, holding the cork handle of the rod with both hands and doing nothing else. The actual fly line was gone from the reel, and now the twenty-pound test backing was vanishing too, the reserve left on the spool getting smaller and smaller. Joel maneuvered the boat into a center eddy that would allow him a few moments away from the oars. He lunged forward and helped her lift the rod, raised the tip to bring pressure on the fish. Lisa said, "I don't know what to do," and Joel assured her she was doing fine, began loosening his grip and transferring the full feel of the trout to her.

The boat nosed into a channel of fast water and started a cockeyed drift, and he did the best he could with one hand and a single oar to keep them pointed at the trout. He reached around Lisa and placed his palm against the reel's spool, making the fish battle harder to earn distance. She had, at best, another ten yards of backing to give, and when that was spent, the fish would break the leader or pull loose or—God forbid—snap the whole works and make off with sixty dollars' worth of fly line.

"Keep the rod tip high, keep your palm against the reel but don't press too hard. Tip up, palm on the reel. Consistent pressure. He's going to come ripping back at you sooner or later, so be ready." Joel had released the rod; the trout was all Lisa's.

In the midst of the effort and excitement, Karl continued to fish. His casts were unpredictable, all over the place, and Joel was afraid he'd get his rig tangled with his wife's, especially if the fish made a run in their direction.

"Karl, please stop for just a second." Joel was crouched over his seat, his butt barely touching, the majority of his weight in his legs. He was struggling with the current, chasing the rainbow and keeping an eye peeled for rocks and tricky swirls, ready for anything. The fish was slowing, and Lisa had a good tight line on it.

"I'm not causing her any trouble. I came to fish, okay? Paid some serious bucks."

"She's got the trophy of a lifetime, Karl," Joel admonished him. "Sooner or later that fish'll make a sudden turn or be up here at the boat, and we don't need your line getting wrapped around hers."

"Hell," he said, "it's going to shake off anyway."

Joel considered grabbing the rod from his hands, simply seizing it, but realized that would most likely cause more problems than it cured. "At least try to keep your casts up there," Joel urged him.

The fish erupted from the water, shot straight up so that its impressive length and brilliant colors were revealed, hung airborne for an instant and then splashed into the water, tipping over like felled timber.

"Oh oh oh!" Lisa squealed.

"Let's try to recover some line," Joel told her, and she took the reel's crank and began fighting the fish.

"Is this right?" she asked. "I don't want it to get loose."

"Nice and easy. No rush."

"This is so exciting," she said.

"If he comes at us fast, you won't be able to play him from the reel. You'll have to strip him in, pull in the line with your hand. Did you see me show Karl how?"

"I think. I think so. Uh-oh—he's doing something."

"He's just turning. Keep the tip up. Keep winding." Joel had the boat in good shape, had found a route upstream and was closing down on the fish. He swung them a few degrees off center to give Lisa better leverage.

Karl hadn't stopped his oafish whips and whiffs in the bow of the boat, and one of his casts had sailed past Joel's ear, the hook so close that Joel thought it might have brushed his skin. Joel heard him shout, and when he glanced over his shoulder he saw Karl's rod bent and his line taut. "I've got one too," he yelled. "A monster."

A monster snag, Joel thought. A log or rock or piece of the riverbed. "You're hung, Karl." Lisa's fish had made it to a sluice of swift water and was rushing the boat. She couldn't reel quickly enough to take up the slack, and her line started to sag, drooping onto the surface.

"Use your hand to strip it. You can't use the reel. Strip!" He pushed them downstream now, reversed his stroke to help her eliminate the loose line between her and the fish.

"I *am* fucking hung," Karl cursed. "What do I do?"

"Nothing. You're exactly where you ought to be. I'll take care of you when I'm done with your wife. Let some line go if you need to. Or better yet just break the leader and reel up."

"Great. I'll just sit here and watch." Karl yanked two or three times, but his fly didn't budge.

Lisa had filled the bottom of the boat with coils of line and managed to catch up with her trout. "Good job," Joel told her. The fish jumped again, but this time it was more of a wallow, lacked the altitude and defiance of the earlier leaps. Joel rowed and Lisa turned the reel, and the fish lost ground.

Karl's line was stretched across the water, stuck in the middle of the river, and when they floated even with it, Joel saw the line twitch and go limp, assumed the leader had broken and the fly was lost. Unfortunately, though, they'd drifted below whatever snag was holding Karl's hook, and the new position had freed his tackle.

"Hey, I'm in business again." Karl checked his nymph and flopped it back into the river. "I think that was a damn nice fish you just screwed me out of."

"Pardon?" Joel was tracing Lisa's line, trying to catch sight of the rainbow.

"I had a big-ass fish. I could feel the son of a bitch wiggling and swimming. And you let it get off, fucked it up with your sorry boat driving."

"I apologize. We'll get you another one." Joel almost added something about there being thousands of other boulders and sunken logs in the river but didn't, kept his tongue.

"Oh, goodness! I just saw him. He's so big and gorgeous." Lisa was on the edge of the wooden board that provided her seat.

"We'll have to leave the boat to land him, okay? I'm going to row us about twenty yards farther, onto that shoal. I want you to step out nice and slow, keep the tip high and watch your line. If he takes off, palm the reel, make him use his energy and don't panic."

"Please don't let him get away."

"He won't," Joel said.

He bumped the boat into the shallows, leapt over the side and gave it two rapid tugs, stuck its front well into a bar of smallish stones and low water. He helped Lisa climb out, watching her and the fish and the river. Karl had finally, thank the Lord, stopped casting and was scanning the water, doing his best to get a glimpse of his wife's fish. The trout made two more runs and thrashed and shook when Joel had her lean into it with more rod, and after five tense minutes the spectacular fish was on its side, sliding toward them. Standing knee-deep in the stream, Joel scooped up the rainbow with a long-handled net, didn't stop the net's sweep until the fish was level with his head, raised high in delight and accomplishment. "All right!" he exclaimed. "Yes!"

Lisa had dropped her rod and was tiptoeing toward Joel. "Let me see. Oh, my goodness. Look, Karl. How beautiful."

"Yeah, it's a fish," Karl said.

The trout was easily twenty-five inches and five pounds. Its gills labored from the fight and the absence of oxygen, fanned and shut, fanned and shut. The length of its back was emerald green dotted with black, and its dorsal fin was almost as long as Joel's middle finger. He took three photos of Lisa and her trophy, then they slipped the fish back into the water and watched it swim away, disappearing in a bolt of refracted color after regaining its strength.

"Thank you so much," she said to Joel as they stood at the river's fringe, the water lapping over an apron of plum-size rocks. She reached around him and gave him an abbreviated hug, her hand pressing against his ribs, her shoulder touching the side of his arm when they came together for a sudden second.

"You're welcome. That's by far my nicest fish of the season. Congratulations."

"That was so neat, the whole experience. I can't begin to tell you." She balled her hands into celebratory fists and danced in place for an instant, squished her soaked tennis shoes up and down several times and stomped out splashes of water. "Yes!" she shouted.

They stopped for lunch thirty minutes later at a jut of bank with a good level patch to accommodate the table, chairs and cooler. They could see straight down the river for a quarter mile, and across from their small peninsula was a phenomenal swath of rock, a tall, powerful fortress that extended well into the river and caused the water to go dead around its base. The formation was almost Gothic, had chunky spires and gaps and recesses and ledges and weird cuts that looked vaguely like animals of some sort, maybe lions or gorillas. The top of the rock was higher than the tallest pine on the bank, and its sides were stained gray, green and white. It looked surreal and rough-hewn at the same time, brought to mind a hobbit's fantastical dwelling, and Joel had taken to imagining it as a home for furtive river imps who were most likely benign but probably had sharp incisors twice as long as a man's.

Lisa and Karl had walked behind some skinny pines and scrub growth while Joel was unfolding the portable table and laying out lunch and blush wine. He saw them arguing again, picked them up in the periphery but didn't stop what he was doing, kept his eyes on the plates, napkins and silverware, minded his own affairs and not theirs. He heard the word "bitch," then heard it a second and third time. The last time it came from across the stream, evidently had carried over the water, bounced off the high, brute stone and doubled back. Joel unfolded a canvas chair and locked its legs.

This set-to didn't conclude like the first one Joel had witnessed, however, didn't stop with Karl glowering and cursing and Lisa timidly surrendering. Joel popped open another chair and twisted it steady, had to twice drag his foot through a layer of small, loose stones to get all four legs stationary. He heard Karl's rabid voice again, saw him pointing at Lisa, the end of his index finger so near her nose it might as well have been touching. Joel put his hands in his pockets, checked the table. He heard her voice—it seemed to come ricocheting from the rock tower as well—and she slapped her husband's hand, skin striking skin. Joel thought *Oh my goodness* and felt his stomach spasm, took a mouth breath and started to shout at them.

Karl punched Lisa square in the face with a full fist. She tumbled backward and landed on her butt, managed to catch herself with one arm and break some of the fall. Joel yelled at Karl to quit it and ran to where they were, lost traction in the rocks and stumbled for the first few strides. When he got to them, Lisa was sitting on the ground, her legs splayed, blood rushing from a gash above her eye, and Karl was glaring at her, completely unrepentant, his fist still clenched. Her blood was all down her cheek and neck and making a mess of her shirt. She felt the cut and attempted to clean her face, but wiped sand and grit into the wound and accidentally spread the blood onto her pants, left a crimson print on her thigh.

"Are you okay, Lisa?" Joel asked. He was panting, more from the shock than exertion. He'd never seen a man hit a woman, only counseled couples about abuse and evil in his study, sent them home with a list of Bible verses to read and a marriage handbook.

She stared at Karl, and he stared at her, and neither of them said anything.

"Lisa?" Joel said.

"You are such a coward." She meant this for her husband. "A common coward."

Karl bent his leg at the knee, cocking it as if he were going to kick her. "You'll see what kind of a coward I am if you don't shut your friggin' mouth."

Joel had watched enough. He felt sure Karl was going to sail into her with his foot, and he stepped between them. "That'll do, Karl. Don't you hit her again."

"Oh—Mr. Fucking Fisherman. Who do you think you are, huh? I'll tell you—a loser who paddles a stinkin' boat for tourist tips."

"Leave her alone, Karl."

"Mind your own damn business," he growled.

"This, Karl, *is* my business."

"So what are you going to do about it, fisherman?"

Joel had lost fifteen pounds of preacher's lard since arriving in Missoula—tuna fish and cereal had replaced Brunswick stew and pancakes—and eight hours at the oars twice a week was beginning to show in his arms, shoulders and chest. He was a foot taller than Karl and was wearing sunglasses and a wide-brimmed hat that kept much of his face obscured. "Try me," he said. "In fact, I wish you would."

"Yeah, right. So you can sue me and get rich? You've got nothing to lose, do you? It'd be like early retirement for a deadbeat like you."

"Be that as it may, you need to back off. Otherwise your next fight's going to be with me."

"You think I'm afraid of a piece of shit like you? Do you?"

"I don't know, Karl." Joel removed his dark glasses. "Are you?"

"Neither one of you is worth my time. You go right ahead and be the white knight and see what good it does you."

"You should be ashamed of yourself," Joel told him.

"How would you have any idea?" Karl snorted. "Huh? You don't think she deserved every bit she got?"

"I'm not going to argue with you. Move out of my way."

Joel used two hands to stand Lisa, took her by the wrist and underneath her armpit and helped her to the boat. He set her against its varnished side and tended to her with sterile pads from the first aid kit and a towel he'd soaked in the river. She was completely silent but she didn't seem outside herself, didn't appear dazed or disoriented, followed everything around her with attentive eyes and flinched when the cold towel touched her cut for the first time. Her blood dotted the path they'd taken to the boat, showed up here and there in the light dirt and on the sides and crowns of stones.

Joel was able to clean her face, but the injury was to the bone and the bleeding difficult to staunch. Every time he peeled back the towel, the gash poured blood, and he felt sure she needed stitches to close the meat and skin above her eye. He told her to hold the towel to the wound and apply pressure, to push until she couldn't stand the hurt.

Karl had picked up a rod and waded into the river, pretending to be unconcerned with his wife and her injury. He was fishing close to the bank, in lifeless, shallow water that couldn't possibly hold trout or fish of any kind, and each cast thwacked the shoal behind him and lost momentum.

Joel put Lisa into the boat and shouted to him. He had to scream his name twice before Karl acknowledged him. "Let's go," Joel said.

"I'm not through," Karl answered and turned his head.

Amazing, Joel thought. "I'm going to say this once. Get over here now—immediately—or I'll leave you where you are. You hear me? It's a long, long walk to the road." Joel didn't wait to see if he was coming or not. He pushed the boat from behind, scraping it over the bottom until he felt it surge and float.

"Okay, okay," Karl said. "Jeez, keep your pants on."

He clambered into the bow, and Joel shot them into the swift heart of the stream, leaned forward and extended his arms with every oar stroke and didn't let up until he saw the rusted iron bridge above the take-out. Karl kept fishing during the trip, never stopped casting, and occasionally he would hum or whistle, mostly songs that were unrecognizable, but once he added words and Joel was positive he heard "Danke Schoen." Lisa pressed her cut with the towel and gauze pads and smiled at Joel when he asked if she was doing all right.

None of them spoke while Joel stored their tackle and the cooler and winched the boat onto its trailer. Lisa sat cross-legged at the edge of the river, as far away from them as the land could carry her, her shirt, hands and jeans sullied, the towel saturated with red in the middle and at every corner, tie-dyed almost. Karl didn't seem in the least embarrassed or contrite, and he slouched against the hood of the truck and provoked Joel with an eye-to-eye challenge every opportunity he got.

When Joel finished loading and packing and they were prepared to leave, Karl walked to where his wife was seated. Joel started to trail him, but he noticed there was nothing menacing or aggressive in the way he was going after her. Joel stayed near the truck, watched Karl sidle up to her and say something, and then she said something and stood, handed him the towel for a moment and brushed the butt of her jeans. She took the towel again, and they walked side by side to the truck. As they got closer, Karl hung his arm around her shoulder. She didn't show any reaction, but she let him do it and waited demurely while he sprung the front seat forward and boosted her into the rear of the cab.

There was nothing anyone could say during the trip from the Blackfoot. Both Joel and Karl would look at Lisa as they drove down the interstate. Speed limits were very much an abstract notion in Montana, but Joel still never traveled above sixty-five, was uneasy going too fast, afraid of losing control and crashing or being the one motorist out of a thousand who actually got a citation from a Missoula cop. He glanced at the speedometer and was doing eighty, as fast as he had moved in a vehicle since he was a teenager joyriding in his cousin's souped-up Gran Torino.

Instead of returning to the shop, Joel took an early exit off the interstate and turned on to Orange Street.

"Where're you going?" Karl asked, the first words anyone had spoken during the trip.

"Shortcut," Joel said.

"Oh."

Minutes later Joel made a sudden right at Spruce, and Karl was on to him, saw the signs for Saint Patrick's Hospital. "No fucking way, my man. Uh-uh. What do you think you're doing?'

"I'm taking your wife to get proper medical treatment." Joel saw Karl eye the steering wheel and tightened his grip, kept his hands clenched at ten and two.

"You're wasting your time. And you're kidnapping us. She doesn't want to be here and neither do I. I'll have your ass for this, you understand?"

"Somehow, I'm not too worried," Joel answered. He came to a stop at the emergency room, shifted the truck into park and set the floor brake.

"She's fine, okay?" Karl said. "You don't want to be here, do you?" He twisted to address his wife. It was bright outside, the middle of the afternoon, and everything inside the truck was clear and precise.

Lisa didn't speak. Half her face was still covered by the towel.

"Okay, look. Here's the deal." Karl's tone changed, lost some of its belligerence. "What'll it take? A hundred bucks? Two?" He took his wallet out. "You tell me."

Joel cut the engine. "Do you want to go in and fetch help or do you want me to?"

"Tell him not to do this, Lisa." Karl thinned his lips and raised his chin, stared straight ahead. "You better tell him."

To Joel's delight, she sat mute, only shifted her towel to place a dry spot over the wound.

"Lisa?"

A young man in uniform exited the hospital and approached them, and Joel knew immediately just what kind of person he was. His hair was shaved to the skin on the sides of his head, and his shirt was a tiny bit small across the chest but was clean and proud and without a single wrinkle. He didn't have a gun, although there were all sorts of pouches and attachments hanging from his belt, most noticeably a radio with a stumpy rubber antenna. He came to the window of the truck, and Joel switched the key to give them power and lowered the glass. The man's silver nameplate said Douglas, the elaborate patch on his sleeve announced he was hospital security. A green kid putting in hours, hoping to catch a ride with the real police, spit and polish and by the book, probably a few credits shy of his criminal justice degree at the community college. There was no way Karl would get loose from this guy.

"Afternoon," the officer said. "Can I help you folks?" He crowded the door, almost sticking his head in the cab, and ran his eyes along the interior, surveyed Joel, then Karl, then halted—bingo—at Lisa.

"Yes sir. You can," Joel spoke up. "Lisa's got a bad gash and needs stitches.

I'm Joel King. I work for Dixon Kreager at the Royal Coachman. They were with me when it happened—I saw the whole thing." He thrust his thumb at the passenger seat. "This is her husband, Karl."

"Saw it, huh?" Douglas said suspiciously. He couldn't have been more than twenty, had a wispy mustache and two pink pimples on his chin.

"Yep," Joel said.

"Yeah, she took a bad fall," Karl interjected. "Scared the heck out of me."

"That the story?" Douglas asked Lisa.

"It's a bad cut," she replied without any hesitation.

"Why don't you help her to the ER?" Joel suggested. He cracked the door and Douglas moved away.

Joel got out of the cab, and he and Douglas led Lisa down from the rear of the truck, braced her when she stepped from the running board onto the pavement. Karl scurried around from the opposite side and went into elaborate ministrations, waved Douglas off her arm and helped guide her toward the emergency room entrance.

"I'll need your name and number," Douglas told Joel as they got closer to the hospital.

"Sure," Joel said. "You finish getting her processed, and I'll wait here and give you all the information I can. I won't leave till we've had a chance to discuss things."

The doors opened automatically, and Lisa stopped at the threshold, smiled with the uncovered portion of her mouth and offered Joel her hand. They were far enough along that Joel could smell the ER, the sterile scent typical of every hospital, mostly alcohol and powerful cleanser for the floors. He accepted her hand with both of his, gently, in the same manner he'd received scores of others in wards and waiting rooms and intensive care units, wrapped her to the wrist with a touch suggesting he could siphon off her grief, take it for himself and shunt it to a harmless place.

"My fish was so much fun. Thank you, Joel," she said.

"You're welcome. Hey, like I said, it's the biggest one I've seen this year."

"I appreciate your taking care of me."

He released her hand. "Sure. You make sure you take care of yourself, okay?"

"Okay. Was he really the biggest?"

"He was. Absolutely."

Douglas steered her to a window and the receiving nurse, and Karl stood beside Joel, waiting until his wife and the security guard were out of earshot. "Listen you stupid bastard, I—"

Joel advanced on him, jumped in his face. "No, you listen." He summoned ire and eloquence and made them stick together, preached words to Karl that were righteous and completely commanding. "I will not be intimidated by you. I'm not your wife. You can threaten and bray all you wish, but it won't faze me. You've done a terrible wrong. You are less than a man, beneath an insect even. I'll tell the truth about this, no matter what, so you need to walk away from me before I wring your craven neck."

Karl immediately realized no amount of bluster or bribery would influence Joel or mitigate his fervor, and the wife-beating dentist wilted, dropped his shoulders and slunk down the hall, afraid to say anything else or return Joel's anger, cowed by the sheer obscenity of what he'd done and the resoluteness in Joel's voice.

When Joel arrived home from the hospital, two identical letters were waiting for him on the kitchen table, both in plain envelopes, both typewritten without any return address. The postmarks indicated they'd been sent from Nevada, and Joel speculated that they were Edmund and Sa'ad's doings, would let him know more about handing over the jewelry so it could be taken back to Las Vegas. Baker's toy dump truck was parked in the middle of the table, and there was a jelly smear and a dirty knife and a streak of bread crumbs near the truck. A bill, a grocery store flyer, another bill, a credit card solicitation and three skinny catalogues were lying in a scattered, picked-over pile next to Joel's two pieces of mail. He took a seat, opened an envelope and unfolded the paper inside:

Dear Preacher Joel,

Thank you for your kind invitation to visit while we are in Montana. We don't have much time to spend in your part of the world but would like to see you if you're free. We could meet you Tuesday at noon near the big carousel downtown. I'll have my grandson Eddie along, and I'm sure he'd enjoy experiencing this wonderful attraction.

Regards,
Lyle Jewel

The second letter read exactly as the first, evidently was simply a fail-safe, a precaution that helped the odds where possible mishaps and careless postmen were concerned. Joel was about to tear them both into small pieces, then thought better of it and crammed the envelopes and papers in his front pocket, deciding to keep them and hide them under his mattress and hang on to them to use as thin, lean proof against Edmund and Sa'ad, if it ever came to that. Not much, but better than nothing. The jewel reference was fairly ham-fisted, and down the road it might strike a detective or prosecutor as incriminating and too clever by half, especially since there was most likely no such person living in Las Vegas.

Joel could hear Baker in the rear of the house, talking excitedly to his mother about going to a pizza party with friends from school. The boy came out of his room into the hall, spied Joel and ran to him full tilt, windmilling his arms as if his shoulders lacked sockets and tendons while he made his approach. He bounded onto Joel's lap without breaking stride, crashed against his uncle's chest and hugged his neck with warm, sticky hands.

The two of them were starting to get along well. When Joel had first moved into the basement, he was a stranger to a child who'd been abandoned by his feckless father, and he never once forced the issue, never bought Baker a baseball glove, or talked to him more than the boy wanted, or chased him through the house like a fake monster and tossed him onto the sofa and tickled his ribs. Joel washed dishes, cued the VCR, said good morning and good night, taught his nephew the "God is great" blessing and let the child take his time, circle closer at his own pace.

"Uncle Joel, would you please drive me to the pizza party? *Please.* Everybody who got a hundred on the reading test gets to go."

"Sure. Unless your mother has other plans."

Sophie had a can of generic furniture polish in one hand and a dust rag in the other. "He may go as soon as he takes his dirty clothes to the basement and puts his shoes in the closet where they belong."

"Sounds fair to me," Joel said, jostling the boy with his knee. "You going to help your mom with that?"

"Yeah, I guess," he answered.

"And what brings Bernie Cornfeld home so early? The rivers run dry?" The question was more mischievous than snide; Sophie's anger and exasperation never lingered for too long, were always overridden by her affection for Joel, and on Tuesday she'd said what she had to say about his throwing in with Christy and his newest folly, and that was four days ago, now far enough past for most of her bile to have evaporated.

"Who's Bernie Cornfeld?" Joel asked.

"Yeah, who's Bernie Cornfeld?" Baker echoed. He was still in Joel's lap, but had undone his hands from around his uncle's neck.

"He's a famous con man. Bilked people out of millions in the sixties and seventies and lived it up with Victoria Principal in the Caribbean. I used to read about them and think it was sort of glamorous and swank, although he did seem old and chunky and hairy as best I can recall. She was about twenty back then, a real siren. I would've thought, Joel, that you'd be aware of all the legends in your new field. You know, Bernie, Jim Bakker, Charles Ponzi, Jesse Jackson, the swarthy carnival guys with pick-up-ducks and teddy bears."

"I'm only halfway through the textbook. Just finished the chapter on selling frozen meat door-to-door and the Irish Travelers' termite scare for the elderly. I'm sure I'll encounter the true masters in another hundred pages or so."

Sophie laughed hard enough that her shoulders shook, and she stuck out her tongue at Joel. "Smartass," she said.

"You said a dirty word," Baker singsonged.

"I did, but it's Uncle Joel's fault."

"Why?" Baker asked.

"I would suggest you go look after your clothes and shoes," Joel told him.

"Good idea," Sophie agreed. "Then Uncle Joel can drive you to the party."

"Where is it?" Joel asked.

"Near Lolo. I've got a map."

"I'll be glad to take him." He nudged Baker forward and playfully swatted his butt. "I'm ready when you are," he said to the boy. Baker slid from his lap and went to his room, didn't carp or fret or trudge across the den, behaved like a smart kid should, and Joel caught the satisfaction in his sister's eyes as she watched her child walk a straight line down the hall, proud of her son and all she'd been able to accomplish in him, by herself, working under considerable burdens, a single woman doing her job and a man's as well.

"Good for you," he said, and she knew exactly what he meant.

"So why *are* you home early? I hope nothing happened."

"Well, nothing happened to me. I took a man and his wife down the Blackfoot, and the man was an absolute ogre. He punched his wife in the face and cut her pretty badly. For no reason, he hit her. I rushed her to the hospital, and here I am."

"How frigging horrible. They should cut his nuts off."

"I agree. He was such a spoiled bully. I had to break them up, literally step between them."

"Did you call the police?"

"I wrote a report for the guard at the hospital. And I left my name and number."

"He just hit her?"

"Basically, yeah. They were in a bad mood when they came to the shop, and it got worse and worse. Part of it was she caught this phenomenal trout, and he couldn't stand it. At least that's my take on it."

"Poor woman."

"Yeah. Her name's Lisa. I feel sorry for her."

"Ought to castrate him," Sophie said, still disturbed.

"But the good news is I brought home an excellent spread—no one touched lunch. Food but, alas, no tip from the wife-beater. At least we can have a nice dinner."

"Can't," she said, her voice returning to normal. "Not tonight."

"Why?"

Sophie mimicked Groucho Marx, her eyebrows wiggling corny innuendo. "Love to, but I have a date." She waved an invisible cigar.

"Oh."

"I was going to see if you'd baby-sit Baker. If you can't, I'll call Joan. I've already mentioned it to her, and she'll do it if you don't want to."

"It would be my pleasure. You go and enjoy yourself. How about that—a date, huh?"

"Yep," she said, and actually raised on the balls of her feet for an instant, a nervous, girlish push of excitement.

"Who's the lucky gentleman?"

"His name is Raleigh, and he seems okay. I met him at Baker's school. He's a teacher and has a kid of his own. Divorced. I've got my fingers crossed."

"This is your first bit of courting since I moved here, isn't it?"

"So?"

"So nothing. Only an observation. I'm extremely happy for you." He smiled and nodded his approval. "Try to behave," he teased. "And be home before midnight. Harpo and Chico will hold down the fort."

"He's making dinner for me."

"Have a blast and don't worry about a thing. I'll take care of my favorite nephew."

"You have anything on the horizon, Joel?" she asked.

"Meaning what?"

"Well, you and Martha have been apart for a while now, and I thought I understood you to say the divorce was almost done, that she just wanted it over."

"True."

"So are you going to spend the rest of your days burning incense and moping about in a long robe and cowl, or are you going to move on with life?"

"That's an odd question coming from you," he replied.

"Why's it odd?"

He grinned at her. "I figured you think I should be sort of permanently suspended where women and romance are concerned. Like certain criminals who can never own a gun or enter the public-housing project or log on to a computer."

"I'm serious, Joel. You should try to find someone. Over eighteen, of course."

"Of course."

"The right woman could make you happy, lift your spirits. I'd hope you've learned your lesson by now and would treat her decently."

"Believe me, I've learned my lesson," he said.

"So have you met anyone? Anyone at all?"

"I'm kind of fond of the lady I work for."

"There you go. Have you talked to her?" Sophie asked.

"Yeah. She told me to drop dead."

"Well, that's a start." Sophie transferred the dust rag into the same hand as the can. "Not a very good one, but a start."

"Why are you dusting? I did the entire house no more than two days ago."

"And I appreciate it. Thank you. By the way—did you know it's well within accepted standards to move things when you clean? To wipe *underneath* objects and *behind* furniture?"

Joel smiled at her, chuckled. "Thanks for the tip. It should really enhance my game."

At noon on Tuesday, Joel was in downtown Missoula, drinking a cup of coffee and taking bites of a Snickers bar left over from Karl and Lisa's Blackfoot lunch. "A Carousel for Missoula" was next to a whimsical, slides-and-chutes play area for children called Dragon Hollow, and a surprising number of people were milling around, many more than Joel expected on an unremarkable weekday. He spent several minutes studying the carousel, walked against the rotation so the parade of horses met him head-on. The horses had pink painted inside the openings for their nostrils and ears, white wooden teeth, and fancy halters carved and lathed to the last detail, and a band organ played "Toot, Toot, Tootsie" as they cantered in their circle.

Joel spotted Edmund and Sa'ad before they noticed him, glimpsed them between the white flank of one horse and the palomino head of another. Edmund looked ordinary, blended into the crowd, but Sa'ad was something else altogether, and Joel started laughing even though he was angry and disgusted with them and on edge about delivering the jewelry. Everything Sa'ad was wearing appeared to be right off the shelf, absolutely new: a hideous red-and-white flannel shirt, stiff blue jeans, impractical leather hiking boots, a wool jacket the color of a ripe summer tomato and a porkpie hat with a curlicue feather in the band. Joel changed directions and followed the horses around to where the two men were and attracted their attention with a pssst that was difficult to form because he was so amused.

"Joel," Edmund said. He kept his head tucked, his hands inside his pockets. He was wearing a baseball cap and dark glasses. "What's so funny?" he asked.

Joel turned so he was shoulder to shoulder with Edmund, both of them staring at the large wooden face of a dragon in the playground. Joel dropped his voice, started singing in a deep, stagy bass: "Oklahoma, where the wind comes sweeping down the plains . . ." He stopped and grinned, shifting his eyes toward Sa'ad.

"What? What's going on?" Edmund sounded uneasy, and he scanned the area, even looked at the sky for some reason. "Why are you singing about Oklahoma?"

"Keep walking," Sa'ad said, a step or two behind them.

"Calm down, Sa'ad," Joel said. "We're in the middle of Montana. I don't think there's much surveillance happening here."

"People never think they're being watched," Sa'ad replied. "That's how they get caught."

"What's so damn funny?" Edmund wanted to know.

"Who the heck dressed Sa'ad?" Joel asked. He laughed again. "He getting ready for a casting call at the college? I thought maybe they were doing *Oklahoma* this semester. Or *Little House on the Prairie,* perhaps that's it."

Edmund stopped short, so quickly that Sa'ad nearly bumped him from the rear. He bent at the waist and slapped his thighs, stood still while he laughed. "No shit, Joel," he said when he straightened himself. "I told him a million times. I think he looks like Eb from *Green Acres.*"

"Or Mr. Haney," Joel said.

"I'm glad I can bring such entertainment to you both. Obviously, this isn't my usual venue." Sa'ad seemed surprisingly good-humored about the abuse.

"Yeah, shiny suits and thousand-dollar shoes don't cut much ice around here," Joel said.

They started moving again, Joel and Edmund in front, Sa'ad trailing.

"I told him." Edmund was shaking his head, still grinning. "God forbid some crew-cut militiamen stop us and discover him dressed like he is. I doubt he'd make it out alive. A yodeling black lumberjack, the lost member of the Village People."

"Do you have my fishing equipment?" Sa'ad whispered, putting his lips close to Joel's ear and aiming the words.

"Fishing equipment?" Joel hesitated, twisted his head a quarter turn. "Oh, yeah. Sure. Right."

"How much?" Sa'ad asked.

"How much?" Joel repeated. He peered at Edmund.

"The value," Edmund offered.

Joel suddenly became anxious, was conscious of every step, every breath, every swallow, felt his skin tingling and his lungs harden. "Oh."

"Three?" Sa'ad suggested.

"No," Joel answered. "Two seventy-five."

"Two seventy-five? Shit." Sa'ad's voice peaked when he cursed. "That's light, my friend."

"Well, Sa'ad, I did the best I could. You want me to go somewhere else? Visit more stores? I could tell them that you and Edmund believe the bag is worth three or four hundred thousand, make a big splash, decorate myself in neon arrows and cause a scene. I went to one place, and this is what I got. Maybe you need to do a little more research on your end." He kept walking but glared back at Sa'ad.

"No problem, Joel," Edmund said. "Everything's okay. Appraisals are subjective, seat-of-the-pants stuff anyway." He removed his sunglasses. "After expenses, we're all gonna walk with close to sixty-eight. Nothing to sneeze at there."

"You have the paperwork handy?" Sa'ad demanded.

"Yeah, Eb, I do. I brought the original with me for you to see. Somehow I guessed you'd be a pain in the butt about things. This isn't my fault, guys." The nervousness was gone, and his breathing was in rhythm again.

"I agree," Edmund assured him. "Everything's cool—right, Sa'ad?"

"We'll see," Sa'ad grumbled. "You turn left," he said to Joel, "and we're going to walk on. We're parked on Higgins Street, near some kind of camping and hiking shop. Blue rental Impala, Nevada plates. Meet us there in ten minutes. Give me the equipment and the papers to examine as soon as you locate us. Then we'll be on the road."

"Fine," Joel said and veered away, nearly bumped into a mother cradling a drowsy child and had to apologize.

Ten minutes later, Joel located the car and found Sa'ad behind the wheel, his hat on the seat beside him. Joel had placed the bag inside a newspaper, and now he leaned against the Impala's door and shook the velvet sack through the window and into Sa'ad's lap. The appraisal was folded small and stuffed in with the valuables. "I'll need the jeweler's statement returned," Joel said. He left and walked the streets without any destination, looked in several windows, strolled close enough to the Clark Fork that he could smell the river and finally made his way back to the blue vehicle and waited for one of them to speak.

"Okay," Sa'ad said. "Let us know if your work schedule changes."

"I will."

Sa'ad cranked the motor. "Sorry about the misunderstanding."

Joel shrugged.

"You did great, Joel. Great." Edmund bobbed his head up and down.

"How long before something happens?" Joel asked. Cars were passing him on the street, the majority of them in no hurry, the drivers making slow, blinkered turns and braking before every stoplight regardless of its color.

"Two or three months," Edmund said.

"Will you warn me?"

"No," Sa'ad told him. "But let us know if your schedule changes. You need to be at work when it happens." He passed the appraisal through the window, and Joel held it concealed in his palm, didn't immediately pocket it.

"I understand."

"Good luck," Sa'ad said, and he sounded sincere. "We're almost there."

"Great to see you," Edmund said. "Just stick to the plan."

"I will," Joel answered, both words spoken softly.

Joel had time to kill and nothing to do, but he didn't want to return home, couldn't think of any attraction there beyond television and the Third Part of Thomas Aquinas's *Summa Theologica* beside his bed, and he wasn't in the mood for reruns or dense reading. He stood where Sa'ad and Edmund had left him, eyeing the streets and businesses, debating where he should go. He decided to wander back to the carousel, stroll around and see if anything interested him. It would be nice to have a magazine or a big-city newspaper to read, and he thought about visiting the library or a bookstore.

He'd started along the sidewalk in the direction of a travel agency, beckoned by a giant poster of a beach and inviting ocean, when he heard a car approaching from behind, louder and more rapidly than the other traffic tooling through the town. The car wasn't quite speeding, but Joel heard it accelerate from a stop and continue to climb. He turned and discovered Edmund and Sa'ad coming down the street in their blue Impala, fast enough that he knew instantly something was wrong, that they had returned in a hurry, looking for him. Sa'ad slowed and pulled alongside the curb, talking out the window to Joel while the car continued to roll.

"Where is it?" he demanded, his face blazing with fury.

"What? Where is what, Sa'ad?" Joel just stared at him. "Why are you here again?"

"Get in the car," Sa'ad barked.

"Why?" Joel asked, a trace of fear starting to appear with the confusion.

"Get in the motherfucking car right now, or I swear I'll get out and drag you in." He stopped the Impala.

Joel studied him and then tried to peek at Edmund's expression. "Calm down. The way you're acting, I'm not about to go anywhere with you."

Sa'ad had traveled as far as he could, had arrived at a parked vehicle that blocked his progress. He ripped open the door, and Joel heard Edmund tell him to quit being an ass and give Joel a chance to explain. "It's okay," Edmund said, leaning across the seat so Joel could see him. "We've got a problem with the bag you gave us. Somethin's missing."

"Missing?" Joel took a step toward the car and crooked his neck to get a better view of Edmund.

"Let's not discuss this here," Edmund pleaded. "Sa'ad's not going to do nothing; you know how he gets, all wound up and full of hot air."

"I don't understand. And I thought we were trying to avoid being seen together."

"I'm going to ask one more time," Sa'ad threatened. "Get in."

"Help us out here, Joel," Edmund cajoled. "We need to clear this up, find an understandin'."

Joel thought about weapons. He couldn't see anything in Sa'ad's hands or the front of the vehicle, but he was still nervous, reluctant. "I'll meet you guys at the carousel. Just leave the car and follow me there."

"You cocksucker," Sa'ad said, but he didn't make good on his promise to come after Joel.

Joel kept watch on them over his shoulder and took longer strides than usual. He was bewildered as to why they had returned, concerned this was some new layer in the con that would lessen his stake or leave him vulnerable, and he was queasy and cotton-mouthed because he believed Sa'ad might really hurt him. He didn't stop at the horses, but instead continued on until he arrived at a chest-high wooden fence in front of the dragon playground, discovered when he looked up that the beast was glowering also, was staring at him with angled green eyebrows and a sour mouth. He rested his elbows along the top of the fence, and Edmund and Sa'ad filled in on each side, so close they touched him.

"Do you think we are morons?" Sa'ad asked.

"No. Not morons," Joel said, and the answer made Sa'ad that much madder.

"We have an item missing," Edmund offered.

"From the bag?" Joel asked.

"Correct."

"That you gave to me and I just handed back?" Joel said.

"Right," Edmund said. "It's not there. It wasn't returned."

"You're wearing my ass out," Sa'ad complained. "You know damn well it's not there."

Joel stepped into Sa'ad. "You're suggesting I stole part of the jewelry?"

"Cool it, guys." Edmund gripped Joel's arm. "Come on now. We're all friends here. Nobody's accusing you of anything."

"He is," Joel said, frowning at Sa'ad.

"Damn right I am," Sa'ad answered.

"I returned everything I got. I darn sure didn't steal anything. Why would I do that?"

"Duh?" Sa'ad said. "Money, maybe?"

Joel relaxed and let out a breath, then another. "Sa'ad, I promise I gave back the whole works, all of it, every bit." Joel held up his hand and spread his fingers, as if taking an oath. "My word on that."

"So where is it, then?" Sa'ad wanted to know. "Tell me."

"What's missing?" Joel asked.

"I did an inventory when Abel gave me the stuff, wrote down the contents of the bag. It would seem we're missing a diamond and emerald ring. Six total stones, platinum setting, small gouge on one side." Sa'ad was now sounding more lawyerly than angry. "Not a great piece, maybe ten, fifteen grand tops, according to Abel. Very much the kind of low-interest item somebody might rogue, figuring no one else would notice."

"Yeah, well, I don't have it," Joel said. "I remember seeing it, though. I have to admit that much—I was going to ask if you were sure *you* didn't lose it or fail to deliver it to me. But I did get it. I remember the big nick."

"So where is it?" Sa'ad asked, less aggressively this time.

"I don't know. Did you check the car? Maybe it fell out."

"Did I check the car?" Sa'ad mocked him. "It's not in the fucking car. And it's due back at its rightful home day after tomorrow, before the owners return from their vacation and discover it's gone."

"Think about where it could be," Edmund encouraged him. "Think where you saw it last."

"I don't know . . . Wow." Joel rubbed the side of his face; he felt stubble resist when he went against the grain.

"You can't hustle a hustler, Joel," Sa'ad said. "Just give it up, and we'll consider it bad judgment and move on, pretend this never occurred."

"I simply don't have it. I don't. I promise."

"Fine," Sa'ad said petulantly. "Have it your way." He paused. "No matter how you break it down, this is your fuckup—you're either dishonest or remarkably incompetent. So this comes out of your cut."

Joel shook his head, sighed. "I never should've gotten into this. Never. What was I thinking?" He whirled and looked Sa'ad in the eye. "And this is what I get, huh? Treachery and backstabbing and everybody questioning everybody, no one sure whom to believe."

"Spare me the sermon and self-pity. You made your choices, and it's a little late to start bitching about them now."

"Joel, I believe you, okay?" Edmund said. "And you can believe me— we're not out to screw you. But you can see our problem. I hope this is no more than a bump in the road. We'll get it solved, though. Yes we will."

"Tell that to your buddy Sa'ad," Joel said.

"It is solved, Joel," Sa'ad said. "For starters, your share is going to be fifteen thousand light—"

Joel interrupted him. "Hey, whoa. Wait. Wait a minute. Remember how you estimated we'd get three hundred and the appraisal came up short? Remember?"

"I've already thought of that," Sa'ad answered.

"So that means—maybe—the missing piece didn't make it to the appraiser. See what I mean? That's why we were disappointed in the amount, got only two seventy-five. Or maybe she took it, the lady at the store or . . . oh, my . . . the guy in Roanoke at the pawnshop. Doc was his name . . . Certainly he wouldn't have been so brazen. But you know, he had the stuff and shuffled it around and did a lot with his hands—and he did try to cheat me, lied about the value. I'll bet that son of a gun took it."

"Or maybe gremlins snatched it while you slept," Sa'ad said. "I don't give a shit how you lost it. Your share's going to be light, and if this thing is reported to the cops, they'll start nosing around and you can be sure they'll spend some time with Abel. If he's compromised, it'll cost me thousands. And if things get nasty, I'll make certain you take the fall. That's a promise."

"Maybe the owners won't notice it's gone," Joel said lamely. "Or maybe they won't report it to the police."

"Right," Sa'ad snorted. "I'll count on that."

"And it's not like you've lost anything, Sa'ad," Joel added. "It's someone else's property, not yours. Why punish me?"

"I'm out my share of the piece you lost, and so are Edmund and Abel. Your share goes for aggravation costs."

"Well, I'm sorry," Joel said. "Surely you don't think I'd do something this obvious, this stupid, to try to take advantage of you and Edmund?" He kept his eyes away from Sa'ad, watched two kids emerge from a tube slide that emptied at the dragon's haunch.

"Check the appraisal and see if the ring is mentioned," Edmund said. "You can tell by the descriptions. We didn't bother to inspect that right off, when you first gave us the papers. We just looked at the amount, the bottom line, and it seemed low but in the ballpark. Sa'ad had me match up the bag with his list as we were leavin' town. There were thirteen pieces in the bag, fifteen on his inventory. We gave you fifteen, you hocked the cheap earrings, we got back thirteen. So we're one shy. I told him you were totally innocent. I stuck up for you."

Joel pulled the appraisal from his pocket and read the contents as Edmund and Sa'ad crowded in, looking along with him. "Only thirteen listed," he said glumly. "The ring never made it."

"Doesn't tell us a thing, Joel," Sa'ad said. "I'm supposed to believe you weren't aware how many items were in the bag? Never counted? Never inspected the pieces?"

"I knew there were several, Sa'ad. I didn't memorize them or write them down like you. I'm a rookie—it never occurred to me. And I was nervous as a cat when I went to the store for the appraisal. You try that sometime, try to seem casual and surprised while you're pulling off a scam and on probation with a jail sentence hanging over your head. I wasn't counting, but I was always careful to watch when the bag was out of my control. It's not like there were two things, and I lost one of them. There were a bunch, and I was darn attentive if they weren't under my mattress."

"You're kidding, right?" Sa'ad chided him. "You hid the shit under your mattress?"

"Where else would I put it?" Now Joel was growing angry.

"I'm not even going to answer that," Sa'ad scoffed.

"I don't know what we can do here," Edmund said. "Helluva dilemma we got."

"You don't think there's any chance of criminal problems, do you?" Joel asked him. "Or jail?"

Edmund spoke in a pensive voice. "I'm guessin' the owners will report it to their insurance company, the company will demand a police report, the police will talk to everyone who has access—including Abel—and get nowhere—"

"You better hope they get nowhere," Sa'ad butted in.

"And dependin' on the people who own the stuff, the police will assume it was lost or misplaced or underneath a sofa cushion. If this was a theft, the cops would expect more to be taken, especially when there's so much more available. Plus they won't find squat on Abel or any of his guys, and Abel's a champ. He'll offer interviews with his staff and let the cops search his home and the whole nine yards. But it does give us a wrinkle we don't need."

"I promise I don't have it," Joel said. "I'm not trying to slip one past you. Either I just lost it, or Doc or the lady appraiser has it. Should I go back and ask? Or should you guys?"

"How smart is that, Joel?" Sa'ad snapped. "Huh? All we need is for you to be running around claiming a hot ring the police are looking for in Las Vegas. As poor as our fortunes have been so far, the damn trails would cross and we—pardon me, *you*—would be in even deeper."

"I don't know what to say," Joel muttered.

"I'll be watching you like a hawk," Sa'ad warned him.

"You do that. See if I care." Joel unwound his features, rubbed his palm against his temple and turned to Edmund, completely ignoring Sa'ad. "You think we should still go through with this?"

"Probably," Edmund answered. "We'll let things slide and see what happens in Vegas. There's still no real link. I mean, a lady loses a ring in Vegas, you get robbed of thirteen different pieces of jewelry miles away. No connection, unless there's the million-to-one chance some insurance company happens to compare your loss claim to the owner's insured list and sees they're similar. Red flag goes up, and we have a problem, but in a sense, we've had that problem all along. It's maybe slightly more possible if the actual owners have just filed a claim and their policy's been in play recently. But Abel can help us with that, too. When the ring's reported missin' in Vegas, I'm sure the insurance folks will want a word with the cleanin' service, and Abel can tell us who has the coverage. If it's not the same company who's insuring you, we've got clear sailin'. No chance of overlap."

"Jeez," Joel said. "Could this get any more fouled up?"

"It's the business we're in, Joel," Edmund replied. "It's what we do."

"You understand you're on the hook for this? Whatever it takes," Sa'ad warned for what seemed like the hundredth time.

"No? Really?" Joel said. "I thought we'd patched things up, and we'd all share responsibility equally."

When Joel arrived home after work, he combed the Taurus for the missing ring, used Baker's Spider-Man flashlight and a straightened coat hanger and checked under the seats and mats and in every crack and recess. He emptied the glove compartment and the trunk, found a dime, three pennies and an ink pen, but no jewelry. He searched the Volvo and his clothes. He looked beneath his bed and raised the mattress off the box springs, propped it with two fire logs. The ring was gone, and the more he considered it, the more convinced he became that Doc was the culprit. He'd been hoodooed by an old pro, hoodwinked when he thought he was the one ruling the scam.

On the first Monday in October, Probation Officer Jack Howard called Joel at his sister's and told him he needed to report immediately. That was how he announced himself on the phone: "This is Probation Officer Jack Howard, and I need to talk to Joel King."

"I recognized your voice," Joel told him. "This is Joel. Good morning."

"You need to come by my office ASAP," he said, his voice all business.

"You mean now? Today?"

" 'ASAP' is what they call an acronym. It means as soon as possible. Like right this instant."

Joel was preparing Jell-O, stirring bright cherry powder into a bowl of warm water with a wooden spoon. He assumed Howard was calling because he wanted to revisit the subject of the probation release, had decided on the shape, size and cost of his corruption. Joel stifled his anger and answered in a subservient, humble tone. "I'll stop what I'm doing and drive right down, if that's convenient for you, sir."

"Yeah, yeah, yeah. It's convenient for me. I'll be waiting."

"Is it about—"

Howard interrupted before Joel could finish. "I'll see you soon," he said, then hung up the phone.

Joel had intended to get back to him, had planned to stop by and genuflect and make peace and negotiate the terms of his buyout, but he'd recognized he needed to let their disagreement cool or he would just make the situation worse, would utter something under his breath or lose his temper again and drive the price of his discharge even higher. It was difficult to kneel and kiss Howard's ring and come off as genuine when he despised the man and everything about him, and despite several prayerful efforts to shed his dislike, he'd been unable to marshal enough will to talk to Howard without risking another ugly skirmish and bruised throat.

He'd say very little, Joel decided during the drive to town, just make his offer and eat crow and meekly say he couldn't afford the price that was originally quoted. He'd look at the floor or the wall when they spoke and divert his face from Howard's line of sight, because even a dullard like Howard could spot the loathing in his expression. He stopped at an Ole's convenience store and pumped three dollars' worth of gas into the Taurus, and when he was standing at the register counting nickels and quarters out of his palm, he glanced at the cashier and saw himself in a mirror behind her, noticed that his hair and whiskers were getting grayer, his face craggy.

Two other people were in the waiting area when Joel arrived, a chunky man with a red beard and a completely average fellow in jeans and a sport coat. Mrs. Heller greeted him by name, got up from her seat and accompanied him to Howard's door. She knocked and then allowed him in without waiting for an answer or anyone to appear.

Howard was where he always was, seated behind his desk, but his feet weren't hoisted and he was sitting like a professional, his hands stacked on top of a file, the arrogant sway in his neck and shoulders absent. A woman was seated on Joel's side of the desk. She had a round face that wasn't the least bit fat or heavy, thick brown hair styled so it didn't appear to require much attention, painted nails and a trace of lipstick that wasn't very noticeable, seemed more brownish than red. She was smartly dressed, and a briefcase with a skinned, dented corner was beside her on the floor. She stood when Joel came through the door, and—remarkably—Howard also rose, left his seat and gestured toward the empty chair next to the woman. She looked to be thirty-five or so, was tall for a woman and had a good deal of presence in the small, sparse office.

"Good morning, Mr. King. Thank you for coming so soon." Howard's tone was new to Joel, the sarcasm and condescension gone, replaced by a businesslike monotone, the voice reminiscent of a salesclerk or an elderly lady making change at the end of a cafeteria line.

"Hello," Joel said. Whatever this was, it couldn't be good. But certainly she hadn't been brought here, some cop or lawyer, to cause him trouble about the probation disagreement or the bribe he'd offered his supervising officer—that would be too stupid and impulsive even for Howard.

"This is Lynette Allen, Mr. King." Howard rolled his hand in her direction, shifted his weight. A flash of malice hopped through his mouth and constricted one of his eyes, and he was careful to make sure Joel saw the old Howard, gave him a cancerous second or two that he kept hidden from Lynette Allen.

"Pleased to meet you," she offered. They shook hands, and she sat down, then Joel, then Howard.

No idea. He had no idea, and the anticipation and dread were beginning to pummel his bowels and cause his head to fill with static and white noise.

"She's with the county attorney's office," Howard said. "A prosecutor."

The jewels. Edmund and Sa'ad. Either they'd betrayed him as part of the scam or something had gone awry or the police in Las Vegas were on his heels, eager to discuss the missing ring. Had to be it. He briefly shut his eyes and sucked down a breath, went limp against the chair. "Okay," he said. Or maybe it had to do with Christy, seeing her at the mall, violating his probation; perhaps word of that mistake had reached the Virginia authorities.

"Thank you for coming, Mr. King," she said. "On such short notice."

"Sure. I came as soon as Mr. Howard called." Leaving the state without permission—that could be it if Howard had found out about Vegas and was proving a point, delivering a shot of payback for the threats about early release. Or maybe he had simply concocted a dirty drug screen or made up a violation from whole cloth. Right now, he'd gladly take either of those and be delighted. Insurance fraud had to be bad, serious, a federal offense.

"I'm here to speak to you about a case, Mr. King," Lynette said.

And I've become such a con and crook and poor probationer, Joel thought, that I'm left with far too many possibilities to know which one you're here to discuss. Could be one of many. "What case?" he asked.

"Ah, a case you're involved in and can assist us with."

"I'm sure Mr. King wants to be helpful," Howard remarked.

"I do. If I can," Joel said warily. He didn't look at the woman beside him.

"As Mr. Howard mentioned, I work with the county attorney's office here in Missoula." Lynette craned her neck, attempting to engage Joel.

He stared at his shoes, relocated his feet. One of the laces was untied, and the string ends were frayed and starting to unravel. "Right," he said and didn't dare look at her.

"I prosecute primarily domestic crimes," she told him.

"Oh, okay," Joel said, distracted, not really listening, still afraid of what was in the offing.

"I understand you might have witnessed a crime. A Lisa Dillen was attacked by her husband, a man by the name of Karl Dillen. They're from South Carolina and took a float trip with you not too long ago."

Joel was counting the eyelets in his shoe. Two, three, four . . . and he stopped, caught up with Lynette Allen's words as they passed through his ears and into his muddled brain. He popped up and faced her, full of relief and surprise. "A witness?"

"Correct. We understand you saw everything and were very supportive of the victim."

Joel wet his lips and twisted so he could better see her, crossed his legs. "Sure. Yes. So that's it? You want to talk to me about Karl and Lisa?"

"That's it for the time being," Howard added. "You and I may need to see each other about some unrelated matters before you leave."

"Okay," Joel said.

"You remember what happened?" she asked.

"I do. I was there the whole time. I drove her to the hospital."

"Would you be willing to testify?" she asked him.

"I guess so. If you think it would do any good."

"We think it would," she said.

"I'm assuming you know my situation, my history and so forth. Won't that be a problem—me being on probation and having a record?"

Lynette shook her head. "Not admissible in Montana. No one will know the difference."

"I'll try to help," he offered.

"Good," she said. "You mind telling me what you know?"

"Now?"

"Now would be great."

"Well . . ." Joel hesitated, decided to give Howard a needle and tweak even though he knew it would probably cost him later on. "Do you mind if we speak in private?" he asked her.

"You mean you and me?" she asked.

"Exactly."

"You don't care, do you, Mr. Howard?" she replied in a way that let him know he'd better not.

"You want me to leave my own office?" he asked, his disbelief obvious by the time he ended his sentence.

"I don't know why any of this matters one way or the other to you, Mr. Howard," she said firmly. "And the county attorney's office will be most grateful. I'll let you know if I unearth anything that affects his probationary status."

"Hey, fine with me. Whatever I can do to be helpful. I'll grab a cup of coffee." He managed to rein in his voice. "But you don't leave when you get done with lawyer Allen, okay Mr. King?" He showed them both an exaggerated smile. "I need to go over official probation business with you, Mr. King, take care of some important details." He displayed the smile again. "And you'll probably have to wait while I see my other appointments, which means hanging around till I can work you in."

"You want to talk now," Joel suggested, "before Ms. Allen and I get started?"

"No. No, no, no. Not at all. I'm sure lawyer Allen is busier than me." He smiled one final time, said goodbye to Lynette Allen and left the room, made a production of pulling the door quietly closed as he crayfished from sight.

"Why do you want to talk in private?" she inquired when Howard was gone.

"Oh, so you enjoy his company?" Joel said.

"He's a little prickly and a piece of work, but I don't know why you care if he hears what you have to say." She made a quick gesture with her hands, flicked her palms.

"I'm just more comfortable with him elsewhere," he said.

"Your call." She repeated the gesture. "So what do you know about my case?"

"Everything, most likely." Joel recounted to her how Karl had hit his wife without any provocation and split the skin above her eye, and how he'd taken Lisa to the hospital despite Karl's objections. After he finished the story, he asked her why it was important for him to testify. "It seems like a slam dunk to me," he remarked. "He hit her, and the proof's right there on her face."

"I'm sorry to say it's not so simple. Like many domestic assault victims, she is extremely reluctant to testify. The case came to us on a compulsory report from the hospital."

"Why's that?" Joel asked. "You'd think she'd want to stick it to him."

"The reasons vary. Sometimes it's old-fashioned fear. Sometimes it's self-esteem—many victims feel they deserve to be battered, that they're to blame. Maybe it's embarrassment, maybe it's love, maybe it's money, maybe it's an effort to keep the kids in an intact home. I can cite you hundreds of reasons, but I'm afraid she'll refuse to testify or simply lie for him. She's already called my office."

"That's a shame."

"So that's why we need you," she explained.

"What does Karl say?" Joel asked.

"He says she fell because you mishandled the boat and caused it to lurch suddenly as you were approaching the bank."

"That's not true," Joel said.

There was a knock on the door, and Mrs. Heller appeared, inquired how much longer they'd need the office.

"Until we're finished," Lynette said sharply. She waited for the door to close and then returned to Joel. "I know it's not. He's got two other dismissals on his record for basically the same offense. Both times she asked for the charges to be dropped."

"Well, I'll do what's right."

"Even if she begs you not to, calls and cries and pleads and tells you it's her fault and that I'm pushing the case against her will?"

"The truth is the truth. If you put me on the stand, I'll tell what I know."

She leaned closer to him, put her elbow on the chair arm and let it hold her weight. "I don't want you to think I'm a zealot or some kind of flamer. I'm not out to eradicate men and distaff the world, okay? I try to be evenhanded. I want you to know as much going in. In fact, I have four rules. I don't become too excited if someone is punched for cheating on her husband; I don't really care if you get hit after spitting in a man's face; and a fine will do if you slap your wife when she calls you a motherfucker for no reason. But you lay hands on a woman without any genuine provocation or in the middle of some everyday spat—you need to go to jail. Period."

"I don't have any quarrel with that."

"Good. So I can count on you?"

"Yes," Joel said.

"This guy's an asshole," she said.

"And evidently pretty wealthy—a dentist or something."

"Right. And you know what you call an asshole with money?"

"Nope."

"An asshole," she said and didn't smile, not one whit.

"Let me know what I need to do."

"I will," she said and took the load off her arm. "Dixon Kreager speaks highly of you."

"You know Dixon?"

"Sure. I think the world of him."

"I do too," Joel said. "Why were you talking to him?"

"To find out what kind of witness you might be."

"Makes sense," Joel said.

"Howard, on the other hand, says you're a con artist and a rascal. 'Just another lying preacher' is how he phrased it."

Joel considered what he should say, searched the floor with the toe of his shoe and then stared at the empty space behind Howard's desk. "I'm sorry he feels that way," he finally answered. "I'm not too fond of him either."

fourteen _____

Joel's divorce became final on November 3, a Tuesday. He got the news
from Sa'ad a day later, received the call while he was watching a PBS special on Frank Lloyd Wright, and when he heard Sa'ad's voice, he turned off
the power to the cable box so the den fell completely quiet. He was in the
house by himself; Sophie was at work, and Baker wouldn't be home from
school for another three hours. It was the first contact he'd had with Sa'ad
since their argument at the carousel, and the sound of his voice—cool, polished and oiled—caused a bitter taste in Joel's mouth and set him on edge.

Sa'ad said hello, politely asked about Sophie and trout fishing and then
went immediately to business. "As of yesterday, you and Martha are divorced," was the way he put it. There was no suggestion of bad blood from
the jewelry battle royal.

Joel didn't respond, just sat there with metallic saliva in his mouth and
replayed the sentence over and over and over, dwelled on the brutal bare-
ness of what he was hearing and what it entailed. The words were stark, to
the marrow, blunt and precise, a handful of syllables and a commonplace
legal result that undid a precious sacrament and made strangers of two
people who'd shared a bed and loved each other so fully they'd vowed only
death would separate them, and even that would be temporary. Such a
grand, remarkable movement of spirit had been reduced to nothing, made
so trite and inert that the ordinary end came from the lips of a dishonest,
silk-stocking Las Vegas lawyer who carefully pronounced every word and
would have his secretary drop the final decree in the mail. And that was it,
the sum total, all that was left of a marriage begun eighteen years ago as
lovely and ineffable—a dab of paperwork and an attorney's phone call. It

was as if the moon had plummeted from orbit and ended up a regular old chunk of rock, merely another gray stone in a field or beside a road, indistinguishable from the thousands of others lying with it.

"Joel?" Sa'ad said after a moment. "Are you still there?"

"Yes." He was crying, his nose was dripping and his throat was filling with spit and disappointment.

"Hey, I'm sorry. I am, all kidding aside."

"The love of my life . . ." Joel said. He wiped his face and nose with his sleeve, stood up from the sofa.

"Hang in there."

"I prayed and prayed over this, and somehow I just never believed it would happen." He sucked back mucus that had run to his lip, sniffed three straight times before exhaling.

"Sorry."

"I don't mean to go to pieces," Joel said. "I knew this was coming—it's not like you didn't warn me."

"And the good news is no alimony, no nastiness. Long term, you'll be damn glad of that much."

"Yeah."

"It's always tough when it actually happens," Sa'ad said.

"Okay." Joel was doing better. He dried his nose and cheeks again, used a paper napkin from the kitchen.

"Let me know if I can do anything else."

"I will."

"I mean it. I realize we've had a few rough spots, Joel, but I consider you a friend."

"You . . ." The hypocrisy caught Joel off guard, infuriating him. He stopped crying. "What?"

"I consider you a friend," Sa'ad repeated. "Certainly more than just a client."

"How about that. How blessed can one guy be?" Joel couldn't help but let the sarcasm fly. He balled the napkin and threw it at the trash can, missed.

"I'm sorry. Did I say something to upset you?"

"No." Joel was curt.

"I've tried to do my level best for you, Joel. I don't know why you would be distressed with me. You're ending up with a no-fault divorce, no alimony payments and basically a new life. I won't mislead you—most of that seems to have been her decision, but it's still an excellent outcome."

"I agree. No alimony—great. Thanks. You've treated me well professionally." He realized it was important to compose himself and keep his rage in check. He didn't need Sa'ad suspicious, not with the church settlement still up in the air. "I didn't mean to be rude. I'm just really upset."

"I understand."

"Sorry."

"Speaking of our professional relationship, I'm having trouble getting a handle on the Virginia suit," Sa'ad said.

"Oh?"

"My associate tells me Mr. Roland wouldn't return his calls and faxes, and when Roland finally does contact us, he claims we've been fired. What's going on with that?"

Joel had known this might happen, and he'd prepared a story, was ready with a practiced explanation. "I didn't tell him I was firing anyone. After everything went so well, we discussed the case and decided I was safe and so was the church." To Joel's delight, his response was sounding spontaneous and blasé. "As badly as Christy did, there's no way she'll get anywhere near the full insurance amount. So I told Roland to manage things by himself. That was all there was to it, Sa'ad. I figured I'd save Edmund some money and, well, you know, uh, just sort of put an end to our connection. Given Edmund's line of work, the fewer contacts we three have—"

Sa'ad interrupted, nearly shouting. "You don't need to explain any further over the telephone."

"Right. So I didn't fire anyone. As far as I can determine, Christy's case is a dud."

"You're certain of that?" Sa'ad asked. "Roland's not telling us diddly, but my associate's under the impression he wasn't very happy with you or your performance."

"He told me he was. And, you know, he seems to be a very cautious, close-to-the-vest kind of guy. Maybe he doesn't want to raise expectations."

"Something's a little odd there—you positive you don't want me to track it down?"

"There's nothing to track down." Joel hoped he sounded confident.

"Well, I guess you're right. Four million's a lot of coverage. But don't come complaining to me if things fail to go smoothly."

"I was there. She'll be lucky to get four hundred dollars, much less four million."

"Okay. I'll close my file and send Edmund a bill."

"You actually bill him, huh? I mean, you know, I thought you did, but—"

"Why wouldn't I? I'll give him a reasonable discount, of course. He's a friend and good client."

"I see," Joel said.

"And you're satisfied everything is under control?"

What is it going to take, Joel wondered. "Yes. I've got complete faith in Mr. Roland."

"Then I guess our business is done," Sa'ad announced. "Our legal business," he added.

"It is. Thanks."

"Perhaps our paths will cross again someday. I've enjoyed representing you. And I regret things didn't work out with your wife."

"Me too." Joel clicked off the phone, didn't say goodbye or mention their other concern.

The leaves, almost all of them, had turned color in Virginia—reds and yellows and fire-oranges were gussying up the hardwood branches—but the weather was still mild and plenty tolerable during the day. Christy was wearing shorts, tennis shoes, socks and a long-sleeve Sweet Briar sweatshirt, walking from the guardhouse down a twist of road that led from Route 29 to the college. She had a pipe hidden in her hand and a film canister of pot in her pocket and had already taken two extreme hits as soon as she passed the scarecrow security cop in his silly hut. It was three in the afternoon, broad November daylight, and she was walking because she had to, had to get outside and smoke a little dope to keep from going mad, completely freaking bonkers.

Despite what he'd said, Henry Clay Hanes still hadn't come across with her money, claimed Roland and the insurance company were stalling and had made a sorry-ass counteroffer of one million, which wouldn't be so bad if she weren't expecting nearly four times as much. He was going to do this and that, set the case for trial and ask for summary judgment— he spelled the term for her over the phone—and tighten the screws, and sooner or later the cash would be on his desk, but it was more money than most people see in a lifetime and it wasn't a big shock they were delaying payment, stretching things to the limit. Maybe before Christmas, he'd said, haughty and patronizing like always.

She was also anxious about Joel, worried that he might be doubting her commitment and thinking she'd double-crossed him. She'd sent him Hanes's bogus letter to Sa'ad describing her poor performance, had awakened with a hangover and the strange residue of a mushroom high and mailed the copy the morning after she'd gotten it, but that was eons ago and he had to be concerned, even though they'd agreed not to speak till after the checks were hers and the case closed, no matter how long it took.

She lit the dope and sucked smoke, held down the pot until her lungs rebelled and coughed it up. She needed to give him a signal, to let him know she was still at school and hadn't seen any dollars. Fuck it—she could just call from a pay phone when she was in Lynchburg, use coins instead of her credit card. But, damn, what was the number at his sister's? So . . . she'd mail him again, send a note, wear gloves, disguise her writing, drop a coded message to keep him sedated and off her ass while the check was in limbo. And who was watching, really? Like the FBI or something? Probably nobody—all this Morse code and *Mission: Impossible* stuff was a joke. It was a safe bet she could drive to his door naked and drunk, and it wouldn't make any difference.

Then there was the matter of a paper due Monday and a test the next day that would halt her weekend and keep her from riding with her new friend Kate to Charlottesville for a deluxe band party on Rugby Road. She'd met a killer guy named Gates who'd invited her to Vail over the holidays, and she'd screwed him at his friend's apartment and he'd sent her flowers but, like always, if she wasn't at the party with him it was anybody's guess where he'd end up or what skank might try to sleep with him. Plus, she'd allowed him to do it without a condom, and even though it was day nine when they got together who knew about that math for sure, and then she hears that Denise who lives across the hall has herpes, caught the infernal shit from a VMI cadet.

There was just a ton on her. It was making her hair fall out and spoiling her complexion.

She put away the dope and sat against a tree trunk midway down the entrance road. She could hear cars and trucks traveling on the four-lane below her, but she couldn't see them. She heard somebody blow a long, pissed-off horn, and occasionally a trucker would let off the accelerator and the engine would make a rumbling pop-pop-pop noise. The pot and the warm sun on her face gave her a small portion of relief, coated her with a soothing, low-grade comfort. She marveled at the brightness of the leaves, running her eyes from hue to hue, and after a while busied herself trying to find patches that were still green, hadn't yet changed. They're all dying, she dope-thought, one final, spectacular, eye-catching flameout, and next month they'll be gone, dry and brown and useless and stuck to the dirt.

Christy had been camped under the tree for a good while when a girl and her boyfriend appeared, startling her. She'd been thinking about the branches and Gates and how it might be cool to have a baby, especially if she was rich as shit and didn't have to worry about some dumbass guy supporting her. Each time she'd find the rare patch of green leaves, she'd stare at them and wonder how long it would be before they fell, whether they'd at least be allowed to boss the sky for a day or two before the wind blew them into nothing . . . like what happened to River Phoenix and Kurt Cobain. The girl spoke to her, said hello, and her boyfriend mentioned what a pretty afternoon it was, and Christy was so surprised that she could barely speak. "Hi," was all she said.

The girl's name was Amy—Christy had seen her on campus—and she was from Ohio, seemed pleasant enough but not too outgoing. She and the boy began strolling up the road toward the school, holding hands, taking their time, swinging their arms. Christy heard Amy ask him if he wanted to stay for dinner and study afterward, and he said yes, let go of her hand and slipped his arm around her waist. The scene made Christy suddenly sad, mixed despair with the pot and her weariness, and caused her to reflect on where she was and where she ought to be—a smart, gorgeous girl who knew a lot and had figured out next to nothing.

Amy and her cute date were going to eat together and highlight pages with yellow markers and kiss and maybe have sex and just know they had life by the tail. They weren't antsy and rushed, didn't have to squirm and grasp and yearn, weren't constantly on patrol for a stronger drink or a heftier buzz or a better party or enough money to conquer the world. The entire time she watched them wooing and nuzzling, she envied their simple contentment, wished she could somehow find satisfaction in picnics, Jane Austen novels, film festivals, cooking, good grades, the Sunday comics, sharing a chocolate dessert or watching it snow at night with the floodlights on. But it's just fucking impossible to leave cocaine for caffeine without being bored to death, and she was where she was, and soon she'd be almost four million dollars improved, all the stress gone, and hand-holding, romance and changing seasons wouldn't concern her, not when she was at a reggae festival in Montego Bay, high as a kite, fresh from the hotel spa.

She stood and followed Amy up the drive, and as she walked she recalled being a child, seven or eight, and playing checkers with her Grandma Flippen, her mother's mother, the elderly lady in a sweater and a knee-length cotton dress, the two of them laughing and pushing the wooden disks around the board, jumping each other's men and getting crowned, making red and black kings that could move backward and forward and almost never got cornered. When the game was over, her grandmother would put away her game pieces in an old, plastic potato salad container with most of the writing worn off its lid, and she'd fix them a country-ham sandwich and a Pepsi, would cut the sandwich in two and press the bread flat with the side of her kitchen knife.

Christy felt a tear leave the boundary of her eye. Only a solitary tear, and she wasn't sad enough to want to cry, hadn't known it was on the way or felt it building. She dabbed the wetness with her index finger, then held her fingertip in front of her face and stared at the dampness as if it were some odd, impossible mistake.

Joel had heard about the Montana winters, had been warned about the frigid, harsh winds that would rampage through the Bitterroot and Sapphire Mountains and gut the valleys and vales. He experienced his first cold snap at the beginning of November when an icy front blanketed most of the state and delivered two days of snowfall, close to eleven inches, an unusual early arrival that didn't augur well for the next several months. He wore double shirts, thermal gloves and his heaviest coat anytime he ventured outdoors, but the chill was unavoidable and very much different than the occasional freezes in Roanoke. The weather covered everything, made walking and starting cars and feeding the chickens and simply drawing breath a strained, bundled effort. The rivers changed color, acquiring grays and bleak blues, and the trees, even the evergreens, lost their vitality, seemed to bow their heads and capitulate to the brutal, stinging air.

In the heart of the cold spell, Dixon was kind enough to give Joel a Thursday morning's work at the Coachman, called him the day before and asked him to clean and sort one of the storage rooms and help prepare Christmas shipments. Joel got to the shop at eight and was finished by lunch, and Dixon invited him to eat barbecue and beans in his office. Dixon had labored over the meat for two days, soaking it in sauce and letting it stand overnight and slow-cooking it on a stove he'd installed in an unfinished garage off his office.

When he sat down to eat, Joel had shucked his jacket, but still was wearing long johns and two shirts, couldn't shiver and stomp the last traces of cold from his legs and feet. Dixon cleared a spot on his desk for their plates, and he kept a space heater plugged in while they ate. They reminisced about fishing and funny clients and the terrible trip with Karl and Lisa. Dixon assured Joel that Lynette Allen was a superior lady and a dandy lawyer and would kick Karl Dillen's tooth-fairy ass, not to worry.

When the conversation wandered to Christmas and religion, Joel invited

Dixon to attend a holiday service with him, perhaps the Christmas Eve cantata at Missoula Baptist or a morning communion at Saint Francis Xavier's. Now that the guide season was finished, Joel made the pilgrimage to town every Sunday, parting Baker's hair and dressing him in a boy's clip-on tie and hauling him along, holding his hand as they climbed the stairs at eleven o'clock while the bells rang and courteous people welcomed them. Baker always sat quietly until the kids were dismissed for the children's program, drew airplanes and bulldozers on the church bulletin and showed them to Joel when he was done. They'd stop at Burger King on the drive home, and Joel would let the boy order whatever he wanted, reward him for being so mannerly, so smart. "I'll be taking my nephew when I go, and who knows, maybe Sophie'll surprise us," he told Dixon.

Dixon shook his head, chewed a mouthful of meat, swallowed, drank and said, "No thanks"—said it in a polite, respectful fashion, but used a tone that didn't leave much room for compromise.

"Why not?"

"To each his own," Dixon answered. "It's just not for me."

"I think you'd enjoy it—especially at Christmas. Have you ever been to church?"

"Yeah, sure. Who hasn't?" He moved some stray beans into a pile with his spoon.

"And you didn't like the experience?"

Dixon took a big bite of meat, then another. "Well, Joel, here's my take on it, for what it's worth. Churchgoin' to me is a lot like blues music. Everybody always talks it up, says great things about it, and you know it's supposed to boost your soul, but when you actually do it, when you go sit in a smoky club for two hours hearing some old brother with a bum leg and a pair of Ray-Bans play the same slow, self-indulgent, strung-out three notes and squeeze his eyes shut, you start thinking, man, this crap ain't so hot. Truth is, you'd rather be down at the Holiday Inn lounge tossin' back dollar shooters, pawing the strange women and dancing to disco—'Brickhouse,' 'Word Up,' something fun and rollicking."

Joel laughed. "I've never heard that comparison before. And I didn't picture you as a disco man. Better not let it slip out; you need to keep your gruff, mountain-man mystique. I'll pretend I never heard it, tell everyone you drink bourbon and dark beer and listen to old bluegrass records. There'll be no mention of disco from me."

"I like the party that comes with it. And, hey, that was the music in my day."

"Fair enough."

"Nothin' against church," Dixon continued. "But it's one of those things—like museums and gyms, for instance—that's probably good for you and earns you kudos from your friends but is only enjoyed after the fact, when it's over and done and you can say you went through it."

"Well, keep it in mind. I'll probably bother you again about it—I'd love to have the company."

"We'll see," Dixon said. "So you like my marinade?"

"It's excellent. What do you put in it?"

"I can give you the recipe if you want." He began hunting through the papers scattered on his desk. "I've got it written down somewhere." Then the old-fashioned, rotary dial phone rang, and Dixon answered it, inter-rupting his search. He soon looked concerned, focused on the call and quit shuffling the invoices and notes and messages and magazines. His eyes narrowed, and he mouthed the word "damn" after hearing something, was obviously listening to serious news. He looked at Joel and said, "He's right here. I'll put him on." He stretched the receiver to Joel, told him it was his sister and she was upset, bawling because someone had broken into her house and robbed them and torn the place apart.

Joel was incensed when he reached Sophie's, speechless with anger, and the kicked-in door and reckless pilfering and turned-over furni-ture and gaping drawers barely hanging in their slots made him despise Sa'ad and Edmund even more, strengthened his resolve to punish them. Sophie was standing beside a uniformed policeman, and another man, dressed in a blazer and slacks, was on his knees examining the splintered door casing.

"The TV, the VCR, the new microwave, my jewelry, Baker's silver dollars—everything," Sophie said to him. She spoke to him as soon as he appeared, talking to him from the kitchen. "They flat wiped us out. And look at this." She waved her hand across the pillaged rooms. "Just look. What kind of animal would do something like this?"

The man inspecting the doorway stood and introduced himself to Joel. "I'm Detective Holman, Bill Holman. Missoula Police." One of his knees was wet from the slush and ice around the entrance. "This is Deputy Ron Graham." He glanced in the other officer's direction. "Sorry to meet you under these circumstances."

"Yeah. What a mess." Joel had never been more ashamed in his life. His knees were weak and spongy, his spine was in flames and he felt sure his face was flushed, flooded with pounding red disgrace. Here it was, all his doing, his sister's home wrecked and violated, as if she'd been tackled and raped, strangers throwing things from their proper places and emptying her bedroom dresser, running wild through her belongings. He put both hands over his face, tipped back his head and shut his eyes. He had no idea it would be so violent and bad, a simple, pretend burglary rigged by his partners. "Unbelievable."

Sophie left the officer and walked to where Joel was standing, had to step over a lamp and detour around the couch. The couch was on its back, flipped by the intruders, its dark canvas bottom dirty with lint and whorls of dust. She hugged him, mashing her face into his chest. "What else, Joel? What's next, huh?" The words burrowed into the fabric of his coat, were muffled and muted.

He patted her hair and stayed silent, didn't open his mouth, didn't lie or hedge or make his own fraud worse. This was a terrible blow, but she'd soon have thousands and thousands of dollars, and she'd be able to leave this bare-bones shack behind if she wanted, buy herself a much finer place to live, a two-story with a balcony and a river view. He hadn't anticipated this kind of impact, hadn't seen it coming, but he'd make her whole again, and an old TV and a battered door would seem like nothing. "I'm sorry. So sorry," he said. "I'll help you get over this and move on. Don't worry." He pushed her away, made her focus on him. "We'll be okay."

"I'm so glad you're here," she said. "I don't know what I'd do. I mean with Baker and all—what if they come back? It's like I'll never feel safe."

"We'll try to keep an eye on things," Holman offered. "Increase our presence out this way for a while. I know how you must feel. It's real normal, especially for ladies."

"Thanks," she said.

"It's rare for the same ones to return," he added. "Very unusual."

"Okay." Her eyes were swollen and she was wearing a matching skirt and sweater, her work clothes. She'd been called home after the postman noticed the door was ajar and looked inside.

Joel's shame wasn't leaving—he continued to feel weak, hot and worthless, far distant from the Lord's touch. He shifted positions, put his arm along Sophie's shoulders, did his best to keep his face blank and his sister reassured. There was no need—none—for Sa'ad and Edmund or their hireling thugs to have been so remarkably malevolent. He bit his lip and shook his head, and the detective acknowledged his reaction, thought it perfectly correct for a man whose pretty sister's house had been torn to shreds by thieves.

"We've got some information that might be helpful," Holman said.

"This is the fifth one in a month. They hit the people who live about a mile from here, family by the name of Evans. You know them? They have a brick ranch with the fine-lookin' pair of quarter horses out front."

"Yeah," Sophie said. "They're good neighbors."

"And we've got some things to work with. There's a partial shoe print on the door, and tire tracks in your drive and the mailman saw a white truck with a camper shell right as he was arriving. That's the same description we got from another robbery—three men in a white truck. We'll have someone try to lift fingerprints, but so far we haven't been too lucky there." The officer was methodical, appeared intelligent and truly concerned about his investigation and Sophie's loss.

"Thank you," she said.

"Thanks," Joel echoed.

"As soon as you can, I need you both to do an inventory and tell us what's missing. Any information about brands, serial numbers or distinctive markings is helpful to us. If you have photos or warranty cards, anything that can help us identify your items, let me know, okay?"

"Okay," Joel said.

"Don't rush. Take your time," Holman cautioned them.

"I understand," Joel said.

The other policeman was in the kitchen, and Joel happened to be watching when he raised from over the counter and called for Holman. "Bill, come here a second. Look at this."

Holman excused himself and walked the four or five strides to the small kitchen. Joel and Sophie followed behind him, straining to see what was so important, Joel's hand in the center of her back, encouraging her.

"Check this out," the officer said. He pointed at the counter where Joel had smashed it and done haphazard repairs and never gotten around to a final fix. The replacement boards weren't completely flush and hadn't been planed, and the Formica covering was sheared and cut on both sides of the break, leaving exposed edges that didn't meet. The counter was somewhere between light brown and weak orange, and there were three dark-red drops and a minuscule smear on one side of the Formica gap, three dots and a smudge that were blood, sure as they were standing there.

"Looks like—" Holman began.

"Yeah," Deputy Graham interrupted.

"Like blood," Holman finished.

"Yeah," Graham said, excited.

"Either of you get cut there?" Holman asked.

"No," Joel answered, and Sophie shook her head.

"What was here, on the counter?" Holman asked.

"The microwave," Sophie said.

Joel watched the detective's eyes travel back to the outlet. "The bastard cut himself when he jerked it unplugged or was lifting it to carry away. His arm would've been directly over that sharp piece of the counter. Now we're talking." He smiled and pursed his lips. "These guys are amateurs—I've known it from day one. We'll get 'em with this, yes indeed we will."

Joel stared at the red evidence and felt his face and neck blink again, imagined three scared slugs—he knew the type, had spent six months with them in jail—sitting across from Holman and selling everyone out, telling the cop how the robbery was a ruse for something much bigger, an insurance scam, and, yes, darn right, they wanted on the train, would be willing to cooperate with the state and testify against the masterminds. "Why wouldn't they clean it before leaving?" Joel asked.

"Sir, they're petty crooks," Holman said. "Why do they do all the stupid things they do? Why do they get caught over and over? Because they're dumb and lazy, mostly. Here, maybe the guy didn't know he'd gotten scratched, or maybe they're in a hurry, or possibly they're dopers who don't think clear, or maybe they aren't too smart about DNA. I swear to you, we got a blood match on a burglar 'bout a year ago—clown cut himself on a store window—and he says, just as positive as can be, that we're trying to trick him, that we can only match DNA from semen." Holman laughed at the recollection. "You wouldn't believe how stupid and, well, *ignorant* some of these people are."

Actually, I would, having seen it firsthand, Joel thought. He wiped his hand across his brow even though it wasn't that hot in the room. "I see," he said to the cops. Certainly though, Sa'ad—foxy, wary Sa'ad—wouldn't have divulged anything to bunglers such as these, let them know the big picture and put everyone at risk. If the robbers got caught—and it seemed they would—the worst that could happen is they'd yammer about some Mr. X or mystery man named Raoul, and the cops would ignore them, assume they were trying to shift blame and save their own skins, simply spinning jailhouse nonsense.

"You have insurance, ma'am?" Holman asked Sophie.

"Pardon?" she said.

"Homeowners' insurance. I wondered if you had any on your house."

"Yeah, I do. I paid it about three months ago."

"They'll reimburse you for a lot of this, the theft and property damage," Holman said. "You need to call your agent and file a report. Make sure you list everything—you know how insurance companies can be."

"Thanks, I will," she replied. Her mood didn't seem to change, however; she remained dazed and glum, her mouth not all the way closed, her arms flaccid. "I think I've got a thousand-dollar deductible, something like that," she added. "And it's not the money, not really. It's this—this terrible intrusion." She surveyed the ugliness, began in the corner of the den and slowly viewed the room, stopping when she reached the couch. She went to it and gripped one of the short wooden legs with both hands. "Help me with this, Joel."

He grabbed on to a leg, placed the palm of his other hand against a seat cushion and pushed the sofa off its back, righted it. Tomorrow, as soon as he got out of bed, before coffee or cereal, he'd expose the bottom again, put the brush attachment on the vacuum and suck off the trash and dust. He looked at Sophie, standing opposite him with her hands in free fall, her fear and dismay beginning to harden into anger, her house trashed, her property in the hands of hoodlums, her plans to write a children's book and a Franklin Pierce article on hold while she hunted secondhand TVs and made lists of what had been taken from her. "Shit," she said, and Joel was glad to hear it, relieved there was moxie still remaining.

Joel waited until four-thirty to call Sa'ad. He and Sophie were able to accomplish a lot before Baker's bus arrived, and Joel met the boy at the end of the drive and told him in gentle terms what had happened, informed him there'd be no videos or TV for several days because bad men had stolen things from their house. He asked Baker to help his mom and be a big boy for her, and the lad promised he would, ran down the snow-slick road ahead of his uncle after Joel had explained matters, dropped a glove on the way to the door and was panting and pink-cheeked when Sophie hugged him. Baker told her not to worry, he'd just read books and color and make the best of the situation, and she started quivering in her mouth and fanning herself with her bare hand, almost cried some more.

The Volvo had all-wheel drive and snow tires, and after Baker went inside, Joel cranked the car, turned the heat on high and drove to a pay phone outside a grocery store. He didn't stop at the first phone or the next one after that, drove farther than he had to, wasted four miles' worth of gas. He had two dollars and seventy cents in his front pocket, all in change, hoped it was enough to get through to Sa'ad so he wouldn't have to bust a five.

As it turned out, he didn't have to wait long. After reciting the code phrase and warning the secretary that his pay-phone minutes were going fast, Joel stood shivering in the awful weather, on hold, listening to a pre-recorded Sa'ad thank clients for their calls while classical music played in the background, the piece heavy with cellos, bass and kettledrums. The receiver was cold against Joel's ear, and he was starting to absorb the air in his face and hands, had left his scarf and gloves in the basement, but he was stranded on hold only for a few moments before the real Sa'ad came on the line. He took Joel's number and instructed him to hang up, then called back immediately.

"Is this Joel King?" Sa'ad asked.

"It is," Joel said.

"I want to verify that. What is your middle name?"

"My middle name? Walker. Joel Walker King."

"Your ex-wife's maiden name?"

"Stanley," Joel answered. "It's me, Sa'ad, okay? You ought to recognize my voice by now. I'm outside and freezing and in a bad mood, so let's get down to brass tacks."

Sa'ad ignored Joel's protests, continued with his litany of questions. "In a moment, Joel. In a moment. Am I correct that you are calling me as your attorney?"

"Yeah, right. Whatever." A pickup chugged by with two shaggy black dogs in the bed.

"You expect this to be a privileged communication, and there is no one else listening or within earshot on your end?"

It occurred to Joel what Sa'ad was doing, building in a legal safeguard for them if their conversation was intercepted or overheard. "Correct. This is a legal call between me and my attorney."

"What can I do for you? Are you sure we don't need to meet in person?"

"No. Not at all. I simply need a bit of advice, Sa'ad, because guess what, some worthless, sorry crooks broke into my sister's house and robbed us. Did you hear that, Sa'ad? We've been robbed. It's not the stealing, Sa'ad, I mean, hey, you almost expect that, right? Crime's everywhere." Joel was becoming agitated. His voice got faster and higher. "So the theft wasn't a surprise. No surprise there. But what really enraged me was the shambles they made of our house, how it's absolutely destroyed."

"Hold on. Wait. You're telling me that your sister's home was robbed? The dwelling in which you now live?"

"Yeah, Sa'ad, the dwelling in which I now live. My sister's house, you idiot!" Joel screamed at the phone. He couldn't help himself. "It looks like a hurricane hit." Another pickup passed by, rolled through a stretch of slushy melt that its tires spun out in small, dirty plumes. "Sophie's at home with her child, crying."

"This robbery happened today?" Sa'ad asked. Joel's shouting didn't seem to affect him.

"Today. A few hours ago." Joel switched the phone to his other hand and jammed the free hand into his coat pocket.

"Where were you?" Sa'ad asked. "As I recall, you don't usually go to work until late in the day. Were you at the restaurant?"

"Well, as it happened—just one of those things—I was at my other job, eating lunch with my boss when the call came."

"So you were at work, and there's a break-in?" Sa'ad was still confounded.

Joel sensed for the first time something might've gone wrong. He'd phoned expecting stock replies and apologies and burnished answers, but Sa'ad was clearly surprised by the information or else was very, very skilled at feigning bewilderment. "Correct," he said.

"I see. And what is missing?"

"Everything. You name it." Joel lowered his voice. He turned up his collar, wiggled his toes inside his boots.

"The police come?"

"Yes. They mentioned there'd been four other break-ins near our place. They think they'll catch the people responsible."

"They always think that," Sa'ad said, returning to form.

"I'd bet on the good guys in this one," Joel said.

"Difficult to tell the good guys from the bad guys sometimes. I'm not sure who to root for in this instance."

"Well, before you buy the pennants and foam fingers, you should know the burglars left some blood at the house, and the cops are planning to do DNA tests. I'm guessing the dolts who did this will be caught, and they'll probably squeal like stuck pigs to save their own worthless hides if they happen to know anything helpful."

Sa'ad was quiet, and Joel could envision him in his office with the guns and mounted animals, twirling his trendy spectacles in one hand, his chair close to his desk, his face metamorphosing every few seconds. "So, Joel, as I'm understanding your circumstances, you were at work with your employer, miles from home, and your sister was also absent, when thieves hit your house, taking everything not nailed down. And one of the thieves leaves behind sufficient blood for a DNA sample and maybe some other clues."

"You got it."

"Well, how about that." Sa'ad's voice was no longer fractured, had regained its customary force. "This must come as quite a shock, my friend. It certainly comes as quite a shock to me, something so violent and random." He emphasized the words "shock" and "random," provided them with thick, rich vowels and elongated them like an elementary school teacher drilling a spelling class.

"I'm pretty darn shocked all right. And mad, Sa'ad. Mad as I've ever been." A cloud covered the sun, and a gust of wind tore through the parking lot. Joel could see his sentences take shape in the freezing air, tiny snippets of warm breath the cold outlined and condensed. "It was so unnecessary, the complete disregard for our home."

"I agree, Joel. It seems, sadly, you have been the victim of a senseless, random crime. You were selected without rhyme or reason."

"Is that so?"

"Absolutely," Sa'ad said with conviction.

Joel hesitated, pondering his next question. "So you don't think these people are part of a ring, something bigger? Working for someone else?"

"No chance. None at all."

"You're positive of that?" Joel pressed.

"Damn right, I'm positive. You get my drift, Joel? Every eight minutes there's a burglary in this country—this one happened to be yours. I'm your lawyer and your friend, so there's no need for you to take out your frustration on me. I thought you were calling for advice, not to vent and complain." Sa'ad was shaping the conversation, steering Joel, covering their tracks, always feinting and dodging and paranoid.

"I'm not convinced." Joel kicked at the ground, hacked through hard mashed snow to the dark pavement. "I'm at a place I don't know who to believe, or what's true and what isn't. I don't trust a single person on this planet except my sister. No offense, but right now you're not someone I'd want holding my wallet or watching my dog while I'm on vacation."

"Believe me, Preacher, if these people were professionals, if they were part of an organized effort, they wouldn't have done four houses in the same neighborhood and been so damn sloppy and inept. You're dealing with kids or pipeheads or rubes. You simply caught some bad luck and that's the end of the story, and maybe it's not so bad after all, huh? Think about it."

"I am."

"So did you yourself lose anything of value?" Sa'ad asked.

"Did I? Well . . ." Joel stopped, unsure what to say.

"If you did, if anything is missing, you should immediately report it to the insurance company and the police."

"Really?" Joel asked.

"Yes. Why wouldn't you? Didn't I advise you some weeks ago to have your belongings insured? That's why people purchase insurance and pay premiums—you should file a claim for your loss."

"What if they catch the people who broke in? You know, what if the burglars say they didn't take my stuff? And me with a record—I might not be believed, might get in trouble."

"Don't concern yourself with that. File the claim."

"I'm worried—"

"Listen to me. Quit dithering and wringing your hands. Quit thinking the worst. If they catch the guys—and here I'm speaking legally—it's actually a positive for you. If they find criminals who've broken into other homes, who admit to some degree of involvement, who actually did several crimes besides yours, there can be no suggestion from your insurer that this was a put-up job. So what if the stupid crooks don't want to claim responsibility for every item missing? This is, in the final analysis, far from a catastrophe."

"For what it's worth, you're giving me your word about this? About it being random, pure happenstance?"

"I am," Sa'ad said solemnly. "I'm as surprised as you."

"What about . . . I seem to have lost a piece. There's one I didn't get insured. Problems there, you think?"

"No. None as things stand."

Joel let down his guard, spoke a little more directly than he should have over the telephone. "That's still a huge riddle to me—I'm not so sure you couldn't tell me what happened, where it went. The more I think about it, the more I become convinced I'm on the sucker end of some kind of bait and switch. Doc's my first candidate, but I won't be bowled over if other folks are responsible."

"Yeah, well, I know the other folks intimately, and they feel exactly the same about you. And those folks have better things to do with their time and effort than get into a pissing contest over a few thousand bucks. Those folks wouldn't fool around with some little infant hustle, especially among friends."

"Maybe it's just the tip of an iceberg," Joel said.

"Or maybe it's merely someone's incompetence or naked greed. Few thousand dollars might mean a lot to a poor man."

"At any rate, it was a horrible sight. My sister's, I mean. I won't ever forget it."

"It's unfortunate when anyone is victimized by a home invasion," Sa'ad allowed.

"Well, in the long run I suppose—possibly—you could be right. I certainly am rid of one problem—there's no doubt we've been robbed. No question there."

"Exactly. And say they catch the guys, and they deny taking your items—who's going to take the word of a bunch of thieves?"

"Well, I'm not sure I want to put it in those terms," Joel said, the irony causing him to shake his head even though he was standing by himself in a frigid parking lot, his cheeks and toes numb, his insides a jittery stew.

Sophie stayed home from work the next day to restore her house and assess her losses and write her list of missing items. Joel helped her, worked without taking a break, and by late morning the two of them had cleaned and organized until rooms and drawers were mostly in satisfactory order, returned to where they'd been. Sophie was sitting cross-legged on the sofa, compiling her list on sheets of notebook paper, using a dictionary as a lapboard.

Joel leaned against the den wall and watched her. He was tired, enervated and frazzled, hadn't slept more than an hour and hadn't shaved or showered, but this was as good a time as any. "I need to talk to you for a second while you're doing that," he said, his voice ricocheting in his ears.

"Okay," she answered without interrupting her efforts. She started using her fingers and counting aloud, calculating how many videotapes were gone.

"I'm missing some things as well. I just wanted to let you know."

"Let me finish this, and you can tell me. I'll add them on."

"They took some jewelry Mom gave me. I had it hidden in the basement." He hated to lie and immediately asked to be forgiven, offered a silent prayer and instinctively glanced upward.

"Say again?" Sophie stopped what she was doing and laid the pen on the couch.

"I, uh, brought some jewelry with me from Roanoke, some pieces Mom gave me. They were for both of us, to be shared. I'm not claiming them for myself, anything like that. I was planning to surprise you with them at Christmas." He'd concocted this twist several hours ago, lying in his basement bed fitful and wide awake, the radio playing low and the persistent cold bleeding through the cinder-block. "It looks like they're missing also. I'm sorry."

"What kind of jewelry did Mom give you? And when?"

"She insisted I have it when she was in Roanoke, still coherent, and Martha and I were taking care of her. I stored it at the bank and brought it with me when I came back from Roanoke."

"And you kept it here? In the basement? How smart is that?"

"In retrospect, not very."

"How will we ever prove what it was or what it was worth? I remember she had a few bracelets and a keepsake ring, but I couldn't begin to tell you anything about the style or value."

"Well, for a change I have good news. Very good news. I had the items insured. All of them. I had them appraised and photographed, and we should get every dime we're out."

"You had them insured?" she asked incredulously.

"Yes." He swayed forward, stopped leaning on the wall.

"When?" she asked.

"Not long after my trip to Roanoke. I didn't want to just leave it lying around here."

"So how much was it worth?"

"That's the other happy news. I mean, I'd rather have Mom's gift than cash, but at least we're not completely out of luck. We should get fifty thousand, or thereabouts. It was insured for around fifty." That would be his cut, after paying Sa'ad and Edmund and Abel Crane and having his share docked for the missing ring, the loss of which remained a complete mystery.

"Fifty thousand dollars?"

"Right," Joel said tersely. "And I'm sorry to have lost something so valuable and irreplaceable, but it could be worse."

"Yeah, could be." She was looking at him, sizing him up. "I thought most of her jewelry was still with her, at High Pines."

"A lot of it is. But the nicer things she entrusted to me for safekeeping and for us to have when she passed away."

"What nicer things that would be worth that kind of money?"

Joel crammed his fists against his sides, spread his legs. Glowered. "I'm not going to stand here and debate this with you. I'm not trying to be rude or disagreeable, but I'm darn tired of you second-guessing everything I do and say." The words were noisy, amped by cheap mettle. "There were some rings and pins and bracelets, okay? You can check with the bank in Roanoke, and the insurance agent has photos of each piece and an appraisal. Why is this such an issue?"

"It's not an issue, Joel," she said, retreating. "All things considered, you can see why I might be skeptical. If you tell me this is a legit loss, then so be it. Get the cash and give me whatever you think is fair for my share."

"Okay." He dropped his arms. "I was planning on you receiving ninety-nine percent, most of the money."

"And you promise me there's nothing crooked going on?"

"Goodness, Sophie, how could there be? Huh? Tell me that?" He hardened his voice and glared at her. Joel's irritation had become genuine, and it occurred to him he'd managed to gain a scoundrel's capacity for indignation, was taking offense at the truth and pistol-whipping his sister and screwing his lips into a pained scowl. The realization braced him, causing him to shake his head in the abrupt way people do when they're groggy or bewildered, like a cat shedding rain sprinkles. He let the belligerence drain for a moment, tried to regain his perspective. "My," he muttered. "I'm sorry. You have every right to ask. I promise I'm not doing anything wrong."

Three days later, at his office in town, poor Scottie the insurance agent looked as if he'd been handed the hot, humming end of a power line when Joel told him about the burglary and the missing jewelry. He was sitting behind his desk, dressed in a loud, bulky sweater, and he did nothing to camouflage his discomfort.

"All of it?" he croaked.

"Sorry," Joel said. "There's nothing left."

"Any leads?" Scottie asked.

"The police are optimistic."

"Crap. I can't believe it."

"Maybe they'll recover some of it if they catch the guys," Joel offered.

Scottie steadied himself and fish-eyed Joel. "So the police are sure about it being a break-in? They've been called and investigated?"

"Yeah. We were the fifth house robbed in our area. Number five. They have some promising clues, though, and one of the thieves was cut and left a blood trail." Joel pretended not to notice Scottie's suspicious look, chattered on as if the notion of fraud was so foreign it couldn't possibly enter his mind.

"Where were you when it happened?" he asked bluntly.

"At work with Dixon Kreager. My sister was at work, too. Postman discovered the trouble." Joel was nodding as he spoke. "I've got the officer's card if you need a copy. He seems darn efficient, first-rate. They wiped us out—took everything. At least you don't have my sister's claim. I'm terribly sorry about this."

Scottie slumped in his chair, picking at a fuzz ball on his sweater. He buzzed his secretary and asked her to bring him a proof-of-loss form and did his best to turn cheerfully professional, but it was difficult to do, knowing as he did the company was going to take a dim view of a smelly two-hundred-seventy-five-thousand-dollar jewelry loss. They might disqualify him from writing their business, might pull out and leave him high and dry, and for sure there'd be no bonus this year, no plaques or banquets or trips to Orlando with the wife and kids. Of all the rotten breaks.

fifteen

For Joel, Sophie, and Baker, Christmas was a blessed time, a two-week period of cheer and closeness. Another strong storm hit in mid-December, but the snow suddenly became appropriate and even magical. The sunlight waltzed across the countryside, causing frozen branches to shimmer and the white ground and hibernating mountains to glint brilliant reflections. The town was lit with colored bulbs and decorated with mistletoe, wreaths, garlands and candy canes, and a neighbor from down the road came to visit the Kings in a jolly sled pulled by two huge bay horses and took Baker and Sophie for a ride, everybody bundled in scarves and blankets and sipping from a thermos of hot chocolate, jingle bells shaking with every stride.

A banquet cancelled at the Station, and Sarah had already paid for turkeys, fixings, cranberry sauce and two hundred dinner rolls she couldn't possibly use, so she gave all the help a cardboard box heaped with food. Joel was the beneficiary of an eight-pound bird, cranberry sauce, rolls and a tin-foil pan of dressing. She also gave him a twenty-five-dollar bonus, added the extra cash to his paycheck without any fanfare or warning. He thanked her twice, and she said he should send his regards to the good folks over in Frenchtown who'd made a deposit and then called off their company Christmas party. She was as aloof and standoffish as ever when she told him that, and she was quick to mention everyone had received food and a pay increase for the holidays. She turned to march away as she always did—practically a soldier's pivot—but she stopped unexpectedly and put her hands in her pockets. "Merry Christmas, Joel King," she said, and then finished her departure without saying anything else or waiting for his response.

On the last day of classes before Christmas break, Joel drove to Baker's school and picked him up an hour early. The elementary school air was hot and saturated and smelled like fuel oil, and Joel walked past reindeer drawings done in clumsy crayon and a long lineup of Santas with glued-on cotton-ball beards. He stopped near the end of the Santa row and fingered a cotton tuft, smiled to himself and hoped some of the innocence might transfer, rub off.

A stout, frenetic lady in a denim dress and running shoes went to find Baker, and the boy was beside himself when he saw Joel, ran to him and banged against his leg, then pogoed up and down, up and down, and asked if he got to leave early, wanted to know where they were going. Joel drove him to a hardware store at the south end of Missoula, and a young man named Billy sold them an old-fashioned wooden sled, a Rocket Flyer with red steel runners and shellacked slats. To Joel's delight, Baker had passed on the elaborate, newfangled models with plastic seats and steering wheels; he had proceeded directly to the genuine article and pointed.

Joel and Baker loaded the Rocket Flyer into the Taurus and traveled to a ridge not far from their house, parking the car on the side of the road. The sky was gray but still bright, and they were dressed in heavy coats, warm wool hats and down-filled gloves. Joel tucked the sled under his arm and set off across a field, and before long he dropped the sled onto its runners and held Baker's hand. The ground crunched under their feet; theirs were the first steps to disturb the snow, and in one spot, tall, colorless blades of grass rose up through their tracks. When they arrived at the height of the knoll, Baker was excited and anxious, his lips trembling from the cold and anticipation, his breathing one rapid puff after another.

"You've never been on a sled, huh?" Joel asked, already aware of the answer.

"Nope. I wasn't old enough before, and then Mom said I didn't need one."

"Well, you've got one now. Let's see how she does."

At first they rode down the slope together, both of them flat on the sled, Joel on bottom, Baker above him, the two of them hollering and screaming as they went along. Then Baker slid down by himself, and Joel ran behind him for a few steps and pushed him, gave him a big shove to build his speed. Joel slipped and fell once, and his coat and knees got wet in the snow, but he didn't care, and he didn't grow any colder because of the accident.

After Baker mastered the sled and their path to the bottom, Joel retraced their footsteps to the Taurus and gathered a newspaper and several sticks of kindling he'd brought from Sophie's woodpile. He used the newspaper and a fast-food bag to start a fire on the crest of the ridge, and he and Baker positioned the sled next to the fire and used it as a seat. The fire wasn't much, was sort of inferior, but that wasn't the point. They sat mute and watched the flames burn and flicker, the wood turning to ash.

Joel soon noticed that Baker was mimicking him, the boy sitting exactly as he was with his head bowed, elbows on his knees and his hands clasped. When Joel changed position, Baker would also. Joel sat up and crossed his legs, rested an ankle on his damp knee. Baker did the same. "You enjoy the sled?" Joel eventually asked.

"Yeah. I want to go again."

"We'll keep at it as long as you like, and as long as your out-of-shape old uncle can pull this thing up the hill for you."

The child looked at Joel, wiped his nose across the arm of his coat. "Thank you, Uncle Joel," he said, and it meant the world to Joel. It was so good to be back to where he'd once been, when he was Preacher Joel and he could do for others and relish life, savor things great and mundane and in-between.

They didn't leave the ridge until it was dead dark, took one last chancy, exhilarating trip together, dropping blindly through two hundred yards of night, quiet this time, not a word as they raced along, the fire a distant orange dot when they reached the end of their ride. Sophie admonished them for getting home so late, but she wasn't really mad, and pretty soon she'd prepared tomato soup and grilled cheese sandwiches for them to eat.

The following day, Joel bought his mother a blue cowboy hat and took it to her at High Pines, wrapped it in green paper and a gold bow. She loved the hat and didn't seem to want to take it off, put it on without hesitation and adjusted the brim until it was to her satisfaction. Joel told her it was Christmas, and the mention of the word and the green-and-gold present cleared her eyes for a moment, snatched her from inside herself long enough to look at him with some recognition in her gaze. Joel clutched her hand, and they walked around the halls and she jabbered about her granddaddy's old mule and a dance at college and the books someone had stolen from the library, volumes she needed to recover or replace without any further delay. He hugged her before he left, told her she'd been a good mother, and she caught sight of herself in a mirror on the wall of her room and said the hat very much suited her.

He bought Tom McGuane's fishing book from a store on Higgins

Street and gave it to Dixon, inscribed it with three words: "Thanks for everything." Frankie received a Delbert McClinton CD, and was so grateful he blushed and sputtered, then became embarrassed because he didn't have a gift for Joel. Besides the sled, Baker got a new pair of boots and a kid's spinning rod that Dixon let go for next to nothing. Joel found a sturdy set of tires for Sophie, purchased them on credit, and he paid for her to have dinner at Blackbird's, wrapped a gift certificate for two in a shoebox and taped on an oversize card.

He and Sophie and Baker attended the Christmas Eve service at the Baptist church, and they sang "Silent Night" after the minister had delivered his sermon, a short message about miracles and the birth of Jesus. The church was at capacity—sons and daughters and relatives and grumpy husbands who never came were there, everyone content, woes and contentiousness suspended for an hour in favor of goodwill and grace. Listening to the choir while the wind gusted outside and thrashed against the doors and stained-glass windows, Joel was proud to have been a part of this at one time, certain he was inside a mighty redoubt, confident he was where he needed to be, positive about the bedrock strength of his faith.

The afternoon of the twenty-fifth, Baker wore his new boots and pretended to fish behind the sofa with his rod and reel, and Sophie cut chunks and slices of leftover turkey and stored them in a Tupperware container. Sophie and Baker had given Joel an electric blanket—the biggest package beneath the tree—and he slept warm in the basement on Christmas night, small currents of heat washing over his neck and chin.

And so it went—they were blessed and happy for two weeks, the best they'd had in months.

But it was a short, brief blessing, and it halted rudely, came to a sudden end and was replaced by misery and tests that flew at Joel with freight-train ferocity, almost beat him down for good.

The first round of torment arrived in early January, when Joel was once again summoned for a meeting with his probation officer. He'd fed a new chunk of wood into the stove and was sitting on the sofa, reading the *Missoulian* and finishing a second cup of fresh coffee, all his chores completed, the house cozy, Tut and the hen pecking at a scoop of scratch, the kitchen tidy. Jack Howard called early, at nine on the button, and Joel was unhappy about having to interrupt his morning, asked twice if he could come later on his way to work and save himself a trip. Howard was having none of that, was churlish and hateful over the phone, insisted Joel get his ass there and quit backtalking him. Joel didn't ask why he needed to report, simply assumed it was to discuss Karl and Lisa's case, and he poured his coffee into a tall thermal mug, collected his coat, scarf and gloves and drove to town.

When Mrs. Heller opened the door to Howard's office, Joel didn't see Lynette Allen, and didn't recognize the people clumped in front of Howard's desk. There were two men wearing suits—dark, respectable suits with cuffed trousers—and a woman whose hair was plaited and gathered and pinned into an insolvable bun.

Howard himself was visibly delighted about something; he smirked and folded his arms and popped Joel with a cynical, mean-spirited look the instant he got the chance. "Guess who's here to see you, Jimmy Swaggert?" he crowed as Joel entered the office.

"I don't know." Joel's eyes began a kinetic hop, twitching from person to person like two captured summer crickets in a child's Mason jar.

"Important visitors," Howard said, coming around his desk to join them.

Oddly, Joel didn't feel the same degree of panic he'd experienced when he'd been put through the wringer with Lynette Allen. This time, he didn't need to speculate as to why these ominous, serious people wanted an audience with him—it didn't matter, the reason. It was going to be bad, very bad, that much was apparent, and Joel went straight to despair, stood under the doorway with his eyes going berserk and the rest of him petrified and shackled, the fear hollowing him out. "I don't know," he said through stiff, deadened lips.

"Well, I'll tell you." Howard's tone was soaked with sarcasm. "To my left is Special Agent Hobbes from the FBI. That would be the Federal Bureau of Investigation. He rode all the way from Helena to meet you."

"Morning, Mr. King," Hobbes said, his voice bland, his posture flawless.

"Hello, sir," Joel answered, and he thought about running, just wheeling on the lot of them and busting out the door and sprinting across the snow until they caught him and subdued him and dragged him away in handcuffs.

"Next to him," Howard continued, "is Special Agent Woods from the Montana State Police."

Woods said hello. He invited Joel to join them and requested that he shut the door.

Joel pushed the door closed and managed a halting, tentative step forward. This had to be about the jewelry. Had to be. He tried to pray, to recite the words in his head, but it was impossible—nothing would come.

"And on the end is Anna Starke. She also works with the FBI—flew here from our nation's capital."

She acknowledged Joel but didn't speak.

Howard took hold of a chair with both hands and drew it toward Joel. "Like the man said, Mr. King, take a load off." He was sideways to Joel, talking from half a face.

Joel stared at the chair and saw it transmuted—Eucharist wafer into flesh, grape juice into blood—into a trap, a tar pit, a four-legged, state-issued crucible. He sat down with Howard still looming behind him, brushed the weasel's arms and could smell Old Spice as he lowered himself into the seat.

The three visitors were in front of him, between Howard's desk and the uncomfortable chair, virtually on top of him in the undersized office. Agent Hobbes began the inquiry, his manner formal and crisp, the military apparent in his bearing. "Mr. King, as your probation officer mentioned, my name is Len Hobbes, and I'm a special agent with the FBI. We're here to ask you some questions about an issue we think you can help us with. You're not under arrest, and you're free to leave at any time. Is that understood?"

"Yes, I suppose," Joel answered. "What's this about?" he croaked, but he wasn't very convincing, sounded guilty and shifty when he spoke, his eyes still spastic.

"Yes, well, we'll get to that. Although you're not in custody, I'm going to read your Miranda rights." And he did, read a list of sentences from a laminated card and frightened Joel even more. When he finished he asked if Joel understood what he'd just recited, and Joel nodded yes. In fact, the warnings were a buzz of disjointed words jetting through his brain, bad-guy clichés his nerves hashed into incomprehensible mumbo jumbo.

"Good," Hobbes said. "Then let's talk. I'm not one for beating around the bush."

"Okay," Joel answered. His eyes were finally slowing, the giveaway darts and skips becoming less obvious.

"In August of last year, you purchased an insurance policy for thirteen articles of jewelry from an agent James Scott here in Missoula, correct?"

Joel offered him a dumb look and didn't respond.

"Cat got your tongue, Reverend?" Howard chided him, and Agent Hobbes melted the probation officer, scowled and glared and blistered him with a blast-furnace stare.

"We know, obviously, that you obtained the policy," Hobbes continued. "We also have the State Farm agent's photographs of the items and the written descriptions of each piece."

Joel deflated through his chest and shoulders, rested his elbows on his knees and dropped his chin into his palms. He was going to jail again. No doubt—he was going to jail, and his sister and Baker would be heartbroken. He should've listened to Sophie and walked away. He peeked at the agent's black shoes—they were immaculate, buffed and spiffy.

"You all right?" Hobbes asked.

"Yeah," Joel sighed.

"In November of last year, you filed a theft claim for these same thirteen pieces of jewelry."

"We were robbed," Joel volunteered. "You can confirm that with Officer Holman at the police department."

"Don't doubt it," Hobbes said, his cadence not changing. "Don't doubt it for a minute."

"Okay," Joel said. He lifted his chin and laced his fingers in his lap. From day one, no matter how much sophistry and rationalization he'd allowed himself, no matter how much bluster he'd directed at his sister, and no matter how often he'd sprinkled holiness over his profane dishonesty and swore it was made righteous, there'd always been a rank kernel of guilt he couldn't dislodge, a nagging throb he couldn't paper over or ignore or talk away or slip by on little cat feet. And now the toll was due, his reckoning at hand. "My," he said almost inaudibly, drowning in his own thoughts, the room and people a blur of background, barely there.

"We know you're not the rightful owner of the pieces you had insured. We know that. We also know you're a defrocked minister who took advantage of an unstable girl in your congregation. We know your history. And we know your mother didn't give you the items in the photos."

"How do you know any such thing?" Joel asked, the agent returning to focus, the room solid again.

Hobbes looked at him. "Today, Mr. King, is the day. Today is when you have to decide if you want to help us out or face the consequences. You're either with us or against us—your choice. You get points for being honest and contrite, and punishment for telling falsehoods and stonewalling. Like I said, your choice."

"What are you accusing me of?" Joel asked. "My mom gave me the jewelry."

Anna Starke had been half sitting on Howard's desk. She stood and spoke for the first time, in a voice that was silky and nuanced, sultry. "Mr. King, I work with the FBI's Criminal Investigative Division. My special interest is art theft. I'm not a police officer as most people understand the term. I have a doctorate in art history and also a master's in museum studies. I devote a great deal of my time to our NSAF program—the National Stolen Art File. We catalogue the theft of certain significant art objects, specifically those of particular historic or artistic importance with a value of more than two thousand dollars."

"I certainly don't have any art," Joel told her. "I'm not following you."

"Bear with me for a moment," she said. "When a piece of fine art disappears, the local agencies contact us and we place the information in our system. We even have a website now. Obviously, we enjoy a close working relationship with galleries and dealers and collectors—and insurance companies."

"Makes sense," Joel said. It seemed to him that Hobbes had slipped nearer, was erect and rigid and cutting off his view of the room. Agent Woods had also crept forward.

"In June of 2001, a Chagall painting entitled *Over Vitebsk* was stolen from the Jewish Museum in New York City. It was on loan from a private collection in Russia, and we very much want to recover it. We want it because it's quite valuable, but also because this is embarrassing to the museum and to law enforcement in our country. People won't lend us their art if we can't protect it, and that's a bad thing for everyone, wouldn't you agree?"

"I don't have it," Joel said. "I promise. You can check my closet." He noticed Hobbes's annoyance and instantly regretted being flippant.

Anna Starke smiled. "We know you don't. But what you do have, Mr. King, is a diamond and ruby ring that was stolen at the same time, from another display that was also on exhibit there. And we want to know where you got the ring so we can find the painting."

"My mother," Joel lied. "She gave me the whole collection."

"No one here believes that," Woods said.

"We really aren't after you, Mr. King," Starke assured him. "Not really. But you'll leave us very few options unless you tell the truth."

"Why do you think my ring is the stolen one? It looks like any other ring to me."

She wasn't fazed by his protest. "Not so. There were two rings taken at the same time as the Chagall. They were given to two daughters by their father, and we refer to them as the red and green sisters. One is set with rubies and diamonds, the other with emeralds and diamonds. The red sister is the ruby piece, the one you took to the State Farm agent here in Missoula. The—"

"You can't tell something such as that from a picture," Joel interrupted. "You're trying to trick me."

"Oh, but you see, I can. I can indeed, because the sisters have been examined and photographed extensively over the years. Moreover, both were photographed and catalogued before they were lent to the Jewish Museum. I know what the filigree down each side looks like, I know the number and sizes of the stones, I know the setting type and most of all I know there are three tiny initials—NWT—inside the red sister's band. When we enhanced the photos taken at the State Farm office and the lab people did their magic, I can see an *N* and part of a *W* in the photo. You've got the red sister, Mr. King, and I'm sure of it."

"So . . . so . . . What you're saying is the jewelry I have—had—is stolen?" Joel sounded truly surprised, and his shock caused a barely perceptible grimace to hurry through Hobbes's face.

"Precisely," she replied. "That's correct. I'll even say it for you: The ring you took to State Farm was stolen from an exhibit at the Jewish Museum. Stolen on the same day as a very important painting and stolen by the same people."

"And we want to know where you obtained it," Hobbes added.

Joel was stunned, speechless. His fingers were entwined so desperately that the blood had fled his knuckles, blanching them.

"This is your day, Mr. King," Woods encouraged him. "We're after the big fish, not you. But you stick to this bullshit, and we're gonna send you to prison again. *Comprende?*"

"Yeah," Joel said. "Are you planning on arresting me now? Today?"

"It's certainly a possibility," Hobbes answered.

Joel slumped well into his seat, struggling to think, to arrive at a sound decision. There was a thumping inside his head, a drumming that pulsed and surged and ached as far down as the bridge of his nose.

"What'll it be, Mr. King?" Anna Starke asked. "Seems to me you've only got one option."

Joel looked at her, then began a progression along the line of faces and merciless expressions. "You know," he said when he reached Hobbes, the last of the four, "I think I want to speak to my lawyer before I say anything else." His voice cracked on several of the words.

"Ha!" Hobbes bellowed. "Your lawyer?"

Woods shut his eyes and wrinkled his lips, released a peeved, disgruntled sound.

"Yes. I'm not trying to be uncooperative, but I'd like to have someone here to speak for me. Someone on my side." Sa'ad's voice was burned into his mind, surfacing through all the muck and confusion: *I want to speak to my fucking lawyer. I want to speak to my fucking lawyer—that's the mantra, Joel.*

"That's your option," Hobbes said, "but the longer you put us off, the worse things become for you. If we solve this little mystery by ourselves, you'll have nothing left to barter."

"I want to help, but I'm going to keep quiet until I have a chance to discuss things with my attorney," Joel said. "I haven't done anything wrong, so I don't think waiting will affect me one way or the other." He was able to mouth the words with a trace of confidence. "I guess you just need to go on and do what you have to do. I sure don't want to be arrested, but if that's what's in the cards for me, so be it."

Hobbes bent forward so his face was level with Joel's, no more than a foot away. "Where are you from, Mr. King?" he asked.

"Pardon?"

"Where are you from originally?"

"Oh. The Midwest. Indiana."

"The heartland," Hobbes said. His breath made it to Joel's nose, smelled clean and cinnamony. "Me, I'm from North Carolina. Greensboro, North Carolina."

"Okay," Joel said.

"You follow wrestling, Joel?" Hobbes asked.

"Wrestling?"

"Yeah, wrestling. Professional wrestling."

"Not really. Can't say—"

Hobbes talked over Joel's answer. "See, I grew up with it—'Rip' Hawk, Swede Hansen, Johnny Weaver, Chief Wahoo McDaniel, the Amazing Zuma, Andre the Giant. Came on Channel Eight when I was a kid, and a guy by the name of Charlie Harville did the announcing. Even traveled right to your hometown, had matches in the high school gym. Yessir. I'm not sure about Indiana, who your champ was. Might've been Dory Funk Sr., but don't quote me on that."

Joel wondered if Hobbes was threatening him, if he was on the verge of asking everyone to leave and close the door behind them and stay gone for five minutes. "I'm not familiar with any of those people," Joel said with an uninflected voice. "Sorry."

"I watch it to this day. It's big-time now, sells out arenas. And you have to buy the good matches on Pay-Per-View." Hobbes leaned away and allowed Joel some space.

Howard was spellbound by Hobbes's narrative, waiting intently for the punch line.

"And you know what I've discovered watching wrestling for almost three decades?" Hobbes asked but didn't wait for anyone to respond. "I've discovered that only the villains, the heels, have managers. I remember a fellow by the name of J. C. Dykes who managed the Infernos. All that sonofabitch ever did was help them cheat—he was constantly slipping them a piece of steel or distracting the ref or grabbing the other side's tights or blindsiding some helpless opponent with his cane. It's the same today. Your Jimmy Harts or your Bobby Henans—they're there for one reason and one reason only. To cheat, to foul up a fair match, to help a lesser man prevail. And you know what?"

"What?" Joel asked reflexively.

"That's what lawyers do, too. They're the assholes in coats and ties trying to trick the refs or get their man into the ring with a loaded boot. To this day, I've never seen an honest wrestler with a manager or an innocent man who asks for a lawyer. You asking for a lawyer is just like saying 'I'm guilty, I've got something to hide, but I hope I can find a shyster to create a diversion and hit the system over the head with a folding chair when no one's looking.' That's what you're telling me. You're the guy wearing the mask waiting for some mouthy lout to save you from a three-count, to rescue your pansy ass when you've been legitimately whipped."

"Exactly," Howard said, clearly impressed by the analogy. No doubt it would soon appear in his repertoire along with the cat-and-train fable.

"I'm not guilty of anything," Joel responded.

"Then why are you squalling for a lawyer?" Hobbes said. "Why won't you cooperate with us?"

Joel dallied before answering, rolled his wrist and checked his watch, toed a small puddle underneath his foot and stared at an ugly brown water stain on the white ceiling tiles. These people were going to do what they wanted, and his answer probably didn't make a great deal of difference. "Isn't all that wrestling stuff fake, just bad theater? Soap opera in briefs?"

"So that's it?" Hobbes asked. "You're shutting us down?"

"I'm not trying to cause trouble, but yes, for right now I am. I'll have to get back to you."

"I wish we could change your mind," Anna Starke said.

But they didn't arrest him, thank goodness, merely asked him when he wanted to meet again and gave him business cards and warned him about departing town and browbeat him for a few moments more and finally let him walk out of Howard's office. Still, it was fair to assume the moment was drawing nigh when Hobbes and Woods and two or three others would appear at Sophie's and take him to jail, slap the cuffs on his wrists and cinch them so they left pink imprints in his skin. It was also a given that his phone line was now tapped and someone would be following him wherever he went. He stopped at a pay phone about a mile from Howard's office, called Sa'ad and left a message, told the secretary there was an absolute emergency in Missoula—he needed a private face-to-face conference about legal matters. Sa'ad was out of the office, and Joel advised her he'd call again, that he was being tailed by the police, his calls most likely monitored by the FBI.

It didn't stop there. Yet another fierce snowstorm had arrived while Joel was being eviscerated at Howard's office, and he lurched and spun his way home, barely able to see the road through the sheets of white that unfurled from the sky. He hit a patch of ice and skidded two wheels into a ditch, fishtailed and slipped and nearly got stuck for good before the tires gained traction again.

The house was comfortable when he finally arrived, the temperature agreeable, and he changed clothes, put on jeans and a flannel shirt and wiped his face with a warm washcloth. He was so agitated that he simply paced, rambling around the house without any intent or route. He tried to recover in bed but couldn't lie peacefully. He wasn't hungry, didn't eat, and time was painful, wouldn't pass, seemed to accumulate in bottlenecks and refuse to leave. The snow kept falling, had piled three inches high on the Taurus's hood by one o'clock.

The phone rang at fifteen after one, and Joel expected to hear Sophie when he answered, assumed she was calling about Baker and school's early dismissal or a change in her own plans because of the weather. Instead, he was surprised by a woman's voice he didn't recognize, asking if he was Joel King who used to live in Roanoke, Virginia. Joel wasn't sure why he was being quizzed, and he wasn't able to think clearly, was edgy and apprehensive and so discombobulated that his mind short-circuited for a moment, went haywire.

"Mr. King?" The woman's voice.

He was lost, didn't respond.

"Mr. King?"

"Huh?" he finally muttered. "Yes?"

"Please hold for Detective Hubbard."

"Who?" Joel stammered.

A male voice came over the line. "Mr. King, this is Detective Louis Hubbard with the Roanoke City Police. How are you?"

"Fine," he lied.

"I'm glad to hear it," the man said.

Joel pinched his cheek until the intentional pain sharpened his attention and jarred his senses. "Who is this?" he asked.

"Detective Louis Hubbard, from Roanoke. Do you remember me? I handled the case involving you and a Miss Christina Darden, a girl from your former church. I interviewed you a couple times and testified at your sentencing hearing."

Joel recalled gray hair, blue eyes, an odd nose. "Yeah. Yes. But I've served my time for that. I've been released. I'm living with my sister, working every day."

"Excellent."

"Why are you phoning me?" His mind was mostly in synch again.

"Do you care if I record our conversation?" the detective asked.

"I guess not."

"You have to give me a positive answer, a yes or no, so there's not any doubt."

"You can record if you want to—it's fine by me. Is this about the jewelry? I've already talked to the FBI."

"Pardon?"

"The, uh, jewelry . . ." Joel stopped, censoring himself. "We were robbed, my sister and I. Lost some things. But the police here are already looking into it."

"No, I'm calling about something else. About our friend Miss Darden."

"Uh-huh." Joel's answer was a grunt, two run-on raspy syllables.

There was a pause while the policeman waited to see if he would volunteer more. "You seen her recently, Mr. King?" Hubbard asked, ending the calculated silence.

"Recently?" Joel asked.

"Yeah. When's the last time you had any contact with Christina Darden?"

"Contact . . . well . . . uh, let's see." Joel was delaying. "There in Roanoke, but I couldn't tell you the exact date. I saw her at a deposition—she sued me and the church because of what happened."

"I'm aware of that. The court case and everything. You see her after the deposition, any other time afterwards?"

"No," Joel said. "Absolutely not. Why would I?"

"You tell me," Hubbard said. The connection waned for a moment, made his voice sound tinny, and a static surge caused buzzing electrical noises underneath the words.

"Excuse me," Joel said. "I'm having trouble hearing you."

The line cleared. "You've haven't seen Christina since Roanoke, months ago? Is that what you're telling me?"

"Exactly. Correct. It's been months. She sued me—why would I have any reason to see her?" Tut flew onto the kitchen window's sill, began tapping the glass with his yellow beak. The hen fluttered up beside him, and they both looked inside, jumped their necks and heads from position to position with no stopping in between.

"I'm asking you," Hubbard replied.

"I don't know much more to tell you. I haven't seen or spoken to the girl since we were at the law firm giving our statements. It's as simple as that."

"Yeah?"

"You mind explaining why you're questioning me about her?" Joel was polite.

"Seems she's gone missing."

"Oh, really?"

"You surprised?" Hubbard asked.

"I'm nothing," Joel answered. "I don't really have any reaction. I hope she's okay."

"Me too. But, you know, it's peculiar. She simply disappeared. Gone. Left her clothes, her car, her money in the bank. Vanished into thin air, we like to say. Rare for a person to up and leave and not take money or clothes or a car."

"How long?" Joel wondered. "How long's she been gone?"

"Eight days now. No contact with anyone, and no credit card activity."

"Huh. Well, as I said, I hope she's safe. She's not a bad girl."

Hubbard was silent for several seconds. "You ever see her before the shindig at the lawyers' office, any time before you went over to Gentry, Locke to give your testimony?"

"Why're you asking?"

"Why do you think I'm asking, sir?" Hubbard said.

"I'm not sure."

"Not sure of what—whether you saw her or why I'm asking?"

"Not sure," Joel answered cryptically, his voice dying.

"You're dodging me, Mr. King. You either saw her or you didn't. Maybe, for instance, you met her at the mall and got into a bad disagreement."

"The mall?"

"So did you meet with Christina Darden at Tanglewood Mall the day before your deposition here in Roanoke? Yes or no?"

"I think I've said enough. I haven't done anything wrong, I haven't seen her since the legal proceedings at the law firm and I don't know anything—anything—about her disappearance or where she might be. That's it, that's the end, that's all I'm saying." Joel wanted to sign off as best he could, make sure the recorder captured his grand profession of innocence.

"Her folks invited us to look through her room," Hubbard said, "to see if we could find any clues."

"So?"

"So we found the cassette tape she took from you at the mall the day before you and her were supposed to testify, the one where you're in a nasty, cursing fight and she threatens to report you to the police. You recall that, don't you?"

"I don't remember," Joel answered.

"The fact you're evading me doesn't help any, Mr. King, causes me to think you know more than you're letting on."

"About what?"

"About her location or what's become of her."

"How's there any connection? Are . . . are . . . you trying to suggest . . ." Joel wasn't able to finish; he felt his esophagus clamp shut and air get scarce.

"Makes sense to me," Hubbard said. "Sure."

"Certainly you don't think I'd do anything violent, that I'm involved with her disappearance?"

"Well, let's see—she's ruined your life and career, stuck it to the church you love despite you beggin' her not to and is plannin' to have you sent back to jail. You could find some reasons in that. A motive."

An eruption of gut-bred anger replaced Joel's choking, enfeebling fear. "For goodness sakes, Mr. Hubbard. Think about what you're saying." Joel was indignant. "It's plain silly—the notion I'd do something to a teenage girl because of a lawsuit and a few days in jail. And why now, huh? Explain why now, the timing. She's already testified, the damage is done and obviously she didn't report me. And the church hasn't lost a penny. It's an insurance matter. You're being foolish. You and I both know—and I'm not trying to be critical—that she's probably on a party binge somewhere or shacked up with a frat boy."

"Or maybe she's headed to Montana to rendezvous with an old boyfriend. There's another possibility for you."

"I wouldn't count on it," Joel answered. "I can't believe this."

"We got you for violating your probation, for seeing her. Clear as day, you're guilty there. No denying it."

"Yeah, well, whatever."

"I'm turning over my info to your probation officer, and setting up a joint effort with the Missoula police. They'll be watching you, and if she doesn't surface soon, I'll be on a plane myself to see what I can find in your neck of the woods. And I'm guessing our commonwealth's attorney will bring you back to court here, no matter what happens. They'll revoke your sentence and send you back to jail for disobeying your probation terms."

"You don't truly believe I had a hand in something so sinister, do you? Seriously? Believe I hurt or kidnapped Christy?"

"I know you're a liar and a sex offender—how big a leap is it to the other?"

"This is craziness. Unbelievable. Insane."

The remainder of the day passed with no word from Sa'ad, nothing at all, and Joel was so distracted at work that he called one of the waitresses "Christy" instead of her correct name and scalded his hand with hot water, forgot which spigot he'd opened and then reached for a pot, shrieked and recoiled and startled Frankie and the chef. They put some balm on the hurt, and he continued working, assured everyone he was fine, not to worry.

For three consecutive nights, Joel dreamed he was being attacked by a wild-eyed, mustachioed cavalry officer with a Gatling gun, the madman cranking the weapon's handle and turning it in a slow sweep, dust and bullets everywhere. He lost his appetite, his stomach burned with waves of tension, his mind collapsed, sunk. There was no contact from Sa'ad or Edmund, and Joel didn't call them again after his first, desperate message from the pay phone, began to believe they'd set him adrift.

He was limping into work on a Thursday when a well-dressed stranger confronted him at the entrance to the Station, asking if he was Joel King and extending his hand.

"Why?" Joel asked, looking past the man into the restaurant. It was cold, but Missoula was clear of snow except for a few spots the sun had avoided and a couple of parking-lot piles that weren't completely melted.

"I'm Christopher Hudgins, a lawyer here in town. I'd be grateful for a moment of your time. Won't take long."

"Don't have long," Joel answered.

"Could I come in?"

"It's a public place," Joel said, but his tone wasn't harsh or impolite.

"Buy you a cup of coffee or a snack?"

Joel briefly smiled. "I work here. The coffee's free so long as I don't abuse the privilege."

They went into the building, but Joel didn't sit down, didn't want the lawyer hemming him in, spending too much time with him and peppering him with questions about rings or missing girls or insurance or probation violations or whatever else might be the tribulation du jour. "What's on your mind, Mr. Hudgins? Seems I've recently been a concern for lots of coat-and-tie legal types. What brings you around?" He flashed on the tat-tat-tat of old-timey bullets from his dream.

"Well, I don't know who else you might've run across, but I can assume one of the individuals was Lynette Allen, from the county attorney's office."

"Yes, I know her. My friend Dixon Kreager says she's a fine lady."

"She is. We have a good personal and professional relationship."

The two of them had wound up at the corner of the bar, and Joel picked up a discarded red-and-white plastic stir stick, began bending it into a square. A group of older men were drinking draft beer and sharing appetizers, and a young couple was kissing and cooing, both of the kids with a mixed drink, sitting on their winter coats, their high wooden stools pulled close together.

"You work with her?" Joel asked. "With Miss Allen?"

"No, I'm a defense lawyer. Usually we're opposing each other."

"Oh."

"Which brings me to the reason for my trip here. I represent Lisa Dillen, the lady who was fishing with you not so long ago. She and her husband, Karl. I'm assuming you recall them?"

"Yes, I do." Joel steeled himself and tossed the stir stick onto the bar. For the first time in days he didn't slouch or mumble or imagine things both crazy and wistful, didn't simply go through the motions while waiting for calamity to overtake him. "He slapped the tar out of her for no reason," Joel said bluntly. "Darn hard to forget."

"I understand that's your take on things."

"It's the truth. Period." It felt good to be honest, righteous. It was a tonic that put spine in Joel's words, resurrecting him.

"Let's assume that's true. I'm not saying it is, but let's assume for a moment you're correct. I can promise you Mrs. Dillen does *not* want to pursue this case. She does not, under any circumstances, want to see her husband prosecuted."

"This is her talking, not you and the wife-beating dentist?" Joel asked.

"Exactly. She's called and written Lynette Allen, as well as the head prosecutor, but they refuse to dismiss the case. That's their prerogative, but we view this as a family dispute, and the only 'victim' is satisfied and doesn't want to proceed. It should be her choice, not the state's."

"Why are you telling me this?" Joel asked defiantly. He was taller than the attorney, peered down on him.

"I merely want you to know the whole picture. These good folks have two kids, one who's handicapped and requires a wheelchair. Every single person in their neighborhood will attest to the fact that Karl Dillen takes care of those children, loves 'em and shares the burden. If he goes to jail, Lisa's got twice as much responsibility and twice as much pressure. But that's not the worst of it. Say Karl catches a conviction. And Lynette's charged this as a felony because of the cut and the tiny scar it left. He gets a felony, he most likely loses his dental license and his livelihood. So we end up with him in jail for thirty days, her load doubled with the kids, one crippled, and the family with no money and probably no health insurance, which needless to say is critical to their situation. And you want to tell me this prosecution is for her benefit? It will absolutely destroy her and her kids if Karl gets in trouble."

"He should've thought of that before he hit her," Joel said.

"Well, maybe so, but that's way too pat an answer. So we punish his wife and kids because he made a mistake—a mistake she's begging everyone to forgive? If Karl Dillen receives a felony conviction, Lisa and their children will suffer far more than he does."

"What do you want me to do?" Joel asked.

"Nothing, really. It might be helpful if you spoke with Lynette and persuaded her to see reason. Also, depending how the case breaks, Lisa may refuse to testify against her husband, so it comes down to you. What you saw, what you heard, what you remember. For instance, did you witness everything that led to the disagreement?"

Sarah walked through the bar with a salad bowl perched atop a column of dirty dishes, a water glass in the bowl. She said hello to Joel and studied Christopher Hudgins as she whisked by, paused and asked if he was being helped. Hudgins told her he was, thanks, and was about to leave.

"I saw what I saw," Joel said.

"Did you see what happened immediately before you claim Karl threw a punch?"

"Well, uh, I heard them arguing, and when I looked up he hammered her."

Hudgins rubbed his hands together and bobbed his head up and down. "So you didn't see what happened the whole time? What Lisa might have done?"

"I was doing my job and preparing lunch."

Hudgins continued to bounce his head. "Right. So you couldn't see her go after Karl and throw the first punch?"

"What?" Joel was incredulous. His voice rose, his features compressed and he drew back, viewed Hudgins's full length. "You can't be serious."

"Karl is prepared to testify she came at him swinging. He acted in self-defense. She's not going to contradict him, and from what you're telling me, you can't say one way or the other."

"What a load of bunk. I know what happened, and he's the one who's wrong, absolutely wrong."

"But you didn't see the moments leading up to his punch, now did you? Can't say what Lisa might've done to him?"

"I know what I saw," Joel snapped, "and so does your client."

"Not to put too fine a point on this, but we've been speaking in the abstract here. Hypothetically. You're aware, I'm certain, that Dr. Dillen has said from day one this was entirely your fault, that you were reckless with the boat and your negligence caused his wife's injury."

"A giant lie," Joel replied.

"Maybe. But Mrs. Dillen has instructed me to file suit against you and Royal Coachman Outfitters for civil damages. It will come down to your word against theirs."

"Theirs?"

"Theirs," Hudgins assured him. "Mrs. Dillen wants this over and done."

"So I play along and sit on my hands and soften my testimony or you're going to sue me and Dixon? You're here to threaten me?"

"Those are your words, not mine. I'm simply reciting possibilities. I'm certainly not threatening you. No sir."

Joel stuck Hudgins with the belligerent, devil-may-care stare he'd seen Edmund use on Will Cassady when the inexperienced jailer boy had threatened an arrest for obstructing justice. "You're bluffing." Joel crowded him. "You can't have it both ways. How stupid do you think I am? Karl can't say he hit her in self-defense and then claim the next day, for another suit, that I wrecked the boat and cut her. It's one or the other."

Hudgins commenced again with his hands, rubbing and rolling and churning. "Good point. I'm glad you understand that. Glad indeed. You see, Mr. King, you go first at the criminal trial. We listen. I'm sure our trial strategy, what Karl and Lisa say or don't say, will be very much linked to what you state, how you present things. If the door's left open for Karl to claim self-defense, I predict he will, and then he'll retract his statement about your handling of the boat, tell the court he didn't want to embarrass or implicate his wife and attempted to protect her by describing the episode as an accident. You and the Coachman walk away unscathed under that scenario. If there's no chance of self-defense, I see the Dillens—both of them—pointing the finger at you and suing the bejesus out of you."

"No way. She wouldn't lie and turn on me like that," Joel's expression lost some of its verve. "I helped her. I kept him from kicking her and doing more damage."

"It's you or her kids, you or her house, you or her health insurance. I don't think you want to put her to the test, Mr. King. And, hey, all we want is the truth, right? The truth without any editorials and slant, the truth that she was arguing and upset and she could've rushed him when you were distracted. The truth that she hit him first."

"She slapped his finger away from her face," Joel said. "Hardly justification for his beating her."

"After she's already swung at him when you weren't watching," Hudgins added, smiling. "And she was advancing on him. He was trying to keep her at arm's length, and she ploughed ahead, knocking his peacemaker's defense out of her path."

"You know that's plain poppycock," Joel said.

Sarah was in the bar again, this time with her hands free. She asked Joel when he was planning on clocking in and starting work, and he told her he was as good as there. He stared at Hudgins before leaving, asked the lawyer if he followed professional wrestling, informed him lawyers were akin to crooked managers trying to sabotage the good guys and were nothing but charlatans. Hudgins departed, and Joel plodded through the doors to the kitchen, nowhere else to go, completely trussed by frauds and worldly machinations, some of his own doing, some just sent his way and delivered to him—evidently—as an object lesson, a little extra from his Maker so he could discover how it felt to be shaken and buffeted in the slipstream of other people's treachery.

There they were, big as life, sawing through thick red steaks, buttering rolls and drinking highballs, sitting at a table next to the rear bar. It was Friday evening, five days after Joel had called Las Vegas and left his urgent, frantic message, and the Station was jammed and chaotic, loaded with skiers, loggers, locals, college kids, the office staff of a huge chiropractic firm and a rowdy bachelorette party ordering purple hooter-shooters by the dozen, the bride-to-be soused and sloppy even though it wasn't yet eight o'clock. Sa'ad and Edmund were seated in Laura Hinton's section, and she was pouring ice water into their glasses from a sideways pitcher, smiling at Edmund, inquiring about their need for more bread or alcohol. Strangely, though, it had taken a while for the two men to sink in, to register on Joel; they were expert at turning bland, chameleons, absolutely unremarkable despite the fact Sa'ad was the dining area's only dark-skinned customer, and Joel hadn't seen them arrive and didn't know how long they'd been at the table.

Edmund was wearing a twill hat that advertised an overrated Missoula fly-fishing service, and he'd grown a full beard, dense, barbered and the same length all over his face, gray at his chin and temples. Sa'ad was dressed in ski clothes with a knit cap pulled to the middle of his forehead and was hiding behind a pair of wire-rimmed spectacles that were completely pedestrian, cheap, functional glasses he would never have purchased except as a disguise. Joel had looked in their direction once before, when he'd stepped from the kitchen to retrieve a tub of dirty dishes—stared right at them and not recognized what he was seeing.

After riding out a surge of anxiety and lickety-split pulse, Joel walked by their seats and locked eyes for an instant, but he didn't linger or interrupt his task, kept moving. He delivered a rack of clean glasses to the bar and retraced his route. When he passed their table this time, Sa'ad said, "Bathroom—five minutes" while waving his fork in a little conversational circle and pretending to talk to Edmund, never so much as glancing at Joel.

Joel checked the kitchen clock and started scraping food scraps from plates. Someone had left most of a chicken entrée untouched, and the meal hit the trash can's bottom squarely, the chicken and fancy sauce first, then a potato skin, then a sprinkle of al dente string beans. A thud followed by pitty-pats. Frankie was singing and gyrating his hips, picking up snatches of a radio song through the din of simmering skillets, knives beating chopping boards, mixers, oven buzzers and the steel double doors banging against the shoulders and knees of waiters passing through with precariously balanced trays. Joel filled a coffee cup with cold water, drank it without pausing, removed his apron and left for the toilet.

Edmund was already there, pressed against a urinal. Another man was at the sink, combing his hair and admiring his mirror reflection. Sa'ad came in, and the stranger finished arranging his head, wet his hands, yanked two brown paper towels from a wall dispenser, dabbed his palms and fingers with the towels and disappeared. Sa'ad bolted the door and motioned for Joel to join him at the front of the sink. Sa'ad opened both spigots, and two separate streams splashed in the basin and quickly got ahead of the drain, began to flood the bowl. Edmund joined them, clapping Joel on the shoulder and hooking him into a one-armed hug.

"We have major trouble," Joel announced.

"Indeed we do," Sa'ad said quietly, speaking toward the water.

"The authorities are all over me," Joel complained. "I'm sure they're watching me, eavesdropping, tailing me, the whole package."

"Correct," Edmund said.

"What took you so long?" He glared at Sa'ad. "I called you days ago."

"I was on vacation, okay? Out of the office. I don't stay there twenty-four seven, awaiting your commands. We came as soon as we could."

"Arrived yesterday," Edmund added. "Did a little reconnaissance work and took the lay of the land."

"You've been here since yesterday?" Joel asked, peering at Sa'ad and Edmund in the mirror. "Why didn't you contact me right away?" The sink was over halfway full, rising.

"You think we're complete fools, Joel?" Sa'ad said. "Think we would roll into Missoula with our guns blazing not knowing jack about the situation here? Maybe you've switched sides, maybe it's a trap, maybe it's one of a million things. At a minimum, you'd told us there was surveillance."

"It's a trap all right," Joel hissed, "and I'm the one with steel jaws around my ankles, thanks to you."

"Well, you *are* being followed. A guy in a green Explorer tailed you home last night. He's outside now, waiting for you to finish work. I'm sure your phones are bugged as well. They might've even wired this place." Sa'ad suddenly turned, grabbed Joel along the ribs and frisked him, stuck his hands inside his shirt and then checked his trousers, patting down his buttocks, thighs and calves. Joel stood passively, a sullen slouch convexing his torso. "Or they may have wired you," Sa'ad said when he finished his search, unrepentant about his lack of trust.

"Satisfied?" Joel asked.

"So far," Sa'ad said. He stopped the water and allowed the level to decline.

"Nothing personal," Edmund offered. "We gotta cover every base, though. You understand, right?"

"Sure," Joel said.

"And, hey, fair for the goose, fair for the gander. You want to check us, go to it." Edmund raised his hands and stepped away from the sink.

"I'm fine," Joel said.

Someone began knocking and wouldn't stop, and Joel scurried across the room and cracked the door, opening it only enough to give his eyes peeking space. He told two young boys about a problem with the plumbing and advised them to use the other toilet, gave them directions and thanked them for their patience.

"So what's the deal?" Edmund asked when Joel rejoined them. "What's happened?"

Sa'ad began running the water again; he instructed Joel to whisper.

"In a nutshell, the items you gave me were stolen," Joel said.

"We know that," Sa'ad said sharply. "Of course they were. But we've returned them to the rightful owner. Except the damn ring you either lost or pilfered."

"No, it's not so simple." Joel leaned closer to the faucet. "One of the rings you borrowed is famous and itself stolen. You fools gave me the Eiffel Tower of jewelry and had me try to insure it as my own."

"What?" Edmund was perplexed; his mouth soured at the corners.

"One of the rings you gave me was taken from the Jewish Museum in a big art heist, and the FBI is having a conniption to learn where I obtained the jewelry so they can find the rest of the stolen loot, primarily some important painting."

"It was just a bunch of jewelry," Sa'ad protested. "No huge stones, nothing fancy or exceptional. You sure about this?"

"Of course I'm sure," Joel said, his words piercing the water noise. "The stones and whatnot aren't the problem—I take it they're pretty average. It's just that this ordinary piece was stolen at the same time as a big-deal painting, and yes, they know it's the right ring. It has initials on it, Sa'ad. Initials. Like a calling card. Nice job you guys did."

"Believe me, Joel, we didn't know," Edmund said.

"Of course we didn't know." Sa'ad spoke immediately. "Why would we give you high-profile property and expose ourselves to significant risks?"

"I didn't suggest you did it intentionally," Joel replied. "Only that you've screwed up royally. Some experts you turned out to be—I'd have done better partnering up with Moe and Curly."

"Fuck you," Sa'ad said.

"Oh—and from what I can gather, the red ring I showed to the State Farm agent, the one the feds know about, is a mate to the emerald ring that's mysteriously vanished. Red and green sisters, they're called." Joel tunneled in on Sa'ad. "I hope that doesn't affect anyone's plans or finances."

"Why would it," Sa'ad answered, "given that neither Edmund nor I has the emerald piece? It sprouted wings on your watch, not ours."

"What did you tell the FBI?" Edmund asked.

Another customer tried the door, shook the knob but didn't knock and finally went away. Edmund slowed the water.

"Nothing. I stuck to my story and insisted I talk to my attorney. And it wasn't just the FBI—oh no. The visit was with my probation officer and a local cop as well. There's no way this thing is going to pan out now. We, gentlemen, are about to be shown the gallows."

"Damn," Edmund said.

"And I'll get thrown in jail and perhaps even tagged with a major art theft I'm clueless about." Joel shrunk his mouth, gave Sa'ad a withering, accusatory once-over. "Thanks."

Sa'ad pointed at Joel. "Short term: keep quiet and say nothing. I'll have a lawyer here pronto, someone who can't be linked to us. If they had the absolute, one-hundred-percent goods on you, you'd be wearing a jumpsuit already. They obviously can't prove where you obtained the ring or even that you knew it was stolen."

"True," Edmund remarked. "I agree."

"Let's think out loud," Sa'ad said. He took off the ugly glasses, slid the cap closer to his hairline. "Some things I can put together from what you've told me. Let's work through this. The owners never made a claim for the missing ring. Never did. Now we know why—it was stolen."

"Let me repeat how pleased I am about that," Joel grumbled.

"That's why I advised you to proceed with your claim here after you and your sister were robbed—the folks in Vegas, the true owners, never reported the emerald ring gone, never raised a stink. I didn't really know why at the time, but now I do. Abel informs me that the jewelry came from a safe at a residence, belonged to a bimbo showgirl who's married to some ancient troll from Holland. Dumb bitch wrote down the combination and taped it to the bottom of her clock radio. She mentioned the missing ring to Abel once and that was it, asked him if he'd seen it around the house—as best we can tell, no police ever came, no adjusters, nothing. Nobody's bothered Abel, and he'd be the first guy they questioned. Either she was afraid to give her husband the bad news, or she told him and he damn sure didn't want to file a claim." Sa'ad fussed with his chin and pinched a fold of skin between his thumb and index finger. "So it would appear we've been snake-bitten like nobody's business. Abel picked the one house in town with jewels everybody's after."

"Yeah, but you can't blame him, Sa'ad," Edmund said. "Who knew? Huh? We followed procedure—nothing too large or splashy or unique. Just bad damn luck. Un-fucking-believable bad luck."

"What should I do?" Joel asked.

"Like I said, keep quiet," Sa'ad told him. "Don't volunteer a thing and go about your business. All they can prove is you had—maybe—a piece of jewelry that's now gone. Your mother's still not competent, true?"

"True," Joel answered.

"So they can't make any progress there," Sa'ad said. "And if they come to search your house, they won't find any painting or anything else incriminating. It's a standoff."

"That probably won't keep them from arresting me. They left me with the impression it's only a matter of time."

"Don't let them bluff you, Joel," Edmund encouraged him. "Talkin' to 'em never helps. Don't open your mouth. Make them prove their case. All they know is you most likely had a stolen ring—can't say where you got it or that you stole it or knew it was part of a burglary. You're an innocent bystander caught up in somebody else's wrongdoin'."

The water had reached the lip of the sink, was about to spill onto the floor. Joel shut both spigots and studied the two men next to him, pausing a good long while after he twisted toward Sa'ad. There wasn't the slightest speck of betrayal or duplicity in their expressions—the same cads who'd sent Christy Darden to snare him in a nasty insurance scam were now giving him self-serving advice and doing it with forthright eyes and solemn, earnest lips. "An innocent bystander—amen," Joel said flatly, the sentence without pitch. "Don't you know it."

Several lopsided bubbles rose and glubbed in the sink, and the water dropped through the drain, made a muffled, sucking noise as it poured down the pipes.

"I've got to get back to work," Joel said. "I'll keep you both posted."

Sa'ad completely removed the cap and revealed his whole face. "You understand, Joel, that there's no way you can sell us out. It would be your word against ours, and there's not a single piece of physical evidence to support your story, nothing to connect all of us when the nitty-gritty comes. There's really very little for you to offer them, you see, beyond tall tales and wild accusations, and those won't mean shit for you in terms of a deal. So, please, don't be getting any brilliant ideas."

The letter from Gentry, Locke was waiting for Joel, propped against the salt shaker, when he arrived home at one in the morning, the FBI on his butt, Sa'ad and Edmund gone, headed out of town four hours earlier, the two of them haints of a sort, who probably began to fade into mist and vapors the instant they stepped outside the Station and hit the night air. Joel opened the envelope with a butcher knife, withdrew several sheets of paper and positioned them at an angle, bent them toward the sink so they would catch the ceiling light. The correspondence was from Brian Roland and tersely informed Joel the case against him and the church had been settled and dismissed. Attached to the letter was a four-page release, signed by Christy. She'd received three million, five hundred thousand dollars.

The release had been completed on December twenty-first—weeks ago—and Joel felt his jaw fall slack and lost the tension in his hands. The papers went to the floor, landing with a small plop and folding up at each end. She had betrayed him, cut his throat, taken the money he'd helped her earn and left him behind, abandoned him. "Oh God," he said out loud. He looked around the inside of his sister's tiny house but was unable to discern very much with only one bulb burning, saw lumps, shadows, outlines and the concentrated reflection of the overhead light on the silver side of the toaster. He was, right then, at absolute nothing, played out and cornered, all his strategies gone to naught. It didn't do him any good, but he kicked the pile of papers, kicked them twice before he collected them and went belowground to his bed.

The following day, Agent Hobbes and Anna Starke appeared at noon, rapped on the door and announced themselves from outside. Joel opened the door only as far as the safety chain allowed, and they inquired about coming in. He told them no, asked what they wanted. Hobbes seemed oddly serene, as if he knew something Joel didn't, and Anna Starke told Joel time was expiring, that they knew he was up to no good and he needed to help them and help himself. "You're looking at twenty, thirty years in prison if you grab the short end of this particular stick," she warned him. He promised her he'd contacted a lawyer and was eager to meet, would soon make arrangements. Hobbes didn't have much to say and began to whistle as they walked away and climbed into their dark blue sedan. They sat in the drive fifteen minutes before leaving—just sat there with the engine idling—and Joel watched them through the window, rubbernecking around the fabric hem of the curtains so they couldn't see him.

There was nothing left for Joel to do but hunker down, just retreat and cover himself with his forearms and elbows to stave off as much of the avalanche as he could and hope he didn't smother underneath the rush of lousy breaks and curdled fortune. After Hobbes and Starke finally disappeared, he phoned the Station and reported sick, and Sarah came on the line to speak with him, sounded solicitous and concerned, promised to save him a pint of the chef's minestrone and cautioned him not to rush his recovery. He spent the remainder of the afternoon trying to figure an escape from the labyrinth he'd wandered into, found a pen and paper and drew diagrams and scribbled plans and stared at the walls and walked outside in the frigid air but came up with nothing, could think of no more tricks or clever subterfuge, was done.

When Baker and Sophie arrived home, he was sitting on the sofa doodling, not dressed for work, his hair poorly groomed, his skin sallow. Baker hurried to the couch and hugged him, oblivious to his ratty appearance and the bigger issue of his not being at the restaurant. He wrapped the child with both arms, kissed his head and asked him to go to his room for a moment while he spoke with Sophie, made the request quietly but with enough iron and adult intonation in his words that the boy knew he meant business.

"I'll do my homework and you can check it for me," Baker said brightly. He lifted his backpack from the floor but didn't loop it over his shoulder, just carried it at his side and commenced an obedient trek through the den, down the hall.

Sophie knew an unhappy report was imminent; the only question was its breadth and length and how much it would affect her. She dropped her purse on the kitchen table, walked around to the front of the sofa and frowned at her brother, looming above him. "Let's have it," she said, her voice ready to rupture.

"Want to sit?" Joel suggested.

"No, I'll stand for the present, thank you."

"You're sure?" He raised his face, looked at her full.

"Out with it, Joel. Say it and get it over with. What is it this time?"

"Well, it's not really 'this time,' I'm afraid. It's an accumulation of events, and it's pretty awful."

"Why am I not surprised?" She sounded irritated, upset, but there was a trickle of pity in her tone as well. She took a seat on the edge of the coffee table and crossed her legs.

"I hate to have to tell you," he said. "I hate being such a failure."

"Just say it."

Joel melted into the corner of the sofa. "Okay," he said, and he told his sister what he'd done, laid out the stories in a monotone, described the jewelry scam and how it had gone awry because of rotten happenstance and the initialed "red sister" ring, admitted the police and FBI were about to arrest him. Then there was the problem with Karl and Lisa, their threat to sue him and ruin Dixon unless he went along with their outright lying—which really wasn't his fault, he hastened to add, made sure he had his sister's eye and showed her his innocence when he finished this part of his yarn. The worst, though, was Christy, who was missing, and he was a suspect evidently, and at a bare minimum they'd heard him on tape arguing with her and that was good enough to get him returned to the Roanoke jail. And to beat all, Christy had screwed him out of the money he was planning to donate to the church and to hand over to her—to Sophie— well over one point five million dollars, the money he'd generated with his Elmer Gantry shenanigans at their deposition. In retrospect, the saga was so hapless and amateurish that Joel finished with a rueful, winsome chuckle, swiped his fingers through his hair and left his hands atop his head, his arms flopped out and resting against the sofa cushions. "A lot of sound and fury, toil and trouble, for nothing. Nothing," he concluded. "You were absolutely right—I should've simply let things be."

Sophie was tearful, but she seemed rational and remarkably emotion-less. Her shoulders were still, her breathing normal, her mouth steadfast. "To start with," she said, "how could you have ever in a thousand years trusted a crazy bitch like this Christy girl?"

"I never really trusted her, Sophie, but, you see, at least I had a chance to turn the situation around. A chance, like buying a lottery ticket or taking a swing at bat. Can't win if you don't play. If I do nothing, I get nothing, and the bad guys—Christy and Edmund and Sa'ad—stroll off with everything. Did I completely trust her? Of course not. Did I figure she'd split the payoff with me? I guessed it was fifty-fifty, and that was better than where I was, at zero and a chump."

"I told you from the first that you were out of your depth," she said.

"I know."

"And this idiotic jewelry plan to defraud insurance companies," she continued, her voice gaining volume. "What were you thinking? Huh? You weren't forced into that, now were you? You signed up for it, and it's pure laziness, greed and impatience, the same faults you're supposed to know so much about conquering. A lot easier to preach it than to live it, isn't it? Words versus deeds, Joel. I've struggled to put food on the table for my son, been broke and ass-kicked and abandoned, but I've never so much as taken a stamp from work. Never. The first time things get tight, you go to pieces. And the clincher is you lied to me and flew self-righteous when I questioned you about where you got thousands of dollars' worth of jewelry—crawled all over me, yelled and wagged your finger."

"I'm sorry. I've made mistake after mistake, but I did have a long, difficult stretch. I didn't simply walk out of church and stumble into a deck of cards, an eye patch and a bottle of sweet wine. Give me a little credit. Some of this is my fault, some isn't."

"If you hadn't hit on a seventeen-year-old girl, then *none* of this would be happening, correct? The way I see it, everything flows from that shining moment, and you're damn sure responsible for your bad decisions and midlife libido." There was no bitterness in her voice, no spite. She seemed more amazed than angry.

"I am, and maybe this is part of the Lord's will. What I did was bad, and I'm perhaps still paying my debt."

"The saddest part, Joel, is Baker." She wiped her cheek. "He's going to be devastated." She sounded nettled now, emphasized the last word.

"I'm so sorry, Sophie," Joel said. He took down his hands and placed them in his lap. "Believe me, I've considered that. I love him. I truly do."

"Yet another man walks out of his life and disappoints him. Thanks, Joel. Thank you."

Joel pushed off the sofa, joined Sophie on the low, wooden table and molded his hand over her knee. "Through the entire thing, from my first foul-up with Christy to this very moment, I have kept faith in God and believed—believed absolutely—that He can deliver me from any abyss. I've prayed again and again that He would bless you and this house and Baker, and I've knocked at His door and begged Him to grant me wisdom and let me get money for you and Roanoke First Baptist and, most of all, for Baker. It makes me sick to realize I've been so inadequate and will end up hurting a wonderful, beautiful boy. I'm not altogether sure why my prayers have remained unanswered, can't explain it."

Sophie stared at him, astonished. She opened her mouth to speak and a guttural groan made it to the top of her throat, but nothing else came, not another sound.

"What?" Joel asked. "What is it?"

"Gee, Joel, isn't that a lot like asking for chocolate icing to spread on a bowl of shit? Or the dope addict asking the Lord to sanctify his needle, or Sirhan seeking a special blessing for his pistol, or my cheating husband praying he won't get caught sneaking into the house as the sun comes up? I like your take on this, Joel, your particular brand of the gospel—do what the hell ever you want and beg your Good Lord to put His imprimatur on it, then sulk and pout if He doesn't." She shook her head, tossed off a mystified, derisive laugh. "Damn."

He removed his hand from her leg.

"I mean, I don't have a degree in this crap, didn't go to friggin' grad school and write term papers on the Council of Trent—you're the expert. But common sense might suggest you try praying for guidance rather than doing as you please and whining to have it validated. Have you thought about how foolish your position is? You supposedly believe in this great, gracious divine hand, and the moment things turn a tad sticky you jump ship and start lying, cheating and stealing, hit the sin trifecta, really ring the bell, and then you wonder how come you and your snake-oil friends aren't prospering." She was looking at him in the same way she looked at her son when the boy clung to some immature foolishness, her expression mostly bafflement.

"You can't simply quit, Sophie, close your eyes and cower and do nothing and wait for the Lord to throw you a lifeline. I had to act, to try to rectify things and overcome my mistakes. I'm not expected to sit about passive and defeated, watching people run all over me. The Lord wants us to carry a little of our own load."

"Yeah, and to carry it honestly, Joel. I'm not going to debate this with you—I'm not the one who quotes the Bible and got paid out of a collection plate to be an example for others. You've conned yourself if you truly believe half the bullshit you're saying, and that's tragic."

"I bent the rules for the greater good, to do justice," Joel protested.

Sophie didn't respond, allowing him to keep at his explanations.

"I mean . . . Well, for instance, if Ted Bundy were asking where you were, I think you'd agree it would be permissible to mislead him, to lie, rather than have you abducted and killed. But I'm supposed to let Sa'ad and Edmund make off with millions of dollars at my expense?"

"Whatever, Joel. Or you could tell the truth and trust Providence, huh? Who knows what would've happened to Sa'ad and Edmund, how this would have finished—as it stands, you've probably managed to triple their take. Seems the question is how deep your faith runs, and yours is fairly shallow. How long did you last before you signed up with this crook Edmund? A week or two?"

"A month," he mumbled. "And that was after half a year in jail and the kitchen catching fire."

"A regular Job," she chastised him. "Congratulations."

"Well . . . ," he said.

"Well?"

"I suppose there's some truth to what you're saying," he admitted.

"Hey, I'm the one who thinks everything is relative and believes in a great big gray area and compromise and leniency and flukes over divine order. But lying and breaking the law can't be too noble, especially lying to me. I'm not as sold on religion as you are—far from it—but I do believe in decency and a few absolutes. You're the one who was complaining not so long ago that people do what the hell they want to and then ask the church to tell 'em it's okay and award them gold stars."

"There's a big difference. I'm trying to do the right thing, to fix my error and serve the Lord. It's not as if I'm out whoring and drugging and preying on innocent folks."

"And I'm sure He's mighty proud of your efforts. Delighted. It was especially good of Him to suspend all the normal rules for you and still let you use His name while you were setting affairs in order here on earth. Doing *His* will, right? Lying and conniving and stealing to promote God's agenda. Yessir, I'm sure the banquet table is arranged and the goblets are ready with wine—you've done well, carried the banner high."

"There is a difference," he said feebly. "I was at least trying to do the Lord's mission, was aware of right and wrong and the big picture. Maybe my tack was misguided, but I've always meant to arrive at the ultimate good. I wanted to repay the church as best I could, give you and Baker a life and put a stop to Sa'ad and Edmund's corruption. And, like I told you before, I hardly feel guilty about beating an insurance company at its own game. They're all dishonest corporations, and you and I and the church deserve the cash more than they do. Certainly you don't disagree with me there?"

"I never said you didn't have fine intentions. Your sincerity almost makes it scarier. I'm recalling Jim Jones and David Koresh and that freakish Marshall whatever, the spooky, castrated guy whose disciples all went to the mall and bought Nikes for the final trip through the Milky Way."

"They're obviously crazy. That's an extreme example. Unfair."

"And you're what, Joel? Merely opportunistic? Step back and think about where you've wound up. Think. Isn't that the proof of the pudding—there's no way you're in this dilemma if you've been making sound, moral choices. Obviously something's pretty screwed up."

Joel paused and considered her point. "It all just crept up on me piecemeal, and before I know it I'm in a quagmire and there's no escaping. But I'm still not sure where the train jumped the tracks. I'm not denying I made some questionable decisions, but, my goodness . . ." He sighed, shook his head. "Virtually everything you're saying is true. As much as I'd like to quarrel with you, I can't."

"I'm not claiming I have all the answers, okay? But it's time to play the rest of this straight and quit pretending you're someone else."

"I plan to," he said.

"Good," she replied.

"So what do you recommend?" he asked.

"Get an honest lawyer, tell him the truth and see what happens. This insane plotting is only making the situation worse."

"Okay," he said.

"Promise me," she insisted.

"I don't really have any other option," he said sadly. "There's nothing else left to do."

"The honest lawyer part might be a problem," Sophie said.

"Yeah. I'm darn sure not going to trust whoever Sa'ad sends."

"No kidding," she replied.

"You realize how much I regret putting you through this?" Joel's eyes watered, but he didn't cry. He kept his gaze directed at the floor. "I'm sorry. I keep having to say that, don't I? You are such a smart, righteous person—I'm proud of you. You're so much better than I, so much stronger and tougher." He took some satisfaction in what he was telling her, perked up, managed to face her. "Thanks."

"Sure." She seemed uneasy, looked away and rearranged herself, moved her legs and feet. "You'll be fine. Don't worry."

They sat there and didn't talk any more, brother and sister at the end of Joel's confession, stayed where they were and grew comfortable again without uttering a syllable, heard the wind gust and cause a loose gutter to flap against the house and Baker start a child's merry, content humming while he worked on his studies, adding numbers together and totaling them in his head, writing three-digit answers for his mother and Joel to inspect.

That night, before he went to bed, Joel recalled the solid sense of Sophie's counsel, and he dropped to his knees, rested his elbows on the mattress, shut his eyes and prayed fervently, first asking to be forgiven, then simply requesting help and an indication of what the Lord wished of him. He furrowed his brow and said the words aloud and with conviction, repeated phrases, pleaded for guidance and promised to be compliant, surrendered. After he finished, he lay in bed and waited, listening and watching, but nothing arrived, no pillar of fire, no paternal baritone, no swooping messenger, no tableau of saints and scrolls, not even a creak in the floor or a rumble when the furnace switched on and filled the ducts with warm air.

eighteen

Joel maintained his prayerful entreaties the following morning, swaying and rocking and worshipping on abject knees for fifteen minutes. He thought of nothing but his mistakes, lit a candle—yellow and slender, a birthday cake leftover—before he knelt and ceaselessly murmured the chastened request Sophie had suggested: He asked to be forgiven and submitted to his Lord's will, the very same Lord he believed in and had preached about, the Lord he had carried into the pulpit hundreds of Sundays and urged others to accept no matter how persistent the affliction or how barren the horizon. He begged for deliverance, and he finally prostrated himself, belly-flopped onto the concrete where he lay spread-eagle, his cheek flush against the floor, the plea to God rote, rhythmic and tranced, the basement awash with Old Testament piety.

He also decided to fast, so he skipped breakfast and drank only two glasses of water during the afternoon. He prepared supper for Sophie and Baker—fried hamburger steaks, browned potato slices in the oven and mixed together a foil bag of processed cheese and Kraft macaroni noodles, made the dish thoroughly soggy the way Baker liked it. He found not eating difficult, but he felt virtuous and holy, somewhat at peace with his circumstances, the suffocating worry that came from struggling to stay a step ahead of a virulent, nipping pack starting to lift.

Sophie noticed right away that he wasn't having dinner. "You're not hungry?" she asked.

"I'm fasting," he answered.

"Pardon?"

"I'm fasting. No food today."

"And there's a reason for this?" she asked, chewing her meat.

"I'm attempting to make amends. To be penitent."

She cut a potato and raked the piece through a pool of ketchup. "Seriously?"

"What's so odd about that? I took your advice. I've asked to be forgiven, and I've surrendered my burdens to the Lord."

A slyness enlivened her eyes and mouth. "I'm certain not eating will solve your problems. Once the FBI gets wind of your decision, they'll turn tail and run, leave Montana forever. And it'll be good practice for your hunger strike if you're sent to prison—you and the other inmates will be able to protest like champs, really show 'em who's boss."

"It's my way of dealing with things." Joel spoke evenly. "I feel better today than I have in months."

"Do I need to keep watch on the rooster?" she asked.

"The rooster?"

"Yeah. You're not planning some kind of sacrifice, are you? A burnt offering? Firing up Tut over a pile of kindling, chanting and writhing and speaking in a mystical tongue?"

Joel laughed, and so did Sophie. "I'll stick to less dramatic remedies for the short term," he said.

"You're not going to hurt Tut?" Baker was alarmed, enough so that he quit eating. His plate was a topsy-turvy medley of colors and jagged cuts, and several yellow, cheesy noodles had tumbled onto the table.

"No, not at all," Joel promised him. "Your mom's only joshing. I'd never do anything to Tut or his hen."

"You better not," the boy warned him.

"Don't worry," Joel answered. "Tut's my pal."

After dinner was finished, Sophie helped Joel wash the greasy skillet and the macaroni-and-cheese pot and stow the dishes. While they were straightening the kitchen, she poured a cold beer into a tall glass and removed an elastic band from her hair and shook loose a ponytail, then scratched her scalp with all ten fingers. "So what have you decided to do?" she asked when they were almost through. "Beyond starving yourself, I mean."

"Well, I think I should talk to a lawyer and tell the whole story, everything, the unvarnished truth, and hope for the best. Isn't that what you recommended?"

"Yeah, I suppose so."

"I spoke to Dixon this afternoon," Joel said.

"Oh?" She swallowed some beer. "About a lawyer? Did he give you a name?"

"Well, sort of. I'm going to see Lynette Allen, the lady who's handling the case with Karl and Lisa."

Sophie placed her glass on the counter and gave Joel a quizzical stare. "Uh, help me here, but isn't she the prosecutor, the person from the other side? Maybe you should consult a *defense* lawyer, the slippery folks who're paid to help you, not the state."

"Well, maybe I should, but what good would it do? Dixon says Lynette is fair, and from my dealings with her, it would appear she is. I think she'll know how to manage the threats I'm getting from Karl and Lisa, and I'm planning to tell her about Sa'ad and Edmund and this blasted red sister ring. Better her than Hobbes or the state police, don't you think?"

"I don't know, Joel . . ." Sophie sounded troubled. She lifted her beer but didn't drink. "You could still be honest and retain your own attorney."

"To what end?" he asked.

"I want you to leave this nonsense behind and shake free from the fraud and sorry people, but I don't want you to go to jail for the rest of your life."

"I don't think I will. I don't think that's the Lord's plan for me. And if it is, I've probably earned it."

"You fly from pillar to post, Joel, from one extreme to the other. Gangster to altar boy. Why don't you simply disavow the stealing and lying, locate a lawyer, keep quiet and shoot for the most lenient deal available? There's nothing wrong with looking out for yourself." She set the beer down without tasting it. "We've only had the contrite Joel for a day—shouldn't you consider this a while longer? Maybe pop a Prozac before you get too rash and swept away by your newfound virtue? A lot of people who leave the tent revival wake up the next morning broke and really regret being seized by the moment and forking over their paycheck."

"Believe me, Sophie, I'm not trying to hang myself. This is a good solution, and an honest one. I'll be careful."

"Have you heard from Sa'ad? Wasn't he going to hire someone to represent you?"

"Right," Joel sneered. "Some shyster named Harper phoned this afternoon and left a message on the answering machine. Claimed he was returning my call and said he was eager to meet with me about my legal woes. It goes without saying I didn't call back. The heck with that—he's working for Sa'ad and Edmund, not me. I'd be crazy to trust him."

"No doubt," Sophie said. "I was just curious if they'd followed through."

"Of course they did. They want to keep tabs on me and have their guy pulling the strings."

"When are you going to see Lynette?" she asked.

"Tomorrow. And Dixon's agreed to go with me."

"Does he understand what you've done?"

"No. He said he's not interested in knowing the details." Joel took his sister's hand, and she held on for a few seconds before pulling away.

"I want to go too." She was determined, her tone emphatic.

"Why? I'm grateful, but you don't have to do that. I'm a grown man—I don't need my baby sister there to tie my mittens and wipe my nose."

"I want to make sure you don't screw up and do something foolish."

"Sophie—"

"Hush, Joel. I've made up my mind."

"It would be sort of embarrassing," he said. "Makes me look like a stupid child who can't take care of himself."

"Tough. And that characterization isn't far from accurate given what I've been hearing."

"You'll miss work," he protested.

"The hell with work. You're my brother."

Driving to see Lynette Allen the next morning, Joel and Sophie became trapped behind two tractor-trailers monopolizing both lanes of the interstate. The truck immediately ahead of them was covered with dust, and someone had finger-written "show me boobs or leg" in the dirt on the trailer's rear doors. The trucks finally pulled to the right lane at the same time so Joel could maneuver around them, and he floored the Volvo, accelerating to almost eighty-five. The eighteen-wheelers' huge, noisy tires were at eye level, and Sophie gripped Joel's thigh as he sped the car past, the trucks not giving any ground. "Hurry up, Joel," she told him, "before they swerve over here and wreck us." After they'd almost made it by and she'd regained her composure, she looked up at the driver of the second truck and scowled. "Assholes."

She was still steamed about the trucks when they met Dixon outside Lynette Allen's office. Joel was actually thankful for the distraction, grateful the inconsiderate drivers had taken their minds off the harrowing, Hail Mary conference he'd arranged. He'd been reduced to one final shot, a let-it-rip meeting with a virtual stranger—a prosecutor—whose reaction could ruin the rest of his life or set him free, and sadly, he was forced to slink through her door as the worst kind of Judas, a traitor betraying his cronies in hopes of hitting the courthouse jackpot. Tension and his stool pigeon's guilt had been gnawing into his entrails all morning, turning him nauseous as he sat solitary at the kitchen table, nibbling a spoonful of Baker's sugary cereal and watching dawn swirl the sky blue, orange, reddish and lavender.

The meeting was scheduled for ten-thirty, and they'd all arrived early. Dixon quietly greeted Joel and said hello to Sophie, and they sat in a sparse waiting room and killed time discussing the snowpack and the prospects for spring, how much water the rivers would hold after the mountains thawed. On the wall, there was a large round clock with a second hand, and Lynette appeared punctually at half past the hour and invited them into her office.

She had no idea why her friend Dixon was accompanying Joel, and she couldn't have known why Joel and Sophie wanted to speak with her. She was delighted to see Dixon, talked to him about mutual acquaintances and getting together for some fishing on the Blackfoot. She offered them coffee, and everyone declined. There was a lull in the conversation after Lynette finished telling Dixon about her sister's successful knee surgery, and Dixon abruptly steered the subject to Joel's problems.

"Joel has some troubles, Lynn," he began, squirming forward and sitting on the edge of his chair. "Some of his situation has to do with this damn fight out on the Blackfoot, and some of it's unrelated. I understand the additional stuff is serious. I told Joel you'd treat him fairly. You and I have known each other for years, and you've always been square with people. I don't know the details of Joel's predicament, and don't care to. But I did want to come with him today. I'm vouchin' for him, Lynn. He's a good man. I'd like to have him at the shop come May."

"Your being here means a lot," Lynette Allen told him. "You know that."

Joel felt a push of emotion, of gratitude, and his eyes welled. Dixon Kreager's friendship was unearned and his help was of the priceless variety, without hooks or loopholes or hope of reciprocation, a donation from the stores of an optimistic man, a handout offered because it was needed and for no other reason. Whatever else might happen, Dixon had made up his mind about Joel King, weighed him by his own set of standards and not found him wanting. "Thanks, Dixon," Joel said.

"Sure." Standing up, he gave Lynette a sharp nod, briefly rested his hand on Sophie's shoulder and, having accomplished what he came to do, left the room, his rubber-soled boots squeaking on the linoleum as he departed.

"I put a lot of stock in Dixon Kreager," she said to Joel.

"He's a remarkable man," Joel replied. "Been awfully kind to me."

"So where do we want to start?"

"How about the case involving Karl?" Joel suggested.

"Whatever makes you comfortable," she said. "I don't mean anything by this, but is there a reason your sister's here?" She glanced at Sophie and smiled warmly. "She's welcome to stay, of course."

"She's just concerned about me," Joel said.

"Oh, okay."

"As for Karl, his attorney approached me and tried to twist my arm, showed up at my workplace and gave me a sob story about Lisa and her kids, then basically threatened to sue me and Dixon if I didn't play ball with them. They want me to say that Lisa attacked him, and that he hit her in self-defense. Otherwise they're both going to claim I mishandled the boat and that's how she got hurt. Do you think she would lie, turn on me after I kept him from beating her even worse?"

Lynette raised and dropped her shoulders, exhaled heavily. "Difficult to say. It's very possible though. Who's the lawyer? Who's representing Karl?"

"His name's Christopher Hudgins."

"Hmm. And he wanted you to lie?"

Joel thought for a moment. "Not exactly. He asked lots of questions and more or less made it apparent what he was digging for."

"Did he threaten you or offer you a bribe?"

"Again, he was very careful. I mean, I certainly felt threatened. There's no doubt what he wants, what he's intimating. He keeps pointing out I didn't see what happened immediately before Karl cracked her—the split second right before—and that she was angry and arguing and slapped his finger away from her nose. Hudgins is trying to make it appear she was the aggressor."

"I'm not surprised."

"He also wanted me to talk to you and persuade you to drop the case."

"He—"

"But that's not why I'm here," Joel hastened to add.

"It's unethical to threaten you with a civil action to gain an advantage during a criminal proceeding. I don't care how he song-and-danced it, it seems obvious he's squeezing you. I think I'll give him a call and let him know I'm considering a report to the state disciplinary committee. Let's see if that rattles his cage."

"I appreciate it, but he's going to say he merely gave me the facts, outlined his clients' position and tried to discover what my testimony would be. He doesn't seem like the type who'll be intimidated."

"We'll see," she said. "Let's call his bluff. You think they really want to go after Dixon Kreager in this town? Think they really want to have Karl questioned about his past record? And what would they receive if they somehow pull off the impossible and win? Hell, she had a cut and a few stitches you accidentally caused—that's their best-case scenario. What's it worth? A thousand bucks maybe? Two thousand? And I'm confident Dixon's insured."

"I'm not," Joel said. "Insured, that is."

"You were working for him. As his employee, you'd be covered."

"I don't want to bring Dixon any trouble. Or myself. I'm scared to death of lawsuits. I want to be clear of this as soon as possible."

"You'll be fine. Our lad Christopher's blowing smoke. You're not folding, are you? Getting ready to take a hike and leave me holding the bag?"

"No. I'm concerned, okay? But I'm sticking with you. I'll take the oath and tell the truth and let the chips fall where they may."

"Good," said Sophie, speaking for the first time. "You put the bastard behind bars, Ms. Allen. Joel will be there to do his part."

"I will," he added. "I'm telling you all this so you'll be prepared and can anticipate problems, not because I'm planning to change my story."

"I appreciate the notice," Lynette said. "I'll mention their threat to Dixon and make certain he's insured. But they'll never go through with it. Never. Not a chance. And I'll light a match under Hudgins and see how he likes a little heat himself."

"There we go," Sophie said, becoming animated.

"I've already alerted Dixon," Joel said. "He didn't seem too concerned, but I still worry about dragging him into a lawsuit."

"Believe me," Lynette said, "he can take care of himself."

"I just hope we don't wind up hurting innocent people," Joel remarked. "Lisa, the kids."

"Yeah—if we leave him alone, they'll have hospitalization insurance every time he punches one of them and plenty of money to pay for her plastic surgery. Or enough cash for a fine funeral with exquisite floral arrangements." The words were steeped in sarcasm. "Am I getting warm? I'm guessing you're hearing the same shopworn argument I've already heard from Lisa and heard in one shape or form a hundred times before."

"I'm not defending him," Joel protested. "I simply feel sorry for her and the kids, okay?"

"Let Ms. Allen handle those concerns, Joel. You're the witness, not their counselor." Sophie paused. "Or their minister."

Lynette lessened her tone. "Believe me, Mr. King, I don't want Lisa to suffer any further. I'm sensitive to her needs and the balancing I may have to consider at some point. Right now, though, the hard line best serves everyone."

"Okay," Joel said.

"Okay," Lynette replied. She glanced at a clock on her desk, didn't make any effort to conceal what she was doing. "And you have some other issues? Something else you wanted to discuss?" She was pleasant, conversational.

Joel rubbed his hands together and felt his joints freeze—his knees, ankles and knuckles solidified, lost their play—and his stomach seemed to vanish, leaving him with a vacant crater in his abdomen. The nausea he'd experienced at dawn briefly boiled, and his mind began to somersault and spew half thoughts and non sequiturs, misfiring. He was watching *Giant* . . . and Elizabeth Taylor was ladling water from a trough . . . and he careened to his mother at the library, reading Dr. Seuss. Then he was stopping to help a man in a green suit change a tire on a Buick, the man's wife wearing her Sunday dress and an elaborate hat, fanning herself and sipping orange soda as she watched them labor beneath the scorching sun. The photo of Baker when he was a newborn, a buffalo nickel, an eight-track of Louis Armstrong singing "Hello Dolly," the scent of his pastor's robe when—

"Joel, tell her." It was Sophie, drawing him back. "Don't just sit there like a bump on a log."

"Yeah . . ." he said, still partly missing, the tangents overtaking him.

Sophie snapped her fingers and barked his name. "Joel!"

"You're sure," he asked.

"I thought *you* were," she answered, agitated. "We came because you decided Ms. Allen was the person to help you."

"It's a big decision. Hard to know what to do. I'm so nervous my head is about to explode," he said, trying to contain the entropy.

"I'll be glad to help if I can," Lynette offered. "You okay? You look pale."

"Yeah. Thank you. I'm just scared. I've gotten myself into a whale of a jam."

"Something other than the difficulties with Karl and Lisa?" Lynette asked.

"Yes," Joel said. He stretched his legs, undid his knees, rotated his ankles. Inside his skull, a stooped woman wearing a purple shirt and straw boater was feeding a swarm of pigeons, tossing the birds stale bread crumbs. "Give me a minute, please."

"Certainly," Lynette said. "Would you care for some water?"

"No," Joel said. Here he was, bottom of the barrel, puny and dependent. How the mighty had fallen. He sat silently, noticed a line of tiny black ants winding out of the baseboard, the insects creating a small, fluctuating *S*.

Sophie was studying him, and it was obvious she loved him, always would. She touched the top of his hand, and the warmth and skin and humanity helped to anchor him and wring the last of the gibberish from his thoughts. "She is a good woman—you're right. Talk to her, Joel."

"I will," he said.

"Don't worry," Sophie encouraged him.

A faint ache flashed at one temple, but the confusion had blown through and was gone, and Joel had control of himself again. "Okay." He filled his lungs and sat erect, glanced at Sophie and began, his voice scratchy at first. He hadn't gotten too far along in his narrative when Lynette waved her hand and interrupted him.

"Whoa," she said. "Hang on here. You need a lawyer—I'm not the person who should hear this. You understand my job, correct? I can't help you or advise you or make any deal for you—I play for the other side. If you tell me something incriminating, I'm duty-bound to use it to your detriment."

"I understand," Joel assured her. "I know what you have to do. I also think you'll be fair about it."

"You want to confess to me? To sign up for some damn serious crimes? I promise you I'm going to march straight to the FBI and the state police. I don't have any other option."

"I recognize your responsibilities," Joel said calmly. He was steady now, his mind intact. "But I believe you'll help me as much as you can."

"Why would you think that? You've spent maybe an hour—total—with me. You don't even know me."

"I had a good feeling about you the first time we met, and Dixon believes in you, and Sophie does, too. And I've prayed over it and decided you're the person to approach with this. There's also the fact I don't have anywhere else to go. There's too much on me, too much weight, and I'm fresh out of escape routes."

"I'm advising you against this. I'll give you the name of a good criminal defense lawyer."

"No need. I'm going to keep talking, and you can either listen or not. Your choice."

"I want to tape you then. I'll record what you say along with my advice to you, and I'm going to read your Miranda warnings as well."

"Sure," Joel replied.

Lynette left and soon returned with a tape recorder. She set it in the middle of her desk, slightly closer to him than her. She asked his name and social security number and cautioned him and told him not to confess and recited his rights and urged him again to see a lawyer, and the machine witnessed it all. He said he fully understood everything and was doing what he wanted, that he had to clear his conscience regardless of the consequences. He started his spiel a second time, went back to his drive from the Roanoke jail and the intentional Cadillac wreck. Lynette cut him off as he was describing Edmund's performance at the emergency room, how there was a gleam in his eye and a reference to a "dollar-collar."

"You're positive you want to do this?"

"Yes," he said.

Joel told her an abridged story, a version that was wholly true but incomplete. He only informed her of his dealings with Edmund and Sa'ad and the jewelry, didn't see any reason to dredge up his fraud and purple-shirted stagecraft in Roanoke, or reveal how he'd combined with Christy to pick the bones of the church's insurance company. As far as he was concerned, Christy had rendered that issue moot when she'd snatched the entire check and left him dangling. He did add, almost as an afterthought, that the Virginia authorities were none too thrilled with him for contacting Christy before their deposition and would probably revoke his probation.

"My goodness," Lynette exclaimed when he finished. "What a swamp. And quite a fantastic saga. As we like to say, crime doesn't pay."

"Hasn't done much for me," Joel said.

"I told him from the outset he was acting like a fool," Sophie remarked. "Warned him till I was blue in the face."

"She did," Joel agreed.

"So what are you expecting me to do?" Lynette asked, the recorder continuing to run.

"Whatever you feel is correct. I'm leaving it up to you."

"Do you think the FBI would offer Joel a deal?" Sophie asked. "Could you check with them? He's a small fish—certainly they'd rather get to Edmund and Sa'ad. There's no telling what they've done. Once you got started, I bet you'd find so much crookedness that you could put them behind bars forever."

"I'll review this with Agent Woods initially. I prefer to stay local."

"Okay," Sophie answered.

"But I can tell you exactly what the cops will want. Evidence. Something hard. Or maybe some cooperation—a body wire or a monitored phone call."

"Never, ever work," Joel said. "They're far too clever. They always frisk me. They never say squat on the phone, and they know the FBI's listening. Sa'ad even whispers in the middle of town and runs the water at the restaurant's bathroom. No, you can forget that, especially now with their antennae raised."

The recorder clicked off, two plastic buttons popping up simultaneously. Lynette flipped the cassette and restarted the machine. "So we have a problem. We prosecuting attorneys don't like swearing contests, and I'm sure the U.S. attorney will share my view if this lands in federal court. We'd have you—a disgraced criminal preacher on the verge of doing a second jail stint—and your words, words that came only when you were about to get arrested for a very serious crime. Sa'ad and Edmund will deny everything, and we have nothing to support your version of events. Can you think of anything to connect these guys to your story?"

"I have a letter," Joel offered.

"Oh?" Lynette keened her head.

"From them," Joel added.

"What kind of letter?" she asked.

"About meeting them to return the Las Vegas jewelry."

"They're so brilliant that they wrote you a letter detailing the crime?"

"Well, uh, sort of. It's in code."

"I see," she said warily. "And let me speculate—it's typed, not signed, and they aren't mentioned by name."

"True," he said. "But it has a Las Vegas postmark."

"Wow. There's the break we'll need," Lynette answered, her tone not as cynical as her words. "Bring it by, and I'll take a look at it. It's probably a waste of resources to check for prints and DNA, but we'll see what happens. Anything else?"

"I know Edmund drove Joel to Montana, to my house," Sophie offered. "I was there, I saw him myself. Driving a white Cadillac that was dented and wrecked."

"We'll require more than Edmund being generous to his former preacher and transporting him across the country as a favor."

"I would think the little things add up after a while," Joel suggested.

"They do," Lynette replied. "They add up to something little. Get my drift?"

"The only other connection is that I went gambling with them in Las

Vegas. I saw a program on the Travel Channel about casinos, how they video everything with this 'eye in the sky' camera, so I'm sure we got filmed. We were playing blackjack."

"How long ago?" she asked.

"Several months. I can check the exact dates. It was at the Mirage Hotel."

"Still doesn't prove much. Unless they gave you the jewels on camera, and I'm certain we're not going to be so fortunate."

"Hardly. By the way, I flew to meet them under an assumed name. At their insistence." Joel's voice was spiritless. "I realize that doesn't help matters any."

"You lie a lot for a man of the cloth," Lynette said.

"I was trying to . . . to get on my feet and take care of my sister and her boy." Joel was ashamed, everything about him downtrodden.

Lynette sighed. "I wish we had more."

"But I do have proof, don't I?" Joel suggested. "I had the jewelry. What could be stronger evidence?"

"*You* had the jewelry. We've got to show some irrefutable link to *them*. Otherwise, the state is left with the last-ditch accusations of a convicted scoundrel stacked against the denials of a member of the bar and a successful businessman."

"But how could I have gotten the jewelry and known how to engineer a scam like this? No judge or jury's going to think I was working solo."

"Doesn't matter. We have to demonstrate beyond a reasonable doubt *who* you were conspiring with, not just leave the jury with a hunch you probably, might have, could have, should have gotten some assistance. We're where we started, Mr. King. We have your word, and it's a very compromised word even on a good day."

"You believe Joel, don't you?" Sophie asked her.

"Actually, I do. But it's not what I believe, you know? It's what I can prove, and I'm afraid the fine folks who call the shots are going to want more than you can provide."

"Meaning what?" Joel asked.

"I'll pass the information along and see what the reaction is. But honestly, you're not bringing much to the dance. My guess is they'll use what you've told them, say thanks, and bust the hell out of you for insurance fraud. They'll take you federal. You can pull the time after you've finished the six-month probation violation in Virginia. Sorry."

"What am I facing?"

"I have no idea. It does help you've come forward, but I wouldn't count on fishing for several seasons."

"You don't think they'll blame him for the museum, do you?" Sophie asked. "The painting?"

"I wouldn't rule it out. They're under a great deal of pressure and scrutiny. And they've got him in exclusive possession of stolen goods and lying about where he obtained them." Lynette wasn't sounding sympathetic.

"You know I didn't rob a museum. I probably could account for where I was, if I have to. There's no way I'm guilty of anything involving their stupid art—you know it and they know it. And what about their promise to me, telling me to help them and they'd take care of me?"

"I guess we'll see," she replied. "It's not like they'll give you life or something. You're smart to come forward, and everyone will appreciate your trying to help. But you're not going to walk away with a new suit, reward money and a certificate of commendation from the president. You can't break the law and act as you please and then have it all wiped clean because you're finally telling the truth and promising not to sin again. The legal world's a little different than the religious world in that regard. We still punish you even if you ask to be forgiven."

"You can assure them I'll be honest and cooperative." Joel hesitated. "But I'll only speak with you. There's no reason from them to call or come by or park in the driveway or harass me at work."

"Your prerogative," Lynette said.

"Thank you, Ms. Allen," Sophie said. "Please take care of Joel. He's not a bad man."

Lynette picked up a yellow pencil and relaxed in her chair. She targeted Joel with the eraser end, held the lead tip between her thumb and index finger. "Maybe not. But I can't see where he's been a real good one, either."

"But you'll look after him?" Sophie pleaded.

"I'll honor my job, as I warned you going in. I'll try my best to see he gets what he deserves, no more and no less. And, yes, I'll probably do a little extra for him, though it will be because of Dixon and you, not because of anything particularly noble I've discovered about the Reverend King."

Despite Joel's requests to the contrary, Hobbes and his posse were at the Station when he arrived for his shift, and they were infuriated because he refused to speak with them and told them point-blank to quit badgering him. For whatever reason, they phoned early the next morning and made a trip to the house to pound on the door and deliver more threats, but they still didn't arrest him. Not long after they roared off, Sophie arrived home unexpectedly, schlepping through the kitchen with a sick Baker and a pharmacy bag full of pills and cough syrup. She put him in bed, poured herself a glass of orange juice and decided not to return to work, pointing out that it would be a bunch of driving for nothing. She called her boss and let him know, then tossed the cordless phone on the sofa.

"He's got a bad fever," she said. "Almost a hundred and one."

"Anything I can do?" Joel volunteered.

"Nope," she said. "A lot of kids at school have the same crud—it's a four- or five-day bug, I'm told."

"Poor guy," Joel said.

"I've got a date tomorrow evening, but if he's still running a temperature, I'll cancel."

"You want me to stay with him? I can see if Sarah will give me the night off."

"No. I already have a baby-sitter, but I don't want to leave him if he feels bad. In fact, I probably should call now and let Raleigh know."

"How's that progressing?" Joel asked. "Must be okay if you're still seeing him."

"Yeah, well, so far, so good. He seems like a nice man and has passed most of the important tests so far. He opens the car door for me; he listens more than he talks; he has custody of his kid; he doesn't refer to his ex as a dumbass or a slut; and when I checked his bathroom cabinet, there were no tampons or women's perfumes or antidepressants or Acyclovir prescriptions."

"I'm not familiar with the last item."

"Herpes medication," Sophie informed him. "Plus his tub was clean, no grime or hair in the drain, and his towels weren't stinky."

"Pretty high standards," he kidded her.

"Actually they are."

"So you looked in his cabinets? Without his knowing?"

"Damn right I did. In my opinion, the finest resume available. And I don't recall his telling me not to." She finished her juice and set the glass on the floor.

"Good luck. Hope he pans out for you."

"I'm having fun and taking it one day at a time. It's difficult to trust someone, but there's a lot to be lost if I don't try. Seeing what's happened to you has made me realize that life is short and tricky. I might as well enjoy it."

"I'm glad I could be helpful."

"Yeah, the supreme example of how I don't want to wind up." She winked. "And you? You're not in chains, so I assume there's nothing to report?"

"Hobbes and his crew stopped by work yesterday and then came out here this afternoon, but I ignored them and sent them packing. According to the information Hobbes bellowed from behind the door, Lynette has arranged a meeting for tomorrow. I'll check with her, but that would make sense."

"Did he say what they wanted? Or what they had in mind for you?"

"No," Joel said.

"Did he sound angry?" she asked.

"It wasn't a bridge-bid tone, so I'd have to say he's rankled, yes."

"Damn, Joel. I'm worried sick about you. I wish I'd . . . I'd . . . I don't know. I wish I hadn't leaned on you so hard to come clean. Now I'm afraid you're going to get screwed."

"I've prayed and confessed my sins and petitioned for forgiveness. Your advice was splendid. I'm okay, better than I've been."

"Splendid?" she mocked him.

"Splendid," he smiled.

"I hate to keep going back and forth and changing my mind and switching advice, but I'm scared to death for you. One minute something seems right, the next minute it seems stupid."

"At a minimum, I won't fall into any more trouble or make things worse."

Sophie started to answer him and was interrupted by the phone. She stretched to the last cushion and grabbed the receiver by the antenna, held it to her ear. She said hello and said yes twice and then blocked the lower part of the phone with her hand. "It's Lisa Dillen," she whispered. "She sounds upset."

Joel took the phone, and Lisa rushed through what her attorney had already detailed, describing her child's handicap and the hardships a conviction would bring to their household, imploring Joel to help her. Karl had promised to undergo counseling, she told him, and it was her life and her decision and why was everyone so determined to butt in? She would be the one punished if Karl got convicted, she and her children. She was the so-called victim, and she was satisfied, so why—why—couldn't this end?

"Ma'am, I've got to be honest with you," Joel answered. "I'm going to iron my good shirt, drive into town, take the oath and tell the truth. And the truth is the man beat you."

"But he won't ever again. And it's no one else's business."

"Lynette Allen's a fair woman—maybe if Karl were to plead guilty, she'd try to find a compromise everyone could accept."

There was a voice in the background, spotty and uneven, difficult to understand. Joel strained to hear, and then Karl appeared on the line, hot and seething right off the bat. "Listen, you piece of shit," he stormed, "I'll ruin your life if you don't get with the program. We've found out the ugly particulars about you and how you enjoy screwing teenage girls, what a freakin' joke you are. My lawyer told you what we're prepared to say, and we're not kidding you. You want a monster lawsuit, you keep right on spouting your bullshit version, and I'll own you and your buddy's crummy business."

"I'm not sure I follow you, Karl. You're planning a suit? What are you going to say?"

"Either you say Lisa started it, or I'll nail you with splittin' her head. Just like Mr. Hudgins promised you." He was still raging.

"Oh. Well, you did hit her, Karl. Punched her like a yellow coward," Joel baited him. "Struck a girl."

"And when I get a chance, I'll give you twice what she got, fisherman. You hear me?"

"I do." Joel was exuberant. "And I'm guessing a few others do too, you fool." He didn't listen any longer, simply held the phone at arm's length and motioned for his sister to take it while Karl's scratchy, long-distance rants bled from the earpiece and died unheard, rose and dissolved into nothing. "Here," he said. "I'm not usually a fan of cursing, but this sorry scum needs a good talkin' to. Lay it to him. Try to remember we're bugged and the FBI's listening. He's already admitted everything, so it's all sport from here on out. Catharsis."

Sophie snatched the phone and lit into Karl, called him a "baby-dicked shithead" for starters, and Joel huddled beside her and laughed and giggled like a gleeful teenager who'd discovered the combination to the family liquor cabinet, enjoyed her going toe-to-toe with Karl, found it perfect that the wife-beater was getting flogged by a smart, fearless woman who had a construction worker's knack for profanity and the courage of a Trojan foot soldier.

nineteen

The meeting with Hobbes, Starke, and Woods took place at Lynette's office, late in the evening, at eight o'clock. Sarah became understanding when Joel explained he was an important witness in a court proceeding— spousal abuse, he informed her, true enough but misleading—and needed an hour of personal time to confer with the authorities. She told him not to hurry, and Frankie promised he'd pull double duty until Joel returned to the Station. Lynette was waiting in the lobby of the Missoula County Courthouse, let him through the oversize security doors and locked the entrance behind them. It appeared everyone had departed for the day— offices were dark, passageways were empty and a headphoned janitor was buffing the floor with an electric machine, the brushes whirling, the cord stretching thirty feet to a receptacle at the opposite end of the hall. Lynette didn't speak as she guided Joel through the somber, musty corridors, stay-ing a stride ahead of him—a detached distance that made it apparent she had no desire for cordiality or friendly chitchat.

The five of them convened in a windowless conference room with an oblong table, seedy chairs, bluish carpet and ineffective fluorescent light-ing. Joel was relieved to discover his probation officer hadn't been invited; there was no sign of Howard, and Joel was grateful the slithering proba-tion newt wouldn't be involved in negotiating his fate. Everyone except Lynette Allen had a file or folder, and everyone was immaculately dressed, especially Anna Starke, who was wearing a fashionable suit and heels that seemed too expensive and suggestive for government work in Washington and were certainly remarkable for Missoula. They all stood as Joel and Lynette entered the room and sat after offering strained, perfunctory greetings. Hobbes uttered a bare "good evening," had difficulty with even that meager politeness.

Hobbes had assumed the head of the table, and he took the lead in speaking to Joel. Hobbes's overcoat was obsessively folded and draped over the seat next to him, his file shut but within convenient reach. "So, Mr. King," he said, "you finally decided to honor us with your presence."

"I've always been willing to help."

Hobbes sped through the standard warnings and rights, and Joel had now heard them so many times that he actually recited the last phrase along with Hobbes—"one will be appointed for you," he mouthed simultaneously with the agent. "I know the drill," Joel remarked.

"Ms. Allen has detailed your story to us," Hobbes said.

"Okay."

"As I understand it, you're telling us you obtained the Jewish Museum jewelry from one Sa'ad X. Sa'ad and one Edmund Brooks to use as bait in an insurance scam, then returned the items to them."

"That's it in a nutshell," Joel replied.

"I see. And you have no proof except the two letters you've already provided to Ms. Allen?"

"I mentioned to her I was at the Mirage playing blackjack with them. I'd hoped the security recordings would confirm we were there."

Hobbes surveyed the table before responding. "We have the cassettes. They do show you, Sa'ad and Brooks. Along with your wholesome dates for the night."

"Hey—I'd never seen that girl before, didn't invite her, didn't lay a hand on her and went home alone. Are we clear on that?"

"Whatever," Hobbes answered.

"So you know I'm being honest," Joel said. "The tapes bear me out."

"The tapes show what they show," Hobbes said. "You and your buddies gambling and cavorting with trashy women. The tape, the letters and a buck will buy us a junior bacon cheeseburger at Wendy's, tax not included."

"I'm sorry I don't have more evidence. But I'm telling the truth."

"We believe you are," Anna Starke said, her voice throaty and rich. "The agency has confirmed that Mr. Abel Crane does in fact own a Las Vegas cleaning business. His given name, of course, isn't Abel Crane. He performs this service for the thirty-thousand-square-foot mansion of one of our old friends, Mr. Peter Van Heiss. Mr. Van Heiss loves fine art and has been on the fringe of many suspect exchanges and disappearances."

"Well, there you go," Joel said, relieved.

She leaned closer, and her watchband grazed the table. "But I'm afraid we're nowhere near the payoff, Mr. King." She adjusted the watch, pushing it underneath her cuff.

"Exactly. My opinion exactly," said Woods.

"We'd get a complete shredding if we went to trial with what we have now," Hobbes said. He stared at Joel, allowed himself a smile that evolved into a chuckling taunt. "You guys—what colossal screwups. Steal—excuse me, borrow—jewelry that turns out to be hot as a two-dollar pistol. What're the odds, huh? You must be feeling pretty stupid. The gang that couldn't shoot straight."

"To be honest, Mr. Hobbes, I've simply tried to forget it and remedy matters to the best of my ability." Joel glowered at him. "And I'm sick and tired of your ridicule. I'm ready to take my punishment, but I'll be damned if I'm going to sit here while you demean my efforts to set things straight." It was the first time Joel could recall using profanity since he was a seminary student.

"I don't need a lesson on manners and respect from a petty swindler and a child molester." Hobbes's voice and expression were implacable. "You can like it or not like it, and it's all the same to me."

Lynette was seated next to Joel. "I'm not sure this is productive, gentlemen," she said. "It's fair to say everyone is aware of your efforts, Mr. King. It's also fair to say they're somewhat self-serving and calculated. But there's no need to dwell on the topic any longer, is there? And there's no need to be anything but professional and civil. At this juncture, the question is how to best accomplish our respective goals. Mr. King, you want the least possible punishment, and the government hopes to recover the painting and arrest those responsible for its theft."

"I hope everyone present realizes I'm in charge of this investigation," Hobbes said.

"No one has intimated otherwise," Lynette answered, her tone matching his.

"Don't you think we've got enough for a warrant?" Woods suggested. "We've got Mr. King's statement, we know he had the ring, his story checks, he has these letters—how much more do you folks need? I'd apply for a warrant, go to Vegas and toss this guy Van Heiss's domicile."

"And if we miss?" Hobbes said. "If the painting's gone or if we can't find it, we're history. The ring might be at his house, but it doesn't follow that the Chagall will be. We reveal our hand too early and we're hosed. Van Heiss could abscond overseas or unload the painting. We know he has it; now we need to know exactly *where* he has it."

"Bust him on the ring," Woods said.

"We don't want the ring," Anna Starke explained. "Besides, he probably has bogus papers and will swear he obtained it legitimately. It would be impossible to do that with the Chagall."

"Why would anyone want a painting he couldn't display?" Joel asked, looking at Anna Starke for an answer.

"To own it, to possess it, to have something spectacular and rare that no one else can duplicate. To be in the same room with genius. It's hardly about displaying it, Mr. King. These people are far beyond that. There's a whole subculture that lives and breathes fine art. Why do legitimate collectors pay millions for pieces that will never see the light of day? It's not like you're going to hang the Rubens above the poker table at the hunting cabin or put it in your den, even if you acquired it honestly."

"Seems strange to me," Joel replied.

"Try this: If you, clergyman that you are, could have Martin Luther or John Calvin or Christ himself secretly live in your basement, wouldn't you do it? Damn straight you would." Anna Starke's tone was didactic, bordered on condescension. "For goodness sakes, people maim each other over Beanie Babies and Depression glass and Secretariat decanters and playoff tickets, and you're asking me why someone would steal a permanent glimpse into sheer, unique loveliness?"

"Maybe," Hobbes sneered, "the illustration would be more instructive for Mr. King if you gave him a chance to meet, say, Larry Flynt or the last living Sadducee."

"What—you take a basic religion class at night school while you were completing your GED?" Joel smirked at Hobbes.

"Yeah," Hobbes answered. "Probably the same course they teach at the pokey. Adult education, it's called. You'll have the opportunity for a refresher real soon."

"How about the ring? Strange your guy'd be so careless there," Woods interrupted, trying to maintain the peace.

"The perils of a bimbo wife," Hobbes suggested. He continued to sear Joel but halted their tit-for-tat.

"And let's not forget," Starke said, "that the jewelry was stolen from their safe. It's not as if she strolled into the FBI office with the red sister around her neck on a chain. Plus, it's the kind of item he could give her and she could wear in certain circles without any suspicion. Out of context, the ring is fairly nondescript. It's not too incriminating unless you have the whole puzzle arranged, although I would imagine our friend Peter told his ditzy wife to keep it under lock and key until the furor died down."

"As was mentioned earlier, it's a piece of cake to get a bogus set of papers and a receipt, claim you've been shanghaied by unscrupulous dealers if you're ever caught. The ring's easy." Hobbes appeared eager to showcase his insight and let everyone know he was as schooled as his fellow agent.

"Gotcha," Woods said.

"So we find ourselves, Mr. King, in a position where you really can't do much for us," Hobbes concluded. "We want the painting, and you can't take us any closer to Van Heiss."

"I would assume the FBI has an interest in halting widespread, systematic insurance fraud," Lynette remarked. "This guy Sa'ad and his buddy apparently are very significant operators."

Anna Starke looked at her. "Not at the expense of my painting," she said, the first time the two women had addressed each other. And—suddenly, instantly—it became obvious to Joel who was calling the shots, despite Hobbes's insistence that he frame the questions and sit at the head of the table and proclaim himself prince of the investigation. Joel envisioned him seated on Anna Starke's knee with an opening in his shoulders for her to insert her hand and manipulate his wooden lips and notched chin.

"I agree," Hobbes said.

"So why am I here?" Joel wondered.

"For us to have a look at you," Hobbes answered. "See if there's anything else you can tell us."

"You know what I know," Joel said, his spirits flagging.

Lynette focused on Anna Starke. "Let me make sure I'm understanding you. You plan to ignore Sa'ad and Brooks and punish Mr. King, who's helping you, because you're afraid of alerting Van Heiss or losing the trail of this painting? Is that what I'm hearing?"

Anna Starke met Lynette's stare and responded in her textured voice. "I want the Chagall. How does arresting Sa'ad take me there? We have a disconnect here, Ms. Allen. I have a global problem, whereas you're concerned with a couple of con men ripping off an industry that hardly has a history of clean hands. We often turn a blind eye when the bad guys shoot each other. If we apprehend Sa'ad and Abel Crane along the way, good for us. If we don't, but recover the art, I'll nevertheless be delighted. And right now I'm not about to roust this Crane guy and pin the ring on him so Van Heiss can see me coming from a mile away and stash the grand prize."

"But you still intend to prosecute Mr. King? Slay the minnow while the sharks swim out to sea?" Lynette packed the question with disapproval.

"The fact Sa'ad and Brooks are guilty doesn't make Mr. King any less guilty, now does it, Miss Allen?" Hobbes said, his air self-satisfied and conceited. "Let one murderer go free because the other two happen to escape the scene? You good people in state court going to stop prosecuting speeding tickets because everybody does it and you don't catch them all?"

"It's the good people in state court who are doin' the dirty work, diggin' the trenches and risking our lives while you guys jet around hunting for a damn hoity-toity painting," Woods snapped. "When's the last time you and the professor here got to arrest a crackhead with a pistol or sat up all night in the woods freezing your butt off doin' surveillance?"

"No one would ever discount the importance of and danger in what you do, Agent Woods," Anna Starke replied. She puffed the "of" and "in."

"There's no need for us to be having this debate," Lynette said. "Mr. King has broken the law and deserves to be punished. I merely hope you will honor your commitment to him and see that he's treated fairly."

"He'll get what he deserves," Hobbes said.

Anna Starke focused again on Lynette. "I will see to it our attorneys are aware of his cooperation. I've never hinted to the contrary. I will recommend he receive appropriate consideration."

Months ago, tending to the predictable problems of his congregation, writing sermons, visiting nursing homes, scheduling bake sales and congratulating new mothers at the hospital—sealed inside the protective boundaries of the cloth—Joel could never have imagined how rough and tumble the secular world really was, how truth frequently took a circuitous route to arrive at its destination, leapfrogging, doubling back, hopscotching, detouring, sometimes becoming lost for days, sometimes disappearing altogether. "Call if you need me," he said to everyone at the table, then walked out of the room and through the gloomy building, by himself until the custodian let him out and wished him a good night.

The following morning was unseasonably mild, and Joel decided to visit the country church he'd discovered upon first arriving at his sister's, embarked on the trip mindful of how satisfying it was to be outside in the sweet winter air, aware that he might soon be returned to jail. He paused at the neighbors' pasture to pet the horses, and crouched and beckoned their skittish mutt to come nearer and have its stomach tickled. The sun had gotten the better of the cold by the time the church came into sight, and a pair of eagles sailed from a stand of trees, beat their wings to gain altitude, then commenced a languid, stately glide.

When Joel got close enough to read the church's sign, its black vinyl letters delivered the week's wisdom: DON'T GIVE UP. MOSES WAS ONCE A

BASKET CASE, TOO. A pickup was parked near the entrance, and the door was unlocked when Joel tried the knob. He went inside, waited for his vision to adjust to the middling light.

It felt as if the heat wasn't working; the sanctuary was chilly, still held the aftertaste of the previous night's cold, the trapped air no warmer than the day outside. Joel didn't remove his coat and took a seat on the front pew, bowed his head, closed his lids and allowed his mind to drain until there was nothing left in his thoughts. He remained on the unyielding oak for some time, pensive and meditative, emptying himself of every notion and impulse, making space for the Lord to alight and suffuse his spirit.

He didn't know how long had passed when he noticed a vibration, a trembling shock in his feet that connected him to the building and made him aware of his arms, legs, and hands again, wrestling him back from his worship. Next there was a boom and then a rough banging, metal colliding with metal, rising from the bowels of the church. He listened for more sounds, cocked his head toward the floor. He waited but didn't hear anything else. A brass cross and two collection plates were arranged on a table beneath the pulpit, the cross's glossy finish muted by the dim surroundings.

The banging started again, this time fierce and sustained, and Joel was able to pinpoint where it was coming from. He left the sanctuary through a side door, followed a set of steps into an ample finished basement and startled a man propped on his forearm and rib cage, repairing an ancient oil furnace. The man was using a monkey wrench to adjust a fitting, and pipes, tools, couplings, a soldering iron and several smeared rags were scattered next to him. He had thick brown hair and was wearing jeans and a flannel shirt, and he fumbled his wrench when Joel spoke.

"Oh my. You gave me a heckuva scare," he said, holding a hand to his chest. "I didn't hear you come in." He stood up and wiped both palms on his pants, slap-brushed the dirt on his shirt.

"I'm sorry," Joel said. "I didn't mean to sneak up on you."

"No problem. I don't think we've met. I'm Harlan Hunter, the pastor here. I'd shake hands, but I'm so filthy I'd make a mess of you."

"I'm Joel King. I live down the road with my sister, Sophie. The door was open, so I came in. I hope that's okay."

"Of course it is. You're welcome anytime. Everyone's welcome in the Lord's house."

"I was upstairs praying and meditating, and I heard the noise. I take it your furnace is on the fritz."

"Yes sir," Hunter replied. "And I'm not sure I can fix it."

"Shame," Joel said sympathetically.

"Yep."

"Can I do anything to help?" Joel asked.

"I might have you grab that tank line while I take a hacksaw to it, keep it from floppin' around."

"I'd be glad to," Joel said.

"If you don't mind."

"No problem," Joel told him.

"And I guess I should properly welcome you to our church and see if I can do anything for you," Hunter said. "Not often we have newcomers stoppin' by to pray on a weekday. Hard enough to get folks here on Sundays." He laughed at his own observation.

"Uh, well, no. I just enjoy the walk from home and the silence and appreciate having a church close by."

"Come anytime," Hunter said, and Joel noticed his eyes were watery, irritated. Probably from the fuel oil or squinting to do fine work on a wire or motor part.

"What kind of congregation are you?" Joel asked. The sign above the slogan board noted the church's name, the TRUE VINE GOSPEL CHURCH, and stated there were services on Wednesday evenings and Sunday mornings, visitors welcome.

"We're a 'Word' church, independent, open to anybody who loves the Lord and believes in the absolute, unerring truth of the scriptures."

"Good." There was a little too much charisma and salesmanship in the description for Joel's taste. "Good for you."

"Are you churched, Joel?" Harlan Hunter asked. "Saved?"

"Yes. I attend the Baptist church in town and was baptized at nineteen." The preacher's pushiness was making Joel uneasy.

"Well, if you're ever of a mind to pay us a visit, the doors are always open. We'd love to have you and your sister, too. Excitin' things are happening here. The Holy Spirit is conquerin' Satan and claimin' lives."

"Maybe I will. Thanks."

Reverend Hunter positioned himself on the floor again, and Joel knelt beside him and held the copper line that fed oil from the tank. Hunter had to access the pipe from underneath, and he was on his back, peering up at Joel. He began sawing into the metal, made cramped half strokes back and forth across the copper while Joel kept it braced. After a few moments, Joel smelled something odd over the pungent scent of the oil, caught a powerful whiff of alcohol, a stray scent that became stronger as Hunter exhaled and continued to labor and sweat. The surprise popped into Joel's eyes and became obvious in his features, and Hunter halted his cutting, wriggled and wormed and said, "Oh, that. That's cough syrup. I've been sick with the flu." The smell of whiskey got stronger when he spoke, belying the hasty fib, and Joel held fast to the pipe, nodded and told the preacher it had been a bad season for sickness.

As Joel departed the building, he assured himself it was meaningless in a sense, this man's drinking, and there was—for Joel—a definite profit gained from the alcoholic minister's plight and transparent lie. Harlan Hunter had an Achilles' heel, sure, but he was nevertheless fighting the fight, not succumbing, not yet. He was where he was supposed to be, tending to a cranky, antiquated furnace, skinning his knuckles and ruining his clothes, and the drinking could have been anything, from a palmed collection-plate twenty to a crack in his faith, but the flaw was still servant to his determination, only an ugly habit or a few stitches in his overall humanity, a petal, a capillary, a piston, a brush stroke, a piece but hardly the whole. Joel drew a guilty comfort from the man's foibles, was able to shed a measure of his own self-loathing, realized that he and the poor fellow and everyone else were alike, clay and dust, forever imperfect, hamstrung by the Fall and a snake's beguiling charm but still precious in the Lord's eyes.

The walk home to Sophie's was pleasant, brightened by a complete stranger coasting to the side of the road and offering him a lift, which he declined. The furnace was operating when he'd left, fixed good as new, and that cheered him as well, knowing that he'd helped warm the church and taken some of the load off Harlan Hunter.

Upon arriving home from True Vine, Joel found Baker's clothes and sheets deposited in front of the washer and dryer, the clothes heaped into a pile, the sheets stretched their full length across the basement floor, lugged by a corner to their destination and dropped, white carcasses that extended ten feet along the cement, the tail ends barely missing the last stair step. Even though his sheets could have used more effort, the boy had turned his pockets inside out, bless his heart, just like Joel had asked him to. It was Sophie who was careless in that regard, left bottle caps, coins, ink pens, tissues, napkins and credit card receipts in her pockets so Joel often wound up with Impressionist loads and saturated specks of paper clinging to every garment in the wash. He'd kidded her about it several times, prodding her to be more attentive. "It would help Mr. French," he'd joked, "if Sissy could perhaps empty her pockets and unroll her socks before tossing everything in the laundry."

"Why don't you check for yourself, Joel? It's not like I have nothing else to do. How difficult is that?"

"I always try, but sometimes I forget or overlook a pocket. It's no big deal—I didn't mean to start a fight."

She'd stared at him, entertained and vexed at the same time. "Damn, Joel, you can be such an old maid. I can do my own clothes if it's going to weigh on you so heavily. I've made it okay by myself so far."

"It was only a suggestion. I'll continue to chimp-pick the clots and paper fleas off entire baskets. Not a problem. It's my responsibility to double-check."

Joel decided to do a load of whites and his own sheets, poured in bleach and ran the water hot. He piddled upstairs and rested on the couch while the machine clicked through its cycles, then tossed the wet lump into the dryer and filled the washer with dark pants and shirts. Immediately after he set the dryer and it began to tumble the sheets and underwear, he heard a scraping inside, and he thought of Sophie, wondered what it could be this time, hoped for quarters or dimes and not another tube of lipstick. He interrupted the machine, reached in and groped along the bottom, didn't discover anything. It occurred to him that the machine might be broken, the knocking from a screw or bolt sheared loose and rattling in the drum, because what in creation could she have left in her undergarments that was causing the racket? He removed the clump of saturated cloth, placed it on the floor and began searching for the problem, separated panties, bras, T-shirts and Baker's briefs from the sheets.

It took a minute—his hands were moist and his knees had begun to ache from squatting—but he found the source of the noise: a hard bump at the margin of the fitted sheet, concealed just under the elastic. He flipped the edge and then stood up, staring at his discovery the entire time. A little head rush hit him, but it really wasn't much, sort of a blip or two, and that was it, all he felt at first even though he was excited. He bit his lower lip, twice, to make sure he wasn't still supine on the sofa, dozing, dreaming, his mind spawning impossibly good fortune.

Returning to the laundry, he bent over and quick-touched the tiny stones and damp metal, used only his index finger and jerked away instantly, as if the ring were scalding or toxic to anyone foolish enough to come in contact with it. The ring. There it was, the ring, the missing ring, the green sister, the gash along its side caught on an elastic thread in the crinkled, bunched lip of the sheet, a thousand-to-one shot, barely snagged. Joel thrust a fist into the air and thanked the Lord. "Hallelujah," he shouted, and couldn't stop smiling. This was a start, he was convinced, the beginning of his delivery, the godsend that would take him away from Pharaoh and out of Egypt. "Hallelujah!"

When he finished his celebration, Joel placed the ring in a sock and taped it to the top side of a drain pipe that bisected the basement's ceiling. He knew the discovery was important, that it held the genesis of his restoration and the answer to his miseries, but he wasn't certain what he needed to do. He'd learned a lesson though, yes he had, and this time he simply hid the jewelry and waited for inspiration, didn't go off half-cocked and by himself, armed only with falsehoods, deceits and his own inadequate devices. He finished the laundry, listened to an NPR story about the cold war and reported to work early, humming a Baptist hymn as he entered the Station's kitchen.

A table of Hollywood producers and movie people visited the restaurant for dinner and ordered every appetizer on the menu. They took drunk and distributed intoxicated cash among the waiters and kitchen staff and paid Sarah to let them remain until three-thirty in the morning. Joel stayed, too, made eighty dollars extra and helped cook late-night hamburgers for the road, packed the food in a lettuce crate and led the drunkest partyers to a cab. As he and Sarah were returning to the entrance, walking side by side across the parking lot, he sneaked a glance at her and got caught, and she told him to cut it out, that it was never going to happen for him. Joel laughed and apologized, said he didn't mean to be a nuisance.

The climate reverted to normal for February, cold during the days and frigid when the sun disappeared and the blue sky turned to pitch with swaths of pinprick stars. Joel heard nothing else from Lynette or the FBI, went about his routine and took Baker to a movie with the extra cash from the Hollywood party at the Station, bought the boy a Cherry Coke and a mammoth vat of popcorn. He'd been at work for an hour on a busy Thursday evening when Sarah appeared in the kitchen and told him someone was asking for him and he needed to follow her. They went into Sarah's unorganized office, not much more than a closet with a minuscule desk and a phone, and Lynette Allen was waiting there, dressed in her work clothes, a gray suit and a blouse fastened at the neck. Lynette was standing, and there was scarcely enough room for the three of them.

She thanked Sarah for the help and apologized for the interruption, and

Sarah left, pointedly remarking as she stalked off that it was a hectic night and they were already lacking a waiter.

"I didn't expect to see you," Joel said.

"No?"

"I was betting on Hobbes and handcuffs." He smiled.

"Sorry to disappoint you." Lynette sounded tired.

"What brings you to the Station?" Joel asked.

"What brings me here is my friendship with Dixon Kreager, my empathy for your sister, my ethical duty as an attorney and my mild dislike of the federal government."

"Well, for what it's worth, I'm indebted to you for sticking up for me at our meeting. Thanks. I should've called or something."

She rested against Sarah's desk, and Joel could see her thigh's outline take shape in the fabric of her skirt. "I wasn't defending you. I was simply trying to make certain you were credited for your efforts and fairly punished for your crimes."

"Dixon was right about you."

"Don't wear that button out, Mr. King. You've pushed it to death."

"Sorry," Joel said.

"So here's where we are." Lynette rose from the desk, stood without support, her arms folded behind her, her hand clasping her wrist. "I'm here in person because I'm not sure about the phones. I think they've discontinued the intercept, but I'm not positive. I've spoken with Alden Hinton, the U.S. attorney for our district. Alden's not a bad fellow for a fed, and he's married to a girlfriend of mine from Bozeman. We've agreed to bypass Ms. Starke and her henchman Mr. Hobbes to some extent. You help us make the case against Sa'ad and Brooks, we delay the arrests so as to give Hobbes and Starke and their Washington handlers sufficient opportunity to corner Van Heiss and the painting, and you receive nine months federal time and a fine, two years probation. A single conviction for insurance fraud. The incarceration will be at a minimum-security facility—you can play volleyball and get pointers for your next crime from tax cheats and greedy CEOs. The Virginia sentence will be revoked, but you get to pull it concurrently—"

"Meaning what? Concurrently?" Joel questioned her.

"You serve the sentences simultaneously, together. It won't lengthen your stay—you'll do nine months, and the Virginia authorities can say they've revoked your sentence and punished you. It's a formality that allows them to cover their butts. The truth of the matter is they don't want to go to the trouble and expense of extraditing you over some worthless misdemeanor."

"That's not what I'm hearing. Detective Hubbard told me it was a done deal, that I was headed to Virginia for a probation violation."

"It's taken care of as part of the arrangement. There's a lot of bluff in our business."

"I don't want to go to another jail. I don't mind the pen, but I think I'd go crazy if I have to serve time back in Roanoke."

"You'll most likely wind up in Arizona, in a federal facility."

"Okay," Joel said. "So it's a given I have to do time?"

"Nine months. No negotiation. Take it or leave it."

"Ummm," Joel winced, the sound guttural and raw, as if he'd been punched in the stomach. "I hate going back. Lord knows I do. I'd thought there was a slim chance, a possibility, some way . . ." Almost a year of his life would be wasted. "Okay," he said softly, sadly.

"Here are the catches. One, you have to testify against Brooks and Sa'ad and tell the truth. Two, you have to work with us to obtain some type of hard evidence against them. This may take months, possibly years, and would include phone taps, wires, perhaps introducing an undercover agent to them. If you don't give us something we consider satisfactory, the deal's off and you're back to square one. We need something solid, something more than your unsupported story. Three, and most important to me, you must testify truthfully in the case against Karl Dillen."

"Sure," Joel said, reviving, his voice gaining character. "I was planning to anyway. Did you hear the stuff he said over the phone?"

Lynette appeared baffled, and Joel told her about his conversation with Karl, how he'd lured him into several incriminating statements. "I figured Hobbes and Ms. Starke would've clued you in, and I meant to tell you myself when we all met, but I got so flustered and disappointed that it slipped my mind."

"I'll certainly research it," she replied, a frown spreading through her lips.

"It should put the last nail in his coffin," Joel said. "He admitted hitting her."

"Great. Finally, we have to know for sure you had nothing to do with Christy Darden's disappearance."

Joel rolled his eyes. "Who put that idea in your head? That whole ridiculous theory is out of left field, just stupid and ludicrous. Did that Hubbard character tell you he thought I was involved?"

"Yes."

"And they're serious?"

"His thinking on it is, and here I'm quoting verbatim, 'it's possible the skunk knows more than he's letting on, but not probable.' Detective Hubbard informs me they have a reliable sighting they're pursuing, a tip that she and her boyfriend took her civil settlement and headed to the Caribbean. I guess they have you and your base instincts to thank for the funding, huh?"

"Wow, there's a big surprise." He wouldn't even respond to her dig about his misconduct.

"We want to start by trying some phone taps, then a face-to-face with you and Sa'ad."

"I've already told you they won't say diddly over the phone, especially now, and they always frisk me before we talk. You're setting me up to fail."

"We have some state-of-the-art transmitters and a few other cards up our sleeve. You do your part and let us take care of the rest."

"How do I know I'll really get the deal? Hobbes may override you, or something might go wrong, or someone might have a change of heart. From what you've said, I'll be banking on Sa'ad and Edmund making a mistake—and that's out of my control. On top of that, there's as much sleight of hand, trickery and lying on your side as there is with the guys in black hats. Hidden agendas, infighting, dissembling—everything but the by-the-book justice I studied in civics class. You blame me for being skeptical?"

"You'll have my word and the written promise of the United States attorney. I hope that'll be adequate. If not, then don't sign the agreement, and take your chances with Hobbes and Hubbard."

"Okay, okay, I'll enroll with you guys. That was my plan when I talked to you and came clean, and it's still my plan today."

"I'll see about the paperwork. And you're certain you want to continue on without a lawyer?"

"The deal is very decent. I don't see how a lawyer could do any better for me. I just wish I didn't have to be incarcerated. I'd thought, because of something . . . well . . . I'd acquired a sort of expectation recently, based on this occurrence several days ago . . . Oh, heck, I'm babbling. I need to shut up. I know I've been saying all along I don't mind going to jail, but when it finally hits home, it's a different story. Difficult." Joel paused. Lynette didn't provide him any relief, didn't speak or offer any sympathy in her body language. "What do you think will happen to Sa'ad and Edmund? Their punishment?"

She shrugged. "I have no idea."

"Edmund's actually a likable guy. I hate it for him."

"You'll get over it."

"May I ask you something?"

"What?" She sounded irate.

"Well, I discovered . . . I went to the library, and like Agent Starke said, there's a website for the FBI's stolen art program. I found it on the Internet."

"So?"

He dropped his head, focused on a cylinder full of pens and pencils at the edge of Sarah's desk. "There's a reward for the painting and jewelry."

Lynette's hands flew out from behind her, her face shrank and her eyes turned incendiary. She pointed at Joel. "Not for the thief, there isn't. Not for criminals. Have you lost your sanity? Do people like you ever stop trying to beat the system?"

"I'm not the thief," Joel said calmly. "And I wasn't planning to collect the money for myself."

"Good, because you won't be. Try to play this straight for a change, Mr. King."

"I am. I will."

"You better," she warned and pushed past him, left without saying anything else, shook her head the whole time she was walking to the exit. "Damn," he heard her mutter as she left the restaurant and merged into the night.

Joel was still befuddled, still uncertain what ought to be done, and he attempted to keep his mind uncluttered, waiting for the Lord's will to become apparent. He would tell the truth and practice his faith and do everything reasonable to remain patient, but the stark mention of jail was depressing him, and the euphoria of the green sister's discovery had totally vanished. He felt stymied, and the basement celebration seemed remote and watered-down, the delight dwindling to dismay as it became obvious he had a stolen ring but no inkling how he could use it to advance himself or mend his mistakes.

To compound his despair, he'd experienced pangs of paranoia the last couple days, wondered if *he* might be the unwitting whipping boy in the script, wind up busted with the stolen ring stuffed in a tube sock and taped to a plastic cellar pipe. He said silent words, asked for direction and aid in making sense of his situation, and watched from the office as Lynette cranked her car in the parking lot, his view cropped by the door frame and the limits of the front window.

As he was leaving, Joel noticed a sign on Sarah's desk, a revised set of guidelines she'd not yet posted. She'd written lost-and-found instructions for the staff, six paragraphs telling them what to do with forgotten hats, glasses, wallets, credit cards and purses. The first sentence advised the Station workers to MAKE EVERY ATTEMPT TO RETURN LOST PROPERTY TO THE OWNER IMMEDIATELY. Ah, Joel thought, now there's an idea, and he imagined himself seated at the foot of Sa'ad's lofty desk, asking questions and getting nowhere, Lynette and Woods eavesdropping from an unmarked car, incensed because Joel wasn't extracting any corroborating details from the cunning, shifty lawyer, he and Sa'ad trading Mona Lisa smiles, sparring silently, each certain he knew more than the other.

Right at that moment, an electrical surge coursed through the Station, and the illumination, machines, fans, stoves, neon beer signs, blenders and ice machines flickered and sputtered and went dead, and then sparked again. Diners glanced at the ceiling, and a pair of bar patrons toasted the power's restoration after the sudden glitch. It struck Joel, as a plan began to coalesce in his mind, that the disappointing events of the last months were beginning to lodge a maul's tapered steel blade between him and his faith, and for the first time since impassioned college union debates and the drowning death of an adolescent cousin, he gagged on his own beliefs and actually considered alternatives, allowed the possibility he might be deluding himself.

He felt flushed, sickly, and he stood faltering at the doorjamb and wondered if his pole star of two decades was celestial hokum, his rituals and litanies on a par with fezzes and Masonic passwords. There was such meager progress toward fulfillment, and his redemption was arduous, and he was staring at nine penitentiary months, and there were so many miles to go, and he was supposed to follow tenets contrary to every instinct known to mankind while agnostics, Hindus and robber barons lived blithely and died peacefully at ninety-five. Pagans prospered and missionaries perished in botched kidnappings. Perhaps the ring was a fluke, no more than a chunk of metal attached willy-nilly to an elastic band, the result of a loose drawstring and an automatic wash cycle rather than Providence's intervention.

Less than two weeks ago he was positive of his fate and good standing, rapturous, joyous and worshipping full throttle, and—snap, poof—now he was on the verge of another retreating-tide drift, unmoored and miserable. Maybe Sophie was correct, maybe there were three or four general rules, along with gravity and the laws of nature, and that was the extent of it, and he inhabited the world of a chaise-longue deity who'd created the earth and retired to mint juleps and a silver centerfold sun reflector. Or worse, perhaps the universe was simply a helter-skelter accident, a collection of atoms, chemistry, big bangs and quirks in the genes of dumb apes, and there was no sentry at the gate—religion was merely a well-executed scarecrow or the ultimate con game, just a grandiloquent hustle backed up by the threat of damnation and pitchforks.

As he added details to the schematic taking form in his head, he decided this was it, that this clear, creative plan streaming into his mind had to be the solution, the answer to his entreaties, and if it wasn't he shouldn't be held accountable for the mistake because the notions were arriving with the pomp and trimmings of a revelation. He was going to toss his homestead deed into the pot and bet the ranch—together with the dogma that had sustained him for so many of his years—on one card from the deck, on a whiff of misdirection and the dexterity of his five fingers.

Near the end of February, Joel and Lynette met with a Las Vegas detective and two Montana cops from Helena and tried to coax Sa'ad into an admission over the phone. They placed the call from the Missoula police station, and Agent Woods, wearing a suit and cowboy boots, arrived as they were dialing Sa'ad's number. The gear was basic, a pair of headphones and a recorder tied into Joel's line, and everyone was gathered around a table. "So this is state-of-the-art?" Joel asked as they were plugging in wires and testing the equipment. "You're going to listen on an extension?" He grinned at Lynette.

"We have to start somewhere," she told him.

"I feel like I'm armed with a slingshot and trying to destroy a Sherman tank."

"You better hope your aim's good," Woods said.

They instructed him not to force the conversation, to speak in code as always, to look at the large canvas and the long term. A word here, a reference there, and sooner or later the slips would multiply and give them what they required. Joel was barely nervous when the number started to ring, convinced the entire enterprise was a farce and there was nothing at stake. Joel recited the "my divorce" pass-phrase to the receptionist, and she promptly banished him to the heavy-duty classical music on hold, left him there for longer than usual and then returned to tell him Mr. Sa'ad was not available. She'd leave Joel's message and have Mr. Sa'ad return his call. "I'm at a pay phone," Joel fibbed, following his script. "Don't worry about it."

They tried again later in the day and got the same stonewall, kept at it for the remainder of the week and never got past the secretary. "I told you so," Joel said during the last attempt as he bounced his head in rhythm with the phone music and waited to hear Sa'ad's prerecorded message for the umpteenth time. Joel imagined a Serengeti beast, its nostrils flared and neck hair erect, sensing a shift in the wind or an aberrant odor and trotting away with springy steps, gone and more guarded than ever.

Next they had him attempt to ensnare Edmund, and this strategy proved equally unsuccessful. When Joel rang Edmund's home in Roanoke, the number had been disconnected, and everyone at the table in Missoula groaned, turning to Lynette with "what now?" expressions. "We go to them," she said, and Joel quickly agreed that was their only chance. "I'm ready," he said.

Joel was careful to keep Sophie abreast of each development, told her about his deal and the jail time and what he'd promised to do. She agreed with him that Lynette was being fair, and that they owed Dixon Kreager the sun and moon. When the phone plan was declared a failure, Joel advised Sophie he'd be traveling to Las Vegas to meet with Sa'ad, and he assured her he was sanguine about the trip, thought something might come of it. She seemed concerned, worried he might work for months and never catch Sa'ad and Edmund, might never satisfy the police. For no reason, she bought him a coconut cake from the grocery-store bakery and a new shirt from Sears, left the shirt on his bed with a silly card so he'd find it when he arrived home from the Station.

Without fail, Joel asked each night to be forgiven of his sins and reiterated the all-or-nothing nature of his plan, made it apparent to the heavens that he'd marshaled the totality of his faith and strapped it to this endeavor, was expecting either Antietam or a parade through the streets of Paris. He was nervous, anxious, keen to leave for Las Vegas.

On the last Saturday in February, they took Baker to High Pines for a visit with his Wild West grandma, and she doted on the boy even though she had no idea who he was, inviting him to her reading circle and saying bizarre things that made him laugh. They tried to persuade her to go for a ride in the Volvo, but she was afraid she'd miss lunch, wouldn't hear of it.

"It's shitty growing old," Sophie remarked on the drive home, cursing in front of her son. "Shitty to wear out like the flattened bristles of a toothbrush, to squirt urine when you cough and have your fingers curl into ghastly hooks." But there was something gentle and upbeat in her short outburst, a lesson imparted to her boy and her brother, a reminder to be thankful for sound health and the immediate moment. There was also a shared awareness of what they'd just experienced, a recognition of how blood and family kept them wedded to a giant continuity, how they were the three center segments in an arc that disappeared below the horizon line in both directions, a mother, her daughter and a whip-smart grandson. "You realize, Baker," Sophie said, "that I knew your grandma's mother, used to help her make chicken and dumplings. And one day you'll tell your kid's children that you knew Grandma Helen." And the boy got it, felt the same visceral bond, told his mom he thought it was cool, wished he could've met his great-grandmother and her mother, too.

That night, Sophie brought Raleigh to town and they went to eat at a pizza parlor, mingled their kids for the first time and carted Joel along as chaperon, jester and buffer zone. Raleigh was a kind, introverted man, and he was attentive to Sophie without being fresh or showy. He paid for everyone's meal and slid a satisfactory tip under the big tin pizza platter. Sophie and Raleigh were going to a student play at the university, and Joel was to take the boys for ice cream and hot chocolate, then home to Sophie's for movies, Sweet Tarts and video games. He was glad to do it, loved children, and Sophie gave him a wink and a compact wave after she and Raleigh had buttoned their winter coats and donned their gloves; she came back to the table and bussed his cheek and told him she loved him.

twenty

The trick, Joel came to realize, was how to differentiate between heaven-sent persuasion and his own wish list, how to separate holy marching orders from the vanities and narcissistic wants that cluttered his brain. The voices in his thoughts always sounded identical, and the ideas that wandered through his mind didn't carry labels or certificates of authenticity; the flashy, peacock counterfeits were just as impressive—at first blush—as the pedigreed article. He'd prayed for guidance and remained passive, malleable, and believed he'd discovered the Lord's will, had kicked tires and examined the fine print on every document. In the midst of his crisis of faith at the Station, wobbly and with his stomach in revolt, he'd been imbued with step-by-step wisdom, and there'd been ample opportunity since then for him to be warned or dissuaded if he were formulating trouble for himself. He'd been given the goods—who could dispute it?

Then again, how many other pilgrims had received their instructions—and been certain—and then done something obviously maniacal or self-serving, set out convinced of their righteousness only to discover the Almighty wasn't buying into their job change or car bomb or blood-transfusion refusal or well-intentioned fund-raiser? He'd been asked this question hundreds of times by his church members: "How can I tell?" they'd plead, so many of them anguished and tentative. Now that he faced the very same dilemma, he reflected on his stock answer and realized how facile it'd been, how he'd given them nothing of value. "You'll know," he'd frequently instruct his congregation, "you'll know because it's the Lord's desire, and it will swell your heart."

Recalling his own worthless advice, he shook his head and tried to imagine what the men and women of his church must have thought when he handed them little more than an open-ended tautology, a soothsayer's can't-miss wisdom. He looked at the keys of Sophie's antiquated IBM typewriter, stuck a sheet of paper on the black roller, pressed the "down" button on the far right side and watched the paper wrap and load. It was the first of March, a week after his last failed telephone efforts on behalf of the police, and Agent Woods would be at Sophie's in four days, ready to travel to Las Vegas for the next shot at Sa'ad. Joel started to type. "This is the hardest thing I've ever done," the letter began. He was using carbon paper, creating a duplicate of the original page. "Here we go," he said to himself. "Lord willing." He finished the letter and put the original and the copy in his sister's dinged metal mailbox, raising the scrawny red flag to signal the postman.

Joel slept well the night before departing for the meeting with Sa'ad, and he was dressed and groomed early, eager to leave for Nevada. To Joel's dismay, Hobbes arrived at Sophie's along with Woods, and the FBI agent was in particularly bad humor, upset because he'd been outflanked to some extent by Lynette and the U.S. attorney. "This is a wild goose chase," he grumbled as Joel put his overnight bag in the Taurus. "A penny-ante operation that'll probably cost us a year of work and ensure the loss of a priceless painting."

"In all fairness," Woods remarked, "you guys must've had a bad year, 'cause it was Mr. King who gave you most of what you know. You'd still be spinnin' your wheels and chasin' bad info if Ms. Allen hadn't done your homework for you."

"I doubt it," Hobbes said, but he didn't bother to elaborate.

Woods rode with Joel in the Taurus, and Hobbes followed them in a silver sedan. It took two days to reach Las Vegas, and Woods and Joel shared a hotel room the first night on the road. They talked about sports, politics, old movies and fishing, alternated NPR and country-and-western stations when they played the radio. Joel did most of the driving, but he became fatigued with three hours remaining to Vegas, and Woods handled the last stretch while Joel dozed with his head against the window, his sleep sterile and dreamless, the arid desert whizzing by at ninety miles an hour.

They'd had Joel make an appointment with Sa'ad under a fictitious name and required him to bring the Taurus in case Sa'ad checked the parking lot or asked how he'd gotten to Nevada. The appointment was at four o'clock. An hour beforehand Joel, Hobbes, and Woods met Harry Winton, the Vegas officer supervising the case, at the Stardust Hotel, took the elevator to the fifth floor and knocked on a door without a number. Winton and a colleague were waiting in a room that lacked a bed and dresser, and they gave Joel all manner of advice as well as a makeshift disguise: a hat, wig and sunglasses, amateurish enough that it would appear to be Joel's handiwork, not the creation of a police sting. They bugged his car and provided him with a fountain pen to place in his pocket, explaining how the miniature transmitter at the top of the device needed to remain outside the cloth, pointed toward Sa'ad. Don't act nervous, they coached him. Don't do anything suspicious. Be yourself.

"I'll try," Joel said. "To be honest, I'm pretty darn jittery."

"You better hope this goes well," Hobbes said, his demeanor menacing.

"No one could possibly want this to succeed more than I do," Joel vowed. He took a heavy breath, then exhaled through his mouth, fretted with his hands and flicked his tongue over his lips.

"I need to talk to you about one other matter," Woods said.

"Oh, what's that?" Joel asked. He stopped his hands.

"You know anything you're not telling us?" Woods asked. His approach was indirect and genial.

"About what?"

"About the friggin' Lindbergh baby. About the one-armed man," Hobbes snapped. "What the hell do you think we're talking about?"

Woods stared at Joel. "Is there anything else regarding Sa'ad or Brooks or the jewelry we oughta know? Information of any kind whatsoever?"

"I'm not following you," Joel said and wrinkled his forehead. He looked at Woods but not Hobbes.

Woods reached inside his sport coat and withdrew a sheet of paper. It was creased vertically, folded only once. "Take a look at this. It's a copy." He handed it over, and Joel feigned surprise, allowed his face to crash and his posture to disintegrate.

"Oh my," he said.

"No kidding, Mr. King," Hobbes said. " 'Oh my' is right. You've been feeding us snacks instead of a meal. Sitting on material facts." Hobbes's features were intense.

Joel pretended to study the page:

To the FBI and Agent Woods:

This is the hardest thing I've ever done. I love my brother Joel and do not want him to get in more trouble than he's already in. What you people don't understand is that he fears Sa'ad. Sa'ad is a wicked, dangerous man, and Joel is scared of him. I'm afraid that Joel will not tell you the whole story, and you'll never catch Sa'ad. I think Joel knows where one of the stolen rings is hidden, that it's somewhere in Sa'ad's office. If you encourage Joel and reassure him, I think he might reveal the location and give you more help. Now, he's just mixed up and frightened. He doesn't know what to do or where to turn. But if you could find the ring, you could put Sa'ad away and protect Joel, right? Please work with him on this, but don't let him know I contacted you.

Thank you,
Sophie King

"So what do you have to say, Mr. King?" Hobbes demanded.

"Well, I've never lied to you guys or anything," Joel said.

"Never lied?" Hobbes boomed. "That's all you *ever* do. A lie's a conscious evasion of the truth, and that seems to be your calling card. Never lied? Ha!"

"Joel, if you know where the dadgummed ring is, if it's not at Van Heiss's, you'd better tell us," Woods encouraged him. "Come on now. We're out on a limb here, especially Lynette, and we don't need you keepin' details to yourself. We can protect you from Sa'ad and his friend, if that's your worry. We haven't seen much that leads us to believe either one of 'em's violent. They're con men, but they hardly seem dangerous, okay? My guess is they'll break and run when we get down to the nitty-gritty. Why're you so scared?"

"You don't know Sa'ad. You guys have no idea." Joel made his voice quaver. "You better believe I'm afraid of them," he said, his words freighted with phony conviction. "He's ruthless. You'll see soon enough."

"Well, tough shit," Hobbes said. "He's a typical con man, and you're a conniving little ferret who's afraid of your shadow. I could tell you about dangerous. You don't know the first thing about dangerous. You're scared of a damn ambulance-chasing lawyer."

Woods looked at Hobbes and waited a moment before he spoke. "We'll do everything in our power to guarantee your safety, if that's what it takes. So will Ms. Allen."

"Let's cut to the chase," Hobbes said. "Do you know where the ring is? Do you?"

"No one asked me that before, okay? Never. I've never once fibbed about it. It's not fair to accuse me of misleading the police. I've done everything you've asked—made the calls, agreed to the wire, whatever."

"Yeah, and you've told your damn sister twice as much as you've told us," Hobbes complained. "You know good and well you've been jerking us around."

"I have not," Joel protested.

"So where's the ring?" Woods asked. "And which ring are we discussing? You told us everything was returned."

"Did you guys threaten my sister?" Joel suddenly said.

"Lord no," Woods assured him. "This came in the mail. Just her tryin' to look out for you."

"How do I know she wrote it? Maybe this is some police hoax." Joel felt he needed to ask this, and he momentarily slipped into high dudgeon.

"It's not a trick. She sent it to the police station and a copy to Ms. Allen," Woods said. "We wouldn't wanna cause your sister any grief."

"So what if it is a ruse, Mr. King?" Hobbes was tapping his foot and smacking gum. "It's fairly obvious you know more than you're letting on. I'm running out of patience."

"Joel?" Woods lifted his eyebrows.

"Why would she do this to me?" Joel said, touching all the bases.

"We can't help you unless you help us," Woods said. "Your sister's got the right idea."

"Okay." Joel paused. "Okay—here's what I know." He ballooned his cheeks and then let the air escape. "Sa'ad feels very secure in his office, claims it would be difficult to obtain a wire tap or search warrant because of his being an attorney and entitled to protect clients and their files and communications. He views the office as a safe haven. He has all sorts of stuffed hunting trophies and this rack of gum machines in there. The place looks like Dante's zoo or something, very foreboding. I think the jewelry's hidden in his office, either in the gum machines or one of the animals."

"How do you know?" Woods asked. "Have you seen it? Has he told you?"

"No, but I've seen Edmund fooling with the machines, removing items while he and Sa'ad discussed business."

"What the hell is that supposed to mean?" Hobbes asked.

"Did you see the Jewish Museum ring?" Woods asked before Joel could respond to Hobbes. "Why would he keep part of the bait? I thought the plan was to return it?"

"No. Honestly, I didn't see it. But if you put it all together—the fact Sa'ad feels his office is off-limits to the authorities, and Edmund taking things from the gum machines, and all the nooks and crannies in these animals—where does it point you? And wouldn't it make sense for them to keep a bonus, a relatively inexpensive piece, a five- or ten-thousand-dollar trinket the owner would assume was lost or misplaced? It's easy money, and it adds up."

"Makes no sense at all that they'd jeopardize the whole plan and risk hundreds of thousands for a few measly grand, " Hobbes said. "They'd be morons to raise flags by keeping part of the bait." He bore down on Joel. "What exactly did Edmund remove?"

"They didn't invite me over for a private viewing, Mr. Hobbes. Edmund took the machine apart and reached inside. I guess he just wanted his chewing gum for free." Joel was sarcastic with the last sentence.

"I don't know," Woods said. "Is this it, everything?"

"Yeah. No offense, guys, but first you berate me for not being forthcoming enough, and when I tell you what I think, you treat me like I'm an idiot. I can't win."

"I can't believe an accomplished operator like Sa'ad would hold on to a mediocre piece of stolen jewelry," Hobbes said.

"Really?" Joel said. "Is it so difficult to imagine a thief getting greedy, becoming more and more emboldened?" He was forceful and argumentative. "I mean, heck, it's nothing to me, but I know there's something other than legal briefs and paper clips in Sa'ad's office."

"But you never *saw* the ring?" Woods asked. "Either one of 'em? Correct?"

"Correct. I never saw a ring or anything else. And maybe our stuff's long gone or never was there or was returned to the owner. I don't guess you'll be asking Mr. Van Heiss, though, will you? But I'll bet you there's something incriminating in those machines. Why else would Edmund be taking off the top while he and Sa'ad talk about the legal system and their so-called projects, how two 'claims' had come to fruition?"

"Did Sa'ad or Edmund ever tell you—expressly admit—they were planning on keeping some of the Van Heiss jewelry?" Hobbes asked.

"No, not exactly."

"Why do I have to drag every single syllable out of your sorry mouth?" Hobbes complained. "Why?"

"What did they tell you, Joel?" Woods asked.

"When they came to Missoula to collect the whole bag, they claimed one piece was missing. A ring. They threw a fit and accused me of stealing it."

"Did you?" Woods wondered. "Steal it, I mean?"

"No, of course not. Why would I?"

"Because you could?" Hobbes said sardonically.

Joel ignored him. "So why are they claiming a ring is gone? Huh? Why are they accusing me? Maybe Sa'ad swiped it and wants Edmund to suspect me. Or one might conclude it's part of their scam somehow, a double-cross. Perhaps they skimmed a taste off the top."

"Why would they even alert you?" Hobbes asked. "Why wouldn't they simply do it and leave you none the wiser? You're not being rational."

"That's the sixty-four-thousand-dollar question, isn't it? I have no idea. You're the expert; I'd hoped you could shed some light on the situation, how the plot progresses. But I know they claim there's a missing ring, the green one. Add that to everything else you know."

"Hmmm," Woods said, thinking.

Harry Winton hadn't joined the debate. He'd listened and peered out the hotel window at the Las Vegas Strip, was watching a teenage hooker wearing cutoff jeans bargaining with a bald, flabby man in a Hawaiian shirt. "Add that to everything else we know, and we don't know anything," he said, speaking for the first time since he'd introduced himself. "That letter was typed, wasn't it? Even the woman's name?" he asked, directing the question to Hobbes.

"Yeah. We sent a copy to—"

"Oh, I got it," Winton interrupted. "I got it. Thank you."

"Yeah. No problem," Hobbes said, uncertain where the Vegas policeman was headed.

Winton returned to the window. "Midafternoon and people are paying for sex," he remarked, still studying the girl and her john. "Me, I'd at least try a few more bars and casinos, keep at it till dark, see if I couldn't find some tourist for free before I coughed up my hard-earned bucks." He kept his back to everyone in the room. "Two things you should know, Mr. King." Winton's voice was weirdly high, as if his Adam's apple were clamped. Joel wondered if he'd been injured, his throat traumatized by an accident or scuffle with a criminal.

"Okay," Joel answered.

"One, almost every cop in this town hates Sa'ad X. Sa'ad. He's a shyster and a crook, and he's always accusing us of shit we haven't done to try and shake his clients loose." Winton swung around as he was talking and gazed at Joel.

"I see," Joel said.

"Second, it's procedure that we have to search you before you go in with the wire." The announcement was brief and deft. He'd intentionally jumped Joel, waylaid him, and he paused to take Joel's measure, studying him for a gasp or erratic breath, field-testing his reaction to see if there was any sign of guilt.

"I'm not surprised by that," Joel said. "I understand you're doing your job."

Hobbes's expression had turned stony. Woods's face also had changed: he was curious, weighing a new hypothesis, following Harry Winton's gambit to see where it went.

"Of course, since it's only a wire and we're respectful of your dignity, we don't want to make too big a deal of it," Winton said, his voice beginning to sound robotic.

"No problem," Joel said.

"You need to use the toilet or anything before we do the frisk?" Winton asked.

"That would hardly be advisable," Hobbes said to Winton. "You can't be serious?"

"I'll go with him if you're worried," Winton said. "Keep an eye peeled for irregularities." He had difficulty producing the last word, chirped it in a cricket octave.

"I'm not certain your supervision would completely cure my concerns," Hobbes said.

"I'll watch him," Woods volunteered.

"I'm fine, gentlemen. I take your point, Mr. Winton, understand what's not being said, and I can promise you I don't need to visit the restroom or hide anything. And you won't find anything concealed on my person." Joel held each of his arms perpendicularly and made himself into a *T.* "Go to it," he told them, attempting to sound flippant and unconcerned while his mouth began to parch and his guts hopped in his abdomen.

"Oh well," Winton said. He sternly reminded Hobbes this was a state case—Woods chimed in to support him—and that the FBI was there as a courtesy, end of story. He hoped everybody understood their roles. "You fellows passed on this one," he squeaked at Hobbes. "Lookin' for bigger game." He commenced a superficial, desultory search, had Joel unbutton his shirt, rapidly patted his legs and butt, inspected his shoes and wallet and made him remove his belt. "Clean," he declared when he finished.

"Hot, Mr. King?" Hobbes asked.

A sweat rivulet was winding down Joel's forehead, swimming toward the slant of his nose. "I'm not used to the heat," he answered. "The dry heat. What's it to you?"

"Always the con artist, aren't you?" Hobbes said. "And it's March, ass-hole."

"Always the skeptic," Joel replied.

The three other officers left him alone with Hobbes while they went to a white van—TOPPS CLEANING AND JANITORIAL was written on each door in bold black letters—and checked the reception from the transmitter.

"Test one, two, three, four, five, Agent Hobbes is glad to be alive," Joel joked after waiting for them to get in position.

"Where is it?" Hobbes said.

"Where's what?"

"Kill two birds with one stone today, eh? How much was the reward on the museum burglary? I heard from Ms. Allen you've been asking."

"I'm sure you already know," Joel answered, "being an ace G-man and all."

Joel looked like a late-seventies rock star in his police disguise—one of the Allman Brothers, maybe, or Pete Townsend—his head underneath a puffy, mushrooming denim cap, his straight black wig brushing his shoulders and his face obscured behind tricolored aviator sunglasses. "Do I get a guitar?" he asked Woods once they'd finished dressing him. "A leather vest with tassels?"

"It's *supposed* to look homemade," Woods told him. "Like you did it yourself."

"I know," Joel said. "I'm only kidding."

The appointment had been made under the name of Sherman Flanagan, and because Mr. Flanagan was a new client, Sa'ad's receptionist presented him with a two-page questionnaire fastened to a clipboard and instructed him to please complete every section. Joel spent five minutes goofing through his answers and was tempted to put "police informant" in the employment blank before finally deciding to stay in character. "Bass player, seventies cover band," he printed. Ten minutes after he returned the forms, the receptionist announced that Mr. Sa'ad was ready for him. She didn't seem to recognize him, although she did ask twice if he was Mr. Flanagan when he first arrived and told her he was there for his four o'clock meeting.

Sa'ad was in full flower as Joel entered his office, hovering and pacing on his raised platform, talking into a sleek cordless phone, animals snarling, growling, pouncing, clawing and prowling all around him. He acknowledged Joel soon after he came through the door, then ignored him while he continued to saunter back and forth and purr sonorous sentences to the person on the other end of the call. Joel kept his distance, held steady near the threshold, and he pretended to scan the office, did a three-sixty that concluded at the gum machines. Sa'ad glanced his way again and spoke into the phone: "Yes you will. Oh, yes you will," he said imperiously.

Joel pivoted to block Sa'ad's view, ran one hand across the top of the machines and sneaked the other into the front of his pants, located the two strips of Scotch tape holding the ring on the underside of his scrotum. He'd practiced for several hours in the basement, had become adept at collecting the jewelry and leaving the tape behind, was able to accomplish the grab with a fluid motion that didn't register in his shoulders or stance. He'd used a yellow-and-white disposable Bic razor to shave the area, had drawn blood because he couldn't half see what he was doing. The cotton fabric of his pocket was cut away on the rear side, replaced with a generous patch of thick black felt. The felt was lightly glued to the rest of the pocket, barely attached.

With the ring in his palm, he jammed his hand into the rigged pocket—looking for coins it would appear—separating the felt and balling it around the ring. He could hear Sa'ad finishing the call, could tell he was being watched now, and he was careful not to panic, didn't rush, doused his nerves with the belief he was doing fate's bidding and operating under the Lord's immunity.

He inserted the wad into the throat of the machine and pushed until he got complete resistance, then paused to make certain the clog hung and didn't fall out. The metal flap covering the shoot clicked closed when Joel withdrew his fingers, made a ting that sounded like a detonation to Joel's tense ears. He spun around and brought his fist to his lips, acting as if he were dropping in gum, and began chewing the piece already in his mouth.

Done. Mission accomplished. Thank you, Lord. This had to be the correct route, he told himself, because so far the plan had transpired flawlessly and without a hitch. Sa'ad could have recognized him or met him at the door or kept him under scrutiny the entire time, but, just as he'd hoped, the hotshot lawyer was too busy showing off and strutting the stage for a new client. Instead of virtually begging him to entrap Sa'ad, the detectives could've searched him rigorously, stripped him naked and pried apart his legs and discovered his hiding place, which was good but far from perfect. Either Winton and Woods didn't care about his potential skullduggery or they were convinced he was on the straight and narrow since he didn't come unglued when the subject of a frisk was raised. It was as if the Lord had snapped His fingers in front of the cops' eyes and rendered them temporarily blind. So what if Hobbes thought he had Joel pegged—he was out of the loop, and he couldn't prove a thing.

"Mr. Flanagan," Sa'ad said. "Sorry to keep you waiting."

"Hello, Sa'ad," Joel said, still standing at the machines. The greeting was brassy and obnoxious. "Great to see you."

"Sir?" Sa'ad was taken aback. "Have we met?"

"Of course we have. Although you don't seem too eager to return my calls." Joel moved closer, away from the treats and novelties. "It's me."

"I'm not certain . . ." Sa'ad hesitated and stepped off his platform. "Joel?"

"Excellent. Good guess." He removed the hat and wig, then the glasses. He patted his hair into place as he approached Sa'ad.

"This is a surprise."

"I'll bet," Joel said. "We need to talk, old pal."

"Talk? About what? Have a seat. Welcome. It's been a while." He touched Joel's shoulder and shook his hand. The surprise and confusion were transient, already waning. Sa'ad's expression was no longer mystified and his voice had healed. "Why are you dressed in this . . . this costume?"

"You know why, Sa'ad. The same reason you're not picking up the phone to call me. I had to disguise myself to slip out of Missoula."

"I'm not sure I follow you." Sa'ad looked at him with a mixture of malevolence and joy, like a tiger about to disembowel a hyena. "Sit. Sit, please." He made a grand production of cocking a chair in Joel's direction.

"Sure." Joel sat and tossed his wig and blossomy hat onto the floor. "You want to search me before we do business? Check the lot for spies and black ops?"

"Are you okay? What's happening?"

"You darn well know what's happening, Sa'ad. The project's in the tubes, the FBI is about to eat me alive and you and Edmund aren't helping me."

"Edmund?" Sa'ad said. "Project?"

"Yeah. Edmund."

"What project are you referring to? Your divorce? Has something arisen there? I received your messages, but I've been very distracted."

"Listen, here's the deal. I need a boost, some help and advice from you guys, and if I don't get it, I'm going to start polishing up my junior deputy's badge. Talk to the cops and see what they can offer. Understand?"

"You've lost me, I'm afraid. Simmer down and let's see if we can isolate your concerns." Sa'ad stood and relocated to his desk, hanging his suit jacket over his chair before sitting back down. "Now, let's start by finding you something to cut the dust—water, or a soft drink? Juice?"

"I don't have time for this, Sa'ad. Are you going to work with me or not? Quit acting so bizarre."

"Let's just relax. How about something to drink?"

"I'm not thirsty. What do I need to do about the FBI? They know the insurance claim's a fraud."

"Did you see my most recent addition?" Sa'ad gestured to his left, where a buffalo's horned head was mounted on the wall.

"Great. You shot a bison. Congratulations."

"I'm very proud of it. Know where it came from?"

"Mars? Mutual of Omaha's Wild Kingdom?" Joel shrugged. "Why would I care about your ridiculous hunting trophies?"

"Colorado."

"So?" Joel grunted.

"They raise them there and slaughter them for meat. You can go to the ranch, pay a few hundred bucks, and they place you on a shooting stand above the pen and let you take your pick. The hunter gets the head and skin, then they process the meat and sell it to restaurants and distributors."

"That's obscene, Sa'ad. Gruesome. You shoot the poor animal while it's fenced in? Do you wait for them to look up from the salt blocks and hay? Sounds about par for your course."

"It's a damn fine arrangement, Mr. King. I don't like risk and failure in any of my endeavors." He paused. "And I wanted a buffalo head. Now I have one. They would've killed him sooner or later anyway."

"Is this some sort of parable, Sa'ad? Something veiled?"

He smiled from behind his desk. "No. Gracious, no. Not at all. I simply thought you'd be interested."

"Well, I'm not."

"Do you want to tell me about your problem? Something about the FBI and insurance? This isn't a divorce concern?"

"I've said everything I need to say," Joel told him. "It's your call now." Joel heard the door open, and he noticed Sa'ad calibrate his attention, tilt his chin and extend his neck. A chubby black man in shorts and tennis shoes entered without knocking or speaking and waddled by Joel. He laid a sheet of paper on Sa'ad's desk and stood waiting while Sa'ad read the message. Sa'ad thanked him and dismissed him, and the heavyset man lumbered back out of the room, his thighs squishing as he passed Joel.

"My goodness, Mr. King. I'm absolutely mortified. I hate to mention this, but we have a problem. And it's my fault, my breach." Sa'ad contorted his face into a clownishly overwrought expression of disappointment.

"What?" Joel felt the stares of the stuffed animals, noticing for the first time how their dead, fake eyes were trained on the seats at the bottom of the desk plateau.

"I treasure my clients' privacy. You know that. It's part of my code, part of my obligation as an attorney, to safeguard your secrets. Confidentiality is a watchword with Sa'ad X. Sa'ad. And because I've whipped the state and the federal government in court so many times, and because I help the little guy and the underdog and the single mom, because I don't fear big insurance companies and huge corporations, I'm often a target of unfair practices. Dirty tricks, unlawful surveillance, harassment, snooping, eavesdropping, intimidation—you name it, I've seen it."

"I can't say I'd blame the insurance companies for coming after you—"

"It's just atrocious," Sa'ad declaimed. "There's a price to pay whenever you champion the common man against the state or the establishment."

"I've never heard such a bunch of—"

Sa'ad talked over him, steamrolling Joel's words. "So I've been forced to take countermeasures, to implement security procedures for my clients' protection."

"Oh?" Joel replied. He sensed Sa'ad was nearing the conclusion of his speech, and he could anticipate the applause line, what was coming.

"Sad but true. I'm sorry to report we're being bugged. My security chief, Melvin, tells me there's a transmission leaving this office at this very moment. Can you believe it? You have my apologies." Sa'ad said everything with a straight face. "My, my."

"You have someone monitoring your office for bugs?"

"Day and night, Joel. Day and night. My house, car, office, the works. Isn't it a shame our government would do this to me? It's retribution, pure and simple. Orwellian in nature, illegal and unconstitutional. I've been forced to pay thousands a year and stay constantly vigilant, just to protect the integrity of my services. Makes you sick to your stomach, doesn't it?"

"You know who you remind me of?"

"Who?" Sa'ad's tone was blue, hurt, but his features were jumping with mischief. "Dr. King? Jackie Robinson? The Weavers from Ruby Ridge?"

"I was going to say Al Sharpton. But how about *Don* King?"

"Fine Americans both. Came from nothing. Thank you." Sa'ad situated his chair closer to the desk. "We're going to have to discontinue our conference until we can eliminate this problem. You can reschedule with my secretary, or if there's something urgent, I can give you a referral. You have my apologies for the inconvenience. But let's not say another word regarding your business—we can't take the chance."

"You think you're pretty shrewd, don't you?"

"I'm sorry. I'm not sure what you mean." Sa'ad's expression became more animated, as if his features were about to evacuate his face and assume their own life. He picked up an extravagant fountain pen and opened a folder. "I'm preparing a file note. I'm going to document this intrusion by the government, record how their illegal snooping has interfered with our attorney-client relationship. Bastards. Or perhaps it's a private entity monitoring us, some conglomerate or reckless chemical company with a courtroom grudge. Once we locate the culprit, I'll contact you, and we'll sue them silly." He squiggled the pen across the opened folder. "Huh," he said, bumping the pen's tip against his desktop. Tap, tap, tap. "I'll be darned."

"What?" Joel was perched on the edge of his chair, the frame digging into his thighs.

"Two-hundred-dollar pen, and the rascal won't write." He puckered his lips and a devilish shine flitted through his pupils. "How about that?" He located another pen and pretended it also was broken. "Guess I'm jinxed today."

Joel tried not to smile but couldn't help himself. He broke into a broad grin, and Sa'ad followed suit, flashed a mouthful of perfect dentistry and a ribbon of moist, red gum line. "You'd think for that much money, it would write," Joel said.

"Hey, how about you let me borrow yours?" Sa'ad said, his smile gigantic and insincere.

"Better not," Joel told him.

"Oh?"

"Nah," Joel answered.

"Come on. It'll save my secretary a trip."

"You can't dictate the message? Or simply remember?" Joel was playing out the string, hitting his marks.

"No, I need to document this immediately, so there's no question about accuracy or whose note it is." He reached toward Joel with an open hand. "It'll only take a minute, and I'd be eternally indebted."

Joel rose and transferred the pen to Sa'ad and didn't sit again. Sa'ad acted as if he were attempting to write on the file, but Joel could see the nib wasn't anywhere near the target. Sa'ad made a number of passes and strokes over the folder, then started shaking the pen and thwacking it against his desk. "Damn, Preacher, this one's defective, too." He beat the daylights out of the pen, tossed it into a trash can and the amusement, every jot and tittle of it, fled his face. The spiteful playfulness vanished and the harmless man-in-the-moon grin disappeared, replaced by a pernicious stare.

"I don't guess I'll be getting my pen back, huh?" Joel asked.

"No," Sa'ad said, his appearance now waxy and stiff, tombish. "I'll have my office manager send you a replacement. And I'm sorry to be no more help with your legal problems."

"I'll be in touch," Joel said. He was certain he smelled formaldehyde cross-stitched with decay, the stink probably emanating from the newly mounted buffalo head.

"You do that, Reverend." Sa'ad sounded and looked soulless, capable of most anything, his conscience evidently assigned to the taxidermist along with the bears and deer and other wild beasts.

Joel drove from Sa'ad's to the Stardust, the Topps cleaning van following at an inconspicuous distance. They reconvened in the same room, and Hobbes ploughed into him as if the catastrophe with Sa'ad was somehow Joel's responsibility. "A total fiasco," Hobbes bellowed.

"Not his fault," Woods said.

"Nope," Harry Winton agreed. "Sa'ad's cagey, I'll give him that."

"Joel probably tipped him or warned him or gave him a gesture or some such," Hobbes argued. He was pacing. "And you didn't have to forfeit the damn pen."

"He caught us with our pants down," Woods said. "Damn it. Now Joel's probably too compromised to ever do us any good. Sa'ad'll never trust him. Never."

"Yeah, Hobbes," Joel said, "I gave him a heads-up, told him to hire a security guy and have everything in place so he could discover your J. Edgar Hoover–era, Maxwell Smart microphone-in-a-pen."

"Be as smartass as you like, Mr. King," Hobbes snarled. "Be my guest. As I see it, your deal just went down the crapper, so you go ahead and antagonize us, keep the sarcasm coming. Maybe when Don Rickles croaks you can fill in here on the Strip. And let me assure you that was *state* equipment you were using. We have parabolic mikes and sophisticated bugs and shit so stealthy that Sa'ad would need a microscope to find it."

"You did your best, Joel," Woods said quietly. "I'll tell Lynette."

"Yep," Harry Winton concurred. "I ain't got a beef with Mr. King."

"Thanks," Joel mumbled.

"You see anything strange in the office?" Woods asked. "Got anything else to report?"

"Sorry," Joel answered, intentionally skirting the question.

"I see," Winton said. Joel couldn't determine whether he noticed the evasiveness.

"Not your fault," Woods reiterated.

"By the way, guys," Joel said. "Did you hear the buffalo story? What did I tell you? That's a threat from a man with an arsenal in his office. Believe me now?" In fact, the last creepy moments with Sa'ad had been unnerving, had prompted Joel to partially accept his own pitch.

"Bullshit," Hobbes said. "You call that a threat?"

"Yeah," Joel answered.

"What a cluster fuck this turned out to be," Hobbes griped. "Let's hope we haven't lost the painting."

"I truly hope you recover it," Joel said.

Joel and Woods said goodbye to Officer Winton and his helpers and walked through the casino to the front of the hotel. While the valet was retrieving the Taurus, Joel and Woods stood without talking and waited for the car. Visitors were coming and leaving, cabs peeled off a line near the entrance to collect their fares, and an elderly couple stopped to ask the doorman how to find the buffet and if their coupons were any good there. When the car arrived, Woods inquired where Joel wanted to have dinner, and for a second he thought about suggesting the Rosewood Grille, but he finally said he was indifferent, mentioned Taco Bell or Subway, anything on the route out of the city. Hobbes was already in his silver ride, parked alongside the curb, the engine idling.

"Nothing else I need to know?" Woods said to Joel in a confidential voice. "Just between us?"

"Can't we please give it a rest, Mr. Woods? I'm trying, okay? I'll contact you if anything occurs to me."

Sophie was eager to know what had happened in Las Vegas. She leaned forward and her appearance brightened until Joel told her how Sa'ad had unearthed their plan and brought them up short. They were sitting at opposite ends of her sofa, Sophie dressed in sweatpants and a rugby shirt, Joel wearing jeans. It was seven-thirty in the evening, and the supper dishes were still on the table, a skillet with blackened hamburger remnants still on the range. An hour earlier, Baker had welcomed Joel home with hugs and a fistful of papers and projects from school, imploring him to look at every drawing and every assignment. Sophie had let the child bound around his uncle and blather excitedly, then dispatched him to his room and ordered him to read a book or play with his Tinker Toys.

"I'm so disappointed, Joel. I really thought you were on the right track, that this would work. Maybe . . ." She hesitated. "Who knows, huh? Does this mean your deal is gone?"

"I'm not sure. Woods was very supportive, and it's not my fault. I did what they told me."

"It kills me that an asshole like Sa'ad, the mastermind, is escaping, and you're going to get screwed. Shit. And I was so convinced that confessing was the best option you had."

"You've given me good advice. And been a great sister."

"Thanks," Sophie said.

"Can I ask you something?" Joel didn't change his position. He stayed slouched in the sofa's frayed corner.

"Sure."

"More advice," he said.

"Okay." Sophie arranged the collar of her jersey.

"I think I have something on Sa'ad. But I'm not a hundred percent positive."

"What? What is it?"

"I'm almost certain he's holding part of the jewelry we took. At his office, hidden there. Maybe other stuff as well."

"Why do you think that?"

"He has this collection of gum machines, and I think he hides contraband in them. I've seen Edmund remove one of the tops and fish out things, heard conversations. So when I was in Vegas, I did some investigating. I didn't have much time, but I swear I think there're jewels stuck in the machines. I felt something strange, like a velvet bag—similar to the one they gave me—jammed in a chute. I only had a few seconds to poke around, pretending to buy gum, since Sa'ad was right there."

"Did you tell the cops?"

"I wanted to, started to. But I'm afraid if I'm wrong . . . well, can you imagine how they'll crucify me if I'm wrong? If they get a warrant and search Sa'ad's office and find nothing, he'll sue them to kingdom come. And they'll hang me, yes they will. Even Lynette will want my scalp."

"How sure are you?"

"Very."

"I say tell them exactly what you've told me, warts and all."

"Well, it's also problematic if I'm correct. The more I'm around Sa'ad, the more I become convinced he's dangerous. What if he discovers I'm the one who ratted on him?"

"He already knows you tried to dupe him, right? Didn't you just describe how he busted you guys?"

"Yeah, but he walked away. He won. It would be different if they catch him. He might try to retaliate."

"Maybe. But if he's like his buddy Edmund, I figure he'd simply crawl under a rock and hide like the slime he is."

"Sa'ad's a lot scarier than Edmund."

Sophie attended to her collar again. "I suddenly have a feeling it's not advice you're after."

"Not entirely," Joel responded.

"There's a subtext, huh? I'm seeing the legendary Joel King Shuffle, aren't I?"

"I wouldn't say that, no." Joel uncrossed his legs, planted both feet on the floor. There was a broken video next to the new VCR, and Baker had unspooled yards of brown tape into a slapdash pile of spirals and coils. "But if you'd call Lynette, all my problems will be solved."

"Call Lynette? Me? Why? And say what?"

"Tell her I've informed you where the jewelry, or something valuable, is hidden. That I literally touched it two days ago, and I've heard Sa'ad and Edmund discussing dishonest business."

"How does that help you? Seems it would make it worse, like you're holding out on them."

"Perhaps. But if you inform them I'm scared, and tell them I'm afraid of what will happen if I'm wrong, they can make their own decision and won't blame me if the bottom falls out. And this way, my name is not connected with the tip—I'm insulated, once removed. If they arrest Sa'ad, I'm sure he'll be able to discover who reported him."

"So you want him to come stalking me? Thanks."

"He won't view it the same. I was part of the scheme—you know, honor among thieves, that sort of crap. You're a sister protecting her brother, and that's a whole different kettle of fish. Besides, you said you weren't worried."

"I am now."

"Well, I have to admit there's some risk. Sa'ad might try something, but I don't think he'd have the same passion where you're concerned."

"I don't know, Joel. It might make things worse instead of better. And none of this really rings true—your reasoning's all screwy."

"It's my only hope, Sophie," Joel said. "Otherwise, Sa'ad walks and I get no deal and who knows how much jail time. Just tell Lynette I'm concerned, afraid of leaving her and Woods vulnerable, and they can decide for themselves."

"Seems it never ends with you, Joel."

"We need to do it soon, tonight even, before the stuff goes missing. Leave a message at her office on the answering machine, or call her at home."

Sophie looked at the phone, and Joel could tell she was mulling what she should do, uncertain. "Remember how Sa'ad and Edmund stuck it to me?" he said. "And how I'm going to jail no matter what?"

"Joel . . ."

"I've got to stop him. He deserves it, Sophie. *Please.*"

twenty-one

Dixon phoned Joel in late May and told him there was work for him, the first clients of the spring, a physician and his teenage son. The big rivers were still swollen and too swift to float, plumped by the runoff from the wettest winter in decades, but there were several creeks they could wade and nymph-fish, and Dixon had recently leased a handsome stretch of private water that would be good for respectable browns and rainbows until June, perhaps even July. Joel took the doctor and his son to three different streams, and they caught lots of strong, fat fish, many of which were acrobatic, came tearing from their pools six or seven times before losing their spirit. The doc gave Joel a fifty-dollar tip and his business card, and Dixon had increased the price for a guide by thirty bucks, so Joel received more on that end as well.

The sky was a blue, winsome miracle, and the stream banks were dabbed with infant green, nascent sprigs and blades of grass that shot up irregularly, higher and more vivid than the beige winter holdovers surrounding them. "Beautiful country," the doctor said, "especially this time of year." Joel thought of Virginia while he and his two passengers were driving back to the shop, imagined the dogwoods with their ivory white and stained corners, recalled the azaleas and wisteria bushes and the irises slicing through the dirt outside the First Baptist parsonage, all the trees and fey perennials reborn as the days grew longer and milder.

Joel accompanied his clients to their rented car and watched them leave, then went to Dixon's office, collected his pay and thanked his friend for the opportunity.

"I love it when the fishing starts," Dixon said. "I can't help it. No matter how long I've been doin' this, I still get butterflies when I make the first casts or hook the first trout."

"Tell me that in August, when the tourists are bellyaching about the heat and demanding refunds if the fish don't bite." Joel smiled at his friend.

"Details, Joel, mere details. The spring weeks are like having a new lady in your life, pure romance and excitement. A fresh beginning."

Joel picked up a large, gaudy fly with deer-hair wings. He studied the fly instead of Dixon, mashed the wings together and smoothed the half-inch tail. "On the subject of fresh beginnings," he said, "I can never thank you enough—"

"Don't need to," Dixon interrupted. "You've thanked me and your sister's thanked me, so let's put this behind us. Makes me uncomfortable talkin' about it so much. I only did what I thought was right, and it probably didn't amount to a hill of beans anyway. Just don't let me down."

"Believe me, I won't."

"When you leavin'?" Dixon asked.

"My court date is August fifth, but I don't have to turn in until the last of September. I shouldn't miss any fishing days."

"Sophie told me you got a deal for what—a year?"

"Nine months, thanks to you and Lynette. They've arranged it so I can do my sentence during the winter and be back here to work most of next summer. That is, if I still have a job after I'm released."

"Long as I'm the owner, you'll be welcome," Dixon said.

It was Saturday, and Joel lingered at the Royal Coachman until closing, organizing stock and mopping a bathroom floor that was already spotless. Sophie was in the yard when he rolled to a halt at the end of their rutted driveway, setting her first warm-weather flowers into spaded, fertilized earth. The former owners had located two car tires at each corner of the concrete porch—not just any tires, Sophie always quipped, but artsy tires, spray-painted white—and Sophie was transferring young petunias and impatiens from plastic containers into the white circles. Joel had offered to haul off the tacky, white-trash planters, but Sophie was defiant where they were concerned, said they were a symbolic, tongue-in-cheek reflection of her make-do life, and there they'd stay. She was wearing her gloves and pouring water from a Maxwell House coffee can, had filled one tire and part of the other. Joel walked to where she was, accidentally stepping on an empty plant container and crushing it. "This isn't any good, is it?" he asked, reaching for the flattened plastic.

"Nope," she said. "Junk."

"I didn't see it. The light's going; it'll be dark soon."

"I hope these live," Sophie said. "I don't have much of a green thumb." She tamped around the stem of a petunia. "How was fishing?"

"Excellent. Nice guys and probably thirty trout. A fifty-dollar tip. And seeing Dixon was a delight."

"I'm glad," she replied.

"It was great to be on the river."

"So ask me about my day, Joel." There was the hint of a broader issue in her voice.

"Okay," he grinned. "How was your day, Sophie?"

She removed her muddy gloves, stopped her gardening and sat Indian-style, peering up at him. "Ah, my day was good, too. I decided on something that's been troubling me."

"Troubling you? I hadn't noticed."

"Guess who called me a week ago?"

"I don't know," Joel said.

"Yeah you do. Think."

"Sophie, I don't have any idea."

"Lynette Allen."

"Okay," Joel said. "What did she want?"

"Hmmm, let's see. You're clueless?"

"I'm afraid you'll have to turn over another letter or two on the board."

Sophie stood. Her knees were dirty, and her shirttail was at her thighs. "The reward. The museum reward. She called to discuss my letters and crime-stopper tips. It seems my most recent correspondence requested the cash since I'd reported my brother's misconduct. There was my first letter, of course, and my phone call. You remember my phone call, when I told them where the famous ring was hidden?"

"I do." He took a long, satisfied breath. "And we were correct, weren't we? I told you as soon as Officer Winton told me. It was right there in Sa'ad's office."

"What a dumbass plan, Joel, even worse than the rest. Writing letters in my name, conning that nice woman? Didn't you realize I'd discover what was happening? Hell, they'll have to give *me* the check. I was bound to piece together what you did." She sounded passionate, but not particularly distressed.

"Of course I knew you'd solve it. You'd have to. I wanted you to, because I want you to have the money. Why do you think I jumped through every hoop known to man and prayed and labored and sweated? You *deserve* that twenty-five thousand."

"I do?" she said, her voice fluttering.

"Yes, you do. If for no reason other than the hardship I've visited on you. And for a million other reasons. Your ex-husband's a miserable cad who, to this day, mistreats you and Baker. You need money. Your son's wearing shoes that are too small, and we're driving our mother's car. You're due a break, and this one's clean, honest and aboveboard. This isn't sag money or insurance fraud."

"Joel, it's another con. I didn't report you."

"That's not what the reward's for." This was Joel's trump, he thought, the argument that would surely convert his sister. "The reward is for any-one who helped them recover the jewelry or the painting. And that's you—you did it. You convinced me to go see Lynette and confess. You went with me to her office and pushed me when I was wavering. You legitimately caused the recovery by persuading me to go straight. There's nothing cor-rupt about taking the reward. Please, Sophie, it's the only thing I can do for you."

"Nice try," she said. "There also may be some dispute about the amount I'm due, since technically I only assisted them with one ring."

"Sophie, for goodness sakes. I busted my butt to make this go. You told me to ask the Lord what ought to be done, and I did—I got on my knees and begged for guidance. And this works so perfectly, you see. You're fairly and legally paid, Sa'ad is punished for his theft and for attacking me with Christy, Edmund's shut down, I get my deal and there's not anything the bad guys can say or do that won't implicate them worse. You think Sa'ad's going to admit he and I conspired to bilk an insurance company, and that I turned on him? It's unassailable. He's stuck. This is heaven-sent, with bows on every package. Take the darn cash."

"It does seem foolproof. A good scam. Your technique's improving."

"Sophie, listen. I haven't lied, I've sought the Lord's will, I've helped the cops, and I've put two swindlers out of business and repaid them for dam-aging Roanoke First Baptist. This isn't tainted, and it couldn't be so perfect unless it was moral and right."

"I don't know if it's perfect or not. That's not the issue."

"Take the reward," Joel urged her. "If not for yourself, take it for Baker. Put it away for his college or something."

"I can't, Joel."

"Why not?"

"Because then I'd be too much like you." She said it without any malice, and there was affection in her expression. She took two steps and was be-side him. The mountains were draped now, the world segueing into sil-houettes and a huge panel of charcoal backdrop. "I'm not trying to be hurtful by saying that." She held his hand and turned so they were looking in the same direction. "I've got my decency and my pride, Joel. I don't want charity, and I don't want to be the beneficiary of my brother's misfortune. We've already been through this with your other schemes. And I especially don't need money that's been filtered through thousands of dodges and hustles, wind up like some gangster's moll or John Dillinger's sister. I appreciate it, I really do. I know you did it for me, but I'm passing."

"Why? I can't believe you."

"I just told you why," she said. "And even if I wanted the money, you're so inept and unlucky I'm afraid we'd somehow wind up in trouble."

"You'll never crawl out of this hole," Joel protested.

"Maybe not. But good things are happening—without manipulation. I like Raleigh, and so far he seems like a reliable man. I heard today the University of Michigan is planning to publish my Franklin Pierce article. Five hundred bucks they're paying me. Five hundred. And the police caught two of the men who robbed us, found our microwave and the old TV and VCR. They contacted me at work yesterday. The insurance agent said I can keep them as well as the replacements because of the deductible and their being so ancient. I'll put them in Baker's room so he can watch *The Lion King* while wearing his undersize shoes." She grinned but didn't face Joel, continued to peer at the inky horizon.

"I can't help feeling the reward's part of a special unfolding, a blessing."

"There's a suspicion, you realize, that you somehow planted evidence to save your own hide and punish Sa'ad. Ms. Allen mentioned the possibility."

"I know. The police don't seem to care one way or the other. Sa'ad's guilty, so what does it matter?"

"It doesn't, not to me," she said.

"You're certain about the money?" Joel asked.

"I'm certain about my decency and my values." She sidled nearer so they hit at the hip. "But I love you for trying. Sometimes, my sweet son gives me a birthday gift or a present for Mother's Day that is so homely I'll never use it. I put it right in the closet and adore him for the sincerity."

"Will you just consider it for a little while longer?"

"Nope, I won't. I've already made up my mind, and I told Lynette the same thing."

"So this is simply another foul-up for me? Another X on my ledger?"

"It's nothing, Joel. A cipher. It's like you've built a toothpick castle or a ship in a bottle—an inordinate amount of effort for a worthless, Rube Goldberg result."

"Ouch."

"If it makes you feel better, you have been helpful to me. Yes you have." She looked at him and double-squeezed his hand. "It's nice to be loved and appreciated. It makes coping easier, and your being here for the last several months has gotten rid of the venom in me. Well, most of it at any rate. No matter how much I pound the shit out of you, your heart never goes cold. There's goodness in you; you just haven't been in the everyday world long enough to know how to set it loose. You've never flinched where Baker and I are concerned. You've screwed up, sure, but you've always been constant. Now I have a boyfriend—God, that sounds adolescent—and I probably wouldn't if you hadn't come, hadn't shown me every foundation's not rotten or floating on quicksand and silt."

"But wouldn't it be better to have happiness and a healthy bankroll, too? The Lord's virtually dropped the sweepstakes winner off at your doorstep. I can tell you the details if you'd like, how I—"

"I've gotten all I want from your pursuits. I've decided. Hush. I'm done discussing it." She hooked her arm around his waist. "Let's go inside. I've got a pot of stew cooking, made it with the beef you brought home from work. And a pie, a chocolate pie."

"Okay."

She hugged him.

"You're remarkable," he said, joining the embrace.

"Do you want me to claim the money and give it to you?" she asked. "I would."

"Huh. Well, I hadn't even considered that. Wow."

"I'm not entitled to it, but you did a bunch of legwork for them. I don't know why you should be disqualified."

"What do you think? Should I?" Joel tried to search her expression, but it was too dark to read the subtleties and crinkles that usually companioned her thoughts.

"I wouldn't, but, you know, that's me."

"You're probably right," he agreed. "Perhaps letting it go will boost my virtue quotient, huh?"

"Can I make one other suggestion, Joel? My gift to you?"

"Yeah, please."

"Dr. Piece of Shit and I went to Las Vegas for our wedding anniversary, and we stayed at the Mirage, saw—"

"I've been there," he blurted. "It's where I played cards with Sa'ad and Edmund. I'd forgotten you and Neal went. And I'm glad to hear you haven't lost all your dander; I wouldn't want to be responsible for that."

"Saw the magic show," she continued, "the gay guys, Siegfried and Roy, before the tiger ate one of them. It was a great show, and it seemed amazing, impossible. They made an elephant disappear, and no one could quite figure how they did it. It was so phenomenal because you had no idea how they pulled it off."

"I saw those tigers," Joel said. "In their habitat next to the lobby." He could anticipate her advice, some warning about loitering with the wrong crowd and steering clear of temptation.

"Word of caution from your sister. Those guys were two showmen with gold lamé suits and face jobs, and we couldn't solve their illusions. You sure you have a lock on the creator of the planet? His motives? You have his briefing book? His finished maps and charts? I thought part of the equation, the Baptist preacher equation, was that God moves in mysterious ways, and we're too damn simple to comprehend what's happening. How else can you continue to explain all the frightful plane disasters and still-born babies? I'd be careful about assuming too much, Joel, claiming I'd connected each and every dot."

"Oh," he said, bemused and surprised.

"Yeah. End of sermon."

"Not all the dots," he answered, regaining his composure. "The Lord does act and sometimes it's not for us to understand. But He also answers prayers, reveals bits and pieces of His kingdom. Heck, you see Him manifest—"

Sophie pinched him at the waist. "I didn't mean to invite a lecture. I'm not interested in the zillion canned responses you memorized at seminary. I wanted you to know what I was thinking—use it as you please. I'm the heathen in the family, remember? You're the theologian."

Lynette had assured Joel repeatedly that Karl Dillen and his swaggering lawyer were posturing and would cave before the trial. On the eve of the hearing, however, her office called to remind him he needed to be present at the Missoula County Courthouse, prepared to testify. When he arrived at the courtroom, it was full of defendants and cops and clerks carrying stacks of files to the bench. The four policemen in attendance had butch haircuts and formidable government-issue shoes, and most of the defendants were wearing jeans and scruffy shirts and appeared permanently dazed or disheveled.

Court began at nine in the morning. Joel smelled alcohol on the man beside him in the gallery, and one poor fellow was so impaired that he never seemed to blink, just sat with his eyes scotched, opening and closing his mouth like a guppy. A pale, fleshy mother had to leave her seat because her baby was crying, and the court's business hummed and pinballed at the front of the room, the law a pedestrian amalgam of quick pleas, lies, pompous soliloquies, remorse, convenience and spur-of-the-moment promises. Excepting the attorneys, Joel was the only man wearing a suit, and he immediately started to fret and perspire, dreaded having to testify and hated sitting with the low-grade criminals who reminded him of his stint at the Roanoke jail.

It was early June, but heat was inexplicably being pumped into the courtroom, making the atmosphere stagnant and sweltering. There was no sign of Karl, Lisa or their lawyer, and Joel attempted to attract Lynette's attention, but she never saw him, was too busy talking to the police, checking warrants, questioning witnesses and dealing with a parade of attorneys seeking concessions for their clients. After an hour, she whispered to a bailiff, who then gruffly advised Joel that the "big-shot dentist's" case was the last one on the docket, wouldn't be heard until eleven-thirty. Joel looked at Lynette, and she raised her hand to acknowledge him before resuming her business. He left and bummed around the town, bought a cold soda and a bag of Cheez Doodles, was so bothered that he smeared the greasy orange powder from the snack on his white shirt.

He was back at the courthouse fifteen minutes early and stumbled into the Dillens and their attorney huddled near the door to the courtroom. Karl appeared sheepish, timid, and he didn't speak. Their lawyer recognized Joel, thrust five spread fingers toward him. "Reverend King," he said. "Chris Hudgins. We met at the Station."

Joel shook his hand. "Good morning," he said.

"Spare a minute?" Hudgins asked. "By ourselves?"

Joel glanced at Lisa. She was petite and frail, the color sucked from her twig arms and bird face. There was a purple-and-black, dime-size bruise on her forearm, and when Joel spotted it, he instinctively isolated Karl, stared down at the hairy ogre in his expensive country-club blazer. "Sure," Joel said, still glowering at Karl.

They walked down a flight of marble steps and stood underneath the building's high ceiling, and Hudgins repeated his spiel, this time much more politely, warned Joel of the dire consequences coming his way if the case didn't go well for the Dillens.

"Your guy's a loser," Joel told him. "He's on tape, Mr. Hudgins. I'm not going to lie, not going to help him, not going to retreat. I'm convinced you and your clients are blowing smoke." He noticed the pillars were painted, not real marble, and he saw an empty red-and-white Coke can discarded on a wooden bench.

"And you observed Karl hit her?" Hudgins probed. "That's what you're prepared to say?"

"Yes. I've already told you."

"I see."

"If you'll excuse me," Joel said, thinking he sounded firm and self-possessed, like Cary Grant or Gregory Peck, a handsome man in Beau Brummell suit and conservative tie, walking off unafraid, his head held high, the villain courteously rebuffed.

The crowd inside had thinned, and Joel took a seat near the railing that separated the spectators from the judge and the court's formal domain. A skinny girl with bad grammar was describing to the judge how her husband "had came home drunk as a hoot owl" and kicked her in the stomach. The husband sat with his head bowed as his lawyer listened and scribbled notes. When the case finished, Christopher Hudgins maneuvered behind Lynette and pecked on her shoulder, bent close to her and whispered. She gazed at Joel while the lawyer chewed her ear, and she shook her head before Hudgins finished talking. Joel could read her lips: "No," she said.

Hudgins stood erect and sighed and then bore in for a second round. The begging became more demonstrative this time, the entreaties accompanied by grimaces and arm flaps, and Joel heard the judge call the case and ask the lawyers if they were ready. Joel prayed he wouldn't have to take the stand and be interrogated and get accused of something he didn't do.

He spied Karl seated in the middle of the gallery. He was holding Lisa's hand and appeared terrified, his breathing nearly a pant, so furious that Joel could see his chest heaving. Lynette was now suggesting something to Hudgins, who'd dropped to one knee beside her chair. They both looked at Joel. "Okay," he saw Hudgins say, and he pushed off the floor and motioned for Karl to meet him outside. Lynette asked the judge for a moment of indulgence, announcing that they'd most likely reached a plea bargain.

Hudgins departed with Karl and Lisa and then reappeared to tell the judge that he and the prosecutor had indeed agreed on a disposition. The bailiff herded Karl and Lisa to the opening between the bench and the witness stand, Karl continuing to hold her hand like some giddy honeymooner. Lynette recited the deal and Hudgins and Karl accepted it: Karl would be convicted of misdemeanor assault, receive twelve months suspended on the condition he attend ten counseling sessions, volunteer a hundred hours at the Salvation Army and pay a five-hundred-dollar fine and the court costs. No active jail time, and the charge was reduced from a felony, Hudgins reiterated when the judge asked if Ms. Allen had correctly stated their understanding.

The judge was a young man with ruddy skin, black curly hair and a wide mouth. He accepted the plea bargain, and after he sentenced Karl, he stared down from his perch and warned Karl that if he ever so much as looked sideways at his wife, he'd be spending a year in jail. In Missoula. With the drunk loggers and roustabouts, none of whom cared for soccer or sailing or opera. Joel grinned when the boy judge laid the opera reference on Karl, enjoyed seeing the lout receive his comeuppance.

As they were leaving, Karl approached Joel—startling him—and extended his hand, said he was sorry and conceded he'd been "a pill." He seemed contrite, and Joel accepted his apology, but he kept mashing his doughy fingers after Karl relaxed his grip, refusing to let him escape quickly. Lisa didn't speak, but she shy-smiled at Joel and briefly touched his arm when she filed by, and she continued to look at him while she walked away, kept the smile uninterrupted and watched him until Karl parted the courtroom doors and she was gone from sight.

Hudgins also checked in, was gregarious and voluble, told Joel "it was nothing personal." Merely doing his job and serving his clients, he said. "I'll treat you to a beer next time I'm at the Station," he promised. He gestured at Joel and thanked Lynette for her willingness to help, then scuttled for the exit.

"Lawyers," Joel said to Lynette as she was migrating in his direction, her attention partly on him and partly on a Palm Pilot she was poking with a stylus. "This clown Hudgins attempts to destroy me, but now we're all backslaps and buddy-buddy. No hard feelings, I hope, about the torture I put you through, those bamboo shoots and jumper cables. You guys are something else."

"Sort of like preachers telling us to forgive the bastard who raped our child or the homewrecker who swiped our husband," she replied, evidently finished with the electronic calendar.

"I'd say there's a difference."

"Tell me. I'm anxious to learn," she said. She'd stopped moving and was reclining against the partition railing. A bailiff asked her if she would be all right, and she said yes, not to worry. "Mr. King is a clergyman," she informed the officer. The officer told her he'd see her after lunch and asked her to switch off the lights when she left. The room was empty, the morning's justice done. "I'd assumed it would be easy for you to overlook Mr. Hudgins's indiscretions."

"Yeah, well, whatever." Joel peeked at the state flag, saw a plough, shovel and rosy mountains. An old woman with stringy gray hair stuck her head in the door, asked if anyone had seen her son, Barry Horton, who was supposed to have been in court at nine o'clock. Lynette told her to check with the clerk, that she didn't recall anyone by the name of Barry. "I'm relieved I didn't have to testify," Joel said.

"I think it's an acceptable deal for everyone," Lynette said.

"Yeah. And Karl seemed chastened, humble enough," Joel remarked.

"He was today. I'm sorry to say it usually doesn't last. Maybe the counseling will help, but wife-beating's a hard habit to break. We forced him to admit he was wrong, though, showed him he has to pay the piper. That's something, an improvement. I'd have liked to seen him in jail, but it wasn't going to happen, not for a first offense with a forgiving victim. And there was some risk if we proceeded to trial, more than normal. I'm satisfied."

"You managed the case well," Joel said.

"Thanks. Oh—I appreciate the quick thinking with the phone call. Hobbes gave us a transcript, and you should've seen Hudgins when I told him we had his client sounding like Mr. Hyde on a FBI intercept. It was priceless."

"I'm glad it helped. Sophie enjoyed cursing him." Joel smiled, glanced at the ceiling and briefly recalled his sister's diatribe. "She really gave him an earful."

"When is your, uh, surrender date?" she asked.

"September," he answered.

"Good luck," she said.

"Yeah, thanks." He hesitated. "So did they find the painting? Believe it or not, I phoned Hobbes twice to see what was happening, but he didn't return the calls."

"I'm not privy to their operations. We basically gave them a three-day lag before popping Sa'ad. I understand from Winton they did in fact search Van Heiss's home in Las Vegas and some other properties in Europe. No Chagall so far, but they did find the red sister ring at Van Heiss's and another stolen painting. I don't know any more than that."

"Huh."

"I don't have any idea about Van Heiss, if he's been charged," she said. "Not in my bailiwick."

Joel swallowed twice. "What about Sa'ad?"

"Mr. Sa'ad X. Sa'ad," she said, exaggerating the name. "Ah, yes. The green sister was right where you said it was. I believe Officer Winton confirmed that for you a day or two following the search."

"He did. He called and spoke with me after Sophie phoned you, wanted to verify my information so they could get a warrant. Afterward, he was kind enough to let me know how things turned out. I was happy to get the news."

"Sa'ad claims he was set up, that he's being framed because he's outspoken and black and a champion of unpopular causes. Swears the ring was planted and tells everyone who'll listen you're a liar."

"He engineered the insurance hustle. He and Edmund. That should be obvious."

"I doubt he'll go without a battle," Lynette said. "He's no Karl Dillen. You might have to testify there, too, if they challenge the search."

"I know—testifying is a condition of my agreement. I'm ready."

"Ready to say you didn't plant the evidence?"

"Agent Winton searched me prior to the meeting with Sa'ad, and I was constantly with some cop or agent. They can vouch for me."

"So I hear," she said.

"Of course, I truly don't want to go to trial and have to answer questions and so forth. You see how nervous this small skirmish with Karl has made me. I hate court. I hate the pressure. Hopefully you folks can keep my involvement to a minimum. A skilled attorney might be able to trip me up. I'm no good in this situation. Let's avoid Joel-the-witness as much as we can."

There was a penny lying on the floor, and Joel and Lynette caught sight of it at the same time. She stooped and collected it, held it in a flat hand and asked Joel if he wanted it.

"You can keep it," he told her.

"I do understand they've uncovered a number of irregularities in Mr. Sa'ad's files. Bogus social security numbers, fictitious plaintiffs, fake medical expenses, reports from the same doctor in hundreds of cases."

"Wonderful. So I was right, wasn't I?"

"Seems so," she said. "He was operating a regular fraud factory—a damn sophisticated one, too."

"I'm relieved he's been caught. Makes my life easier."

"You sure you don't want the penny?" she asked. She gave Joel an enigmatic look.

"You found it," he replied.

"I shouldn't mention it, but given your hesitancy to testify against Sa'ad—and perhaps 'hesitancy' isn't the correct word—I thought I'd let you know Winton and the folks in Sin City don't really give a flip about the ring. They simply needed enough probable cause to allow them into Sa'ad's office, wanted to make it through the door any way they could. No matter what happens, I'd say Mr. Sa'ad's gravy train has departed the station minus its number-one passenger. Even if he doesn't go to jail, he'll be disbarred and lose his law license. And there'll be hundreds of civil suits and years of litigation once the insurance industry gets wind of his schemes. Sa'ad will never plague Harry Winton or the insurance companies again. He's kaput, the dragon slain."

"I appreciate your telling me. And I hope it'll be a feather in your cap. You've been a blessing where I'm concerned."

"Oh, I'm sure they'll arrange a big press conference and news release and everyone will smoke cigars. White-collar arrest—shows the world justice is blind to money and power. The dope dealers and peckerwoods can't scream discrimination. The bread and circuses will continue as scheduled."

"Well, thank you for everything. You're the sort of fair and smart person who should be doing this stuff."

"Some people think so," she said.

"Could I buy you lunch?" he asked. "I'd be honored."

"Thanks, but I'd rather not."

"I understand." There was no mistaking her message or her words: he was a criminal and she was a prosecutor, and the twain would never meet.

She pivoted toward her papers and files, then delayed at the gap in the railing. "You realize everything has tentacles, Mr. King. Blowback and spillage. Consequences. That's the first rule of what I do. See what happens when a husband hits his wife? When a prick like Karl Dillen tries to hijack the system and avoid responsibility? The ripples? See how innocent people can get drowned in the wake? It's physics, a Newtonian by-product. I hope you've learned something, being both a cause and an effect."

Joel worked an eight-hour shift at the Station that evening, and when he arrived home to his basement, he undressed and prayed, thanked the Lord for His aid and wisdom. But for some reason this salvation felt superficial and joyless, banal, along the lines of a fast-food hamburger or prostitute's seduction. There was no milk and honey, no contentment in his soul, no sense that he'd been restored to grace. Despite having put his house in order as divinely instructed, he felt as foreign and rootless as ever.

On a more mundane level, the conclusion to his travails struck him as too neat and staid, a plodding, anticlimactic slog that withered at the finale rather than erupting. He wasn't sure what he'd expected—maybe Sa'ad in handcuffs kicking and screaming, maybe Hobbes and Lynette on the national news with the priceless art, maybe his sister happily blubbering over her reward check—but certainly there needed to be more than snippets of information regarding half-baked successes and the suggestion that a wife-beater might, but probably wouldn't, mend his habits.

He repeatedly tried praying, beseeched Heaven for relief, and he fell asleep the night after Karl's trial and dreamt of Michelangelo's *Creation of Adam,* dwelling on the space between the finger of man and the finger of God, an infinitesimal separation that seemed as immense as a continent. Joel dreamed he was standing on the floor of the Sistine Chapel, and he saw the painted Adam convulse, withdraw his hand from the cloud of cherubs and omnipotent prospects of the Lord, and lo and behold if the first man didn't fall from the ceiling, come hurtling and flailing to the ground, splat.

Joel continued to wash dishes and spray pots at the Station, and he had bookings every weekend in June, rowed fishermen from seven to five and sipped coffee with Dixon in the mornings. He had a short float the last Sunday in June, was finished by two o'clock, and he and Dixon took Baker to a deep, emerald hole on the Clark Fork, let the child fish with bait and kill two chunky cutthroats. Jack Howard didn't utter a peep when Joel omitted the thirty extortion dollars from his monthly probation payment and didn't antagonize him with asinine questions and crude stories, aware as he was of Joel's connections to the county attorney's office and his importance in a major FBI case.

The hen hatched seven chicks, Sophie and Raleigh went camping at Yellowstone and Joel scratched off days on a calendar with a felt marker, circled August fifth in red. Time eventually became satisfying and rewarding, made quintessential because it would soon expire, but he never was completely able to shake the feeling he was missing something critical, sensed that he hadn't altogether gained the Lord's favor. He had the Adam nightmare again, and one night he dreamed he was in the Roanoke jail, lying on a cot while Kenny and Watkins Hudson bickered and talked about making moonshine whiskey.

July Fourth, Joel grilled hot dogs on a hibachi while Raleigh's son and Baker played with a water hose and pedaled their bikes up and down the drive and raced around the house. Joel wore an apron that said "The Cook Is Always Right," made vinegary coleslaw from scratch and told Raleigh a funny anecdote about Sophie's senior prom. Sophie and Raleigh drank too much beer and became giggly and punchy. They watched the moon ascend and teeter on the Bitterroot, like one of those blue yard-ornament spheres on a concrete pedestal, Raleigh suggested, his speech thick, delighted. Sophie told him he wasn't shit as a poet, and the three of them busted a gut laughing and ended the night with bottle rockets and sparklers.

The next morning, Detective Hubbard phoned from Virginia and gave Sophie a message for Joel. They'd located Christy, and she was unharmed, so Joel was no longer under suspicion. The hornswoggling with Christy was a loose end of sorts, but Joel couldn't see where he had any exposure there. It was fortunate for him—another of the Lord's protections—that she'd skipped with his half of the take, because Sophie didn't want the money anyway, would never accept it, and now he didn't have to worry about being arrested for his role in another fraud conspiracy.

He'd occasionally considered Christy and her betrayal, had been plagued by her face and voice as he was unloading the boat at the Saint Regis put-in or tending to a tub of dirty dishes or following a kingfisher's balletic arc from tree to river to tree. She came and went at will, always uninvited and unexpected. Early on, after his Roanoke deposition, he'd allowed himself to imagine her arriving in Missoula, a suitcase pregnant with cash banging against her thigh as she lugged it from her car to Sophie's porch. He'd also sporadically revisited his original sin—even though it should've been taboo—recalling his hand inside her shirt and her breast overlapping the lace cup of her bra. He'd been angry with her initially, "pissed off" to use Sophie's phrase, but he'd finally concluded that she should be compensated somehow, since he'd violated whatever religious impulse she ever had and done little or nothing to expand it. And who could put a price on that?

twenty-two _____

Joel's client the Saturday after Independence Day was a peculiar duck, a tall, powerful man in cargo shorts and a muscle shirt. Blond crew cut, blue eyes, tattoos, hiking boots and no hat. His brother was scheduled to fish with him but was delayed, the man explained, would meet them at the river if Joel would be kind enough to give him directions so he could convey the route by cell phone. Joel told Dixon the guy was a weirdo, wondered if he'd ever hired Royal Coachman before. Dixon reviewed his reservation list and old logs and didn't find anything other than a name, a California address and a phone number for the current booking. He offered to send the man on his way, but Joel shrugged and played it off, noted he'd seen worse. Standing beside his boss and selecting flies for the trip, Joel wisecracked that he was himself a legitimate jailbird, scared of nothing, hard-boiled.

The blond's name was Joshua, and he answered Joel's polite questions and asked a number of his own while they drove to the river. Joel had backed the trailer and MacKenzie boat to the edge of the Blackfoot and was winding the winch crank when a car arrived, a red four-door with California plates. From a distance, Joshua's brother looked much like he did—the same blond crew cut, a forearm tattoo and clunky hiking boots. But the brother was smaller, lacked Joshua's bulk and stature, and he was dressed in a baggy shirt and long pants, his eyes masked by sunglasses that followed the shape of his head. The brothers spoke, and the newcomer locked his car and started for Joel, by himself.

He was older, Joel observed. Older than his brother, and his hair was whiter, appeared dyed. He was careful with his feet, hesitated between strides and seemed extra cautious on the slick slope between the last log step and the beginning of the riverbank. Joel shouted good morning over the river's rushing and pulled a cooler across the gunwale. It was a cinch neither of these men could cast a fly, and that would make for a tiresome day and tangled lines. He checked for life jackets, felt his pockets for leaders and tippet. The brother was at stream level, ten yards removed. "Ready for some fishing?" Joel asked enthusiastically. Most likely not big spenders, but you could never tell. And they'd probably want to use drugs and guzzle beer, fit the profile.

"Howdy," the man said. Joshua was still at the car, loafing near the fender, and his posture and crossed arms and lack of fishing interest caused Joel to feel unsettled again.

"Your brother coming?" Joel asked.

"Yeah. He's slow."

The man was at the bow of the boat, and Joel recognized him—Lord Jesus, he recognized him—and Joel immediately reached for a paddle, didn't make any effort to disguise what he was doing or to downplay his alarm.

"Damn, Joel, is that any way to treat a long-lost friend? Smack him with an oar?"

It was Edmund, Edmund with new hair and bleached eyebrows and a tattoo and a young man's glasses and a novel wardrobe, but unmistakably Edmund when he spoke and Joel was able to hear his voice and draw a bead on his features. "You tell me," Joel said. "Looks pretty appropriate from where I'm standing." He removed the oar from the boat and held it with the broad end skyward. "Especially with you sneaking up on me. You and Dolph Lundgren there."

"I ain't here lookin' for trouble, Joel."

"No?"

"No," Edmund answered. He took off the glasses and hung them at the front of his shirt, stuck one earpiece inside his collar.

"Why the cloak and dagger?"

"I wasn't sure if you'd care to see me," Edmund said. "And, hell, who knows if the cops are still watching you."

"What do you want?" Joel kept the paddle in position. He looked at the boat, trying to calculate how long it would take him to be on the river if Joshua left his post and came toward the water.

"To talk."

"For some reason, I have the feeling Joshua's not a very gifted conversationalist," Joel said.

"Should I have him scram?" Edmund asked.

"Yes," Joel answered.

"He's harmless as a kitten," Edmund said. "He really is my brother. My baby brother. Lives in LA and pumps too many weights. He wants to be in action movies."

"Well, why don't you have him action himself on down the highway?"

"I needed him to make the arrangements and bring you this far, okay? I didn't much see us gettin' together any other way."

"You're right about that."

Edmund walked to the first step and yelled for Joshua, tossed him the car keys and told him to leave and come back in half an hour. "There you are, my friend," he said to Joel when he returned. "Anything else I can do?"

"Take off the shirt and spin in a circle. Toss me the glasses. Take off your pants and underwear and let me have them as well. Shoes too."

"Okay. Sure. The pants'll be a while, what with my bad leg and so forth."

"I'm not in a hurry." Joel rested the large end of the oar on the ground and kept both hands on the knob.

Edmund undressed and surrendered his clothes to Joel, had to sit in the dirt to remove his trousers, and, while he was working the garment over his prosthesis, he asked Joel how his sister was faring. "She's fine," Joel said curtly. Edmund was soon naked, and he seemed surprisingly feeble with his clothes stripped, his usual aura and vitality replaced by two folds of flesh at his belly and a bony, concave chest.

"I'd always been curious about that," Joel said.

"About what? What I'd look like naked?" Edmund laughed, jiggling his stomach and shoulders. He didn't seem too uncomfortable with his circumstances, acted more impatient than embarrassed. A car motored by on the road above them, and they turned in unison to watch it.

"Your leg. If you're truly handicapped." Joel continued to scan the road, wondering if Joshua had really departed or had just driven around a bend and was lurking in the woods, poised to spring some godawful trap.

"I wish I wasn't, but I'm a true gimp, Joel. Yep."

"You probably got shot by an angry husband or tried to cheat the wrong mark," Joel scoffed.

"Nope. Lost it when I was a little chap, exactly like I told you. Coulda saved it too, if the insurance people would've loosened their purse strings."

"So that's not a lie?"

"True as a mother's milk. Can I have my pants? Some of me ain't seen this much sunlight in years. I don't need to wind up fried and sun-poisoned."

Joel searched the clothes and didn't discover anything unusual. He wadded the britches and threw them to Edmund. "Why are you here?"

"My shirt? Shoes? Can I have the rest of my clothes?"

Joel chucked the remainder at Edmund's feet. "You've got one minute, and then I'm going to hop in this boat and be gone."

"I wanna know your next move," Edmund said, buttoning his shirt. "Specifically, what it'll take to be rid of you? The price."

"The price?" Joel leaned on the oar. "Be rid of me how?"

"You gonna cut my throat like you did Sa'ad's?" His tone was wounded, can't-believe-it amazed, like the cocky quick-draws in old westerns who get shot and feel the blood oozing from the bullet hole, discover no one's invincible. "I'm willin' to pay."

"I'm going to tell the truth, and if the truth cuts your throat, so be it. Why are you so worried anyway? Seems you've done a superior job of vanishing." For some reason, Joel was drawn to look at Edmund's deformed finger.

He had regained his pants and shirt but was still shoeless, and his belt and wallet remained on the ground, incongruous among the shoal rocks and fragments of smooth, river-washed wood. "Why'd you do this? All we had to do was keep quiet and circle the wagons, and the cops couldn't have laid a glove on us."

"Kiss my butt, Edmund," Joel said. "Don't come dragging here with your doe eyes and tale of woe and misery. I can't believe you have the . . . the . . . nerve to suggest I'm the one who broke ranks. Claim I've wronged *you*. I know, Edmund. Understand? I had an informative tête-à-tête with your girl Christy." Joel was growing angry, and he could feel the bile dapple his neck and blacken his spit. He choked the paddle handle, rattled the blade in the stones. "I probably wouldn't be here if it weren't for you and Sa'ad. I'd be drafting my sermon and looking forward to a picnic with my wife on the parkway this afternoon."

"I'm lost, Preacher. I don't know what I've done to tick you off so bad." A breeze nipped the peak of his hair.

The denials caused Joel to fume. He armed himself with the oar again, shaking it at Edmund. "You worthless swine. There's no need to keep lying. She told me."

"Told you what?" Edmund asked. He extended his arms and bent his wrists in reverse, a supplicant in search of answers. "I don't know what the hell you're talking about."

"I ought to whip the tarnation out of you. First for setting me up and now for bald-face lying to me." He advanced on Edmund, raised the paddle and slid his hands into a narrower grip.

"Whoa now. Hold on a minute. Somethin's terribly confused here." He retreated a step and dragged each naked foot, one flesh, one plastic, through the dirt and stones, caused two different scrapes. "I'm the one who should be carryin' a grudge. I'm the one who got left high and dry, traded to the police for a couple years off your penitentiary sentence." He kept his arms aloft while he spoke.

"Nothing's confused except you," Joel said. A swell of saliva spilled at the corner of his lip, and he blotted it with his palm and sleeve. "You need to go find your brother before I lose my temper."

"Tell me why you're cross, why you're so damn hot with me. Least you could do that. It's been buggin' me to death why you jumped ship."

Joel wiped his lips again. "I'm hot, Edmund, because you pretended to be a friend and then used me like I was crap, and the Lord will have to punish me, yes He will, because seeing you right now I don't think I can ever forgive you. I'm angry because you cost me my wife and job and church and peace of mind, and because you sent a seventeen-year-old girl to trap me so you and Sa'ad could steal money. That makes you a crook and a pimp, Edmund. A lowlife."

"Christy? You mean Christy from Roanoke?" Edmund dropped his arms and contracted his mouth.

The answer infuriated Joel, enraged him, and he swung the oar, took an energetic, roundhouse cut even though he wasn't near enough to Edmund for it to connect. "Yeah, Edmund. The same girl you trained and educated and sent after me."

"Joel, hey, listen. It ain't nothing for me one way or the other right now, but I didn't have nothing to do with you and Christy. You gotta believe me."

"She told me, Edmund. Admitted it. Confessed."

"Confessed what?" he asked. "Why would I want to get you in trouble with her?"

"Millions of insurance dollars?" Joel was on the brink of walloping him with the oar, couldn't help himself.

"Somethin's wrong, Joel. She's lyin' to you."

"Did you send her to Las Vegas? Provide her and another girl airline tickets?"

"Well, yeah. But that doesn't tell you nothing."

"Mentor her on a few scams, let her cut her teeth with a pro?" Talking helped the rage; he finally felt his anger start to ebb.

"Two or three. A slip-and-fall, some baby stuff. But nothing with you."

"Nothing with me?" Joel demanded.

"Absolutely not. I swear. On my mother's grave, I swear. May God strike me dead if I'm lying."

"He probably doesn't want to waste the bullet," Joel said. "You're not worth it."

"That's why you turned on us, isn't it? You think we somehow hosed you first."

"Explain this, Edmund." Joel rested the paddle on his shoulder, transferred most of his weight to one leg. "How does a spoiled, undisciplined, seventeen-year-old girl develop a sophisticated insurance scam that has her using my pubic hair as the coup de grâce? She thought of that by herself? Didn't get any advice from, say, a professional con man like Edmund Brooks?"

"Pubic hair? Wait . . . Huh. So . . . So you didn't screw her?" Edmund asked.

"No. I didn't." Joel was defensive, his voice not as fevered as it had been. "You didn't?"

"I didn't have sex with the girl. Not then, not ever. She lied." He paused. "Well, basically she lied. There's no chance my pubic hair was on her because of sex." His mood was closer to normal, cooling and receding.

"I always thought you did—I was just tryin' to stick up for you and pretend otherwise. I didn't think less of you for it. Everybody has errors, backslides. Damn, Joel." His expression was stoic, his hands in his hip pockets. "My oh my."

"Well, I didn't."

"You pled guilty, didn't fight, didn't ever deny it," Edmund said.

"It's complicated and none of your business. But I'm not divulging anything you don't already know, huh?"

"I thought you done it," he muttered, plopping to the ground beside his belt and billfold. "Never saw it coming." He laughed, a vacant, mournful clucking that the stream instantly swept away. "Sure didn't." He stared up at Joel. "Go ahead if you like. Beat the hell out of me. I deserve it."

"So you admit it? You gave her the con?"

"You could say I did," he said, the words dismal.

"Could say?" Joel asked.

"Yeah." He kicked at the rocks and bumped a piece of wood with his toe. "We've all been had, Preacher. In the worst way. It's my scam all right, my best one ever. But I sure didn't sic her on you or tell her to use it." He shut his eyes and pressed his head into his knees, and Joel had no doubt he was miserable, truly suffering. He said some more, but his mouth was against the cloth of his pants, and the river overrode his voice, drowning the words.

Joel went closer and strained to hear. "Edmund?" he said, standing above him.

He didn't answer.

"You okay?" Joel asked.

"I'm so sorry, Joel. We shoulda known better."

Joel sat at his feet. "Should have known what?"

"My fault," he said. "Fucked us all."

"Tell me," Joel said. He could smell the damp, fertile river soil underneath the stones.

"See, me and Sa'ad carried her to Vegas and showed her the ropes. Christy. She asked us about our biggest project, the best we'd ever done. Sa'ad's sister—sweet girl, name of Joyce, two kids—was working for a big car dealership in Atlanta and her boss kept hittin' on her, wouldn't leave it alone. So we're at Rosewood Grille and showin' off for Christy, and we tell her how we solved the problem and made money to boot."

"Sa'ad's sister cried rape and just happened to have the boss's pubic hair." Joel unconsciously touched his lips with his three middle fingers. "Lord in heaven," he said.

"Our biggest score. Joyce grabbed some fuzz from the old guy's john and ran screamin' to the police. We got half a million and a new Infiniti. And hell, we simply helped the truth along. The old fart was on her like glue—we didn't create nothing that wasn't already present."

"And you told Christy?" Joel asked.

"Sure did. Sa'ad and me and Dom Perignon. Who would've thought?"

"Yeah."

"Little bitch decided to go into business on her own. She didn't really tell you I was in on the play, did she?"

Joel gazed at the river before answering, saw a lone heron and, farther upstream, a group of mergansers hastening across a sandbar. He summoned Christy's face into his mind, recalled her answers at Mac and Maggie's, recollected how she'd spellbound him with "maybes" and prismatic qualifications and denials so intentionally flimsy they were tantamount to affirmations, how he was convinced he knew the truth even before he asked the questions. "Well, maybe I'm saying Edmund was sorta involved," she'd said, sitting in the restaurant's parking lot and belching beer, and that was everything he'd required, a doubtful equivocation that he'd foolishly fashioned into a rock-ribbed given. "She told me what I wanted to hear," Joel said, gathering a gray-green stone and flinging it into the Blackfoot.

" 'Cause I never, ever would've done anything to you. You're my friend, Joel. You were a great minister, the gold standard. And you buried my dad, rode to Maine round-trip with me and conducted a beautiful service for him. I was tryin' to help by offering you a piece of the sag—to this day, I don't think I'm doin' wrong. How much is a person's leg worth? Huh? They ain't paid me enough yet. All I wanted to do was help you. I never tried to screw you or pull you into somethin' wrong."

" 'And a little child shall lead them . . .' Remember that scripture, Edmund?" Joel sent another stone into the river. He saw the splash but couldn't hear the sound.

Edmund nodded. "Sorta. But I hope this ain't the same little child."

"No, I suppose not. It was the first thing that came into my mind." Joel peered at a section of water violently cleaved by a boulder. White chop roiled and gurgled at the boulder's beakish point. "She's more like the daughter of Herodias, the girl child who danced for Herod and got John the Baptist's head as her payment. Herod was the tetrarch of Galilee, remember? I did a sermon on him. Two, in fact. He was so taken by her, he promised her anything in his kingdom. And here we are, two grown men—me a minister—blinded and led astray by a snot-nosed kid."

"Well, at least we didn't kill no one," Edmund offered. "And everybody makes mistakes."

Joel grunted. He popped his forehead with the heel of his hand. "What a dunce I've been."

"You wouldn't have gone against us if you'd known the truth, would you?" Edmund asked.

"No. I would've taken my lumps and kept my mouth shut."

"Damn straight you would've," Edmund declared. "You're no snitch. You've got more character than that."

"I'm not certain how much character I have."

"This is some crazy shit, like the Marx Brothers or *I Love Lucy* when a person misunderstands one teeny fact and everything snowballs and builds on a wrong idea."

"I'm as much to blame as you are, Edmund," Joel said. "Me and my assumptions." He chuckled, then laughed, then barreled into an ungainly howl. "I screwed Sa'ad for no reason," he remarked after composing himself. "Thought I was in charge and doing big things, tried to put the Lord on terms. What an idiot."

"You believe me, don't you? Believe she did the insurance project by herself?"

"Yes," Joel said. "And you have every right to be upset with me. I'm sorry

I doubted you. It seemed logical, seemed . . ." He gestured with his hands, didn't finish the defense.

"I've had a sour stretch, I can't deny that," Edmund said ruefully. "And Sa'ad, well, Sa'ad's mad as a wet hornet."

"Has he implicated you?"

"Gosh no. He hasn't and he won't. But I'm out of commission these days. Coverin' my tracks, lyin' low, flyin' under the radar. You've put me in a helluva bind," Edmund said, sounding rankled for the first time.

"Can you survive? Moneywise, I mean?"

"I've been workin' the sag for twenty years. I got enough salted away to be okay—you had to know sooner or later the gig would expire. But I didn't plan on havin' to live on the lam and wear fake mustaches and find a home in Tijuana. Lot of what comes next depends on you."

"Apparently, the authorities are primarily interested in Sa'ad and the jewelry and the painting; you're second tier. They had me try to call you when we couldn't rope Sa'ad, but that was it. And since Sa'ad discovered me with a wire, I'm off the team. I'm done."

"So you ain't after me? You're not planning to punch my ticket at Sa'ad's trial or keep workin' with the police?"

"No," Joel quickly answered. "I would have an hour ago, but not now."

"I appreciate it."

"Who could find you anyway? No one even knows your real name."

"I don't need people huntin' for me, stirring the pot. The FBI or state police could make it damn rough if they put their minds to it."

"You don't have to worry about me. Like I said, I'm through, and I don't think they're too interested in you anyway. Sa'ad's the catch—you and I are the tadpoles."

"I sure hope so. Man, I do. And I'm sure grateful to hear you don't have an axe to grind with me."

"May I ask you something, Edmund?"

"Let 'er rip," he replied, his voice tinged with relief, his posture gaining vigor. "I'm all ears."

"This probably seems like a small concern, but I wondered . . . wondered about leaving Roanoke, at the store . . . those kids selling doughnuts. Did you clip them?"

"Well, yeah, uh, I did. Hell, Joel, the sag in an enterprise such as that would take your breath. Major profit and cushion built into every box. They've got no more than a buck invested and they're sellin' 'em at four, and the damn school's already takin' my tax dollars and I don't have kids and—"

Joel spoke before he finished. "Enough already. You don't have to justify it to me. I simply wanted to know."

"Fair game, definitely sag," Edmund added, his voice barely above the river's flow.

"One other question—your tie. The tie you wore the last day I preached. Remember?" Another boat was in view. Two anglers were unfurling casts, and a guide was rowing them to one of Joel's favorite riffles, an extended seam that widened into a pocket of placid water beside a shady bank.

Edmund was studying the boat and the fishermen. "Tie? You're referrin' to a necktie?"

"Yes," Joel said.

"Why's that important?"

"Do you remember the tie?" Joel asked. He scooted forward, felt the stones stab his butt and thighs. "The color? Did you do that on purpose?"

"I'm sorry, but you've lost me again."

"Red," Joel said, and he could see the hue in his mind's eye, joining Edmund to the church's carpeted floor. "Identical to the rug, the exact same color. Like some dandy flourish, coordinating your clothes to match the sanctuary."

Edmund pondered the question. "Red tie?"

"Yeah. You were sitting in your usual spot. It was uncanny, and I have this ingrained image of you I'll never forget. I was struggling, reeling, try-ing to make it through the service, and I'll never forget looking at you and seeing this red bond between you and the floor."

"Must've been someone else," Edmund said without inflection.

"No, it was you. You and a red tie. I'm positive."

"Not possible, Joel. You must be mistaken. I don't own anything red, especially a tie. It's a jinxed color for me. Haven't worn red in years—lost ten grand in Atlantic City playin' blackjack, and that cured me. I wear green and silver, the color of money. But nothing red—no ties, shirts, coats, pants, underwear, hats, nothing. It's cursed for me."

"I wasn't hallucinating, Edmund. I saw what I saw."

"You must've been stressed or confused me with another member. Maybe Oliver Rakes—he's a sharp dresser, and he sat in my pew."

One of the men in the boat had hooked a trout, and the guide was wait-ing with a long-handled net.

"It was you," Joel insisted.

"Impossible. But I don't want to argue with you. Who cares, huh? It doesn't make any difference, does it? Could have been an optical illusion, too, with all the stained glass in those windows. Why're you so agitated about what color tie I happened to wear? You're sure askin' me a bunch of bizarre questions."

"You're one hundred percent, absolutely certain it wasn't red?" Joel asked.

"Goodness sakes, Joel," he laughed, "how many ways can I say it? I haven't worn a red tie since Reagan was president, okay?"

"It . . . It was for me, wasn't it?" he said, more to himself than Edmund. "The Lord was calling His shot, tipping His hand in advance so I'd know when the dust cleared that He authored this." Joel leapt to his feet. "Ha. Darn. I'll be darned." He felt queasy and ecstatic and his stomach was pulsating. "Now I see."

"I reckon the tension had to be nearly unbearable," Edmund said, remaining a beat behind. "Someone in that situation, your eyes could play tricks on you. Or your memory could fail. We're talkin' . . . my goodness, we're dealing with a tie I wore months and months ago. I sure as heck can't remember it."

"Doesn't matter," Joel said. "I didn't have any idea at the time why it was significant, and I wasn't supposed to."

"You goin' to share the secret with me, Joel, or leave me in the cold?"

"Edmund, there's an artisan's accomplishment in our intersection and our resolution, an astounding glory. This was my trip, my journey, and the Lord snared you with red bonds and marked you early on so there'd be no mistaking His intent when everything was said and done. You were His instrument. This all happened *through* you, and I know that—now—because I literally saw the church take hold of you."

"Sounds to me like a polite way of sayin' I'm the one who dragged you into this mess. And, hey, red might be someone else's callin' card."

"It's all in how you read it, Edmund, and what you do when your time comes."

"I suppose you know better than me what you saw."

"Remarkable. And I've lived to tell the tale, huh? It was the premium package, too. Platinum, A-1. I sinned and suffered and caved in, lost patience and faith the first time I was truly challenged, resorted to graft and gypping insurance companies, sank deeper into the pit when matters got worse, lied and connived and claimed it as heaven-sent, questioned the validity of my beliefs when I didn't discover instant responses to my prayers, tried to manage the Lord's shop and usurp His prerogatives, and wound up ineffectual and dumbfounded, like a pygmy attempting to solve the sun. I was so distant from influencing events it's ridiculous. What a marvelous, unbelievable display I've witnessed."

Edmund stood and jammed the tail and sides of his shirt into his pants. "What are you saying? Ain't any good whatsoever I can find in you goin' to jail and me tiptoeing on eggshells, worried the police are on my butt and my projects shelved forever."

"Are you a fisherman, Edmund?" Joel asked, his face inspired by the realization, his hands active and darting with useless bustle.

"No, I've wet a line before, but none of this stuff. I fish with worms and a spinning reel. Why're you changing the subject?"

Joel grinned. "Today you're a fisherman. The trip's on me, on the house. I'll row you over some spectacular water, teach you to cast and we'll catch trout, have the float of a lifetime."

"You and me?" Edmund asked. "Go fishin'?"

"Exactly. You'll enjoy it. We'll wait for your brother to get back and let him know, so he won't be worried."

Edmund bent down for his belt and wallet. "If you want to, I don't see why not." He threaded the belt through its loops and buckled it at the second notch on the leather. "And me and you, we're straight, right? Whatever else, we're on the same page? You'll let me be?"

"What name was the reservation in?" Joel asked. "Beeler, wasn't it?"

"At the outfitter's?"

"Yes," Joel said.

"Yeah, George Beeler."

"Well, Mr. Beeler, as far as I'm concerned, everything is sealed and understood. Edmund Brooks is a million miles away, an old friend I haven't seen in a coon's age and will never see again."

"Amen to that," Edmund said.

Joel's disposition was so upbeat in the weeks prior to his September surrender that Sophie twice inquired if he was going bonkers and told him his humming and singing and cheerful "good mornings" were creepy, the kind of graveyard whistling that precedes a nervous breakdown or the casual massacre of innocents at a rural post office. He'd been lark-happy since he'd arrived home from fishing with Edmund Brooks and informed her of Christy's artifice, how she'd snookered two confidence men and a college-educated pastor. He gave Sarah plenty of notice and told her the absolute truth about his circumstances, thanked her for her generosity and apologized for his advances and improper interest in a married lady. At the conclusion of his final shift, she told him he'd been a capable employee and she'd enjoyed meeting him, remarking as she presented his wages that he'd be eligible for rehire if he needed a job. Before he could leave, Frankie enticed him into the kitchen, everyone shouted "surprise," the chef unveiled a farewell cake and Joel kicked around for another hour while the staff drank beer, munched cake and cracked raunchy jokes about prison sodomites.

He couldn't help but cry when he put Baker in bed the night before his departure, and once he started bawling the boy did, too. They were reciting their prayers, knees and toes on the floor, elbows denting the mattress, chins tucked, and the child asked God to take care of Uncle Joel and thanked Jesus for the fishing pole and sled and promised to obey his mother. He'd scratched his face on a briar and his pajama bottoms were too snug and he had a cowlick that no amount of water or hair tonic could tame, and as soon as he concluded his childishly stilted version of the Lord's Prayer, the tears rolled.

Joel sat at the foot of Baker's bed, and the little boy cried in the fashion that little boys of tender years cry, the sobs and wails unabated and made more poignant because he had an intuitive sense of what was happening but couldn't completely understand it, couldn't fathom why his bear of an uncle was weeping with him. Sophie had explained that Joel was going to Arizona to satisfy a debt, to work sort of, and he'd be returning to their house for the summer, before he was even missed. They'd agreed not to bring the boy to the penitentiary, but Joel would write and mail him knick-knacks and phone whenever the opportunity arose. "It won't be like your dad," Joel promised him, broaching this subject for the first time ever. "I'm not leaving for good."

"Cross your heart?" Baker whimpered.

"Cross my heart," Joel replied, attending to the boy's wet cheeks with the knuckle side of a gentle hand.

The morning of his turn-in, Joel and Sophie traveled to High Pines to visit their mother. They didn't speak during the entire trip, kept to themselves but were at ease with the quiet, had no need to talk for the sake of talking. Joel wasn't sure what he wanted for his mom, whether her life was worthwhile or simply a painful bog, but he desperately hoped she wouldn't die while he was in prison. They ate breakfast with her in the communal dining area, and she called Joel "Sheldon"—a reference that baffled both her children—and devoured a second serving of bacon and scrambled eggs. She raided the Smucker's jelly containers from her table and the adjacent table, smuggled eleven foil squares—predominantly strawberry— to her room and added them to her supply of sugar packets, salt, straws and paper napkins. They made conversation for ten minutes, and she put on her Christmas Stetson as they were leaving and in a lucid interval told Joel she loved him and the hat was a treasure for her.

Sophie turned glum and dejected as they drove home, remarking that it was difficult to be party to such pervasive sadness—a mother whose mind had decayed beyond any hope of reclamation, a beloved brother headed to a federal penitentiary, a son abandoned by his own father. Joel did what he could to console her, reminding her of Raleigh and her talents as an essayist and her dedication to Baker, mentioning how noble she'd been in spite of the hardships and inequities she'd seen.

"I'm heartbroken things didn't go better for you, Joel," she said. "I know you must be disappointed. You're at zero again: no job, no money and nine months in jail. And I've been a bitch sometimes, especially at the beginning."

"Oh no," he protested. "I'm not dismayed or unhappy, not in the least. Don't be concerned about me. I'm a million times better than I was a year ago, and you've been a wonderful sister. We've all been improved, and I'm where I need to be. I'm a rich man, Sophie, wealthy in the sense I've always desired to be."

"Well, I *am* worried about you," she said. She quit watching the interstate and stared at him. "I am, despite the fact you've had this wacko, sunny bearing and perma-smile for the last two months." She returned her attention to the road. "You've been acting like a Stepford wife. Or like the friggin' pod people have captured you."

"Listen. I didn't want to say a lot till it was time for me to go, but this experience has been a cure for me. An antidote. I truly am content. I feel grounded and at peace, okay?"

"Joel, you're going to jail. Today. For the second time. You're penniless. You're divorced. You'll need to enlighten me as to why you're so chipper."

"Two reasons. First, before I came here, before the trouble with Christy and Sa'ad and Edmund, I spent year after year after year in this vacuum of a world where I had not one adversity, not a single assault on my religion. My faith was like a hothouse flower or a laboratory invention that busted the first time it was hit by a strong wind. Now it's galvanized, reinforced, a shield that will hold no matter what. I'm secure because I've been walked through the valley, not because I've done an exegesis on the Book of Nahum or touched the parchment pages of some original manuscript or been paid a salary to do a minstrel show every Sunday. Can you imagine what an asset that is? How relieved I am?"

"So if I rob a liquor store, I'll become wise? I can grow secure in my view of the universe by pulling moronic stunts like fondling a juvenile girl from my church?"

"Everyone's different, Sophie. I was an economics professor who'd never dug a ditch, a musician who'd invested decades in reading scores and never sung a song. It was a harrowing ride, I made every bad choice imaginable and I'm paying a price, but, hey, now I know. I'd hoped to avoid prison, but that's part of the calculus."

They were at the secondary route that led to her house, a tar-and-gravel road in ill repair. She slowed and activated the blinker, lifted from the gas. "You made several poor choices, but you're human, Joel. We have frailties—you, me and the guy next door, and we do dumbass things and hopefully learn a lesson. What does that prove? You were in a pinch, desperate, and you clawed and fought and did what you could. You've touched the hot stove and been burned, and you're smarter for it. So? You're still broke, your wife left you and you don't have jack to show for your sojourn in Missoula other than a fresh conviction. This is the wellspring of your happiness?"

He chuckled. As Sophie was accelerating onto the two-lane road, he saw a deer lope across a field and traverse a knoll. "Here's the other thing I've learned. Look at how these various people, events and results were orchestrated. I've discovered the Lord doesn't need lackeys, lieutenants, minions, representatives and envoys to carry His water and discharge His affairs. You even told me as much, months ago. From the prologue with Christy at Roanoke First Baptist to my curtain call with Edmund on the Blackfoot, I've been so far behind the curve it's pathetic. Funny, actually. We're oriented with our noses pressed into this intricate mosaic, so close we fog the tiles, and we're aware of a square or two but have no idea as to what the whole display looks like. My attempts to deliver punishment and fine-tune justice were about as significant as the doodles of a preschooler or the downstroke of a gnat's wing."

"It's nice to have all these abstract notions, and I'm sure you'll receive the Moses suite in the mansion with many rooms, but what are you planning to do come June and everything you own is in a green trash bag and you're waiting for the Greyhound, ten bucks and a pen pal's address in your pocket?"

"Don't you see? How perfect it is? I'm getting another chance, a do-over. And to answer your question, I'm planning to let others manage the sag and the secular world, and I'm going to remain anchored to my beliefs and manage Joel King. I'm wiser these days, Sophie, a better person. This has been a grown man's coming-of-age story. Remember Saul on the road to Damascus, or Oedipus, how he lost his vision but became insightful? I might even go into the ministry again—I've got a story to tell, and I've earned my stripes. I believe I could bring something to the table. It'll be a different table, I imagine, no more retirement packages and cushy parsonages, but there's a slot for me somewhere."

"Yeah, well, remember all the dumbass rock stars and actors who pop up on talk shows and say they've learned their lesson and done their three weeks at Betty Ford and they're sorry because they've been so selfish and self-destructive? The audience applauds and the celeb eats humble pie, and then six months later it's the same old tune and they're back on the TV sofa and they say this time they've *really* learned their lesson, and on and on it goes. Sound familiar? Correct me if I'm wrong, but you've seen the light and been converted and gotten it together—for sure—at least two or three times since Christmas."

The Volvo hit a pothole, and Joel felt the suspension dip. "I don't blame you for doubting me," he said. "I can't honestly promise it's going to be smooth sailing. But I'm positive I've seen the Lord's hand move in my life, and I have a good idea what He expects of me from here on out. When it comes right down to it, that's about all a person can ask for, especially if you're a Baptist preacher."

A prison van was scheduled to collect Joel in Helena, and he and Sophie resisted leaving home until the last moment. He'd tidied his basement quarters, washed sheets and towels and cleaned underneath the bed with a dust mop. Baker was at school and would be spending the night with Raleigh and his son, and Joel left a chartreuse Rooster Tail spinner for his nephew's new fishing rod, placed the lure on the boy's nightstand along with a note carefully printed in block letters. He wrote that he loved Baker very much, penning the "very" double the size of the other words.

He'd saved four hundred and nine dollars in cash. He kept a hundred for the prison canteen and left the rest for his sister; he deposited it in the flour canister, planning to alert her later, after he was incarcerated and she couldn't refuse him. He'd replaced the rotten cold-water hose on the washer, inspected the locks and dead bolts since Sophie would frequently be by herself, packed his Bible and a few necessities in a duffel bag and put his key on the antique dresser. The lone key lying on a slab of polished cherry was the last image he would recall from the basement.

They drove out of Missoula at evening's cusp, bound for Helena. Joel was behind the wheel and Sophie rode with her seat reclined and her eyes closed, talking every so often so Joel would know she was awake. They ate a ninety-minute meal of chicken-fried steak, mashed potatoes and garden tomatoes at a mom-and-pop diner and stopped three times for candy and sodas. When they arrived at the Helena jail, a federal van was waiting, and the two of them didn't fuss or fall emotional when Joel circled around to the Volvo's passenger door and opened it.

They held each other and broke the embrace with pats and rubs, and a tear wandered from Sophie's eye, but the scene wasn't dramatic or over-wrought, probably appeared restrained to the corrections officer watching from the mesh-windowed van. Joel marched to the van, into the night and low-beams until he became indistinct to his sister, and he stopped and talked to a man in a uniform who'd alighted from the vehicle. The man gestured apologetically, and he clicked cuffs to Joel's wrists and a chain to the cuffs, and the spectacle caused Sophie to grieve, to loosen her grip on the shifter and slump in the seat.

The first glimmer came right then, as she considered Joel and his shackles, and she immediately knew what was in store for her, heard the breeze grow to wind, smelled the rain and saw distant, intermittent flashes that were skimming the hillcrests and playing cat and mouse in the sky. She knew a storm was being ushered into Helena, a whopper if the verve and breadth of its first flickers were any indication.

It was late in the season for such an outburst, and it was arriving, strangely enough, from the east. She was surprised and would have to drive fast, ignoring the speed limit, to keep the turmoil behind her. It was in the ephemeral, muted light of this approaching weather that she viewed her brother's face as the officer assisted him into the van, and she saw him—the lightning almost a strobe—as preternaturally calm and serene, his metamorphosis so fierce he was difficult to recognize, a man formed and reformed. She cranked the engine, there was another burst of illumination, and Joel glanced at her and the car. His features came and vanished, but his deliverance was obvious and undeniable even in the transient light, and she was at that instant convinced, believed in the truth of his content-ment and that his coffers were full of the coin he most desired. "Okay," she said, despite his not being able to hear her. "Goodbye."

The storm never caught her, and Tut woke her early in an empty house, he and his hen and their chicks waiting for their buddy Joel to scatter a scoop of cracked corn and pour them fresh water. That evening, she and Raleigh were treating the kids to the county fair, and Uncle Joel had advised Baker he was indeed old enough to ride the Octopus, but as excit-ing as that prospect was, the boy had declared he wasn't budging until he'd heard from Joel, would sleep by the phone if that's what it took. The call came at six-thirty, was the first of many over the next nine months, and after hanging up, Baker looked at his mom and Raleigh and said, "We can go now." He stuck his unopened fishing lure into the pocket of his jean jacket and ran to the car, didn't bother to latch the door behind him.

Christy and her boyfriend, Gates, had been flushed from Montego Bay when her berserk, obsessed father discovered where she was residing, and a black man in a droopy seersucker suit and Panama hat appeared at her bungalow and announced he was Bill Darden's agent, forced a cell phone on her and connected her to her father's office. Initially, her dad was nice and conciliatory, promising her a condo, a minimum-wage allowance, a new car and a platinum card if she'd come home, but she wouldn't go along, and he railed and seethed and threatened her with fantastic bullshit he could never bring to pass. "Have me arrested for what?" she mocked him after he'd resorted to that outlandish threat.

So they'd departed Jamaica and sampled Aruba and Saint John's and ultimately docked in Freeport because Gates had a cousin from Florida who could visit them in the Bahamas and because they loved seeing other Americans and eating the fries at McDonald's. They would smoke dope and lounge around Count Basie Square, entertaining themselves with the weigh-ins from the wahoo tournaments and the bartenders machete-splitting coconuts for piña coladas. They'd chat with college kids and secretaries from Cleveland and sunburned men on golf vacations, and they felt happy and hip, ninety-mile expatriates, took to calling themselves Jake and Lady Brett although they both knew better and it was just for sport. Christy was bright enough to realize she'd eventually become bored, but she hadn't yet; she was loving their footloose junket, and she and Gates had suffered only two squabbles, neither of which amounted to much.

On the first evening Joel King sat in his Arizona prison cell, reading his Bible and highlighting scripture for the sermons he'd be obligated to preach upon his release, Christy, Gates, and their drug dealer Gregory were at a deserted stretch of Xanadu Beach. They weren't in sight of the trinket huts, T-shirt vendors and hair braiders, had taken their pot and their cooler of beer to a patch of sand well removed from the mainstream. The sunset was remarkable—that's why they'd come—and they passed a joint and drank without any more of a plan than to do precisely what they were doing. The sky to their left was majestic, the colors drenching the horizon and partly merging into the ocean, and Gates was gripping

Christy's hand, swigging beer. It required nearly half an hour, but the hues, no matter what shade, eventually turned to red, a bold, striking crimson that subsumed the world and rendered them speechless.

"I've never seen a sunset like that," Gregory finally said. "Never in my life."

"Cool, man," Gates mumbled, stoned and amazed. "So damn red."

"Remember the saying?" Gregory asked. " 'Red sky at night, sailors delight; red sky in morning, sailors take warning'?"

"Shit, Greg, we're landlocked folks—we wouldn't be too versed in nautical stuff," Gates replied.

"I've heard my father chant it a hundred times," Christy said. "He has a boat and fancies himself a captain. I can never, like, keep straight which sky is good and which is bad."

"We need to eat," Gates remarked. "Did you bring any cash, Christy?"

She didn't answer. She was stuck on the image of the commanding sky, not listening to him. "Do you think I should give some of my money to the church like I promised Mr. Hanes I would?" she blurted, ricocheting from thought to thought.

"We've been through that before," Gates said. "It's your freakin' money but, I mean, why would you? The whole religion thing's nothing but bullshit. You'd be payin' money to people like the guy who hit on you. What brought that up?"

"I don't know. It, like, just surfaced all of a sudden. Weird."

"That kind of money'd pay for a lot of good drugs and partyin'," Gates said. "Or a nice boat. And you can always make a contribution to a *real* charity, like an orphanage or the food bank."

The Atlantic was blank now, a monolith of somber green with occasional breaks of white surf along the reefs, and the sky was no longer so regal and extraordinary.

"Screw it," she said. "You're right. They'd probably just waste it." And having said that, suddenly she grew paranoid—must've smoked too much pot, she assumed—and she noticed Gates was totally stoned, close to zoning out. She glanced at Gregory and realized she didn't care for the way he'd been eyeballing her lately, brushing against her and stopping by without being invited, and she was sure he'd seen her changing clothes, shimmying from her shorts and wiggling into a bathing suit. The wind blew in from the sea, aggravating the sand and scrawny pine trees behind them, and Christy felt a chill climb her backbone, sinking in until she couldn't help but shiver.

_____ acknowledgments

So many good people helped me with this book and also my first one. Joe Regal is the best literary agent on the planet, part Henry Kissinger, part Max Perkins, and has never failed to do right by me. Gary Fisketjon is a stone-solid genius who lives up to his billing, and his edits made every single line of this novel better—thanks. A big tip of the hat, once again, to Captain Frank Beverly, Charles F. Wright and the incomparable S. Edward "Smilin' Ed" Flanagan. Eddie and Nancy Turner have never let me down, no matter what, and I know that'll never change. I'm grateful to my minister David "Bucky" Hunsicker and his wife, Matilda, for their friendship and help with the first drafts of my manuscript. And my gratitude to: Gabrielle Brooks for her Herculean efforts and good nature; my buddy Renee Louis; Edd Martin (who spent as much time on _Many Aspects_ as I did); big brother Dave Melesco; my boss, David "Hollywood" Williams; Reverend George Goodman; Robert Earl Keen and Bill Whitbeck; General, Danny and especially Ken Knox; Kelly and Beth; Daniel Wallace; John Boy, Billy and Jackie (the fuel for this book was JB&B Grillin' Sauce and House of Raeford chicken); Charles "The Baron" Aaron; Skip Burpeau; Barnie Day; Rob McFarland; FBI Agent Lynne Chaffinch; Federal Marshal Albert Smith; Chris Corbett; Bess Reed; Len and Nancy Wood; RAMA; and, most of all, to Deana G. Heath, who read and read and read, took care of me and always looked like a million bucks—I couldn't have done this without you. Finally, like my protagonist, I believe in both the Old Testament and the literal truth of the Gospels, and I thank the Lord for His blessings, forbearance and patience.

_____ a note about the type

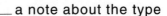

This book was set in a modern adaptation of a type designed by the first William Caslon (1692–1766). The Caslon face, an artistic, easily read type, has enjoyed over two centuries of popularity in our own country. It is of interest to note that the first copies of the Declaration of Independence and the first paper currency distributed to the citizens of the newborn nation were printed in this typeface.

Composed by Creative Graphics, Allentown, Pennsylvania

Printed and bound by Berryville Graphics,
Berryville, Virginia

Designed by Johanna Roebas